A serial killer is on the loose in La La Land,
but *you* may die laughing before the next victim is found.

BAD VIBRATIONS

Dan Anderson

AWARD WINNING AUTHOR

**The first book in the acclaimed series and
recipient of five literary awards, including:**

The Independent Publishers IPPY Book Award -
Silver Medal, Best Regional Fiction (West-Pacific) 2009

The Florida Writers Association Royal Palm Award -
First Place, Published Mystery 2008

Books and Authors -
Murder Mystery Book of the Year 2008

Praise for

Bad Vibrations

The concept of Dan Anderson's Bad Vibrations is unique, fresh, and totally unexpected. Mr. Anderson has created a captivating book with interesting characters who are well motivated from the beginning to the end. The front cover is eye-catching, with the titillating image of a woman on a stark white background. The title and author name are boldly displayed, making it easy for readers to locate. The blurb on the back is intriguing enough to compel readers to open the book, and the opening line will keep them turning pages. The characters are well drawn, and the dialogue is strong and natural to each person speaking.

—*Writer's Digest*

Boom Boom' Saperstein, an exotic dancer at one of North Hollywood's gentlemen's clubs, is found dead floating in her bathtub. Electrocution by vibrator is the cause of death.

Chauncey McFadden, private investigator, is hired by Rubella Saperstein to find the killer of her niece, 'Boom Boom.' With the police not interested in the death of a stripper - it's clear if justice is to be had, it will have to be bought and paid for. The incredibly wealthy Judge Barrington then hires McFadden when the Judge's daughter, Justine, is also murdered by electrocution by vibrator. 'Boom Boom's' roommate is the next victim found murdered. McFadden's homicide experience is limited… actually, non-existent. He's a penny-ante player swept into a high-stakes game. He's playing with the big boys now and needs to find the vibrator killer before they strike again and he finds himself sleeping with the fishes. With his number one suspect now a victim, he must look deeper for the common denominator.

Bad Vibrations is a very well-written and entertaining mystery. It is creative and humorous with McFadden's wise-crack sense of humor and will have you laughing out loud several times throughout its pages. Bad Vibrations will grab your attention from the very first sentence hold it all the way to the shocking whodunit ending.

—MyShelf.com

The main character of Bad Vibrations is Chauncey McFadden-a short, balding PI with no money in his pockets until an amazing stroke of luck lands him in the middle of one of the most bizarre murder cases in the history of southern California. Within the same week, two unrelated and entirely different individuals hire McFadden to solve the murders of female family members. While searching for clues, Chauncey discovers that the victims have more in common than their means of demise, and a frighteningly funny tale begins to unfold.

McFadden is required to visit seedy motels, brave his way into conversations with the owner of the Glad Gland strip joint, and stand up to Lieutenant Del Dotto of the L.A. police department in his search for clues. With his reputation, and sometimes his life, on the line, McFadden struggles to find the connections between the murders he was hired to solve and the deaths that are continuing to occur.

Not a book for the easily embarrassed reader, Bad Vibrations is filled with adult humor and quirky scenarios. Anderson vividly describes his colorful assortment of characters and gives each their own distinct personality. I especially enjoyed the forgetful butler, Montrose, who never seems to remember what was just said in a conversation yet has an uncanny ability to describe past events from his murdered mistress's young years.

Author Dan Anderson has combined his love of comedy and mystery into an original work of art in Bad Vibrations. He currently resides in Orlando, Florida.

Armchair Interviews says: This book could be in all these genres: Mystery, Thriller, Fiction, Suspense, Drama, Comedy, and Adult Humor.

A Great Whodunnit – 4 stars
By John J. White "J J White" (Merritt Island, Florida) -
A wonderfully written book that will have you scratching your head trying to figure out just who is the murderer. Written in the grand style of a Christie novel, yet with a contemporary twist similar to Stuart Woods's book. Like Woods, Mr. Anderson has written in his share of zany characters, not the least of which is Chauncey McFadden, an odd duck to be sure. It takes a chapter or so to understand the protagonist, but then you'll soon feel right at home with him, silently urging him take the correct path in the murderous maze. A good mystery in need of a sequel.

This book is a classic – 5 stars
By Mystery Addict (Florida)
"Woman murdered with vibrator." That's how Bad Vibrations opens and with your attention captured, it never lets go. This book is, without a doubt, one of the funniest mysteries I have ever read. The humor is great, the characters are vividly drawn and the conversational exchanges will put you in stitches. You simply can't put the book down once you start reading it. The dialog is mesmerizing and catchy; it reminds me of Raymond Chandler in places. You get a double bonus- the book is very well written as well. The scenic descriptions of the Los Angeles area are beautifully painted and riveting. There are a number of scenes that you will reread several times because they are so poignant. I hope there are more Chauncey McFadden mysteries to come. This is a very original, creative piece of work.

Bad Vibrations is a great beach read – 5 stars
By B. J. Macecsko "B.J." (Kenilworth, NJ)
I loved Bad Vibrations. Chauncey is an unusual PI that gets the job done. I'm a big fan of the Clark's mysteries but Dan Anderson puts a little more fun into his stories. Great read for a beach or a long ride. It's a great story line too.

From *Barnes & Noble.com*

Bad Vibrations – 5 stars
Bad Vibrations is one of the funniest, most well-written mysteries I have enjoyed in some time. The dialog is snappy, the characters are hilarious, and the descriptions of the scenery are memorable. This book is very creative in plot and style and is one of the most original mysteries I can recall. This book would make an excellent screenplay and someone should make a film of it. I hope we see many more from the author; please don't stop.

One You Can't Put Down – 5 stars
This book is a great mix of humor and mystery. Chauncey McFadden is an unlikely type to be involved in a serious murder investigation. The other characters involved are equally entertaining as we follow Chauncey through the investigation into the murder of 'Boom Boom' Saperstein. Hope to see more of McFadden in the future.

A Fast Moving Intriguing Mystery That Will Prove Interesting to All Readers – 5 stars
A diverse crowd of well developed characters provide a historically under-employed detective continuous challenges and intrigue. Fast paced, fun reading!

Bad Vibrations – 5 stars
I don't usually read mysteries but a friend raved about the book so much I had to give it a try. Am I glad I did! Bad Vibrations is one super-funny, well-written piece of work. The crazy characters, beautiful scenery descriptions, and humor are woven into a fascinating plot. That bar scene in Long Beach is a classic. This is one of the most entertaining books I have read in some time, and I hope that more are to come. Get this author on Oprah.

A Mystery With Humor and Punch – 5 stars
Four young and attractive women are found murdered in a most bizarre manner (No, I won't tell how), and the bored and stumbling cops don't seem to have a clue. So, it is up to our hero and protagonist, Chauncey McFadden, private eye, to unravel the complex case. Unfortunately, Chauncey is not too swift himself, but as expected, he lurches forward and finally solves the murders after many detours into strip clubs and all night diners. This is a very funny (yet serious) novel by a new author. Chauncey is about 75% Guy Noir and 25% Mickey Spillane, so the reader has some idea of what a character this PI really is. The story is told in the first person through the eyes of Chauncey, which gives the novel a lot of added punch.

Wow! This Book Is a Rare Gem. I Am a Fan for Life – 5 stars
I picked up the book and was captivated from the first chapter. The turns and the twists of the plot were countless. The book was funny. The work is a cross of David Letterman, Get Smart and Sherlock Holmes wrapped up in a fun package. Recommended reading for anyone with a funny bone.

Great Beach Read – 5 stars
Wonderful use of descriptive phrases. Funny with pathos, serious with hilarity. I want to read more of Chauncey.

DEATH CRUISE

ALSO BY DAN ANDERSON

Bad Vibrations

DEATH
CRUISE

A NOVEL

DAN
ANDERSON

 Publishing Group, LLC

Phoenix, Arizona

DEATH CRUISE
Copyright © 2009 by Dan Anderson
dananderson305@gmail.com
www.facebook.com/dan.anderson2
www.murdermayhemmalice.com
All rights reserved.

INDI Publishing Group, www.INDIPublishingGroup.com.

Printed and bound in the United States of America. First printing 2010

Published by INDI Publishing Group in association with the author, Dan Anderson.

Cover design by Sarah Spencer

Interior design by Julia Baumann

ISBN 13: 978-1-935636-01-4

Library of Congress Control Number: 2010922283

Dedication

Death Cruise is dedicated to my loving wife, Virginia,
from whom many creative blessings either flow or are stimulated.

Acknowledgments

There are many people to whom I'm indebted for the second launch of Chauncey McFadden and his misadventures in mystery. First, are Sandra and Dawn Cantrell who served as sounding boards for the creation and development of the outré plot and characters. Second, is Jerry D. Simmons, publisher extraordinaire and patron saint of authors. Third, are the many cruise lines sailing the Caribbean whose vessels, staffs and itineraries provided not only superb entertainment but rich material which was mined for fictional inspiration.

CHAPTER 1

"HIS THROAT HAD BEEN CUT FROM ear to ear, McFadden— he was almost decapitated. If I live to be a thousand, I'll never get over the police pictures of poor Lars Amundson, lying there with his head dangling from his body. I get nauseated just thinking about it."

Not as nauseated as I was becoming. I wrapped the remainder of my sandwich in the Food section of the Los Angeles Times and tossed it into the wastebasket at my feet. Taking pains not to drop the telephone receiver I'd wedged between my cheek and shoulder, I tried to be empathetic.

"That's understandable, Mr. Erickson." I picked up my glasses and wiped away a mayonnaise smudge from the left lens. "It must have been a terrible shock seeing one of your most valuable employees under such tragic circumstances. Before you continue, let me grab a pen and some paper."

"Speak a little louder if you will, McFadden. I'm calling from Miami, and the reception on my end fades in and out."

"All right," I agreed, several decibels higher. I was scribbling frantically with the second ball point pen I picked up to accelerate the flow of ink—if it worked at all. "You said your name was Anders Erickson, right? And that you are president and chairman of the board of directors of the Nordic Caribbean Cruise Line?"

"Yes. That's correct."

"And that this Amundson fellow was the chief officer senior of your ship, the *Oslo Aphrodite*... and he was brutally murdered two days ago in a bizarre fashion—"

"Right, and right again." The replies were filtered through static.

"Before I go any farther, how did my detective agency come to your attention if I may ask? I've never done any work in South Florida."

"Judge Alfred Barrington, one of our board members, is from Los Angeles. He recommended you. He told me how you captured the killers of his two daughters a couple of years ago and suggested I contact you."

"Ah, yes," I replied, basking in the warm glow of remembrance. "That was an investigative coup of the first magnitude, if I may say so myself." I saw no point in confessing that prior to the Barrington case, I had accumulated very little experience in the investigation of homicides; that my usual cases were mundane fare such as matrimonial infidelity, missing persons, evidence procurement, insurance fraud, surveillance, and background checks for pre-nups and child custody cases.

"Where was the body found and by whom?" I continued.

"The *Oslo Aphrodite* arrived at the Port of Miami two days ago and had cleared customs and inspection. The passengers and many of the crew had disembarked, pre-boarding maintenance had been performed, and provisions were being loaded aboard for our next departure. Lars' body was found that afternoon... in a car at the port parking garage by a customer picking up his vehicle.

"And, here's the scary part," Erickson continued. "I'd no sooner returned to my office from answering questions at the Miami police precinct yesterday when I got a phone call..." He stopped speaking, in obvious hesitation.

"And..."

"That voice—I can't get it out of my mind. It was a deep bass voice, it sounded like a man, and it rumbled, like it was coming through an echo chamber. It had a heavy accent that I couldn't identify. It was sinister and... and chilling."

"What did he say?" I asked on cue.

"He said... that... more of the crew would die... unless Zunimba was appeased." Erickson sounded shaken.

"Did it say who or what 'Zunimba' was? Did he mention what it might take to appease Zunimba?"

"No, he only said that one sentence."

"So, the name Zunimba doesn't mean anything to you?"

"No," the president said before another pause. When he resumed, his voice had taken on a more businesslike tone. "McFadden, the problem is, the *Oslo Aphrodite* sails day after tomorrow for a thirteen-day cruise of the Caribbean. If this Zunimba makes good on his threat, our company could suffer irreparable financial damage. This is the high season for the cruise business, and any adverse publicity could turn the *Oslo Aphrodite* into a ghost ship."

"I'm surprised your ship is still in port. Wouldn't it usually have sailed out the next day after arrival?"

"Normally, yes, that would be the case. However, three dozen passengers from the last cruise came down with a viral infection and we were impounded by the Centers for Disease Control and Prevention. We're required to report to U.S. health authorities when cases of gastrointestinal illness exceed three percent of the ship's population. We had to sanitize the ship from top to bottom which added a couple of days to port time."

"A virus... which could have come from natural origins or possibly have been introduced aboard the ship deliberately. Did the caller say anything to make you believe you were a target for future sabotage or blackmail?"

"No. Again, the voice said only those few words. Listen, McFadden, if this Zunimba makes good on his threat, it could occur while the ship is at sea outside of U.S. territorial waters. The FBI won't dedicate manpower to a cruise solely on the basis of a telephone threat, and the Miami police don't have jurisdiction at sea. We have ship's security, of course, but it's minimal and Judge Barrington and I felt an outside private investigator may be more effective since he could move freely among passengers and crew without arousing suspicion."

"Point well taken," I said. "Did the Miami police share any information with you regarding their preliminary findings in the murder?"

"No, just the pictures taken of Lar's body by the crime scene investigators. But, besides his head being nearly severed, there were two other things particularly disturbing about the body."

"Go on…" My pen was poised to record the details of this morbid forensic melodrama.

"First, his shirt had been unbuttoned to his waist, and on his chest… a circle had been carved with a knife. Inside the circle were several strange markings—they were drawn with blood, presumably symbols of some sort."

"That is macabre," I agreed. "What was the other disturbing—"

"He had a chicken—"

Static on the line drowned out the remainder of the sentence. I waited for it to subside and yelled, "Erickson, are you still there?"

"Yes," he acknowledged, but his voice sounded distant and remote.

"You started saying something about a chicken?"

Some loud crackling and a few pops cleared up the transmission problem and the president's voice came through loud and clear: "I said his tongue had been cut out, and the head of a dead chicken had been stuffed in his mouth."

I dropped my pen and coughed nervously, while peering under the desk at the wastebasket—and the remainder of the chicken sandwich I'd been munching on when his call came in. "This sounds like some sort of cult-styled execution. Did Lars dabble in the occult?"

"Knowing Lars, I would strongly doubt it."

These strange proceedings stirred my imagination. Quasi-facetiously, I said, "Perhaps he stumbled upon a secret ceremony in the steamy interior of some cursed island and escaped with his life, only to be hunted down by avenging assassins intent on punishing him for his sacrilege."

"You've been working around Hollywood too long, McFadden," Erickson snorted. "Lars was a square shooter; as good as they come. He wouldn't be involved in anything like that.

"Look, I'd like you to come to Miami right away. I want to know who murdered Lars and why. And, I want you to be on the *Oslo Aphrodite* when she sails. Maybe the threat by this Zunimba guy is a bluff, but I'd feel better having someone on board who had some experience in these matters. Will you take the case?"

I wasn't too crazy about the risk that a homicide investigation might entail, but my income flow had been on sabbatical recently and I had to do something with the bills that were accumulating on the corner of the desk, something other than watch the stack grow taller each day.

"Well," I started to think aloud, "there's the question of my fee…"

"I'll pay you $3,000 for two weeks of your time, throw in a free cruise, and pick up any reasonable expenses."

"You've got a deal. I'll take the red-eye out of LAX and be in your office sometime tomorrow afternoon." I decided to entertain a sudden thought: "Would you have any objections to me bringing a female operative along? Her presence will help disguise my true identity and cover up the intent of the mission."

"Be my guest and… hey, can you hold a minute, McFadden? I've got an incoming call on my personal hotline."

While he attended to his other call, I began to fantasize about the voyage. I had heard that cruise lines served eight meals a day and promised myself that I would strive for nothing less than perfect attendance at all seatings. Anything else would be a distinct disservice. My gastronomic euphoria was interrupted by a shout loud enough to make the receiver jump from my hand.

"McFadden!"

"What is it?" My daydream destroyed, I secured the phone in my hand and refocused. "You sound alarmed."

"You better get here tomorrow," Erickson shrieked, "as soon as you can."

"Why? What's wrong?"

"They just found another member of the *Oslo Aphrodite* crew— dead—murdered the same way as Lars!"

CHAPTER 2

WE LEFT LOS ANGELES INTERNATIONAL AIRPORT at nine o'clock that night, which meant a scheduled arrival in Miami at five-thirty the following morning, Friday. The other half of the "we," my "female operative," was in actuality my girlfriend, Girtha Roote. For eons, I had been promising to treat us to a vacation, and this was an ideal opportunity to fulfill my obligation at someone else's expense.

The flight was only partially booked and most people were sound asleep within an hour of takeoff. Girtha, struggling against repose, unfastened her seatbelt extender and cuddled next to me, squeezing my arm with anticipation.

"Oh, Chauncey, this is *too* good to be true," she murmured. "I can't believe that Cosmo gave me two weeks off on such short notice." Cosmo was her employer, the owner of an antediluvian neighborhood diner in downtown L.A.

"I suspect it's because you haven't had a day off since you've worked there," I commented dryly, unimpressed by Cosmo's generosity. "I'm sure you must have fulfilled the terms of your indentured servitude by now."

"Two weeks in the Caribbean. I just can't *believe* it," Girtha rhapsodized. "I'll have to do some shopping tomorrow afternoon, though. I didn't pack enough to last two weeks. I even brought along an empty suitcase to hold clothes I'm gonna buy."

"Don't go overboard, no pun intended. I understand cruise ship cabins are small and don't have much storage space. We'll probably have to sleep curled up as it is."

Girtha pooh-poohed this notion and pulled a blanket over her short, plump frame. The excitement and events of the day had finally caught up with her and a yawn caused her large, green eyes to close and their long lashes to cease their constant fluttering. The monotonic drone of the engines and darkness at thirty thousand feet were all the sedatives she needed. In a moment, she was fast asleep, no doubt dreaming of white, sandy beaches caressed by warm tropical waters, coconut palms stirring gently in soft evening breezes, and an oversized moon bathing the paradise below in a passionate glow. I placed a pillow behind her short, brown hair and bestowed a good-night peck on her rosy, heavily dimpled cheek.

Not quite the romantic, I pulled out some books on ships, nautical terminology, and the city of Miami that I had salvaged from a used book store and began to brush up and research.

Several books later, we arrived at the Miami International Airport on schedule and took a taxi to the Sand Conch Hotel, where the cruise line's passengers were being quartered during the ship's sanitation delay. I got a little more than an hour of sleep before rising to quietly shower and dress. I wrote the still-sleeping Girtha a note and ventured downstairs to hail a cab outside the hotel. It was about 8:45 in the morning and already shaping up to be a hot, humid day.

The North American headquarters of the Nordic Caribbean Cruise Line was not far from my hotel or the Port of Miami. The offices were inside a tall glass and steel skyscraper that commanded a panoramic view of Biscayne Bay and was surrounded by fountains of dancing waters and ubiquitous Canary Island Palms. I located the cruise line listing in the lobby directory and hopped an elevator to the top floor, where a receptionist confirmed my appointment with a quick call and gave me directions to Anders Erickson's office. A short trudge later, I came across his personal secretary leaning back in a chair with her left leg elevated and outstretched, examining a run in her stocking.

"Is that Mr. Erickson's office you're pointing to?" I asked, nodding toward a nearby door opposite her big toe.

She blushed, then quickly lowered her leg and stood up.

I tried desperately to focus on the run in her stocking, but my disobedient eyes kept drifting upward as she stood and smoothed her tight, short skirt.

"Please, follow me," she mumbled while avoiding eye contact.

She could walk point for me anytime. Judging from her figure, she must have been an underwear model moonlighting at the cruise agency to earn some extra coin. We entered an office and found a short, stocky man, hands clasped behind his back, pacing back and forth across a burgundy carpet. A red flattop and ruddy complexion gave his agitation a chromatic dimension.

"McFadden! You made it. Have a seat," he greeted. I shook his sweaty hand and parked myself at the end of an uncomfortable, burnt-sienna colored, leather chesterfield. As I sat, I noted that Erickson had already unbuttoned his collar and loosened his tie. I suspected, however, that the cause of his damp shirt was unrelated to the May humidity. He plopped down behind his desk.

"I see what Judge Barrington meant," he said, likely in reference to my five-foot-eight, two-hundred-forty-pound frame. "He said you didn't look much like a detective—but then, I don't truly know what a detective is supposed to look like."

"We come in all shapes, sizes, colors, and genders," I replied. "You can, however, be confident that my appearance, disarmingly deceptive as it may be, is supported by a keen mind. Let's get down to business," I suggested, changing the subject. "Why don't you start at the beginning?"

With a sigh, he tilted his head back and let his arms dangle over the sides of his chair. "The day before yesterday, I received a call from Captain Nelson informing me of the discovery of Lars Amundson's body in a parking garage."

"I believe you mentioned that Amundson is the chief officer senior."

"Yes, he's the second in command aboard the ship."

"And, I assume that 'Captain Nelson' is in charge of the *Oslo Aphrodite*?"

"That's right. The commander of a cruise ship is actually called the 'master,' but 'Captain' is so well entrenched in the public's vocabulary that everybody uses it."

"What did you do then?" I asked.

"I met Captain Nelson at police headquarters, where we answered some questions about Lars. Nelson had just come from the morgue after identifying the body. I'm still a little shaken as you can tell. I hired Lars years ago, myself, when I was head of human resources."

I noted that he tapped a folder on the top of his desk, which I hoped was a personnel file. "Who's handling the case for the Miami police?"

"A woman by the name of Alameda—Lieutenant Constancia Alameda," Erickson replied after glancing at her business card.

"What did she ask you?"

"Things like, did Lars have any family, how long had he worked for us, what was his job at Nordic Caribbean, how was his job performance, did he have any enemies, who were his associates... things like that."

"What did you tell her?"

"That Lars was thirty-two years old, a bachelor, born in Oslo, Norway; that he'd been with us for eight years, initially as first engineer senior, then as chief officer senior for the past three years; that he was from a wealthy Scandinavian family with large interests in a number of mining and manufacturing companies. Lars was very personable; he had no known enemies or bad habits—other than an occasional fondness for *akvavit*."

"I assume *akvavit* is either kinky sex, a game of chance, or Danish moonshine."

Erickson reacted with an ever-so-slight smile, probably his first in three days. "It's the last one."

"Did his drinking ever get him in any trouble?"

"Not directly," Erickson began. He wrinkled his brow and rubbed his chin. "But there was one incident..." He paused, obviously laboring over his next words. "He got into a little scrape in the Dominican Republic several months ago. It seems he became romantically involved with the daughter of a local magistrate, which didn't sit well with her family. You can see Captain Nelson for details."

Acting on my earlier suspicion, I asked if Amundson's personnel record was available. The president tapped the folder on his desk to confirm my hope. "May I see it for a moment?"

Erickson passed me the file which I scanned in some places and closely read in others. "This file is pretty thorough," I complimented. "It even has his medical records."

"All officers have to take annual physicals. Their fitness is an evaluated component of their performance reviews," Erickson explained.

A few minutes later, after mentally noting some pertinent data, I handed the file back to Erickson. "What can you tell me about Captain Nelson?"

"Isak Nelson is our most experienced master in the fleet," he answered while opening one of his desk drawers and reaching in to pull out another thick brown folder. After opening it to an appropriate section, he used his finger to scan the pages.

"He first went to sea as a teenager in 1950. He served on a few tankers and some freighters for six years before spending two years in the Royal Norwegian Navy. He entered the Norwegian Merchant Naval Academy, graduated as a junior officer, and served on a variety of merchant ships until 1963, when he returned to the academy for his master's certificate. Since 1964, he's served as chief officer senior and captain aboard passenger ships. He joined the Nordic Caribbean fleet in 1971 and has served on all six of our vessels over the past eleven years."

"It sounds like he can row a boat and tie a sailor's hitch," I deduced. "Moving on, over the phone you mentioned that a second crew member had met the 'black camel'—"

"The 'black camel'?"

"I beg your pardon," I replied sheepishly. "It must be the climate. Charlie Chan once said that death is a black camel that kneels unbid at every gate. I was referring to the second murder."

"Oh, I see," Erickson said, suppressing any discernible excitement about Oriental philosophy. "Yes—the call I received yesterday, when I was talking to you. It was Captain Nelson. He'd just been notified that one of our waiters, Victor Dubonnet, had been found in the rear of a warehouse. His throat was cut, his head almost severed, and he had the same design on his chest, as well as a chicken's head in his mouth."

"What can you tell me about Dubonnet's record?"

Erickson picked up a folder from underneath Amundson's. "I just had his file sent over." Again, highlighting with his finger, he determined that the waiter was twenty-six, unmarried, and a citizen of Haiti who had been employed by the cruise line for the past three months.

"Any family?"

Erickson flipped through the file until he located the employment application. "It says Victor was born in Port-au-Prince, but his parents and nine brothers and sisters now live in Plaine-du-Nord, Haiti. He applied for political asylum in this country several years ago and apparently received it. No spouse is indicated." He closed the file and looked up. "The head of our food service staff said Victor was a good employee who got along with his co-workers. It's hard to know any member of the wait staff very well because of their high turnover."

"What kinds of background checks are performed on employment applicants?"

"The officers and senior staff typically have years of experience in their fields and are hired directly by the cruise line from Canada, the U.S., and Western Europe. They're subjected to intense scrutiny and investigation."

"How about the rest of the staff members?"

"Not as much as you might suspect," Erickson acknowledged. "Over eighty nationalities are employed by Nordic Caribbean Cruise Line. Cruise ship staff members are only required to have C1/D1 U.S. Visas, which are little more than a formality. This type of visa is for seamen only, and allows them to enter the U.S. for a limited number of hours and days—primarily time when the ships to which they're assigned are in U.S. ports. They don't need a regular work visa or green card to work on most cruise ships since the majority of vessels are registered in other countries.

"It's important to note that most of the rank-and-file cruise staff, like waiters and cabin stewards, aren't employees of the cruise line. They're hired by crewing agencies who forward the workers' pay to their families while they're at sea. They work on contract periods of three to six months.

"Most large cruise lines hire people from developing, third-world countries where earnings expectations are lower and employment regulations are lax."

"So," I said to sum up his discourse, "*you* do not screen most employees because they don't work for the company, and it's highly unlikely that the crewing agencies subject them to any kind of rigorous background check."

"That's about the size of it," Erickson replied. "Plus, when you get right down to it, even if the agencies *did* do checks, how reliable would any of the information be that they uncovered in those countries?"

"Good point," I agreed. "How often do deaths occur on cruise ships?"

"In the past few years, the cruise industry has experienced an uptick in passenger deaths because of the increase in the number of ships, growth in passenger volume, and expanded itineraries in economically challenged countries.

"The deaths that happen *onboard* are usually such events as accidental falls over the rails, suicide leaps, health problems—heart attack and stroke—and an occasional homicide. Actually, more deaths happen in the ports-of-call, frequently during shore excursions. We've had passengers drown while swimming, snorkeling, scuba diving, using Jet Skis, and parasailing. Others have been killed while driving rented motorcycles and mopeds. Some also die on tour boats that capsize, tour busses that crash, and sightseeing helicopters that fall out of the sky… if you can have fun doing something, you can die in the process."

That's the way I always wanted to go, I thought. "But death threats made against ship personnel—I gather *that* is a new experience."

"It's new for our company. That's why we're so concerned," Erickson said.

"Getting back to the victims, Amundson and Dubonnet… I don't see any apparent connection between them…"

"Nor do I. They were from separate worlds—socially, culturally, financially and racially," Erickson agreed.

"So much for that. Where do we go from here?" I asked.

"Tomorrow afternoon at one, busses will pick you, your

associate, and the rest of the passengers up at your hotel. It will take you to pier three, where the *Oslo Aphrodite* is berthed. I have your cruise schedule here someplace," he said, rummaging through some papers on his desk. "Here it is," he said, handing me the ship's May 1982 bulletin, which reflected the following itinerary:

Day One	Saturday	Miami, Florida—Boarding—At Sea
Day Two	Sunday	At Sea
Day Three	Monday	Ocho Rios, Jamaica
Day Four	Tuesday	At Sea
Day Five	Wednesday	Willemstad, Curacao, Netherlands Antilles
Day Six	Thursday	La Guaira, Venezuela
Day Seven	Friday	At Sea
Day Eight	Saturday	Bridgetown, Barbados
Day Nine	Sunday	Fort-de-France, Martinique
Day Ten	Monday	St. Thomas, U.S. Virgin Islands
Day Eleven	Tuesday	Santo Domingo, Dominican Republic
Day Twelve	Wednesday	At Sea
Day Thirteen	Thursday	Miami

"Nice selection of islands and ports," I commented. "I hope nothing as tawdry as a murder pops up to spoil the cruise."

"I'll second that, McFadden," he said as he bent to rummage through a desk drawer. "As a matter of security, only Captain Nelson and a few other select individuals, such as the security officer, will be made aware of your mission. Not only is Nelson one of the finest officers who ever graced a bridge, but you'll need someone in high command who has the authority to provide you with any support you might need."

Having located the target of his search, he closed the drawer, stood, and polished an object against the leg of his trousers. Satisfied, after a third glance, he handed me a shiny gold object. "This badge will identify you as a ship's inspector. Keep it on your person and flash it if your authority is questioned."

"Thanks." I got to my feet, pinned the shield to the leather in my wallet over my PI license, and prepared to leave. "If any further news regarding either murder should break after we've left port, be sure to let me know.

"Also, please forward your passenger list to Lieutenant Alameda and ask her to run the names through the FBI and Interpol databases. If Zunimba does have anything planned this trip, it would be good to know who the players are. You can contact me with the results as soon as they're available."

"Will do," Erickson promised as we shook hands. His palms were less sweaty and he appeared to be much more relaxed than when I arrived. "We've got cablegrams and ship-to-shore radio telephone service. And McFadden..." he added as I reached the door. "Be careful. I don't want any burials at sea—and that includes you."

"My sentiments, as well. But I do have one concern: Zunimba would have a field day finger painting a mural on a stomach the size of mine."

CHAPTER 3

WHEN I RETURNED TO THE HOTEL ROOM, Girtha was stepping out of the shower. I pointed out a nearby mall from the hotel window and suggested she do her shopping while I took a taxi to the local precinct to look up Lieutenant Alameda. I'd concluded after leaving Erickson's office that Miami police and I might forge a better relationship if we knew each other.

When I arrived, I was informed that Alameda was giving a deposition in a criminal court trial so I slouched in the waiting room for the better part of an hour reading articles from *True Detective* magazine. I was on the last page of a lurid story about the mutilation of a migratory farm worker in an Indian River orange grove when a pleasant voice interrupted its resolution.

"I understand you've been waiting to see me?"

I looked up into the largest pair of brown eyes I had ever seen. Their owner was an almond-complexioned woman of above average height whose curvaceous figure was ill-disguised by a dark blue skirt and jacket. Her coal-black hair was long, straight, and lustrous, and nearly matched the shade of her partially concealed shoulder holster.

"Lieutenant Alameda, I presume?"

"In the flesh."

I stood and shook her hand, admiring the flesh that I could see. "I'm Chauncey McFadden, a PI from Los Angeles. I've been retained by the Nordic Caribbean Cruise Line to look into the murders of their two employees. I'd appreciate a few minutes of your time, now if possible, since we sail tomorrow."

She glanced at her watch. "I can spare you twenty minutes. Come back to my office."

Following her was not hard duty. She had long well-toned legs, a compact derriere, and a walk that would have diverted any randy Hamlin rat from the Pied Piper's entourage.

Her corner office was relatively spacious for her rank. The light gray walls were covered with framed diplomas, advanced degrees in criminology and sociology, and certifications in specialty areas of police science from state and federal law enforcement authorities. Interspersed among those academic accolades were a number of framed articles from the *Miami Herald* in which her career exploits were prominently featured.

"Would you care for some coffee?" she asked. She slid into her chair, her split skirt enabling her to cross her legs effortlessly. Still, I almost managed to maintain direct eye contact. I declined her offer and she punched a button on her intercom. "Brannigan—bring me a cup of java, in my mug."

A moment later, a tall man in a deputy's uniform sauntered in with a steaming cup that had the word "*reina*" emblazoned on the side in bold letters. He set it on her desk and left. His facial expression indicated that he wasn't too thrilled with this aspect of police work.

"So, what's on your mind, McFadden?" she asked with more than a tinge of suspicion in her voice.

"As I mentioned, Nordic Caribbean Cruise Line—in particular, Anders Erickson, the company president—has asked me to investigate the murders of his chief officer senior, Lars Amundson, and a waiter by the name of Victor Dubonnet. I'm sailing on the *Oslo Aphrodite* tomorrow at one o'clock and would appreciate any information you may have uncovered on these homicides."

She looked at me warily. "You're not at all what I expected. When they said a PI was waiting for me, I had a different image in mind."

"Let me guess: an ex-professional football player, forced into early retirement by injuries, who sports a jaw of granite, fists of steel, and biceps the size of frozen turkeys."

She smiled. "Something like that."

"Guys like that may be camera friendly, but the advent of the pistol gave blokes like me a level playing field. You can't tell a detective wannabe from a real detective by sight alone."

She continued her visual evaluation for a moment and then, her mind apparently made up, resumed. "Erickson requested that my department extend you every professional courtesy. Since your inquiry will be beyond our borders, I have no objection." She then added, "Don't take it personally, McFadden, but I'm glad your visit to our colorful little burg will be a brief one. I have enough problems without having a dick under foot."

Her double entendre didn't go unnoticed, but since our time was limited, I wanted to get back on topic. "Regarding Amundson and Dubonnet—"

"Doesn't Erickson think the Miami police department is capable of investigating those murders?" she asked sarcastically. "We may have a high crime rate in Miami, but we also have one of the highest solved crime ratios in the country for a city our size…"

I jumped into the conversation to assuage her suspicion. "The competence of your department's not in question, lieutenant. But because of the telephone threat he received, Mr. Erickson is afraid that additional murders may be in the pipeline—and that those murders will occur at open sea, on the decks of the *Oslo Aphrodite* and outside your jurisdiction. I'm simply looking for information that might help me anticipate such events and more adequately discharge my responsibilities after we leave port."

Assured that I was not the professional threat she had initially perceived, the lieutenant seemed to lower her guard. "We suspect the murders were committed by followers of Zunimba, and that—"

"Excuse me," I jumped in, "but I'm particularly interested in learning about these followers." Based on the censorious stare that followed, I doubted I would interrupt her again.

fI started taking notes as she leaned back in her chair and assumed a professorial posture.

"I'm a little puzzled, lieutenant, by this fusion you speak of. Religion and crime don't normally swap spit."

"From an affluent, industrialized, Western, Judeo-Christian standpoint—no, they don't. But, to ignorant, superstitious souls wallowing in abject poverty, the distinction isn't nearly so clear."

"In other words, Zunimbism offers the poor a way to attain both secular comfort and spiritual salvation."

"Something like that."

I sensed her agreement to my oversimplification was reluctant.

"Its followers seem to find what people everywhere demand of their religion: comfort in the present existence and hope for a better life in the hereafter. The cult's been hard to stamp out, primarily because of the difficulty of infiltrating it with any success. Its members are very close-mouthed. They're brainwashed into believing that if they reveal anything about their secret organization or its activities, they'll be stalked and viciously murdered, and their souls will suffer eternal damnation."

"Is Zunimbism anything like voodoo? I mean, since they both have their origins in Haiti…"

"Yes, and no. Voodoo's pretty harmless. It's no more than a folk religion that was born on the slave plantations of eighteenth-century Haiti. It brought together and blended several major strands of Central and Western African religion and later, elements of French Catholicism. Its concerns were venerating ancestors and dealing with the dead—since the followers believe that those who have died influence the lives of those who are living.

"Voodoo's a powerful and intimate religion because it focuses on transpossession—an altered state of consciousness in which a spirit can speak and act through a family member. Followers also gather at ritual ceremonies, where people sing and dance, during which spirits will occasionally take possession of someone, usually the priest or priestess. The attendees can then talk to the spirit and receive advice."

"This isn't the voodoo I've seen portrayed in the movies," I said.

"No, it isn't. Voodoo's been the victim of negative stereotyping. True voodoo has no such thing as zombies—'living dead' raised from the grave to become mindless servants to some sorcerer who's gained an evil power over them. Neither does it promote the use of voodoo dolls—pushing pins into a victim's image to inflict pain and suffering."

"I'm glad to hear that." And, I was. "And Zunimbism…"

"Zunimbism also claims to have roots in West African culture. While the founders of Zunimbism borrowed much of their terminology and concepts from their voodoo neighbors on the island, it is far from an innocuous folk religion. Zunimbists do not believe in a god, per se, however, they do worship *loas*—spirits that exist in natural elements such as earth, water, wind, and fire.

"As long as an individual stays in harmony with these spirits, he or she will achieve the supreme goal, which is the attainment of pleasure and protection from pain. Zunimbists do have priests and priestesses—*oungans* and *mambos*—who are believed to have powers of sorcery and black magic; but they use those alleged powers to influence the spirits in rewarding or punishing mortals. And they can direct the use of violent means to achieve their objectives."

"This is fascinating, but how does it relate to the two murders?"

"Legend has it that a cocaine smuggler fleeing from Haitian police got lost in the mountains around Ville Bonheur a couple of decades ago. There, he stumbled across a *lien saint*, or holy place, where a Zunimba ritual happened to be taking place. He only managed to avoid execution by sharing a little of his 'cargo.' The white powder filled the ritual participants with such a *loa* that all their past *loas* paled in comparison. Needless to say, it didn't take long for the candy man to have the *oungans* and *mambos* eating out of his hand. Over the following years, he organized and trained a gang that's become second to none when it comes to drug trafficking.

"In no time, the smuggler even became the *oungan rexis*, or head priest, and has now become known as Zunimba. Before long, he was using the natives' newly acquired addiction to cocaine and their longstanding fear of the powers of the *oungans* and *mambos* to develop a loyal group of unquestioning subordinates.

"This oungan rexis, or Zunimba, is brutal in his treatment of rivals as well as those he believes guilty of betrayal. His band of oungans and mambos and their disciples have no fear of personal danger as long as their acts occur in the service of Zunimbism. As long as they don't feel intimidated by death, they feel invincible— a competitive advantage in a cutthroat business that's allowed them to make substantial inroads into the drug trade in this part of the hemisphere."

"Any idea who this messiah of murder is? I hope he doesn't get his own evangelical show on the religious channel."

She shrugged. "No, but we suspect he spends a good deal of his time in Miami."

"Why is that?"

"Zunimbism is too big an operation to be run from a Caribbean island. Plus, drug dealers flock to Miami like ticket scalpers to the Super Bowl. Most of the flow of illegal drugs into this country is coordinated from South Florida." She leaned back in her chair and, ignoring her short, split skirt, plopped her feet on her desk.

This time, I managed to maintain eye contact. "Have autopsies been completed on Amundson and Dubonnet? If so, what was given as the cause of death?"

"Let's see what the ME says," she replied. She lowered her legs to my disappointment, swiveled around to the credenza behind her, and rummaged through a stack of folders, pulling one out of the middle of the stack and another from the bottom. By the time she turned back around to face me, she was flipping through the pages. "Ah, here's the medical section... According to this, we don't have all the results in yet, but the medical examiner says that in both cases the cause of death was exsanguination, a fancy name for the victim bleeding to death.

"The report says, 'A preliminary look at the velocity and type of blood splatters indicates that severe arterial truncation occurred.'" She looked up and, for my benefit, explained: "Arteries spurt freely, resulting in a linear and cascading splatter pattern." Satisfied that she'd demonstrated her intellectual superiority, she glanced back down at the folder and continued reading. "'The wound appears to be a homicidal incision administered by an assailant who was behind the victim.' The ME knows this because the cut started high up on one side of the neck near the ear, swept downward across the front of the throat, and up the opposite side," she paraphrased. I saw her flip through a few photos and study some sketches before she spoke again. "The path was left to right so we know the assailant was right-handed. The depth and angle of the cut, and the fact that only one incision was made, indicates that the assailant was taller than the victim, strong, and used a heavy knife. There were no cuts on the arms or hands of the victim which indicate that the coup de grâce was accomplished so quickly that the victim didn't have time to put up a defense."

"Good summary," I complimented. "My next question may call for some speculation: why do you suppose the murders were executed in such a brutal, ritualistic way? What's the significance of this modus operandi?"

"We don't have a lot to go on here. Apparently, the head is sacred to Zunimbists—it's considered to be the residing place of the soul. After a killer dispatches an enemy, severing his head condemns him to eternal damnation."

"Sounds like overkill to me. What about the markings?"

"The circumscribed symbols painted on the victims' chests haven't been deciphered by cryptologists yet. They could be a warning to others or they may be an explanation of why the victim was killed. Possibly, they're instructions regarding how the deceased is to be treated in the hereafter."

"If this keeps up, it's going to give graffiti a bad name. How about the bit with the chicken's head?" I asked. "Got anything on that yet?"

"It seems that chickens are held in low regard by the Zunimbists—possibly because of their skittish behavior or the fact that they're scavengers of a low order, since they'll eat just about anything on the ground. The Zunimbists also act out a little superstition called *pase poul*, which means 'to pass the chicken.' Once the assassin has completed his work, he rubs a dead chicken all over his own body. Any impurities or evil spirits are transferred to the chicken through this bodily contact. The act, in effect, purges the Zunimbist of his transgressions. Decapitating the chicken and stuffing its head in the corpse's mouth condemns the victim to serve as a substitute in an eternity of torment and anguish."

"The chicken's probably not too crazy about this procedure, either. Remind me not to buy a KFC franchise in Port-au-Prince. One final question, lieutenant. If members of this gang are so secretive, how did you manage to find out so much about them?"

"I'm an adjunct professor and guest lecturer at Miami Dade Community College where I teach criminology with an emphasis on the Caribbean and Central and Latin American regions. I've been gathering a lot of research on the subject and hope to write a book." She paused as she pointed to a framed certificate on the wall beside me. "I was also appointed to head a Zunimba Task Force that is comprised of representatives from law enforcement agencies throughout Florida. We're in the process of expanding our information base on Zunimbism. To date, most of what we know has come from FBI bulletins and our own street experience. It's been difficult getting information from Zunimbists because they'll commit suicide rather than be captured."

"Why? Are they afraid they'll be served chicken as their last meal on death row?"

"Actually, you're on the right track—not about the chicken but death row. The one fear they do have is the death penalty for a couple of reasons. First, they believe the electrical interference generated during an electrocution destroys their ability to receive spirits. Second, once executed, their bodies can only be released to licensed morticians, not fellow cult members who'd whisk the corpses away to jungle locations to perform three-day spiritual ceremonies before burning them in a funeral pyre."

"Digressing for a moment, I wasn't aware Florida had a death penalty."

"We didn't have one for fifteen years, but it was revived in 1979 after a favorable Supreme Court ruling three years earlier. We now use an electric chair, 'Old Sparky' as it's affectionately called. I'm afraid its days are numbered, though."

"Why is that?"

"Criticism from right-to-lifers has been mounting, and the attorney general's office in Tallahassee has been giving some consideration to lethal injections. I don't think that's a good idea, though."

"Because…" I prompted.

"Lethal injection, or what I've read of it, appears to be a complicated, nasty process that has plenty of issues all its own," she replied, her voice tinged with skepticism.

"How's it different from any other shot with a needle? Pardon my ignorance but we still use gas pellets in California."

"According to what I've read, the prisoner is first injected with sodium pentothal, which is pumped throughout the body by the heart and induces sleep. Then pancuronium bromide, a muscle relaxant, is administered to paralyze the diaphragm and lungs and halt breathing. The final step is a third injection of potassium chloride, which stops the beating of the heart."

She glanced at her watch before resuming with some impatience. "Getting back on topic, we did manage to corner a Zunimbist a while back while trying to serve a warrant. He wrecked his car during a police chase but survived, and we were able to get him to a hospital for treatment and interrogation."

"Was it difficult obtaining a confession?" I asked.

"That was actually the easy part," she confided. "All we had to do was walk in the hospital room, waiving a long knife and a plucked chicken."

"And he spilled his guts... in a manner of speaking," I finished with a laugh. "If you have no objections, lieutenant, might I borrow your chicken? I'd like to question the prisoner."

"I'm afraid that won't be possible," she replied.

"Oh? So, he died later?"

"No."

"He was released on bail?"

"No."

"Then what?"

"He grabbed a male nurse's scrubs from a linen closet and escaped. As he was crossing the street, he was hit by a truck carrying live chickens to a poultry processing plant."

"If you live by the chicken," I philosophized, "I guess you die by the chicken."

After briefly pondering the little ironies of life, I was preparing to leave when I thought it advisable to ask about my weapon. "I brought a firearm with me to Florida, a .38 Smith & Wesson. Will that cause anyone a problem?"

Alameda sniffed derisively. "Are you kidding? Florida is a pistol-packer's paradise. We call it 'the Gunshine State' instead of the Sunshine State. You don't need a license or permit to purchase a handgun, rifle, or shotgun in this state. If you're twenty-one, you can buy a handgun from a licensed dealer. If you're eighteen, you can buy from a private party. Our waiting period is only three days, and the criminal background check is a joke.

"Furthermore, firearms don't have to be registered with the police and can be kept in the home without any type of permit. You can even carry a firearm in your vehicle without a permit or concealed-weapons license as long as it's 'securely encased' such as in a glove compartment or someplace where it's not immediately accessible. You can go to any school in Dade County and find more guns than lunchboxes and backpacks."

At that, Alameda buzzed Deputy Brannigan who again lumbered in without relish.

"Take my cup and wash it out," she commanded.

He reached over, picked up the mug, noticed that the contents hadn't been touched, and left.

"Lieutenant Alameda, if you'll permit a suggestion. Authority, once acquired and established, doesn't have to be so blatantly exercised."

"Excuse me?"

It wasn't that she hadn't heard me; she was just surprised that I had challenged her.

"And, what do *you* know about authority?" she asked rhetorically. "Tell me: *what* do you know? I've got three strikes against me. First, I'm a woman working in a man's world. Second, I'm of Cuban origin, working in a city whose power structure is still adjusting to being overrun by Hispanics. The Mariel boatlift in 1980 brought 125,000 Cubans to South Florida, many of them hardened convicts released by Castro from his worst prisons. Bias against Cubans has been a fact of life ever since. Third, I'm smart—smarter than most of the guys in this department who resent it.

"I've worked like hell to get where I am, and I'll be damned if I'll give anyone the upper hand again. Chauvinistic abuse at the police academy didn't stop me; crooks who didn't take me seriously until I cuffed them didn't stop me; police commissioners who patted my ass and called me 'honey' didn't stop me. So, don't tell me how to handle authority, McFadden. I've had to buck it every step of the way in my career."

I rose gingerly from my chair. "Well, I believe my twenty minutes are up. Thanks for the information, lieutenant. I hope you get whatever it is you want, and I hope it's everything you want it to be."

CHAPTER 4

WHEN I GOT BACK TO THE ROOM, I FOUND Girtha sprawled in a chair in front of the air conditioner, fanning herself with a magazine and taking sips from a small paper cup. I marveled at the collection of department store bags scattered around the room. "Finish your shopping?"

"I just got in. That spree almost did me in," she gasped. "The temperature is the same as L.A., but the humidity is murder. I'd barely gotten ten feet from the hotel when it felt as if someone had set off a sprinkler system inside my clothes."

I looked from her bags to my single suitcase as she spoke. "We're only going to be gone two weeks, Girtha. It appears you've prepared for a millennium."

"If that's longer than two weeks, it is *not* true," Girtha said. "A girl can't be seen wearing the same outfit twice, you know. But I bought a few mix-and-match coordinates that should last me a few days."

Only a few moments later, I was taking a much needed nap while Girtha read a book on cruise etiquette. I woke up around eight in the evening, freshened up, and escorted Girtha out into the Cuban section of Miami. The first restaurant we came to—*El Sol De Havana*—looked "ethnic" enough so we walked up to a menu that was posted outside the front door. Unfortunately, we had to lean over the body of a weather-beaten, sleeping indigent who was propped against the wall. He sported a scraggly beard and thinning, stringy hair, and the ash-laden remains of a delicately balanced cigarette hung from his dry lower lip. In his lap, a bowl containing a few coins was nestled. After reading the menu, I pulled a couple of singles from my wallet and stuffed them into his shirt pocket.

"Is that a good idea, Chauncey?" Girtha asked. "Aren't you just encouraging him to continue panhandling?"

"I'm just hedging my bet. A friend of mine once told me that you should always give money to a homeless man: he could be Jesus working undercover."

Inside, the restaurant was almost empty and nothing like its sun-inspired name—its darkness was illumined only by flickering candles wedged in wine bottles that were layered with multi-colored wax drippings. In spite of the darkness, a thin elderly waiter with skin like cured horsehide successfully maneuvered us to a small table without incident. We had even squeezed into our rattan chairs by the time I realized the gentleman was not just hard of hearing, but spoke no English. Fortunately, the smattering of survival Spanish I knew from L.A. was adequate enough to secure two glasses of water and identify several items from the expansive menu.

Girtha suddenly squeezed my arm. "Chauncey," she whispered, "a moment ago, I noticed that those two men getting ready to leave slyly exchanged briefcases. When they opened them, one guy looked like he was counting paper while the other guy licked his finger tip. It looked awfully suspicious if you ask me."

I turned my head only slightly and looked out the corner of my eye, trying to remain as discreet as possible, at a couple of slick-haired gunsels in the far corner. "It could be the consummation of a drug deal," I whispered back.

"In the open like that?"

"This is Miami. According to some of the background reading I did in preparation for the trip, we're at the center of international intrigue and conspiracy. One news article said that if you see two or more men huddled together, chances are they're working out a drug deal or plotting the overthrow of some banana republic—or both.

"According to professional pundits, Miami is a hotbed of lawlessness," I said tongue-in-cheek. I decided to play off some of her naïveté so she wouldn't worry so much about the truth. "Columbian cocaine cowboys, Guatemalan godfathers, Honduran heroin *jefes*, Mexican mafioso, and past Peruvian politicos often meet in obscure corners of neighborhood cafes or aboard posh yachts to link their mutual interests."

"My word, Chauncey. I never would've guessed. I thought Miami was an oceanside Palm Springs."

"There are several Miami's," I responded. I didn't want to scare gullible Girtha, but I did want her to be aware that even paradise has warts. "There's the one that tourists and snowbirds see: South Beach, Collins Avenue, Ocean Drive, and the Art Deco District. Then there's the sprawling condo hives where retired New Yorkers mark time waiting for death, sipping kosher wine in their cabana outfits. There are also the wealthy exclusive enclaves where celebrities—free from a state income tax—collect mansions that are immune from bankruptcy judgments.

"Finally, there's the darker side where espionage is commonplace, guns outnumber people, and drugs flow like tap water; where, more illegal money is laundered than hotel towels; where exiled Latin *caudillos* and strongmen abuse their asylum by plotting the overthrow of those who overthrew them, and illegal arms are *de rigueur* for self-styled revolutionaries."

I was on a roll and, having Girtha's enraptured attention, saw no reason to stop.

"Miami's a city of stark contrasts, from the ritzy mansions on Key Biscayne to the peeling stucco cottages in Liberty City and Little Havana; from bronzed, youthful hard bodies on roller blades to elderly denizens who seem to have been shrunk by years in the sun. Someone once remarked that Miami is a mecca for people-watching because without effort, you can see the tree-ripened grapes and the dry raisins they will become. The flashy and the trashy co-exist in a metropolis so complex and diverse that anyone can call it their own."

Girtha shuddered. "I'm glad we're only going to be here one night."

I smiled and continued my act. "Most of this is transparent to the average citizen. What do they know of contraband being flown into remote Florida landing strips in the dead of night… or bands of mercenaries who regularly use the Everglades to break in new weapons or train recruits in guerrilla warfare? Down here, even the waiting rooms in doctors' offices have *Soldier of Fortune* magazines on the tables.

"Miami is the only city I know where a street was named after a drug dealer, and motels near the airport gave 'freedom fighter' discounts to mercenaries en route to battle enemies of our government. Did you know that during the height of the drug wars, it was reported that the morgue ran out of room and bodies had to be stacked in a refrigerated truck borrowed from a hamburger chain?"

My dissertation was curtailed by the arrival of our order. Girtha and I plowed into the food, and, after devouring generous portions of *moros y cristianos, bistec de palomilla, plátanos maduros,* flan, and espresso, we waddled back to our hotel.

When we got to our room, my heart skipped a beat as I fished the key out of my pocket: our door was ajar. "Girtha, you were the last one out. Did you shut the door?"

"Of course," Girtha replied. "I live in East L.A., remember? I even twisted the knob to make sure the door was locked."

"Wait here," I instructed. "I better have a look."

It was a short look. Besides the room and bath, I only had to scan the closet and underneath the bed. We went through our luggage but found nothing missing.

"No harm done," I said. After one more sweep of the room, I sat on the bed and removed my shoes. "You want to use the bathroom first?"

"Absolutely," Girtha said, "otherwise, there'll be no hot water left."

While she prepared to shower, I turned on the television, hoping to catch a late weather report. I had just leaned comfortably back against my propped-up pillows when a blood-curdling scream erupted from the bathroom! Instinctively, I grabbed my Smith & Wesson from under the mattress and headed for Girtha. As I approached the door, she slammed into me while fleeing the steamy room.

"What's the matter?" I asked with alarm.

"Who'd do such a thing?" she cried. "It's horrible."

"Do what?" I asked. "What are you talking about?"

"There," she exclaimed, pointing behind the coffee maker.

I looked and couldn't control my own gasp—submerged in one of the hotel water glasses was the head... of a chicken.

The SPCA wasn't going to like this.

CHAPTER 5

AFTER FINISHING LUNCH—AND CONSPICUOUSLY avoiding any chicken parts as a menu selection—we and 800 other passengers were picked up by a fleet of buses in front of our hotel and transported to pier three at the Port of Miami where the *Oslo Aphrodite* was moored.

The ship was a breathtaking sight—it stretched longer than two football fields and towered more than ten stories into the air. It was a pristine vision in white, rising majestically above murky harbor waters, ignoring the waterfront flotsam and jetsam which bumped profanely against its haughty hull.

We followed the excited and boisterous crowd up the gangway and, obeying instructions on a sign, headed directly to the main lounge to make dining arrangements. We signed up for the second seating at each meal and learned we would be sharing a table with six other voyagers.

Our cabin, number 700, was amidships on the Promenade Deck, and we were delighted to find that our luggage had already been delivered. The size of the cabin was a disappointment—*either* of us would more than occupy one of the petite, twin-sized bunks. The shower was another revelation—it was smaller than a Gotham telephone booth.

"Oh, Chauncey…" Girtha wailed. "We won't be able to shower together."

"'*Together*'? We won't even be able to shower *individually*! I'll have to wash my front side on odd days and my back side on even days," I lamented.

Our chagrin was dispelled, somewhat, by the discovery of a large floral bouquet and fruit basket thoughtfully provided by our host, Anders Erickson. After we unpacked and stowed our suitcases under the twin beds, we ventured topside to grab a couple of large tropical drinks and take part in the festivities surrounding our departure from port.

We found a place at the stern of the ship, a starboard side rail, just as the vessel's horn bellowed, sending the seagulls into a tizzy and precipitating a flurry of activity. With the retraction of the gangplank, the raising of the anchor, and the release of the mooring lines, we were prepared to get underway. Hundreds of helium-filled balloons were released into the air, colliding in space with brightly colored streamers and confetti. Although no one was seeing us off, we joined in the revelry and waived gaily at the crowd along the quay.

We stayed by the rail for the better part of an hour, enthralled by the embarkation activities, as the land receded into nothingness and we were surrounded by an identical horizon on all sides. By that time, our drink glasses were empty, so we returned to the cabin to review our selection of scheduled activities for that evening. Unfortunately, our debate over possible options was too soon interrupted by a phone call—Captain Nelson requesting my presence in his cabin.

The illusion of holiday abruptly shattered, I was reminded of the grim reason I was on board in the first place.

As I made my way to the Captain's quarters, the image of last night's chicken head returned to my mind. I had seen plucked chickens hanging upside down in Chinatown markets, but the previous night's experience in our hotel bathroom was nonetheless unnerving. The head in our water glass was an obvious indication that my cover had been blown. It was also, perhaps, even a warning, which led me to regret bringing Girtha along. I was still wrestling with that issue when I arrived in front of the Captain's door.

My knock was answered by a tall rawboned man, dressed in white from head to toe except for the black-and-gold epaulets on his shirt. His hair was blond, close-cropped, and flecked with gray. His deep azure eyes were positioned between a chiseled, weathered forehead and a full, neatly trimmed beard, also blond.

"*Velkommen ombord*, Mr. McFadden," he greeted. "Come in."

I followed him back to a sofa that commanded a gorgeous view of the ocean. On a large table in front of us lay several nautical maps, a sextant, and a pair of calipers.

"Plotting our course, Captain? I thought these floating palaces were equipped with state-of-the-art computers?"

"The ship line insists on that fancy equipment but if it was up to me, we'd use constellations and stars to guide us across the seas, like my ancestors, the Vikings."

"You'd need some mighty large sails and a terrific gale of wind to get this goliath island-hopping," I gibed.

"It depends on how much ballast we jettisoned," he hit back, looking at my paunch.

"Ouch," I said merrily. "This is a nice boat you have here."

Captain Nelson turned his head to a large watercolor of the *Oslo Aphrodite* that hung above his bunk and gave it a look most men reserve for young children or old mistresses. "She is a nice ship," he corrected firmly. Despite the name, the *Oslo Aphrodite* was built in Helsinki, at the Wartsila shipyard. She has more than 23,000 gross tonnage, measures 635 feet long, and has a 22 foot draft. She is driven by twin-screw variable-pitch propellers, powered by four Sulzer diesel engines and seven auxiliary engines, uses two Sperry stabilizers, and can reach a service speed of 21 knots."

"I'm afraid you're wasting those engineering details on me, Captain. I was thirty before I could build an oil derrick with Tinker Toys."

He smiled while packing tobacco into the bowl of a well-seasoned meerschaum pipe. "In a way, we're even then—I was thirty before I learned that a private detective was a real occupation and not a figment of some American screenwriter's imagination."

I returned the grin. The Captain was a serious man but, his ship and command aside, he had a lighter side I could relate to. We were going to hit it off okay.

"One question before we begin, Captain. I didn't notice any tugboats helping us out of the harbor."

"The *Oslo Aphrodite* maneuvers through the use of a combination of mechanisms, not just a set of rudders like in the old days. The two main propellers have four blades each and a diameter of twelve feet. We also have two electrically driven props mounted sideways near the bow of the ship. These bow-thruster propellers are used to turn the nose of the ship and, in combination with the aft engine-driven variable-pitch propellers *and* the ship's rudders, we can weave our way in the narrowest of ports without a tug."

"I suspected something like that," I joked.

He continued to gaze at the ship's picture with awe and passion, like a boy's first exposure to his father's hidden stash of girlie magazines. Handing me a large envelope, he said, "I've taken the liberty of anticipating some of your professional needs."

I accepted the envelope, sat down, and emptied its contents, item by item, on a coffee table.

"The first two documents are rosters. The first one contains names and room numbers for all the passengers on this cruise. The second one lists all the crew members on this trip as well as their function. Next is a complete diagram of the ship, which may come in handy. Last is a pass that will admit you to all areas of the ship, even those normally restricted to crew only. I've told my senior staff that you're a ship's inspector from the cruise line. That should enable you to receive all the cooperation you require. If that turns out not to be the case, let me know."

"How many passengers are on this cruise?" I asked.

"Eight hundred and twenty. Our capacity is 1,038, but things have been a bit slow this season. We have a staff of four hundred so you shouldn't find service lacking."

"Can you brief me on the key members of your staff?"

"Certainly," Nelson replied, his face partially obscured by an aromatic cloud of smoke. "There are a dozen 'key' personnel. I'll start with the four senior officers. First, is my right-hand man, the chief officer senior, or COS. That position was filled by Lars Amundson until his murder. His replacement is a fellow who just flew in from Oslo: Leif Jurgens. We've chatted briefly, but as you can appreciate, I know little about him, although his excellent reputation precedes him.

"Second, is our ship's doctor, Piers Lagervist. Our third senior officer is the chief engineer, Arnolf Hansen. He's assisted by the first engineer senior, Rolf Staagland. They run the engine room and ensure that the vessel has enough power to move comfortably through the water. Our final senior officer is the hotel manager, Klaus Mueller. He's in charge of all passenger areas and comforts.

"Other key staff members are the chief radio operator, Bruno Helmje, our link to the outside world. He monitors the ship's radio and will help you with any cablegrams or radio telephone calls you need to make to shore. The chief electrician is Helmet Jorgensen who is responsible for seeing that necessary electrical power is available throughout the ship.

"A gentleman *you'll* come to appreciate a great deal is our 'Chef de Cuisine,' Jules Dumas. He runs the best galley in the Caribbean. The food is outstanding, especially when you consider that he oversees the serving of 22,600 meals a week." Nelson paused and pointed his pipe stem at the straining buttons on my Hawaiian shirt. "Most people tend to gain ten pounds or so during a two-week cruise, so you may want to watch yourself—it doesn't appear you've reserved much room to store them."

"I was planning on walking around the deck every morning," I mumbled. But I still couldn't help squirming in my seat.

"Jogging is better," Nelson commented with a wink. "We also have one of the finest gyms on any cruise ship," he noted, "*if* you're interested."

I think he awaited a response that was not forthcoming. After an instant, he continued.

"Our next staff member is probably the most popular one with the passengers: Cruise Director Ingrid Larsen. She's the mistress of ceremonies who directs the programming and supervision of all passenger activities and shipboard entertainment.

"Bill Graham is the chief purser. He oversees the ship's finances and clears the passengers and crew through the various foreign ports. His office also serves as a general information center.

"And, the last two positions are important, but somewhat less visible to the average passenger. The food and beverage manager is Jean-Charles Beauchemon, and the chief passenger steward is Ugo

Cabrazzi. He's in charge of all passenger cabin services, as well as the general cleanliness of all interior areas of the ship.

"Our security officer, Bo Hatfield, isn't really an officer but you'll want to take him into your confidence at some point. He's been made aware of your real mission and charge."

"Thanks for the thumbnail sketches, Captain. Your crew has quite an international flavor," I commented.

"We have twenty-seven nationalities represented on the crew," he added proudly.

"How many of the crew do you actually know?"

"I only *personally* know the thirty or forty who play some sort of key staff role or hold supervisory positions. The vast majority of the crew is service personnel, of which ten percent or so turn over with each cruise."

"Then you wouldn't know anything about the murdered waiter, Victor Dubonnet?"

"No. I asked Jean-Charles about him but learned little. He had only been in our employ about three months. He was a quiet Haitian man who kept to himself. His performance was viewed as satisfactory. We never received any complaints from passengers seated at his tables."

"How about Lars Amundson? As one of your foremost subordinates, you must have known him pretty well."

Nelson rubbed his beard thoughtfully and sighed. "I was quite fond of Lars. He'd served on the *Oslo Aphrodite* for eight years, the past three as COS. He had a quick mind and wit, good traits to have in this business. We used to share watch on the bridge at night and try to stump each other with riddles. He was a great competitor. He had become an expert in the Rubik's Cube and played a solid game of chess. I'm a ranked player in chess, but he won his share of matches over the years." The Captain halted for a moment of reflection.

"Lars was a born leader… people were naturally attracted to him because of his personality and generosity. We were stunned by his death. He won't be easily forgotten."

"Would you comment upon his shortcomings? I, of course, mean no disrespect for the dead, but his faults may be more relevant to finding his killer."

Nelson shifted his pipe to the other side of his mouth and looked at the ceiling. "Well..." Following another awkward pause that proved to be reminiscence, he spoke but without pleasure. "On the job, his performance was *always* exemplary. But, like most extraordinary people, Lars did have weaknesses that were the flip sides of his strengths...

"His major weakness was boredom... He mastered most things easily... too easily in fact. When things lost their challenge, they lost their fascination for him. He would just grow bored, which occasionally manifested itself in self-destructive behavior... Yes, boredom was his nemesis. It could change him from a romantic to a womanizer, from being witty and clever to satirical and sarcastic, from self-confident to conceited, and from outgoing to overbearing...

"Fortunately, those periods when his dark side was in control were few in number and short-lived. Those closest to him could recognize the symptoms early on and work to get him re-involved in some new mind-consumptive activity."

"How about his recent scrape in the Dominican Republic?" I asked.

Nelson's eyebrows arched, and then lowered. "I was upset with Lars over that little fiasco. I expect my officers to be professional at *all* times—especially when they are in ports of call—and not behave like sailors on liberty..."

"Your answer to this question could be very important, Captain: what kind of trouble did he get into?"

"He got romantically involved with a young girl three or four months ago at a party at the American embassy in Santo Domingo. Unfortunately, she turned out to be the daughter of the *alcalde*—the mayor—of a little town, Santa Cruz de Concepçion. I suspected you would be asking, so I jotted down the names of the family members."

He handed me a piece of paper on which was written Rigoberto Sotomayer, father; Isabela, mother; María Cristina, daughter; Julio, son.

"I'm sorry, Captain—I must be missing something here. What's wrong with a little 'romantic expression' among consenting adults?"

Nelson looked pained. "She was only sixteen, still a minor. To make the matter worse, they were discovered in a room at the embassy by family members—locked in a naked embrace."

When he paused, I thought he was finished speaking. "So she was a minor. Why not rap Lars' knuckles and be done with it?"

"It's not that easy. Among socially prominent Hispanic families in that part of the world, more than age and consent are at issue... having sex before marriage is an unpardonable sin."

"It's amazing what a difference a few degrees in latitude make," I remarked. "In our country, fathers buy condoms for their sons before they're out of junior high, and mothers have their darling daughters outfitted with the latest in birth control devices before their braces are off."

"Unfortunately, the situation grew even worse," Nelson went on with chagrin.

"How so?"

"It seems the young lady became pregnant, and the family threatened legal action to establish paternal responsibility. They wanted Lars to take her hand in matrimony or at least provide a substantial trust fund for child support."

Nelson was busy re-lighting his pipe when I asked, "How did Lars react to this little dilemma?"

"He steadfastly maintained his innocence. He admitted to the romantic interlude, which he asserted was spontaneous and only occurred on that one occasion. However, he denies any responsibility for her pregnancy."

"Was Lars charged with statutory rape?"

"No criminal charges were filed to my knowledge, and Lars wasn't planning on setting foot on the island of Hispaniola again any time soon."

Redirecting the questioning to new ground, I asked, "Lars and Dubonnet were killed a day apart in the same bizarre manner, presumably by the same people. That suggests a connection, but no connection is discernible to me—they don't appear to have any logical association."

"As far as we know, they didn't even know each other," Nelson said. "Their only link appears to be their employer."

"Or, more specifically, their place of employment: the *Oslo*

Aphrodite." An idea was beginning to take shape in my mind. "The call Erickson received said more of the crew would die unless Zunimba was appeased. That suggests that the ship is somehow involved in an activity of interest to Zunimba, or more specifically that other members of the crew have something in common with Lars and Dubonnet which will cause them to become additional targets of violence at the hands of this nasty group of poultry provocateurs.

"The Zunimbists deal in drugs, so we have to suspect that is the common thread. Has the *Oslo Aphrodite* ever had a drug problem or scandal?"

"Never," Nelson snapped defiantly before softening. "I'd be naïve, however, if I didn't think that some marijuana isn't occasionally smuggled onboard by crew members and passengers for personal recreational use, but our penalties are stiff. Crew members who are caught are summarily dismissed. Passengers are evicted from the ship and have to make their own way back to the port of departure at their expense. So, the possibility that drug dealing on the *Oslo Aphrodite* could take place on a large scale does not seem reasonable.

"What happens on shore, even a tragic event like murder, is not my concern. But, here on my vessel, civil order and propriety *will* prevail and be enforced with unflagging zeal."

"I'll do my best, Captain, but barring some *deus ex machina*, quick and tidy solutions aren't usually easy to come by. Investigations usually involve a lot of sweat and, sometimes, more than enough blood to go around."

I left Nelson to grapple with his *weltanschauung* while I pursued a less lofty philosophical matter: how to succeed without being killed in the process.

I envied the Captain in a way. He was monarch of his kingdom; master of his domain. While the land had become contaminated and corrupt, long surrendered to the forces of moral malaise and physical decay, his realm, the sea, remained pristine and pure; the *Oslo Aphrodite*, in his view, the embodiment of perfect universal order.

At some point, perhaps soon, he would come face to face with the reality of evil and his terror would be greater than mine.

CHAPTER 6

"WAS THE CAPTAIN NICE?" GIRTHA ASKED UPON MY RETURN. "I just love men in uniform."

"That's good to know. Remind me to pick up an orange jumpsuit from the L.A. County jail."

"Not that kind of uniform," Girtha replied in exasperation, thwarted in her attempt to make me jealous. "Let's go to dinner. I laid your jacket and tie out on the bed."

The dinner bell tolled, beckoning calorie worshippers to the linen altar, and we joined the throng of fellow passengers at the second seating. Eventually, we entered the Camelot Dining Room and spotted our table number—in the far corner. It was a table for eight, and we were the last to arrive. I introduced Girtha and myself and was waiting for reciprocation when Girtha grabbed my arm, gulped, blinked, pointed, and stammered at the gentleman sitting across from her. "Aren't you… aren't you… aren't you…"

Fortunately, he smiled and mercifully put an end to her reiteration. "Quite possibly, my dear lady. Whom did you have in mind?"

Girtha tugged excitedly at my sleeve. "Help me, Chauncey," she implored. "We watch him all the time on those late show reruns. He's always a swashbuckling buccaneer, a mysterious spy, a dashing infantry captain…"

"Or down-and-out detective," I mumbled. "I believe Lamont Darling is the name you're searching for."

I thought swoons had gone out of style, but Girtha's rendition was as good as any ever captured on film.

"Oh, Mr. Darling," Girtha squealed upon recovering, "I can't believe it's really you. I've been a fan of yours for years. My closet is still full of magazines with your picture on the cover."

"Thank you, my dear. You're very kind." Darling flashed his patented celluloid smile and Girtha went under for the second time.

Begrudgingly, I had to admit that Darling's physical features hadn't exactly been ravaged by time. He was still tall, slender, and debonair with much of the magnetic profile and charm that had made him a top box office draw during the Roosevelt, Truman, and Eisenhower years. A rented tan highlighted his thin mustache and silver hair, which was styled in carefully arranged disarray. His silk sports shirt was fashionably unbuttoned to display several gold chains snuggling in his silver chest hair.

I woke Girtha from her rapture with an elbow to the ribs and suggested that perhaps we should meet the *others* at the table.

Darling introduced his companion, a statuesque early twenty-something blonde with a ponytail, as Fifi. He claimed she was his publicist but she would have looked more at home doing the bump and grind and getting dollar bills tucked inside her G-string. Every time she moved, she threatened to spill over the top of her sundress.

The man next to her, dressed in a white Nordic Caribbean uniform, introduced himself as Piers Lagervist, the ship's doctor. Of medium height and build, he had thinning light hair and small, wire-framed glasses perched on the end of his angular nose. His distinct Scandinavian features made me think of a frontispiece from an early edition of Hans Christian Andersen.

"A doctor? Oh, thank god," Girtha said, clapping her hands together. "I've been dying to talk to someone about my sciatica."

I felt sorry for Lagervist, though I suspected he was accustomed to being bombarded for pro bono medical advice and second opinions. Restricted by the ship's confines, I imagined his nautical medical practice had been reduced to little more than dispensing placebos to peripatetic hypochondriacs, which these longer cruises allegedly attracted. He explained that his presence at our table was for this evening only as officers of the ship were required to rotate among the passenger tables at dinner.

The other couple at the table was a disagreeable-looking pair. The woman, tall and fortyish, had raven-black hair and heavy white makeup that gave her a ghoulish appearance. Her hair had been pulled into a bun so tightly that it stretched the corners of her eyes as well. On the corner of her mouth was a small dark mole that had tiny hairs protruding from it, like the legs of a fly under a microscope. She looked slowly around the room through hooded eyes, like a snake on stakeout outside a mouse hole. She would have been more at home opening the door of Dracula's castle to a stranded traveler during an evening thunderstorm or kicking Cinderella in the ass for not scrubbing the floors fast enough. She was wearing a long-sleeved, burgundy velour dress with a high collar—not typical cruise attire.

The man with her was no bargain, either. He radiated unpleasantness the way overripe cheese gives off stench. Tall and lanky like his wife, his long black hair was combed straight back and fastened into a ponytail. His most arresting features were long sideburns, which almost crept to his jaw, and a long, jagged scar that connected his left temple to his chin. He had eight gold rings on his fingers and enough dirt under his nails to grow potatoes. He was dressed in an expensive-looking, double-breasted silk suit and complementary designer tie—but neither helped the image: he still looked like gift-wrapped sleaze. He had apparently succeeded at something in life, but it wasn't something I wanted to know anything about. When he smiled, I shuddered… as if someone had lifted a manhole cover to hell.

"I am Arturo Del Muerto," he said in a heavy Spanish accent, "a businessman from Bogotá. This is my wife, Castrada. You must pardon her… she does not speak English."

"What kind of business are you in, señor Del Muerto?" I asked.

He looked at me suspiciously; squinting with his left eye and lifting his upper lip until his top row of yellow teeth were bared. "In your country, I would be called… a headhunter."

Whatever the señor was hunting, I had a feeling it wasn't conducive to human health or longevity. A glance at Del Muerto had cured Girtha's swoon, and she had picked up her knife either to butter a roll or in anticipated self-defense.

"The señora," Del Muerto said, referring to Girtha—"my scar... it seems to make her nervous. I should explain—I cut myself shaving."

I managed to control a guffaw, but a question slipped from my lips: "What were you using—a dull machete?"

His deep chuckle sounded like an occupied coffin thudding down steep stairs. "The señor is a funny man. Me... I like funny men. Some people in my country... they don't like funny men so much. They think if you kill a funny man, it will bring you *buena suerte*... good luck."

"I'm a little large for a rabbit's foot, but I'll keep your quaint national custom in mind," I quipped.

With that, everyone turned to the last guest at the table. He was getting along in years and sported snowy white hair with a similarly colored handlebar mustache and goatee to match. He was dressed in a three-piece white linen suit and a black string tie.

He cleared his throat and spoke in a deep Southern drawl. "You all have the honor of addressing Colonel Cicero Augustus Beaufort Talbo of Divine Oaks, Mississippi."

"Oh, a military man. I just love military men," Girtha said. "What branch of service were you in, colonel?"

The Colonel gave her a patronizing look. "Ma'am, the title is an honorary one, given to me by the state militia in appreciation for my active support over the years. I would hardly have borne arms for anybody else. There hasn't been a cause worth fightin' for since the War of Northern Aggression six score ago. Granddaddy Talbo carried the family banner in that conflict."

I wondered if news of World Wars I and II had trickled down to Divine Oaks yet.

"We were sold out at Appomattox and lost everything but the house and the land under it. Even that was overrun by carpet-baggers during Reconstruction. We finally got control of our courts again and brought that passel of vermin to justice."

"Are the bodies still hanging from the tree limbs?" I asked innocently.

"No, suh, we cut 'em down," the Colonel answered without pause. "Didn't want the vultures to get sick."

"Is there a Mrs. Talbo?" Girtha asked.

"There was," the Colonel replied. "She was thrown from a horse while chasing some poachers off the land. She got her head caught in a forked tree branch and broke her neck."

My elbow slipped off the table at the irony: a white Southern matriarch losing her life on a tree limb, but I straightened up and regained my composure.

"Are you in the market for another wife?" Girtha asked.

The Colonel looked around the dining room to assess the plethora of unattached potential partners before replying. "The odds are good, but the goods seem odd."

We were unfolding our napkins when a tall black man with menus under one arm approached our table and coughed politely. He took a deep bow and came up with a broad smile which displayed a wide row of teeth, every other one gold.

"Good evening, dear guests. Allow me to welcome you again to the *Oslo Hermaphrodite*…"

"Aphrodite," I corrected. "Although there are hermaphroditic boats—two-masted vessels that are square-rigged in the fore and schooner-rigged in the aft—this ship isn't one of them." I beamed after proudly displaying my recently acquired nautical knowledge—a prize gained from in-flight reading.

The waiter frowned and looked at the cover of the top menu. "Ah, the gentleman is correct. It is the *Oslo Aphrodite*. I beg your pardon. This is my first cruise aboard the *Oslo Aphrodite*. I am a last-minute replacement for a waiter who recently met an untimely death in Miami."

Startled, I realized he must be the replacement for the late Victor Dubonnet.

"I also beg your indulgence for being late. I am Toussaint L'Enfant, your server, and it will be my pleasure to wait on you throughout your cruise. I am certain you will find our cuisine superb," he touted as he distributed the menus.

It was my turn to frown as I eagerly scanned the bill of fare. "Toussaint, my friend, isn't this the breakfast menu?"

Our affable waiter peered over my shoulder, slapped his forehead with his hand, and emitted a couple of phrases in a foreign tongue that sounded like French.

"How stupid of me," he groaned. He ran around the table collecting the errant menus, apologizing profusely all the while. He sprinted back to the galley and returned with the correct bills of fare.

This first evening out was French night and the entrees were limited but interesting. Girtha and I decided to share a bottle of Chambertin, a favorite of Napoleon and Alexander Dumas, to go with our orders of *carre d'agneau aux herbes pour deux*—a loin of lamb that sounded delicious. Darling navigated the menu with ease, facilely ordering for Fifi and himself in perfect French.

"Your fluency in French is impressive, Mr. Darling. Where did you learn to speak it so well?" I asked.

"I was born in France and lived there until I was discovered in a local film by Hollywood scouts. They gave me a screen test and the rest is, as they say, history."

When the food arrived, it was, fortunately, better than the service. Poor Toussaint, trying valiantly to get through his first meal, had a difficult time matching the orders with the appropriate diner. Everyone was understanding until Toussaint, in his haste to compensate for slow service, spilled a bowl of *consommé queue de boeuf* in Lamont Darling's lap. Darling was enraged and jumped up; "Idiot!" he spat, "Look what you've done to my slacks!"

The scene resulted in a prolonged awkward pause during which we all quietly put down our forks—except, that is, for Del Muerto, who continued to eat with his mouth open. He wiped his chin on his wife's sleeve and tossed his napkin to Darling. "Take mine. I no use these things anyway. The waiter is lucky: in my country, we drag the dumb *mesero* into an alley and cut off his *huevos*."

Girtha gasped, the doctor rolled his eyes, and Colonel Talbo said, "That strikes me as a mite harsh, suh. In Divine Oaks, I'd just restrict him to the plantation for a month and not let him go into town." Compared to the punitive suggestions of Del Muerto and the Colonel, Darling's loud reaction didn't seem so harsh.

The actor quickly apologized and mumbled something about "overreacting" as he sat back down with a blush, no doubt annoyed with himself for his loss of self-control. I permitted myself a brief smirk, luxuriating in the manifestation that Girtha's golden idol had feet of clay. It was doubtful that she would palpitate so easily again in Darling's presence. I looked in her direction, out of the corner of my eye, and caught her staring into her lap, her fingers demurely folded. Her disappointment hung like a pall, and I now felt guilty for having emotionally frolicked in something that had caused her such unhappiness.

Conversation at the table rebounded slowly, but it was predictably restrained and boring. The remainder of the meal passed relatively uneventfully—the best moment coming when the Colonel asked Toussaint what the chef had ladled on his *pomme de frits,* and the waiter scooped some up on his index finger, licked it, and offered *béchamel* sauce as his best guess.

Girtha and I left the table as quickly as decorum allowed and ambled to the Starlight Room and the comedy act of Joey Morton. His jokes pre-dated the Magna Carta, but they were enthusiastically delivered and enlivened with vaudevillian showmanship. He was having such a grand time that it gradually became infectious and the audience sent him off with a respectable round of applause. He was followed by a songstress who apparently harbored a deep-seated grudge against Cole Porter and an accordionist who, eschewing updated material, squeezed out "Lady of Spain." Now I knew where entertainers wind up after their careers hit rock bottom and their agents stop returning their calls.

The highlight of the evening was the next, and final, act: an energetic limbo artist. Encouraged by the beat of several drummers, he managed—after much fanfare and concentration—to slide, slither, writhe, and wriggle under a horizontal bar that was gradually lowered until it was less than two hands high.

"I saw it but I wouldn't have believed it," Girtha exclaimed, dumbfounded. "How did he do that without his butt or shoulders touching the ground? How did something like that get invented anyway?"

"Limbo has a long history," I said. "Some historians claim the limbo mimics the body motions of a slave trying to escape from his dungeon. Other wags say it was invented by a Scotsman trying to sneak into a pay toilet. Take your choice."

After the show, we started to take a turn around deck but found it a bit breezy. "Let's move from the windward side of the ship to the leeward side," I suggested.

"What's the difference?" Girtha asked.

"The windward side is the side of the ship exposed to the wind, while the leeward side is sheltered from the wind," I explained.

We passed by the cabin and picked up Girtha's wrap just in case but she didn't need it. We leaned against the railing and had our breath taken away by a full and silvery moon. Crouched just above the horizon, it was larger than we had ever seen it, and the water captured in its band of light sparkled like diamonds on black velvet.

We stood shoulder to shoulder, speechless and enraptured, and would have remained so indefinitely if a glance at my watch had not disclosed a critical event—the opening of the midnight buffet.

CHAPTER 7

AN EARLY RISER BY HABIT, I AWOKE AT DAYBREAK. I gently pushed back the covers and, without disturbing the softly snoring Girtha, donned a sweatshirt, walking shorts, and tennis shoes to take my morning constitutional topside. The dawn was barely out of its womb, and the early-morning sky was streaked with red, orange, and yellow hues. A few runners were out, thudding around the wooden decks, continuing their terra firma regimen.

When I got back to the cabin, I could hear Girtha working to pry herself out of the shower, and since the door into the room and the door to the bathroom couldn't be open at the same time, I waited in the alleyway until she could make good her escape. When I heard her release the air in her lungs, I walked in to find her slipping on a terrycloth robe, the perfect complement to the white towel turban she'd wrapped around her head. While she put on her face, I struggled with a washcloth in the tiny shower, and then we went to early breakfast. None of our fellow diners were there, so we enjoyed the table to ourselves.

"What do you have planned for today, sweetie-kins?" Girtha asked while unfolding her napkin.

"Hmmm... Sunday and we're at sea—I think we can relax and take it easy by the pool. I also want to review the material Captain Nelson gave me."

"Suits me," Girtha said. "My apartment doesn't have a pool, so I'm going to take advantage of this one all I can. I'd also like to…"

"Good morning, Mr. and Mrs. McFadden." The friendly voice of our neophyte waiter, Toussaint L'Enfant, interrupted the unveiling of her plan. "I see you are dining alone this morning. Would you care for some coffee?"

"Mr. and Mrs. McFadden—it has a nice ring to it, don't you think?" Girtha teased.

"Toussaint, do you have any of those breakfast menus from last night by any chance?" I pretended not to notice the presumptive and erroneous reference to our marital status.

Toussaint moaned and, as expected, slapped his forehead in a repeat of his debut performance. "I will get them at once."

"Girtha," I said in continuation of our conversation, "with luck, I'll be able to spend the day with you, but tomorrow we dock in Ocho Rios—"

"Oh! Our first port. Isn't it exciting?"

"I'm afraid I'll have to ask you to go by yourself."

"By myself? Where will you be?"

"Since almost all passengers and most of the crew will be ashore, it'll be an ideal opportunity to check out some things on the vessel. Remember, a threat has been made against the cruise line and I need to know a lot more about the *Oslo Aphrodite* than I do now."

Girtha frowned but acquiesced, realizing that I did have responsibilities that required attention. "What do you make of things so far, sweetie-kins?" she asked.

"I don't think anything, yet—that's the problem. I only have three bits of divergent information. First, two employees of a cruise line have been similarly butchered in a unique manner, which suggests a common perpetrator. Second, the victims have nothing in common as far as anyone can tell. And, third, a drug-dealing crime cult is believed responsible for both deaths, though even that is only a prima facie assumption."

Toussaint arrived with our menus, which we glanced over while he waited, looking over my shoulder. After submitting our orders, I turned back to Girtha.

"I don't want you to be alarmed, but…" I reached over and took her hand, "you need to watch yourself in Ocho Rios. Stay with others from the ship and don't wander off by yourself."

She jerked her head back and dropped her fork.

"Why, Chauncey? What're you expecting?"

"Nothing, really, but remember the chicken's head that was left in our hotel room in Miami? I'm afraid somebody's been tipped off about why I'm here. We may be under surveillance at this very moment."

"Are we in danger?" Girtha asked, suddenly shaken.

"If I thought so, you'd be on the first plane back to L.A. The threat specifically targeted the ship's crew, so I don't have any personal concerns. Let's just exercise caution, that's all."

Her face relaxed and she was relieved enough to stop twisting her napkin and dig into her *omelette aux girolles*—omelet with mushrooms—while I polished off several orders of *pannequets*—large thin pancakes filled and rolled with fruit. Thirty minutes later, I pushed myself back from the table and groaned.

"What is it, Chauncey?"

"My pants are feeling tight, already, and the cruise has just started. I better start pacing myself. Being fat is worse than being a felon. When you're fat, you carry your prison around with you," I lamented.

We returned to our room, changed, and headed for Lido Deck. I followed silently, marveling at the large carry-on bag with which Girtha struggled. As she staggered to a chaise lounge and collapsed on her back, I knelt down and pawed through the bag's contents: three books, a box of chocolates, some stationery and a pen, two bags of potato chips, a pillow, a portable radio, some underwater goggles, a pair of fins and a mask, a snorkel, a bottle of suntan lotion, *and* a sand pail and shovel.

"Girtha!" I gasped, pulling her into a sitting position. "What're you planning to do—open a concession stand?"

"Don't be silly," she panted. "I merely brought a few little items to see me through the afternoon. Help me drag this lounge away from the umbrella, will you? I want to catch some rays."

"Don't overdo it," I advised. "You have sensitive skin and the sun is stronger here than you're used to." I helped her get situated, confident that she had enough provisions and amusements to last her through the cruise. I needn't have worried; in a moment, she was fast asleep.

We arrived early enough to still find a good selection of seats. Shortly after, however, the poolside area quickly swarmed with sunbathers anxious to acquire tans that would be the envy of friends back home. By mid-morning, the hot sun and clear sky were cooperating to bake masses of undraped bodies that formed a doughnut of flesh around the pool and open-air bar. In the background, a steel drum band from Barbados had finished performing "Yellow Bird," "Peas and Rice," and "The Big Bamboo" before moving on to lesser-known tunes. Throughout the area, several young, nubile staff members in abbreviated white shorts and tight T-shirts displaying the ship's logo scurried around overseeing scheduled passenger events and improvising impromptu activities.

Obscured by my Panama hat and dark sunglasses, I engaged in one of my favorite pastimes: people-watching. I could justify not buckling down to read with the hope that, in scanning my fellow passengers, I might identify a crazed killer. However, the only person I saw with a knife and poultry was the chef at the roast turkey carving station in the buffet line.

Nonetheless, while the exercise was without benefit, it was not without interest. A young couple wearing matching "honeymooner" shirts had their lips glued together like a snail's belly on the glass wall of an aquarium. Next to them, a man and woman in their fifties were doing their best to chaperone a young woman I supposed to be their overdeveloped granddaughter.

The man I cast as the grandfather had jowls that were separated by an oversized cigar that occasionally dropped ashes down his convex leghorn-white torso. I barely restrained a chuckle when he stood up—he resembled a golf ball on two tees. His wife's appearance was no less intriguing. Her lipstick, which looked like it had been applied with a paint roller, was smudged beyond the perimeter of her mouth from chain-smoking through a cigarette holder long enough to play billiards with. Her hair was frazzled, most likely from a surfeit of tint jobs, which, sure enough, I could make out after she let it down. Distinct layers defined where it had been dyed different colors at varying lengths. It resembled the strata of Earth from a geology textbook. Between her lips and her hair, a pair of oversized sunglasses with rhinestone-encrusted frames attempted to cover a slightly swollen face. I guessed the bandages had recently been removed from her latest bout with cosmetic surgery. In fact, as I looked more closely, it appeared that her face had been lifted more often than a five-pound barbell at a busy gym.

The object of their devotion, the presumed granddaughter, was a precocious teen nymph who repeatedly jumped in and out of the pool, coyly tugging up her top after its contents had received sufficient exposure and admiration.

Beyond those highlights, all the expected components of the passenger pool were present, as well. I picked out matrons that were trying to peddle their spinster daughters, hoping to achieve at sea what they had failed to do on land; nubile ingénues who displayed their assets under the pretense of working on stubborn tan lines; retired CEOs who were enjoying the fruits of their golden parachutes; recent divorcees who found themselves back on the market, their reentry financed with hard-won alimony awards; couples hoping to jump-start their boring marriages with a change of scenery; widows heavily involved with gin—playing it half the time and drinking it the other half. I noted women with their gigolos, hoping for love but settling for checkbook sex; and men with their rented mistresses who moaned on cue and stroked sugar daddy's ego like a racehorse's groom. I even spotted some gays, cavorting in thongs, rubbing lotion on each others' bodies with fawning gusto and bitchy delight. Relatively few families ventured into my line of sight, probably because of the length and expense of the cruise. I could have observed indefinitely, but my attention was suddenly captured by the appearance of a familiar figure.

Bellying up to the poolside bar, and ogling all that lay before him, was señor Del Muerto. Martini in hand, he strutted among the sunning beauties, flexing his biceps and holding his stomach in whenever he made eye contact. In spite of his efforts, he wasn't getting much response—though I couldn't have guessed what part of his appearance was to blame: the black lace-up street shoes he was wearing with a pair of dark dress socks held up by red garters;

the crotch of his black nylon swimming suit, which sagged and swung obscenely from side to side like the pendulum of a grandfather clock; or the large jagged scar on his hairy chest that resembled a fire break through a dense forest.

"Señor McFadden!" he greeted upon seeing me. "What brings you out in *el sol*, amigo? You look like you be more at home in a bakery, *no es verdad?*" He laughed at his own humor before spitting an olive pit into the pool.

"And you'd look more at home in a lineup, Del Muerto. What do we have to thank for your appearance today—early parole? Or did you break out of the pen in the laundry truck again?"

His response was a sneer that curdled the coconut cream in my piña colada.

"You funny man, señor McFadden. You lucky I like you, *el gordo*," he said, while pulling a switchblade from the front of his bathing suit. "This knife is not the only lethal weapon I keep in here, you know." Unfortunately, I couldn't look away quickly enough to avoid seeing him grab his crotch. Fortunately, this conversation about Del Muerto's testicular excess was short-lived.

"I must go now to shoot some skeets. You want to join me?"

"Why would I want to shoot skeets? They taste like clay and they're hard to tenderize, no matter how long you marinate them."

He turned and resumed his barrio mating strut, and I heard the words "funny man" as he wandered out of range.

"Excuse me, pal, but is this chair taken?"

I looked up and shook my head. "Help yourself."

"Thanks." The gentleman slumped into the adjacent chair and stretched out. "Nice crowd here today. I wish I had the drawing power of the pool."

Drawing power? The words clicked as I said them to myself. "I caught your show last night. I thought it was quite good. Mr. Morton, isn't it?"

"Joey's the handle," he replied.

He extended his hand, and I shook it.

"Chauncey McFadden's mine."

"First cruise, Chauncey?"

"Yes, as a matter of fact. Girtha, my girlfriend, and I are taking a honeymoon—we skipped the wedding part."

He smiled. "The *Oslo Aphrodite* gets a lot of honeymooners—first, second, and beyond. I'm through with honeymoons, myself. Five trips to the altar kind of soured me on them—not the honeymoons themselves, but the part that followed."

"Five marriages and no visible scars… that's quite an accomplishment. What's your real name, Joey?"

He looked at me suspiciously. "Why do you ask?"

"Your signet ring has the initials 'CA' on it."

"Oh," he laughed, somewhat relieved. "My real name's Carmine Alponicelli—not exactly the kind of moniker that fits on or lights up marques. I changed it on the advice of my agent, Sam Gold—who is really Saul Goldenberger—and my business manager, Stan Kramer—who is really Stanislavski Kruschenovich. I picked 'Joey' because all Jewish comedians are named Joey, and 'Morton' because a box of salt was on the table when I made the decision."

"Hmm," I mused. "It's a good thing a box of sanitary napkins wasn't on the table—otherwise we'd be calling you 'Joey Tampon.'"

"Yeah, close call. Hey, pal, I like your material. Maybe you should join the act. The pay's good and you get to travel a lot."

"No, thanks. Success would be an uncomfortable mantle on my shoulders. Besides, I've become used to the low-paying job I already have."

"Hey, maybe you should try the employment office over at Nabisco. I hear they have some job openings."

"Doing what?" I asked on cue.

"Punching assholes in animal crackers!"

I grimaced. "Joey, the first time I heard that joke, I spit my pacifier halfway across the nursery. That's not from your act, is it?"

"Are you kidding? The cruise line would drop me in two seconds flat if I used language or material like that. This ain't a lounge act in Vegas or Atlantic City. I can't say anything that might offend a minister's wife from Buzzard's Breath, Idaho."

"May I ask you a question, Joey?"

"Sure. I'm out of the closet now."

I was surprised at the turn in the conversation and offered my support. "Congratulations on being so open about your homosexuality—"

"I'm not gay. I'm a recovered agoraphobic," he chortled. "Gotcha!"

I sensed it was going to be difficult getting Joey off the stage. "What's your employment arrangement, if you don't mind me asking? Do you just work an occasional cruise when you feel the need to get away?"

"No, I'm under contract to Nordic Caribbean; I'm not a freelancer. They have four ships that work the Caribbean and two positioned in the Mediterranean. I'm booked about six weeks a year on each of them. I spend half my life at sea; sort of a saltwater borscht belt."

"Then you must have known Lars Amundson, the ship's officer who was murdered in Miami just before we sailed."

"I knew him well enough to speak to him but that's all."

"Joey, did you—?" I was interrupted by the sound of my name being paged through a megaphone carried by a crew member who had been circling around the deck. "Over here!" I yelled.

The courier lowered his megaphone and approached my chair. "Mr. McFadden? I'm Bruno Helmje, the chief radio operator. I'm sorry to disturb you, but you have a phone call in the Radio Room. If you'll follow me, please, I'll guide you there."

"Excuse me, Morton," I said, grunting to my feet. "I'll be back in a minute."

I left the snoozing Girtha undisturbed and followed Helmje to the ship's Radio Room which was on Main Deck. It was difficult keeping pace at first. Although Helmje was a short man—about five feet tall—he took quick strides and darted around and through traffic more efficiently than I did. I noted that he appeared nervous, and constantly glanced over his shoulder but avoided eye contact. When we arrived, a radio operator handed me a receiver and courteously retreated to another room.

"McFadden here."

"McFadden—Anders Erickson. What's the situation on board?"

"Uneventful thus far. I gather from your call that the same can't be said at your end."

"That's an understatement," he sputtered. I could envision Erickson, phone in hand, pacing back and forth within the rut in his carpet.

"Why? What's happened?"

"Another man was found murdered Zunimba-style this morning."

"Was he an employee of Nordic Caribbean?"

"No, he was an employee of a waste management facility at the Port of Miami; fellow named Jacque Destang."

"Was there anything to indicate that his murder is related to our case?"

"That's the interesting part. Destang had a telephone number in his wallet that belonged to an apartment in the Little Haiti section of Dade County."

"So?"

"The apartment's owner is Victor Dubonnet. Metro Homicide thinks it's more than a coincidence, and so do I."

"Have they run a background check on Destang?"

"He was a small-time thief with a record of petty offenses. He'd been employed at the waste management facility for a little over a year."

"Was his nationality Haitian?"

"Yes, *and* he was from Plaine-du-Nord, the same town as Victor Dubonnet."

"If the murders continue to accelerate at this rate, they'll be able to hold their class reunion in a phone booth," I remarked.

"Also, Lieutenant Alameda finished running the passenger list through the international and national crime databases and the results are in."

"Anything interesting?"

"I'll say. There must be thirty people who're of interest to the authorities. Alameda is having warrants taken out on some of them. Don't be surprised if you find paddy wagons backed up to the dock when you disembark in Miami."

"What have you gotten me into, Erickson? Thirty scofflaws? There're more crooks on this cruise than prisoners on the barge to Devil's Island! What type of charges are you seeing?"

"Let's see, one is wanted for suspected embezzlement, one for perjury, three for jumping bail, one for flight to avoid prosecution, one for witness tampering, six for child support arrears, eight are illegal aliens—"

"Erickson, you can skip the white-collar peccadilloes. I'm not interested in people with unpaid traffic tickets. I'm looking for a sadist who can methodically and dispassionately carve people up like a Pacific Northwest totem pole."

"All right, all right, give me a minute," I heard Erickson say over the sound of rustling paper.

"Are you interested in rape, sodomy, or incest?"

"Only as a voyeur. Skip those, too—our crimes aren't of a sexual nature."

"Wait a minute… I may have something here. Here's a passenger who's been arrested eight times for first degree murder and never been convicted!"

"*That* sounds like the type of desperado we're looking for—someone who might be performing chicken transplants without a license."

"Cabin 1124… From Bogotá, Columbia…"

"Who is it, Erickson? What's the name?"

"Arturo Del Muerto—"

"Del Muerto? That's actually not surprising."

"Do you know him?"

"He and his wife are assigned to our dinner table. They are one strange couple—they make Gomez and Morticia Addams seem like Ward and June Cleaver."

"According to this sheet, he's an international hit man… well-known to Interpol… his crimes overlap several member countries. He must be an independent, though; they've never been able to link him to a specific mob or cartel in any country."

"He bears watching, that's for certain," I agreed. "Does your information indicate if Del Muerto is a card-carrying member of Zunimba's gang?"

"Nothing here about that. But, say, there's another person on the passenger manifest I should mention."

"Who's that?"

"Buck Tolleson from Dallas," Erickson said.

"Go on."

"A Texan by the name of Buck Tolleson offered to buy Nordic Caribbean a year or so ago. His price was well below our book value so the board turned him down. Then he got nasty and changed from friendly suitor to hostile raider. He started buying up our stock on the open market and quickly got control of ten percent of it."

"What did you do?"

"We fought back, of course. First, we made an offer to our shareholders to buy back their stock at an above-market price."

"Did it work?"

"Yes and no. We were able to retire about fifteen percent of the outstanding shares that we didn't already own. But then Tolleson started issuing junk bonds."

"What did that accomplish?"

"It gave him an influx of added capital from high-yield, low-quality bonds that he issued in the name of a shell corporation; he then used that money to buy more shares, thus increasing his stake and voting power in Nordic Caribbean."

"How did you counter that dastardly deed?"

"Through the creation of a poison pill."

"Poison pill?"

"A poison pill is a tactic intended to make a hostile corporate takeover too expensive to pursue. In our case, once the hostile suitor acquired more than ten percent of our stock, we authorized our existing stockholders to acquire additional shares of our stock at a bargain price. Doing so immediately diluted the percentage of stock that Tolleson owned."

"Then the pill worked?"

"Not exactly. Tolleson ran ads in all the business and industry publications. They were aimed at our stockholders and attempted to discredit our management. He basically wanted to put the board on the defensive and rally stockholders around his unsolicited offer with promises of changing some items his investigations had uncovered."

"What sorts of items?" I asked.

The president was quiet a moment before continuing, evidently choosing his words carefully. "He made allegations such as conflicts of interest, insider stock trading, bribes to foreign officials, and improper asset and expense accounting, as well as accusations of underfunding and making improper withdrawals from the employee pension plan and backdating stock options. He also accused us of mortgaging corporate assets to increase the executive deferred compensation plan."

"Were any of these charges true?"

I noted another moment of silence before he answered. "Everything's relative, McFadden," he stated with a sigh. "The truth is what's told by the last man standing. Anyway, his smear campaign began to work, as the tide of stockholder opinion started to turn against us… particularly after he blew the whistle on one of our tax shelters."

"Tax shelters?"

Instead of a pause, this answer flew fast and furious in one ear and out the other—with nothing sticking in the middle: "The shelters were ruled by the courts to be an elaborate tax dodge because of their questionable investment strategy and the fact that they allowed loans to executives. In addition, the IRS decreed that they lacked economic substance because they were designed to create bogus paper losses that would help wealthy executives evade millions of dollars in income taxes." He stopped briefly to take a breath before summarizing. "We feared a bitter proxy fight and were running out of money, so we did a 'pump and dump.'"

"A pump and dump…"

"We circulated positive but false rumors to boost our stock price and then sold off shares at the inflated market price to reap big profits before the truth was discovered and the stock tumbled into a freefall."

I was almost wishing I'd paid better attention in third-year economics class. "Did this additional funding allow you to prevail?"

"No—it actually backfired. After our stock price fell, Tolleson bought a ton of it and increased his pressure to put some of his cronies on the board. By this time, too, the financial press was chewing us up, so we turned to our last ace in the hole."

"I can't wait—"

"Greenmail. We had to resort to greenmail."

"Greenmail… I'm afraid to even ask…"

"We paid a premium price—well above market—to buy our stock back from him with the stipulation that he not acquire any more of our stock for ten years. He made $115 million from our repurchase of his shares."

"Sounds to me like he'd be a happy camper."

"One would think so, but Tolleson is more interested in power than money. He made it clear, even after the negotiated settlement, that he was bitter over the outcome of his attempted takeover bid. He's a fearless competitor. Well, that's only partially true. He has one fear: he won't fly. He has to take some other form of transportation wherever he travels."

"To be frank, he sounds like an okay guy to me. His actions seemed to be directed at getting your company to clean up its act. Based upon your own testimony, you guys at Nordic Caribbean have done just about everything but flagellate nuns and burn the crutches of crippled children."

"Don't be fooled, McFadden. We may not run the cleanest corporation in the business, but we're not the only company who's had trouble with Tolleson, either. He's ruthless—as ruthless as they come. The corporate highway is littered with the bodies of companies and investors he's sucked dry."

"So you think this thwarted megalomaniac may be a suspect because he might still have it in for Nordic Caribbean?"

"I'm just alerting you to the possibility, that's all. I don't even know for sure if this is the same Tolleson."

"All right, I'll check him out, but he doesn't sound much like a Zunimba disciple to me. Anything else?"

"No, not at present."

"Okay, then. Thanks for the intel. Over and out."

I couldn't help thinking that if Tolleson's charges were true, Nordic Caribbean had become a modern-day version of seventeenth-century privateers... or worse. Pirates used to pillage and plunder the high seas, but they stole from colonial imperialists who were shipping wealth to rulers in their mother countries—wealth acquired from the blood and sweat of New World natives, whom they almost extinguished through decades of subjugation and exploitation.

Nordic Caribbean, on the other hand, had only transformed the pirates into lawyers, accountants, and investment bankers who hopped down from the yardarms and now perched on Wall Street lampposts. I wondered how many widows and orphans had lost their savings to the corporate shenanigans engineered by these scoundrels. How many employees, having reached the ends of long careers, received nothing but a gold watch after their pensions had been decimated by corporate miscreancy.

Erickson would say that everyone makes out, but everyone never makes out. Where there are winners, there are losers. I recalled one fact of life that is ineluctable: when elephants fight, the grass gets trampled. Everybody can't be above average. As I walked back to the Lido Deck to rejoin Joey and check on Girtha, I was glad the only stock I ever owned was in my Junior Achievement club in high school.

"Hi, sweetie-kins," Girtha greeted me. She'd been laughing hysterically and was now trying to catch her breath while Joey luxuriated in audience appreciation. "I was telling Joey about the used condom I saw floating in the spa this morning, and do you know what he said they call them in New York? Coney Island whitefish! Isn't that a hoot?"

I hoped seafood wasn't on the menu at this evening's dinner. "Trying out some new material, Joey?"

"Naw, that's old stuff; it's on one of my comedy cassettes. I just sold Girtha two of them," he said with a smile, waving a ten dollar bill.

Girtha had finally recovered. "Joey said you had a telephone call. Who was it?"

"I'll tell you later," I said. "You better get out of the sun. You're as pink as a lobster, and you're going to be ill if you're not careful."

Girtha pressed her forefinger to her skin, removed it, and watched the little white circles fade immediately back to pink. "My skin *is* hot to the touch. I think I'll go see that cute doctor and have him rub some lotion on me—the sunburned areas and any other places his naughty fingers might wander to," she said mischievously.

"If he's not in, see Slutskya, the Russian nurse," I retorted with feigned indifference. "She's taking a sabbatical from shot-put training for the next Olympiad. She used to moonlight at the Kremlin car wash and can give your grill and trunk a *good* work over."

I helped pull the huffing Girtha out of her lounge chair just before another appearance from chief radio operator Helmje. This time, however, he approached Joey instead.

"Mr. Morton, you have a telephone call."

Joey's face clouded over and he looked nervous as he grabbed his bag of cassettes. "Gotta go. Catch you later, pal."

Alone and with nothing better to do, I ambled over to the poolside bar. I got the mixologist's attention and ordered the daily special—a 'Paradise' cocktail.

The bartender was a young black man with a broad smile that showcased two rows of glistening ivories. The name tag above his left pocket identified him as Henri Durban. I watched as Henri poured dashes and shots from several bottles into a blender, added some shaved ice, and produced a frozen mixture that he transferred to a cocktail glass. I took a sip of his concoction and rotated it around my mouth with my tongue.

"Do you like it, sir?" He asked congenially and with an indecipherable patois.

"I'm afraid this is 'Paradise lost' on me—it's a bit sweeter than I care for."

"Sorry, sir. It is the guava nectar, a new taste to many people. Let me dump and I make you mai tai."

I handed the glass back to the affable Henri.

"This is second rejection I have today. The other came from man over there." I followed his pointing finger to a white-suited figure sitting by the rail, staring out at the sea. "My mint julep—he doesn't like."

"That looks like Colonel Talbo, a remembrance of things past. Just give him some bourbon and branch and tap dance a little so he won't get homesick. He's probably searching the horizon for signs of the Confederate navy."

"Strange man, that Colonel. When waiter take him change, he refuse to accept five-dollar bill. I have to give him five singles instead."

"He's never forgiven Lincoln for freeing the slaves," I said. "You have an interesting accent, Henri… where are you from?"

"Haiti. I am one of the fortunate ones to escape Baby Doc Duvalier and the Tonton Macoute."

"The Haitian secret police?" I asked.

"Yes. The ones that wear dark glasses, carry machetes, and leave victims hanging in trees as warning to others."

"It sounds like the Macoute and Colonel Talbo's ancestors have something in common."

I swirled my drink, listening to the ice clink in the glass as I tried to make my next question sound as casual as possible. "The fellow who was murdered in Miami—a waiter from this ship—he was Haitian also, wasn't he?"

Henri's smile faded faster than wet red underwear hanging from a clothesline in an August sun. I worried I'd been too abrupt but, fortunately, he spoke.

"Yes, Victor was homeboy. We both born and raised in Cité Soleil, one of most dangerous slums in Port-au-Prince. His family live in Plaine-du-Nord now." He grabbed a cloth and started wiping the counter, even though it was spotless.

"Did you know him well?"

"'Well'? Who can say what is well," he answered before pausing. "We—Victor and I—escape from Haiti three year ago. We are given asylum in Miami. Friends there persuade Immigration and Naturalization people we are political refugees. We get to stay in U.S. and get jobs. I am very happy."

"What about Victor?" I asked. I intended to press on as far as I could.

"Victor and I get in fight over girl," Henri replied. He looked pained and uncomfortable. "Then, she dump both of us, marry rich man, and move to California. Good riddance, but damage done—our friendship never the same after that."

I had one final question, for which I wanted a reaction as much as an answer. "Have you or Victor ever been contacted by a member of the Zunimbist cult?"

Henri's head jerked back and his eyes widened, but he recovered and answered softly. "There are things not to be discussed. I can say no more." With that, he turned and walked to the other end of the bar to serve a new arrival.

"Chauncey! I've been looking all over for you," Girtha said. "Doctor Lagervist gave me some aloe cream to apply. He put some on my back and I feel better already."

Her eyelashes were fluttering at near-hummingbird velocity but I didn't take the bait. I didn't even tell her that the lotion made her skin slick and shiny like an albino manatee. I couldn't have anyway—we were interrupted by a public address announcement alerting us to a lifeboat drill in fifteen minutes. By that time, we had to be at our assigned boat stations, which corresponded to our cabin location, so we proceeded to the Promenade Deck and received our orange life jackets.

During the drill, we were informed that the exercise was mandatory—required by international law—and had to be conducted within twenty-four hours of departure.

As Girtha and I struggled unsuccessfully to lash our jackets around our ample waists, we concluded that, in the event of an actual emergency, we'd be going down with the ship.

CHAPTER 8

T HE NEXT DAY WAS MONDAY, THE THIRD DAY OF THE CRUISE, and I sat up in my bunk, looking out the porthole. The beautiful reef-sheltered bay of Ocho Rios was coming into view and was breathtaking to behold. A white expanse of beach stretched as far as I could see, separating aquamarine waters to its fore from lush vegetation and emerald foliage to its aft. Several rivers tumbled down wooded mountainsides to the sea, meeting in coastal waterfalls of visual splendor. The impact of water meeting water produced a mist that captured the ends of rainbows in an early morning sun.

I could hear Girtha singing in the shower, though she was occasionally drowned out by the ship's horn and the flurry of docking activity noises. She still wasn't thrilled at the prospect of going ashore alone, but she had conceded that a near-empty ship was more conducive to the execution of several plans I had in mind.

"What time do we land?" Girtha asked after escaping the bathroom and starting to remove rollers from her hair.

"Nine o'clock according to the *Sea Compass*," I replied, referring to the daily information and activities bulletin the cabin steward slipped under the door that morning. "The two tours you signed up for should keep you busy most of the day."

"I still wish you were going," Girtha said, her small lips pursed in a quasi-pout.

"Hopefully, I can make the next port on Wednesday. Remember to keep your souvenir purchases to a minimum and a tight grip on your pocketbook."

Girtha looked up, dropping the new sandals she was trying on. "You mean I could get mugged by Jamaicans?"

"It's not the natives I'm worried about; it's the other passengers!" I chuckled. "If the information I received from Erickson is any indication, we would've been in better company on the convict ships England sent to Australia in the eighteenth century."

"Chauncey, you should be ashamed, trying to scare me like that. I have the willies enough as it is." She gave me a peck on the cheek. "I'll see you tonight, sweetie-kins."

With Girtha off for her day, I left the room myself, in pursuit of the Captain. I went first to his cabin, but when my knock wasn't answered, I proceeded to the bridge, where I found him, pipe in mouth and arms folded, surveying the bustling pier scene at the Ocho Rios quay.

"I'm puzzled by something, Captain," I said as I approached him. "Whenever I come to the bridge, I never see anyone steering. Is everything *that* computerized?"

"The ship is on automatic pilot almost all the time. Hand-steering by a quartermaster is normally confined to traveling in narrow channels or heavily trafficked waters. He's also at the helm during bad weather and from sunset to sunrise."

"Good information to know," I said. "Not venturing ashore today, Captain?"

"No," he replied. "When you've been in these ports as many times as I have, you develop immunity to their charm. What can I do for you today?"

"I would like to search the cabin of two of the passengers— Arturo and Castrada Del Muerto in 1124. How can I determine if they've gone ashore and, if so, how might I arrange to gain brief entry into their room?"

The Captain stroked his beard a moment. "What you're asking is highly irregular, Mr. McFadden."

"So is murder, but it could become more 'regular' with each passing day."

The Captain picked up a phone by the helm and punched an extension. "I'll check with the shore excursion manager first."

"Lorenzo? Nelson here. Can you look at the list of passengers who signed up for tours today and tell me if Arturo and Castrada Del Muerto in 1124 signed up for any?"

Pause.

"They didn't? Thanks."

"No luck there," he informed me. "Let me try the chief passenger steward." He punched another extension. "Ugo? Need a favor. Have the cabin steward for 1124 drop what he's doing and check that cabin. I need to know if it's currently occupied or vacant—call me right back." He replaced the phone into its cradle and turned his attention to me.

"The Del Muertos didn't sign up for any tours but they still may have gone ashore," Nelson explained.

In a few minutes the bridge phone rang and the Captain picked it up. "Nelson here."

"The cabin is empty? Thanks, Ugo. Have the steward leave that cabin unlocked and remain there until the ship's inspector gets there."

Nelson turned to me. "The Del Muertos *could* still be aboard ship, but chances are they've gone ashore. For now, they've vacated the cabin and it will be unlocked in a moment if you want to take the risk. Your unrestricted security pass should provide some cover should you be caught."

"Thanks, Captain. I'm on my way."

I arrived at cabin 1124, on Constellation Deck—the high rent district—and found the door had been left unlocked as promised. Other than a few stewards milling about and some passengers getting a late start for shore, the alleyway was deserted. I knocked as a precautionary measure, awaited a response, and then ducked inside when none came.

You could have fit two of my cabins inside Del Muerto's. In addition to a double bed, he had a large closet, several pieces of swanky furniture, a separate sitting area with a loveseat and armchairs, and even a refrigerator. I could have marveled another few minutes, but doing so would have only fueled a growing tinge of jealousy—and I needed to get to work.

I wasn't sure what I was looking for, so I started with the obvious—some clothing that was on the bed, the credenza drawers, and the pockets of garments hanging in the closet. Nothing attracted my attention except the apparent fact that Del Muerto loved beige and tapioca: he had two suits of each color in his closet. I opened the luggage, but struck out there as well.

I had to be missing something, I decided, and sat down on the bed to scan the room from a different angle and collect my thoughts. In doing so, an empty ashtray fell off the nightstand and, to my dismay, rolled under the bed. I slid down the edge of the mattress and positioned myself so I could grope blindly under the box springs. As I stretched into the darkness, I touched something that felt more like a handle than an ashtray. Grasping it, I pulled the object out of its hiding place and discovered it to be a briefcase. It was unlocked, so I opened it and began sorting through the contents.

A chill went up my spine when I realized what I'd found: the equivalent of an assassin's scrapbook! Beneath Arturo's and Castrada's passports, some travelers checks, and an appointment book were clippings dated over the past five years from major newspapers in Miami and Central and South America.

Many of the articles had yellowed with age, and some were written in Spanish, but the graphic pictures and my limited familiarity with the language made it clear why they had been collected: they were reportage of the sensational murders of people in the public eye—judges, police officials, national and local politicians, prominent businessmen, kidnap victims, and even members of crime cartels. They had all been stabbed in the heart by the single thrust of a knife.

I opened the much-traveled passport of Arturo Del Muerto and discovered that he had been in and out of almost every country below the Rio Grande over the past decade. The most recent activity was his entry into the U.S. four days prior to the sailing of the *Oslo Aphrodite*.

Did Del Muerto have anything to do with the murders of Lars Amundson, Victor Dubonnet, and Jacque Destang? Did he freelance on his own or was he a disciple of the Zunimbists? Was he responsible for dispatching victims according to the group's prescribed methodology?

I turned my attention to the appointment book. It was sprinkled with names and places, none of which were meaningful until I got to today's entry. There, in the Monday column were the handwritten notations "Buck Tolleson" and "Ocho Rios, Jamaica"—what was Tolleson's name doing in Del Muerto's appointment book? Was Del Muerto working for Tolleson? Had Tolleson hired Del Muerto to perform acts that would bring adverse publicity to, and deliver a financial blow upon, the *Oslo Aphrodite*, the Nordic Caribbean's flagship and jewel of the fleet? Had Tolleson joined the cruise to personally witness the event?

Particularly discomforting was the realization that Tolleson and Del Muerto could be potentially working together as a duo—that idea was not to be taken lightly. The former had amassed a personal fortune beating the best minds in corporate America at their own game while the latter had proven quite adept at cheating justice by avoiding indictment for a lengthy series of signature murders. Del Muerto's perfected insidiousness could only be strengthened by Tolleson's financial backing.

I looked back down at the book and saw only one future entry in the book: under the upcoming Saturday, "Simon Cartier" and "Bridgetown, Barbados" had been written in. Was Cartier another employer? Or was he simply a personal or business appointment? I made a mental note to check his name against the crew and passenger lists then decided it was time to go. I carefully replaced the contents of the briefcase and pushed it back under the bed, retrieved the ashtray in the process, and straightened the bedspread. At the door, I listened a moment for noises in the alleyway, then opened the door just a crack to peer outside and make certain it was deserted before stepping into it. After locking the door, I navigated gracefully around the service carts and dirty linen bins that were in use by the cabin stewards. I eventually reached the elevator where I stopped and thought for a moment.

Tolleson's importance in the case had suddenly been elevated and an interview with him was clearly a high priority. I removed the cabin list from my jacket pocket and learned that Tolleson was in cabin 1080, fifty feet from Del Muerto's. I proceeded to the cabin door and knocked. After a moment, I knocked again, harder, and was surprised to see the door open a crack to the extra pressure.

After making sure my entry was unobserved, I slipped inside. The layout and furnishings were identical to Del Muerto's cabin—with one important exception: this room had been cleaned out.

I checked all the drawers and eased to my knees to look under the bed. I heard a sound behind me. Holding on to the mattress for support, I turned my head to investigate the noise. I was greeted with a blow to the back of my head which bounced me off the bed before I landed on the carpet with a thud. I was clinging to consciousness by trying to focus on the thousand colored lights that swarmed before my eyes like a kaleidoscope gone berserk. I heard a second noise—perhaps the door closing—before I lost the fight against unconsciousness and total darkness set in.

The next thing I recall was hearing voices in my head. I imagined them to be dissenting morticians, debating how to best prepare my cadaver. "A little rouge here—a little rouge there—a little cotton behind the cheeks..." "Thank goodness he's bald—we won't have to worry about which side to part his hair." "Should the glasses be left on?" "Yes, that would be more natural." "No, wait a minute—a lens is broken. Let's leave them off—who's to notice?" "You're right; the service won't be well attended anyway." "Wait, here's a pair of bifocals left over from that cremation job. Let's use them." "Let's bury him in a dark suit—that way, he won't look so fat." "Homer quit last Friday and turned in his black suit—we can use that one." "That's a nice looking watch he has on—no need to bury it when we could pawn it to defray our expenses."

The voices subsided and I gradually regained consciousness, groped around the carpet until I found my glasses, and struggled to my feet. By holding onto the wall for support, I made it to the bathroom where I splashed cold water on my face. A bit steadier, I grabbed a hand towel from the rack and crept to the refrigerator/ freezer for some ice to make a cold compress for the back of my head.

That major task accomplished, I looked at my watch—I had been unconscious for half an hour. Other than a bump on the back of my forehead and a cut underneath my eye, I didn't look any worse for wear; without the dull throb, I wouldn't have felt any worse, either. Satisfied that I might live after all, I refocused from self to situation.

What had happened? My assailant had either sneaked into the cabin while my back was turned, or he had been hiding inside all along. The room didn't appear to be any different, except I didn't remember the closet door being open.

My interest aroused, I went to the closet and peeked inside. Unlike the rest of the room, it contained one item: a large gray canvas, misshapen duffle bag—the kind used by maritime personnel the world over. I dragged the heavy bag out of the closet and loosened the rope drawstring at the top, expanded the opening with my fingers, and peered inside.

Revulsion started at the bottom of my stomach and almost made it to my throat. Inside the bag, a pair of eyes looked back up at me from the body of a small man. His throat had been cut, the head dangling to one side and looking up. The eyes were wide open, frozen in the terror of his final moment.

Something was stuffed in the mouth and, overcoming my extreme reluctance, I gingerly tugged at the object until it was visible. It wasn't hard to identify. I knew what it was already. Once you've seen one chicken head, you've seen them all. The shirt was soaked with blood from the gash across the neck.

Any final doubts had now been removed: Zunimbists were on board.

I pushed the duffel bag back into the closet and left the cabin. The Captain wasn't going to be too thrilled with this development. A serpent had entered his Eden and the garden would never be the same. I headed for the bridge with the bad tidings.

When I arrived, the Captain was absent. I checked out a few of his favorite haunts before finding him in his quarters.

"McFadden, what happened? You have a bump on your head that's beginning to swell and a welt beneath your eye."

"As bad as I look, there's someone who's in much worse shape. Can you come with me, Captain? I've got something to show you. How's your stomach today?" I led the ship's master back to Tolleson's cabin and pointed to the closet. "Check that out," I said, easing myself into an armchair to relax while I observed his reaction.

Nelson opened the sliding glass closet door. "What do you want to show me, McFadden? What am I supposed to be seeing?"

"A large gray duffel bag. Open it up and look inside. Tell me if it's anyone you know."

"There's nothing here," he repeated, looking at me quizzically.

I got up and joined him at the closet. My chin dropped: the duffel bag was gone!

"If this is your idea of a joke, I don't find it amusing," Nelson said curtly.

"What was in the closet a while ago wasn't the least bit funny, I assure you," I defended weakly.

"All right," Nelson said. "I'll play along. What did you see in the closet that isn't there now?"

"A corpse that appeared to have been dispatched Zunimba-style. I didn't check for markings on the chest, but his throat had been cut and he had a chicken head stuffed into his mouth. You might as well face it, Captain. This nasty business has found a home on the *Oslo Aphrodite*."

Nelson was adamant. "Without something other than your word—something like tangible proof—I'll not be convinced a murder has been committed on this ship."

I got down on my hands and knees and closely examined the interior of the closet. The walls were clean except for a few scuff marks, and I almost gave up finding anything unusual when I noticed two things of interest. The first was a tiny green stone that resembled an emerald that was on top of several loose carpet fibers next to the baseboard. I palmed and pocketed it for later examination. The second was a dark stain on the carpet. I asked the Captain to retrieve a white hand towel from the bathroom. When he handed it to me, I blotted it against the stain.

"Take a look, Captain. That looks like fresh blood to me. Unless someone nicked themselves while shaving in the closet or a cockroach had her period, I suggest we proceed under the assumption that a homicide's been committed. I recommend that we start trying to identify any missing passengers or crew members. By now, that gray duffel bag has probably found its way to Davy Jones's locker."

Nelson was visibly shaken. "I'll do as you suggest, but I must insist upon one thing: this must be handled in a low-key manner. Only you and I are to know anything about this for the time being and until more creditable information is obtained. I don't want the passengers and crew to be needlessly alarmed and have panic unleashed. Once that genie is out of the bottle, it's hard to get him back in."

"Are you trying to avoid panic or bad publicity? I'll go along with your gag order, but for two other reasons. First, with no corpus delicti, I can't prove a crime *has* been committed. Second, I don't believe that innocent bystanders are in danger."

Nelson sighed. "Fair enough." He placed his unlit pipe in his mouth; a gesture I deciphered as relief.

"I need a couple of concessions, as well, Captain. First, I need you to instruct your chief passenger steward to inspect all the dirty-linen hampers used by the cabin stewards for blood stains. I'd like to know how a heavy duffel bag got removed from this cabin, and I believe one of them provided the transportation.

"Second, according to the passenger manifest, this cabin belongs to a man by the name of Buck Tolleson. I was beginning to check him out, based upon information I received from Erickson, when I found the body. I'm wondering if it's possible the body is his since the room is empty and he's not here. And, speaking of empty, isn't it odd that no personal effects, like clothes or luggage or toiletries, are in the room? Can we get Tolleson's description from his room steward or assigned waiter?"

Captain Nelson looked bewildered but recovered somewhat as a lightbulb switched on in his head. "Let me check something..." He dialed an extension from the room phone and waited. "Ugo, this Captain Nelson again. I need some information about a passenger named Buck Tolleson in cabin 1080; what was his itinerary?" There was a brief pause before the Captain said "Thanks" and hung up.

The look on his face was one of relief. "It's as I suspected. Tolleson embarked in Miami but his trip ended in Ocho Rios. He packed and departed this morning. We arranged a local limousine for him and escorted him and his baggage to the dock. He's scheduled on the Ocho Rios to Miami segment of another ship in three days."

"You can take a partial cruise?" I asked.

"Certainly, it's done all the time. Although the full cruise is round-trip, passengers can buy a one-way ticket or any port-to-port segment in between if we have the cabin space. They pay a pro-rata fare plus an added premium. Business has been a little slow for this time of season so this cabin will remain empty until we return to Miami."

"I guess that explains Tolleson's whereabouts but it leaves two questions unanswered: whose body was inside the duffel bag, and why was the body found in Tolleson's cabin? Have your purser's office see if they can locate a missing passenger or crew member and let me know what you find out."

"I'll get started at once," Nelson agreed. Before turning to go, he evidently noticed my furrowed brow and asked, "What else is the matter?"

"A couple of things are still bothering me. I only got a brief look at the face—and it was in anything but a natural state—however, I'd swear I'd seen the victim before. Hopefully, it will come to me. Also, I'm wondering why the killer didn't remove the duffel bag from the room while I was unconscious. Why did he wait until I came around and left to get you?"

Nelson shrugged his shoulders. "Perhaps the alleyway had too much traffic at the time he knocked you out. At about that time, any passengers who stayed on board would have been leaving their cabins for the first seating of lunch; or they may have come back to their cabins from a morning at the pool to change for the movie matinee, the art auction, or the bingo tournament. The alleyways can be deserted at one moment, then—with so many people on similar schedules—be flooded with traffic only a few minutes later."

"Your points are logical," I confessed.

"If there's nothing else, I suggest we get started on our assignments. And," he suggested as we departed, "I suggest you consult Dr. Lagervist and get those bumps and that welt tended to. They're starting to discolor."

Before I took Nelson's advice and paid the ship's real doctor a visit, I made my way to the poolside bar and ordered green Chartreuse on the rocks from doctor Durban. Unlike the previous day, I had the pool area practically to myself—only a couple of dozen others had abstained from trekking about the third largest island in the Caribbean. I took a seat by the Jacuzzi and closed my eyes to concentrate on reducing the dull pain in my skull.

When a third drink still had not done much to evict the pain, I headed for medical services. The good doctor had gone ashore, but in his place an amiable nurse provided a few aspirin and applied some antiseptic to the affected areas. As she finished up, I glanced at my watch and noted that the second lunch was still in progress. I eased myself down from the aluminum infirmary table and made my way to the dining room.

Only two others were at our table: Lamont Darling and Colonel Talbo. The Colonel was dressed in his plantation uniform, giving the amiable Toussaint instructions on how service could be improved. Darling was nattily attired in a mauve silk jacket with matching ascot, signing autographs for two elderly matrons who were gushing with schoolgirl delight.

"Good god, man, what happened to you?" Darling greeted as I backed into my chair. "Did you refuse the aggressive entreaties of the island's beggar population?"

"Nothing quite so dramatic, I'm afraid. I merely slipped on a wet spot on the deck." Without pausing, I changed the subject. "Why didn't you two go ashore?"

"I," Darling swaggered, "was reading a script for a television cameo."

"I went ashore earlier this morning," the Colonel informed us while tucking his napkin under his chin. "I visited Prospect Plantation, and I've got a good mind to ask for a refund. That place wasn't a plantation at all—just a tourist trap. I didn't see any nigras out in the fields picking anything; and no overseer in sight. All I saw was a pickaninny taking tickets."

I was tempted to tell him that an article in that morning's bulletin had described how a fellow named Nat Turner had organized a few slaves for the purpose of emancipation and had commandeered a steamboat heading down the Mississippi to foment insurrection. But, I refrained for fear that it might prompt the Colonel to cash in his Confederate war bonds and pull his grandsons out of college so they could suit up and assume command of their local militias.

"Excuse me, sir, Colonel," Toussaint interrupted. "The chef managed to locate some 'fatback' to season your turnip greens, and he has even agreed to cook a 'pot of grits.' They will be out shortly.

"However, this 'red-eye gravy'... *je ne sais pas...* he is at a loss."

"Never mind, then," the Colonel said. "Just bring me some bacon drippings. I'll use that instead."

"*Oui, mon Colonel,*" Toussaint said with an exaggerated smile and his best Step'n Fetchit imitation as he shuffled away from the table. Evidently more comfortable this afternoon, he was having a field day with the old Delta patriarch.

"What did you say you do for a living, Mr. McFadden?" Darling asked.

"I'm a quality control inspector for cruise lines," I said. I took advantage of the situation and flashed the badge I'd been given by Erickson.

"I see," Darling said. "That explains why I saw you walking around with the Captain this morning. I was curious, that's all."

The rest of the meal was consumed in idle and leisurely chit-chat without incident.

After lunch, I lounged for a while before taking a stroll around the decks. Upon hearing some commotion, I stopped and looked over the rail to observe a parade of passengers returning to the ship in intermittent bunches. They dotted the long pier leading to the ship and were laughing and talking merrily while struggling to carry their purchases on board. Their passage was made more difficult by hordes of mendicant children making their final pleas, and persistent street vendors slashing their prices in a last-ditch effort to peddle their wares. I thought about the perennial tourist's dilemma: were our tourist dollars perceived as supplying an appreciated and needed infusion to local economies? Or were they resented as constant reminders to the underprivileged of their poverty and our conspicuous craving for consumption?

My self-imposed guilt trip was interrupted by the ship's public address system. "Will passenger McFadden please report to the bridge? Thank you."

I found Captain Nelson hanging up the phone when I arrived.

"What's wrong, Captain? You look distressed."

"We haven't located the duffle bag but I have a lead regarding the body stuffed inside of it." He sighed, folded his arms, and leaned back against the bulkhead. "It may be my chief radio operator, Bruno Helmje."

"I met him yesterday when he fetched me for Erickson's call. What makes you think it's him?"

"According to the assistant radio operator, Boyd Fowler, no one's seen him today. Come to think of it, he wasn't at the officers' mess this morning. At first, it was assumed he had gone ashore on some personal business. But when he didn't show up by noon, Fowler informed Jurgens, the new COS. We're certain he didn't leave the ship because he didn't sign out on the log and the guard posted at the exit gangway didn't recall seeing him disembark. We've searched the ship from stern to bow, but he's nowhere to be found."

"What's your normal procedure governing an officer's absence, Captain?"

"Fortunately, Fowler is experienced and can run the communications center, so the cruise will continue as planned. I've entered Bruno's absence in the ship's log as an AWOL until a final disposition can be determined. I've also notified the Nordic Caribbean office in Miami and alerted the Bahamian authorities who will issue an APB on him."

"Why the Bahamian authorities?"

"The *Oslo Aphrodite* was in Bahamian waters when the body was discovered and reported missing, so they have prima facie jurisdiction. Erickson will notify the FBI since Bruno had become an American citizen. Nassau authorities always welcome the assistance of the FBI."

"You know, Captain, the more I think about your suspicion, the more I think it could be correct. The body in the bag must have been a short person— assuming all the parts were there—and the look on the face was so distorted by terror that I might not have recognized it… but I'm pretty sure it could have been Helmje. I'd like to talk to his assistant, Boyd Fowler, if you have no objections."

"Be my guest, though he won't be back on duty until tomorrow morning. You can catch him then." He glanced at his watch and added, "The ship will be weighing anchor soon, and I've got duties to attend to. I'll leave word for Fowler and instruct him to give you his complete cooperation.

"Oh, there's one more thing," Nelson said as he picked up the phone. "We did locate a dirty-linens hamper with dark stains in the bottom."

"Good. Have your security officer swab the stain with a cotton swab, put it in a sealed plastic bag, and mail it to the FBI in Miami. Their crime lab might be able to confirm if the blood type is the same as Helmje's."

I returned to the cabin to check on Girtha and almost collided with a mountain of packages being juggled by two short arms. "Girtha! I thought you were going to exercise some shopping restraint," I remonstrated.

As quickly as I reached around the stack and opened the cabin door, Girtha rushed in, dropped her cargo on my bunk, and collapsed on hers. "It's not my fault, Chauncey. You should have seen the bargains. The prices were a fraction of those in the states. It would've been criminal not to take advantage of 'em."

Then, noticing my face, she asked, "What in the world happened to you?"

She was clearly unnerved—her face turned white and her hands clasped together to keep them from shaking—as I described the discovery of the body in the duffel bag and my subsequent assault. I was finally able to calm her fears by convincing her that the attack had been an impromptu reaction and that I had never been the intended target of the assailant—just an obstacle to be immobilized until the duffel bag could be safely removed.

She felt better. I only wish I had been able to convince myself as easily.

CHAPTER 9

D URING THE NIGHT, A THICK LAYER OF CLOUDS FORMED overhead. The billowy masses darkened, tumbling in playful mirth at first, but soon becoming increasingly ominous, a condition highlighted by dramatic flashes of distant lightning. As the lightning neared, a gale-force wind whipped up the surface of the water and howled across the battered decks. The sea heaved and dipped, spawning whitecaps that arched momentarily toward the heavens… only to collapse into swirling froth an instant later. The flags on the yardarm were repeatedly whipped into a frenzy, released to surrender in exhaustion, whipped back into a brutal crescendo, and released again to wrap their tired fabric around their metal host. On deck, the crew members were much in evidence as they scurried around in their yellow rain garb, securing movable objects before they were blown overboard. Finally, the skies were torn asunder and sheets of rain slammed into the ship.

The next morning, Tuesday, was the fourth day of the cruise and found us still at sea, en route to the colorful port of Willemstad, Curacao. Girtha and I were seated at breakfast. We'd finished our fare and were watching our coffee sway back and forth from one rim of the cup to the other.

"How long is this hurricane supposed to last?" she asked apprehensively. "I had my heart set on shuffleboard today."

"This isn't a hurricane," I corrected, "merely a tropical squall. It'll be over before you know it."

"I still get the jitters, thinking of what might have happened to you yesterday," Girtha said with a shudder. "Knowing there's a killer walking around the ship doesn't make me feel any better. I think you should withdraw from this case so we can go home safe and sound. Does your head still hurt?"

"Only when I breathe, my eyes blink, or my heart beats."

"Chauncey—" she started to protest.

"Just kidding. I wonder where everybody is this morning." The other chairs at our table were still empty.

"Probably putting on their life preservers and fighting for seats in the lifeboat, like we should be doing," Girtha said.

While she worried about our futures, I stared back into the coffee cups and reflected on the case. "You know, Girtha, enough pieces of this puzzle should have fallen into place by now to give me an idea of what's behind it all."

"Such as?"

"Well, let's think about it. First, a ship's officer and a waiter are barbarically murdered in Miami. Shortly thereafter, a worker at the waste disposal facility in Miami, the ship's home port, is found dispatched in similar fashion. But while the method of death appears to be the same in all three situations, nothing suggests that Lars Amundson actually had anything in common with the other two victims.

"Then, the chief radio operator disappears, and we strongly suspect he's been murdered as well—probably in the same way, if the slashed neck and chicken head stuffing are any indication—only the body disappears and we can't be certain of its identity. The corpse I discovered did have a chicken head in its mouth, but I didn't have a chance to check the chest for finger painting. We also don't know if the killer is still on the ship, or if he disembarked in Jamaica."

"If Tolleson wasn't the victim, maybe he was the killer," Girtha offered while spreading preserves on a piece of toast.

"His profile doesn't suggest his direct involvement. He gets his kicks from the financial emasculation of his opponents and the aggrandizement of personal power. He may have hired the knife, but it's not likely that he wielded it."

"Excuse me, Mr. McFadden, may I see you a moment?"

I looked up into the stoic features of Captain Nelson. "It's all right, Captain; you can speak freely in front of my operative. Won't you join us?"

Nelson looked around, paused a moment, then pulled out a chair and seated himself. "I received something interesting over the wire this morning," he said, just above a whisper. "As you may know, we're hooked up to the Associated Press news service. That's where we get the contents for our daily *Ocean and Shore News Bulletin.* Anyway, one of the items on the news service caught my eye this morning."

"And it was…"

He looked around the room once more before responding with another morsel of whispered information. "The body of Buck Tolleson was found in Ocho Rios yesterday afternoon on the grounds of an oceanfront resort where he was staying."

Girtha and I dropped our forks and exchanged surprised glances. "What else did the article say?"

"Not much. All we get are five or six sentences per article, in capsular form. It did say that the victim was stabbed in the heart and suggested—rather comically, I thought—that the death occurred under suspicious circumstances and that foul play is suspected. It concluded by saying that the international investment community is in shock at the sudden loss, et cetera, et cetera. Thank god, Tolleson was no longer a passenger and the *Oslo Aphrodite* wasn't mentioned."

I pondered the Captain's news with some embarrassment. The real meaning of the Tolleson entry in Del Muerto's appointment book was now clear. "Captain, I suspect a passenger aboard this ship may be involved in Tolleson's murder; a hired outlaw by the name of Arturo Del Muerto. You may have seen him and his wife dining at our table."

"It's coincidental that you mention him," Nelson replied. "When the Jamaican police learned that Tolleson had been on board our vessel, they examined the passenger manifest and spotted Del Muerto's name immediately. They were waiting for him at the gangway when he returned to the ship, took him to the customs office at the dock, and interrogated him for the better part of an hour. However, he could prove that he'd been drinking at the Reggae Cantina all afternoon. The bartender and a room full of local barflies remember him well. It seems that Del Muerto bought a lot of friends by springing for one round after another. The police couldn't shake his alibi so they released him back to cruise ship authority."

"An all too familiar scenario, played out once again," I recalled from the newspaper articles in his cabin. "Was his wife, Castrada, with him at the cantina?"

"There was no mention of her," Nelson replied. "Maybe she was shopping or sightseeing. In any event, I've got to be off," Nelson said, rising to his feet. "We're experiencing some turbulence, as you may have noticed, but we expect to be through the system by fourteen hundred hours."

Nelson turned and bumped into an approaching figure. "*Hola*, Captain," greeted Del Muerto with the taciturn Castrada in tow. "This ship... she not like the *Titanic*, we hope."

Nelson smiled, tipped his hat to Castrada and left.

Del Muerto snapped his fingers for Toussaint and sat down. "Well, well, the McFaddens. How goes it señor *y* señora?" Arturo actually looked a bit dapper in a white turtleneck and double-breasted blue blazer, but his wife looked like she had just jumped off the embalming table halfway through the process. I was going to compliment him for his sartorial upgrade to vampire's pimp but thought the better of it.

"Not well," I replied. "I had my heart set on waterskiing lessons this morning, however, the surf's a little rough. Why are you so cheery, Del Muerto? Did you find a duty-free knife sale in Jamaica?"

"You funny man, McFadden," Del Muerto said with a grin last seen on a Transylvanian gargoyle. "The cruise... she is all pleasure for the moment. I took care of my business in Ocho Rios." The carnation in the table's vase centerpiece suddenly began to wilt and Girtha slid her chair closer to mine.

Watching Del Muerto closely, I asked, "Did you hear that one of our passengers had a little accident in Ocho Rios? I believe his name was Tolleson. He won't be able to continue the cruise."

Del Muerto gave his breakfast order to Toussaint and pulled out a cigar. I could tell from the band it was a pricey *Romeo y Julieta*.

He removed the wrapper and his wife, dutifully, struck a match and lit it. He then took the spent match from her and tossed it in the water pitcher.

"Yes... yes, I heard the same thing," he replied, inhaling deeply and releasing parallel columns of malodorous smoke through his nostrils. "That is unfortunate."

I picked up the used napkin from my lap to place it on the table and saw a business card fall from between the starched creases into my lap. "Automobile accident wasn't it?" I asked as I slipped the card discreetly into my pocket—I assumed it was intended for my eyes only.

"No, I don't think so," Del Muerto replied. "Me... I hear he was mugged. Some local thugs wanted his wallet and he resisted, so they stabbed him."

Girtha wobbled to her feet. "Chauncey, I'm going back to the cabin. I think the movement of the ship is getting to me."

I knew what was getting to Girtha; the same thing that was getting to me. Del Muerto had information about the murder to which others on the ship were not privy; information that had not even been contained in the AP newswire.

"How do you know the cause of Tolleson's death, Del Muerto? The ship just received a late-breaking newswire, and it was silent on the cause of death."

"Didn't I mention it?" Del Muerto asked with feigned innocence. "When I was returning to the ship, I bump into a couple of policemen talking about it. The news... it travels fast on a small island. They say that a gringo from the ship got himself killed."

"How did you know he was stabbed?"

"The knife... they say it was found next to the body. That makes sense, you know? The killer... he wouldn't want to keep anything that could be traced back to the scene of the crime. Terrible thing, this murder," Del Muerto mocked, shaking his head. "One cannot be safe; even on vacation."

"The man who was killed, Tolleson, did you know him?" I asked.

"No," Del Muerto shrugged. "No, this man... he was a complete stranger to me. Maybe I see him on the ship, or his picture in the paper... I don't know," his voice trailed off.

"You look familiar as well, Del Muerto. I think I've seen your mug shot in the crime sections of newspapers. Your picture doesn't do you justice I must say."

"I agree with you, señor. The lighting... it is so bad in those lineups. And, they always publish the side of my face with the scar. In my country, I am what you call a—" Del Muerto paused, and then snapped his fingers, "a scapegoat." When the police have a murder they cannot solve and I am in the area, they bring me in for questioning. Thanks to my good fortune, I always have an alibi, and they have to release me. They will never catch the artful Arturo."

"That sounds like harassment; it must be annoying and inconvenient."

"It is bad publicity... it would break my poor mother's heart. Once in a while I sue for... how you say... defecation of character?"

I was going to correct him, but stopped myself: in his case, "defecation" of character was probably a more accurate term than *defamation.*

Having learned about as much as I was going to from the Colombian, I excused myself and headed to the Radio Room to talk to Boyd Fowler who should have been on duty by then. I found him leaning back in a swivel chair reading a letter, his feet propped up on the impressive communications console. I guessed him to be in his early twenties; he was tall and lanky, had short, curly blond hair that partially covered his ears and forehead, and a cleft in his chin in which a dime could be buried. Relaxed in this position, he seemed to extend appendages in all directions, like a vertebrate spider.

"I can tell you're an American, Boyd, and that you just received a letter from your girlfriend."

He sat up and looked up at me with a puzzled look. "That's right. How'd you know?"

I pointed to an envelope laying face down on the console. "From the letters 'S-W-A-K' written on the back flap of the envelope. That little endearment, 'sealed with a kiss,' is distinctly American.

"I'm Chauncey McFadden. I believe Captain Nelson told you I might be dropping by to see you."

"Yes, sir," Fowler replied, taking one last, longing look at the letter before slipping it into his shirt pocket. "You're the ship's inspector."

"That's correct, but at the moment I'm more interested in your boss than the ship. When was the last time you saw him?"

"Sunday night, when my shift ended and my replacement arrived. Bruno and I left the Radio Room about eighteen hundred hours and went to mess. After we grubbed down, I went to the staff lounge to shoot pool and Bruno returned to clean up some things."

"Was that his normal routine—to work the second shift as well?"

"Bruno was married to his job—a real workaholic. He spent most of his free time in the Radio Room. I've never seen a guy so wrapped up in his work. If he wasn't eating or sleeping, he was in his office back there or here at the console."

"Was he ambitious? Was he bucking for a promotion?"

"I think he just liked the work. I don't think he was looking to get ahead. He knew he didn't have the educational background or credentials to get him to the next level. He'd put in a couple of tours of duty with the Danish navy—he ran communications on one of their warships. When his military time was up, he spent some time building a communications network for a new pharmaceutical company on one of the islands, and then came to work for Nordic Caribbean."

"What exactly is it that you all do here, in the Radio Room?"

"Our primary job is to maintain ship-to-shore telephone and radiogram services—those are wireless telegrams—twenty-four hours a day, while the ship is at sea. We close up shop while in ports of call due to international regulations.

"As soon as we receive radiograms, we personally deliver them. We transmit outgoing radiograms as soon as the forms are filled out by passengers here at the Radio Room. When passengers place a phone call to shore, they dial our extension, and we put them through; when calls come in, we direct them to phones in the passengers' cabins.

"We also sort incoming mail and give it to the stewards who deliver the letters to the passengers' cabins, though outgoing mail is handled by the Purser's Office."

"Do you stay busy?"

"We stay fairly busy," Fowler said. "It can be slow at times, then pick up in a hurry, though, particularly when the stock market drops a hundred points and the rich old codgers need to issue sell orders to their brokers."

"What was Helmje's job? How was it different than yours?"

"He did the normal supervisory and administrative stuff. He had to write reports and attend the Captain's meetings to report on the Radio Room and its activities."

"It doesn't seem those duties would require as much extra time as he was devoting to the job."

"He spent a lot of time decoding and encoding messages and telegrams, too."

This was an unexpected and intriguing bit of information. "Decoding? Encoding? Messages?" I was excited to finally feel a lead taking shape. "About what? From whom?"

"He didn't share any of that information with us, so we were never involved," Fowler replied. "He handled it all personally. All I know is, they were coded messages. He used to get a half dozen or so a week, usually from islands in the Caribbean, places in Central and South America, I think, and Miami."

"Being coded, you wouldn't know whether they were personal or ship's business?"

"Nope. Bruno said they were classified and made sure we knew we didn't have the appropriate security clearances to see them. He was touchy on the subject, so we learned not to bring it up. Funny thing, though."

"What's that?" I asked.

"Bruno was kind of nosy himself. In fact, he read everything that came to or left the ship, no matter who it was addressed to or who was sending it. He would even monitor incoming and outgoing calls from time to time."

"Did that strike you as being normal?" I suspected something more than simple paranoia was at work here.

"I don't really know what normal is, sir. This is the only communications job I've ever held on a cruise ship."

"Do you have to keep a log? I assume some record of communications is kept."

"Yes, sir, we have a log of all incoming and outgoing communications—"

"May I see it?" I interrupted.

"You can look at it, but it may not do you any good," he warned me.

"Why not?"

"Because Bruno never recorded any of these classified messages in the log."

I was beginning to see a classic psychological profile starting to emerge… a worker who was involved in secret transactions that no one else was privy to… a worker who was always on the job, who was ostensibly afraid to leave it because someone covering for him might discover what he'd been up to… a worker who didn't leave any record of transactions… I thought of the proverbial accountant who never took a day off because he was afraid that an audit in his absence would uncover that he'd been "cooking the books."

"How long have you known Bruno?" I asked, trying another approach to gain insight into the mysterious Helmje.

"About two years. That's how long I've been here. The two other radio operators are newer, so they wouldn't have much else to tell you."

"Did you know him very well on a personal level?"

Fowler toyed with the St. Christopher's medal around his neck. "Not really. He was a feisty little guy. He was barely five feet tall and he always seemed to be moving; he could never stay still. Sometimes he gave the impression of being nervous; he hopped around like spit on a hot griddle. But he was a decent enough guy; he seemed to get along pretty well with most people."

"Did he go ashore much?"

"At every port of call, since the station is closed while the ship is berthed."

"Who were Bruno's close friends? Who did he socialize with?"

Fowler thought for a minute. "The only person I saw him with a lot was Joey Morton, the comic. Joey stopped by the radio station pretty often and they'd go into Bruno's office and close the door. And, sometimes, I'd see them in the staff lounge, huddled together over in a corner."

"Thanks, Boyd. I may need to talk to you again, but you've been very helpful." Before I left, I grabbed a blank radiogram form and penned three requests to Lieutenant Alameda. My first request was that she mail me CSI pictures of Amundson, Dubonnet, Destang, and any other suspected Zunimbist victims as soon as possible. In particular, I wanted to see close-up shots of the markings on their chests.

Next, I asked that she have the Del Muertos checked out—in-depth, from their births to the present day; not only their police and other public records, but as much personal biographical data as could be accumulated.

Lastly, I requested that she look into Simon Cartier—his current and past occupations, where he had lived, and his association with Bridgetown, Barbados. In view of Tolleson's murder, the presence of Cartier's name in Del Muerto's planner had given him a higher investigational priority.

When I was through, I handed my requests to Fowler. "Send these out right away. Make sure I receive any responses as soon as they come in."

"You got it," Fowler said as he took the form. "Has any information turned up about Bruno? Is he all right?"

"He's just missing at this point," I said. "As soon as we know anything different, I'm sure you'll be among the first to know."

I left the youth to pant over his recent love letter while I went to look for Joey Morton. A steward directed me to the Skylight Lounge, a swanky watering hole on the uppermost deck that extruded out over the stern of the ship, affording a panoramic view of the scenery behind us. Joey was there, all right—slumped over the bar, alone. An overflowing ashtray by his smoking hand indicated that he'd been there for some time. A corresponding pyramid of empty shot glasses by his drinking hand told me he'd been killing time by the ounce.

"Joey," I greeted, hoisting myself up on an adjacent stool. "Isn't it a little early to be drinking lunch?"

"It's vodka and vodka—the latest Soviet diet fad… the rage of Caspian fat farms." Joey lifted his head from his crossed arms on the bar.

"Judging by the number of shot glasses you've stacked, you'd better fasten the seat belt on your bar stool."

"It's the weather. "Storms at sea make me nervous. It's either vodka or Dramamine, and I ran out of the latter hours ago. Look out there," he pointed to the wall of glass being buffeted by howling gusts of wind and water. "It's raining like a cow pissing on a flat rock."

"Don't worry," I comforted. "The Captain's name isn't Noah, the cruise isn't scheduled for forty days and forty nights, and we're one comedian short of the required pair."

"You'll do in a pinch," he complimented. "But, to what do I owe the pleasure of your company?"

"I'd like to talk to you about Bruno Helmje. I understand you two were close friends." My question caught him at a bad time. He was inhaling and my request triggered a gasp which exacerbated into a coughing fit.

When his wheezing had subsided, he picked a tobacco shard off the end of his tongue and shot me a glance that teetered halfway between wariness and suspicion. "Helmje?"

"One and the same."

"The radio man?" He ignored the burning cigarette in the ashtray and lit a successor. "Who are you really, McFadden?"

"I'm a ship's inspector," I replied flashing my badge of identification. "I'm sure you heard that Helmje is missing. I'm trying to find him. What do you know about his disappearance?"

Morton, to his credit, processed this new information quickly. "I knew Helmje, sure. But I don't keep tabs on him. He's probably passed out in the engine room someplace. You could hide for a week on a ship this size. Or maybe he went ashore to knock the cobwebs off his joy stick and couldn't find his pants until after cast-off. He wouldn't be the first crew member to miss reveille."

"It's not reveille I'm concerned about, it's taps."

Morton looked like he was peaking for an anxiety attack. "You think he's pushing up daisies?"

"Water lilies are more like it. If his body isn't on board, it's been tossed over the rail like cold coffee."

Morton turned pale quickly and I didn't think it was because of the weather. "We were friends but I don't know anything that might help you find him." Waving the bartender over, he said, "A couple more of these, Freddy, and make them doubles."

"I'm hearing a different story, Joey. I'm told you and Bruno were as thick as thieves… no pun intended."

"What if I told you we grew up together? We went to the same high school and dated the same girls. We hadn't seen each other in years until I landed this gig. We get together now and then to rehash old times… harmless reminiscing."

"You're trying my patience, Joey. Helmje grew up yodeling in the fiords of Oslo; you were stealing hubcaps in Flatbush as soon as you were weaned. He was in the Danish navy buggering sardine-mongers while you were diddling old Jewesses in the Catskill resorts between shows."

"Whatever," Morton blurted, "but the bottom line is I don't know anything."

"I hope, for your sake, that you're telling the truth, Joey. Money says that Helmje was involved in something that turned out badly and made his disposal necessary. If you were also involved, or you know anything about Helmje's involvement, I wouldn't count on you being around long enough to receive your pension from the Comics' Relief Fund."

Joey looked a little unnerved and rushed to sign his room charge slip for the drinks, then left. His steps were missing their usual spring as he walked quickly to the door. I wondered how long the eternal footman, not known for his patience, would hold Joey's coat.

Once he was out the door, I returned to my cabin, where I found Girtha sprawled in a chair. "What did you do this afternoon?" I asked.

"I went to the art auction since you were tied up. It was fun but most of the paintings were weird. You used to work in a museum and art gallery. What's your opinion of this picture?" Girtha asked, showing me a seated nude in the auction catalog.

I looked at the objet d'art in question. "That's a famous piece by Pablo Picasso. He was a Spanish artist and one of the pioneers of the Cubist movement in the early twentieth century."

"To me she looks like something you'd see in a carnival house of mirrors," Girtha said.

"Cubism holds that the essence of an object can only be captured by showing it from multiple points of view at the same time," I explained. "Cubists will take an object—such as a woman—and break her up into components, analyze her, and then reassemble her in an abstract form."

"I think he'd been sniffing too much paint thinner. Not even Frederick's of Hollywood could make a bra for those knockers," Girtha concluded.

Remembering the business card I had slipped into my trouser pocket at lunch, I pulled it out for review.

"What's that?" Girtha asked.

"A card for a palm reader named Madam Draconia, 14 Breedestraat Street, Willemstad," I read.

"There's writing on the back. What does it say?" Girtha asked, peeking over my shoulder.

"It says I must see her tomorrow without fail; my life may depend on it."

Girtha turned pallid for the umpteenth time.

"Probably a joke," I said, trying to speak with reassurance. "This looks like something Joey Morton would do. He knows I'm a ship's inspector and he's probably stringing me along. I think I'll call his bluff and check out the good madam."

"And, if it isn't a joke?"

She was obviously not convinced.

"Well, then, at least I get my fortune told."

CHAPTER 10

A BRIGHT MORNING SUN STREAMING THROUGH THE porthole caused me to blink myself to consciousness the next morning. It was Wednesday, the fifth day of our cruise. After rubbing my eyes vigorously—my version of calisthenics—I ambled to the door and picked up the daily news and ship's activities bulletins that had been left by our steward. My rising had awakened Girtha who moaned and stretched.

"Why are you getting up in the middle of the night?" she queried between yawns. "It's still pitch black."

"That's because you still have your sleeping mask on," I replied. I slid it down her face and, for good measure, I pulled the elastic band and let it snap against her chin.

"You *stinker!*" she yelled. I had barely squeezed into the bathroom before a flying shoe landed with a loud thud against the door.

We skipped early breakfast and rushed to the starboard rail of the Promenade Deck as the *Oslo Aphrodite* slipped into the world's fifth busiest harbor, Willemstad, the capital of both Curacao and the Netherlands Antilles. The ship was just entering the narrow channel that separates the two districts of the city—Punda on the right and Otrabanda on the left.

As the city came into view, we thought we'd been taken back in time, to seventeenth-century Amsterdam. The largest apparent difference was that Willemstad had modified the Dutch colonial architecture to reflect its warmer, more tropical environment. The Caribbean accents included verandas, porches, fretwork, and shutters. The color scheme had been modified as well, showcasing neatly painted bright and pastel colors. Still, the steeply pitched red tile roofs and gabled houses reflected a distinct Dutch urban architecture.

Ahead were two unique bridges: the Queen Juliana, one of the highest ever constructed, and the Queen Emma, the largest floating pedestrian bridge in the world. The Queen Emma—a pontoon bridge connecting the two districts—swung open up to thirty times a day to admit more than 6,500 ships a year into St. Anna Bay, the entrance to Schottegat Harbor.

Girtha and I got in line and finally disembarked, barreling through the photo op station at the bottom of the gangway. The less aggressive and nimble were helplessly corralled and coerced into smiling for the high-priced pictures that would be publicly available for purchase later in the ship's gallery.

After stopping to ask for directions a few times, we found our way to Breedestraat Street, where we spotted Madam Draconia's place. It would have been hard to miss: the structure was a bright yellow building shaded by purple awnings. One window displayed a giant human palm while a tarot card was centered in the other.

As we approached the building, a tall figure dressed in a long black dress and head scarf walked hurriedly out the door. We let her pass, but when she paused to look back over her shoulder, we recognized her: Castrada Del Muerto. We called her name and waved but she quickened her pace and disappeared into the throng of shoppers on the street.

"I wonder what *she* was doing here?" I asked. "She doesn't seem the type to be curious about her future, and her husband has demonstrable competence in determining the futures of others."

Girtha didn't say anything but pulled the brim of her hat down over her eyes—furtively looking around as if she was entering a speakeasy during Prohibition—before we entered the eerie silence of the shop and looked around. We were immediately fascinated by the merchandise on the shelves and under the glass counters.

At the entrance to the shop, a large selection of incense and burners for home ceremonies was centrally positioned to attract initial attention. These items were located next to a section of "Creole Voodoo Love Spell Kits" and other packaged ceremonies, some with accompanying satin altar cloths and props that enabled buyers to concoct the spells themselves if they didn't want to employ the services of a paid psychic professional. Beside them was an entire shelf devoted to love potions, essential oils that had been "hand-blended and consecrated."

Overhead, dangling from a horizontal rod, was a wide selection of *gris-gris* bags—lucky charms full of herbs and powders that are to be worn around the neck. Their purpose—to help one achieve an object of their desire—was accomplished by spiritual activation, launched by a special chant and blessed candle, both included in the price, of course.

To the left, one cabinet held a large display of "Love Spell Dolls" for which a large sign boasted that replacement kits of all the required herbs and oils could be ordered to permit limitless reuse. Next to that, a rack of silver-chained talismans, amulets, and mystic charms was suspended, each with a design that depended upon the purpose a buyer needed to fulfill.

The largest display of all was on the opposite wall: candles. They were designed in many shapes, even male and female profiles, and in all primary colors, each expected to serve a specific purpose.

Anyone wishing to dabble in the occult—witchcraft, Wicca, sorcery, astrology, or paganism—would find all the supplies they needed right here. For those simply seeking information, or wanting to gain psychic power through self-study, the shop was stocked with a myriad of books on the black arts. Probably not the sort of thing one should read before bedtime.

I was further intrigued by some of the artwork for sale. The creators must have been tormented souls in institutional care who were trying to describe recurrent nightmares to their clinical psychiatrists. I'm not sure where a buyer could comfortably hang any of the pieces, except in the green pellet room at Sing Sing.

"Look, Chauncey," Girtha said, looking up from a bottle she'd removed from a shelf. "This is Mambo Maybelle's Magic Love Elixir. It says on the back label that if you 'slip a couple of drops of this secret formula into your lover's beverage, it promises to turn him into a human tripod.'"

"Forget it, Girtha. The only way I could become a human tripod is if my two legs were amputated."

Girtha looked puzzled, replaced the bottle, and pulled down a cookbook. After thumbing through the pages a moment, she appeared infused with sudden enthusiasm. "This cookbook has recipes for ritualistic cooking. You can induce spells of love... pain... whatever... by using certain herbs and consecrated ingredients. Here's a recipe for 'Grab His Groin Gumbo'—I'm going to copy that one," she said, searching through her purse for a pad and pencil.

"Might as well; that won't be on the menu at Waffle House. Hey, here's one— 'Jump Her Bones Jambalaya'."

A deep, rich voice with a slight accent—probably a Papiamento patois, a combination of Portuguese, Dutch, Spanish, and English with a couple of African dialects thrown in—responded: "May I help you?"

Girtha and I had identical reactions: we turned toward the source of the voice and jumped.

Staring at us from an interior doorway was a tall black woman—over six feet in height with skin was so black it had a bluish tint. On her head, she wore a purple turban with an upright peacock feather wedged between its crisscrossed bands of cloth. A flowing robe of many bright colors enveloped her large-framed body—its colors reminiscent of what I would expect on a drop cloth from the floor of Jackson Pollock's studio.

In a moment, her piercing, penetrating eyes softened and she said with a smile, "*Bon bini*. I am Madam Draconia. Please step into my reading parlor."

The reading parlor reeked of psychic atmosphere. The walls of the square, twenty-by-twenty room were concealed by sections of black velvet drapery. If someone was going to step out from behind one of the curtains, I imagined it would be Bela Lugosi rather than Monty Hall. From the folds of the drapery hung various types of dolls, perhaps effigies to be used in pagan practices. In contrast to the ambiance of this room and the shop we'd passed through, some soothing music—a sort of yoga mantra—set an inviting auditory mood; a waft of burning incense eased the olfactory senses. In addition, a number of candles flickered in floor sconces that were scattered around the perimeter of the room. Dead center, illuminated by a bright overhead light, a round table and three chairs sat without additional fanfare. The madam sat down in one of the chairs and, with a hand gesture, motioned for Girtha and me to occupy the remaining two.

"Nice place you have here," I commented. "I'll admit, though, it's not what I expected."

"What did you expect?" she asked.

"I thought you'd be standing over a boiling cauldron, muttering some incantations, and stirring a brew of snake snouts, toad tongues, and bat brains."

She responded with a smile. "The city fire code forced me to dispose of the boiling cauldron, and I lost my last reliable, cheap source of snakes, toads, *and* bats. So, assuming you are not too disappointed, do you wish to have your palms read, or are you here for one of my other psychic services?" she asked.

"What are your 'other' psychic services?" I asked.

"I provide readings from Tarot cards, tea leaves, or a crystal ball, and I am qualified to practice numerology and to offer Chinese and Western horoscopes."

"A palm reading will be fine."

"That will be ten dollars American or twenty-six Netherlands Antilles gilders—in advance, please."

I scrounged through my pockets until I found a couple of fives, which she slid from my fingers effortlessly. She folded them and stuck them down the front of her robe, banking them between her ample bosoms. I doubted I would have asked for a refund anyway.

"I also cast spells if you're interested," she said. "They are guaranteed and effective within twenty-four hours."

"What kinds of spells?" I asked.

"Love spells are the most popular. I can return a lover, ruin the romantic attraction of a competitor, entrance someone to want you, make you irresistible, or stop a divorce. These spells range from $7.95 to $10.95.

"I can also provide money spells—make your career blossom, bring you fame and fortune, or help you realize that success you've always wanted. These spells range from $8.95 to $11.95.

"Revenge spells are the most extreme. These spells can only be cast upon someone who has hurt you or someone you love. The hurt can be physical, emotional, or mental. These spells bring curses upon your enemies: they will suffer physically, face financial ruin, or have their love life and sexual function destroyed. These spells range from $16.95 to $25.95.

"Please note that I do not offer death spells.

"If you desire a revenge spell, I will need the names and addresses of those upon whom the spell is to be cast. If you have a picture of them, their date of birth, or handwriting sample, that's even better. For maximum spell strength, a biological sample is best: fingernail clippings, strands of hair, or bodily fluids on a tissue."

Following a pause that I'm certain was premeasured, she finalized her offerings. "Are you interested?"

"I guess not," I replied, resisting temptation. "I have a nemesis in Los Angeles—a police lieutenant by the name of Luther Del Dotto. I was thinking that a good dose of gonorrhea would do him good. Or pernicious hemorrhoids might be nice. I would prefer a maximum strength spell, but I'm not up to securing one of his used condoms or toilet tissues." Girtha kicked my foot under the table.

"As you wish," Madam Draconia replied, sensing that her sales pitch had fallen upon deaf ears. "Before we begin, what is your name?" she asked.

"Chauncey McFadden. This is my girlfriend, Girtha Roote."

"He means girlfriend of long-standing who hopes for a more permanent relationship," Girtha quickly clarified in apparent hopes that the madam might be able to assist her in this quest.

"Do you have specific questions or concerns for Madam Draconia?"

"No, nothing in particular. Just give me the old generic, run-of-the-mill, plain-vanilla palm reading. I'm here for curiosity more than anything else."

"Are you right or left handed?" she asked.

"Shouldn't you know that already?" I joked. Girtha kicked me again. In response to a stern glare, I mumbled, "Right."

"Then, give me your right palm, please."

She took my palm in her hand and studied it closely. Her fingernails, which were painted with metallic pink polish, measured at least an inch long and could have impaled a small rat. "You are a non-believer, Mr. McFadden. You believe that palmistry is a hoax. You do not believe that one's future can be foretold by the lines, patterns, and formations on a palm."

"Let's just say, I'm skeptical but open-minded. How does palmistry work?"

"Palm reading is an ancient science whose veracity is unquestionable. It is based upon the analysis and interpretation of many factors, all of them revealed by the characteristics of a person's hand."

"Such as…"

"Primarily, we look at the major lines in the palm. There are twelve: the life line, the head line, the heart line, the health line, the fate line, the fame line, the marriage line, the money line, the sex line, the spirit line, the travel line, and the luck line."

Girtha finally spoke up. "I'm particularly interested in the marriage line and the sex line," she let it be known. "Specifically, does the first one even exist, and will there be more activity in the second one?"

"These concerns will be addressed in due time," Madam Draconia answered with a slight smile. "I do see an intense romantic involvement twenty years ago."

"That was before we met; you never mentioned her," Girtha quipped, more with sudden interest than jealousy.

"Nothing to tell," I told her. "She was memorable but short-lived—like a rented prom dress."

Having sparked some interest, Madam Draconia continued. "We also look at the shape of the hand. There are five major shapes: pointed, square, cone, spade, and mixed. You, for example, have a mixed hand.

"Your fingers also have diverse characteristics. Some of your knuckles are smooth in some areas and knotty in others. Such people tend to be generalists who have creative and practical personalities. Typical occupations include journalists, teachers, and researchers."

"Or private detectives," Girtha added. This time, it was my turn to kick her—for blowing my cover.

"Yes," Madam agreed after brief thought, "a private investigator could have these characteristics as well.

"When looking at fingers, we especially note their length, the spaces between them, their smoothness, and their shape. Looking at the attributes of your fingers, for example, reveals the following about you. You are intellectual, creative, and imaginative, but not always comfortable in your work. You are uneasy with commitment and in structured environments characterized by strong authority. You are honest, direct, and clear-headed, but not obsessively so. You sacrifice material well-being for independence."

Girtha's mouth was agape. Poking me in the arm with her index finger, she said, "Chauncey, that's a perfect description. She couldn't have gotten any closer."

I had to admit that several of the traits were on target... well, many of them anyway... okay, most of them... all right, she nailed me good.

Madam Draconia then peered more closely at my palm, clutched her chest and gasped.

"What's the matter?" I asked. "Did my palm tell you that the bills I gave you were counterfeit? Or is this the part where you are so distraught by an event in my future that you can't continue unless I grease your palm with another ten spot?"

"Worse than that, I'm afraid," she said with a look of distress that totally ignored my jibe. "Your life line tells me that you are in danger. You are pursuing something that will place you in extreme peril if you continue. You are wandering into a web of evil spun by people of unspeakable cruelty. The signs say you must stop now or suffer mortal consequences."

Girtha had fallen from the peak of excitement to a look that told me she was ready to faint. I had to confess to some apprehension myself, despite the fact that I wasn't convinced palmistry was an exact science. To save Girtha from further distress, I asked, "Madam Draconia, may I see your palm a minute?"

She extended her hand reluctantly. Looking into her palm, I said in a soft, mystical tone: "I see a figure in a dark cloak paying you some money to give me a reading intended to scare me off the case I'm working on." I glanced up, winked, and asked innocently: "Am I a quick learner or what?"

"You *profane* spiritualism," she hissed. "The spirits will not take kindly to your blasphemy."

"It won't be the first time. As a kid, I used to sleep during sermons, stick my used chewing gum in the hymnals, and pretend to put ten percent of my allowance in the collection plate.

"A final question—these 'people of unspeakable cruelty' that you mentioned: are they Zunimbists by any chance?"

Madam Draconia lurched to her feet. "This reading is over," she said stiffly. "I cannot tell you more even if you greased my palm with a couple of *C* notes."

"I had to pay ten bucks for that warning," I grumbled on the way out of Madam Draconia's little shop of horrors. "They could have plopped a chicken head on my pillow for nothing."

At least Girtha was in a lighter mood, so we took advantage of being ashore and ambled through the waterside attractions. We passed an outdoor fish market whose metal bins were teeming with catches of the day. Snuggling in crushed ice were crevalle jack, Spanish mackerel, bluefish, snook, grouper, bonito, and cobia. Some customers left with the whole fish in woven baskets; others waited for the vendors to remove the scales, heads, and entrails.

A bit farther, we found a small restaurant off a side street and, being adventurous eaters, we opted for local cuisine. We were not disappointed by the *sopi juana*—iguana soup; the *keshi yena*—baked Edam cheese stuffed with fish; or the *java honden portie*—an Indonesian dish of two fried eggs on a mound of rice encircled by potatoes, vegetables, and steak.

We left our lunch spot, belts loosened a notch, and soon spied an old tour bus, which we joined for a spin around the island. I hoped the tour might provide some additional distraction to Girtha. I was doing my best to get her thinking about something other than the Madam's subsidized and disingenuous prediction.

I'm not usually a fan of local tours. First of all, people sign up for them at inflated prices. Second, the passengers grumble every time they reach a scenic or historic site and have to exit the air-conditioned coach. Their desire to learn and explore, but only in supreme comfort and convenience, is another paradox of the American tourist.

Through the dusty windows, we were able to observe some of the unique topography of Curacao's *cunucu*, or countryside. The flat landscape was dotted with wind-bent *divi-divi* trees, a few varieties of cactus, and some other drought-resistant plants. It became clear that Curacao's location in the Caribbean was both a blessing and a curse: a blessing because of the cooling trade winds that maintain a moderate year-round temperature; a curse because of the paucity of annual rainfall. The arid landscape of the interior was a stark contrast to the sparkling beaches and clear ocean waters that rimmed the island.

Returning to the beaches, we saw an occasional skiff parked between sand dunes, its colors faded by the relentless sun and punishing salt water. Scattered around tufts of plumed grass, were great egrets, white ibises, brown pelicans, and herring gulls—all engaged in grooming or finishing the remains of some delicate repast. They paid scant attention to the marauding shell collectors, who whooped and hollered as they filled their plastic buckets with whelks, conchs, sand dollars, cockles, and sharks' teeth.

My favorite tour stops were the Amstel Brewery, maker of the only beer made with distilled sea water, and the Curacao Liqueur Distillery where we had more than a few tastings of that delightful orange-flavored liquor made from the fruit of the *laraha* tree. Girtha, a nature enthusiast, enjoyed the sea aquarium, where she was able to view more than six hundred species of native sea life that make their homes in the local reefs. She also enjoyed the ostrich and game farm, where she played with newborn offspring of that large, flightless bird. My main thought while we were there was how fortunate for the Zunimbists that they based their cult upon Haitian traditions that employed chickens in their ceremonies. If the cult had been founded in Curacao, the poor assassins would have had to stagger around crime scenes toting dead ostriches.

We still had some time left after the tour's conclusion, so we visited the maritime museum, which was burgeoning with historical artifacts and special exhibits, and Fort Amsterdam, which was originally built to repel invaders but now served as the official residence of the governor-general, the ministry, and government offices.

We got back to the ship the requested thirty minutes prior to departure and limped to our cabin to soothe four aching feet. While Girtha used the restroom, I opened an envelope that I had stepped on when we entered—evidently, it had been slid under the door in our absence—and read the contents.

It was a hastily-scrawled note from Joey Morton. He'd been thinking about our earlier conversation and asked that I meet him in his cabin after the second show. He had a matter of utmost urgency to discuss.

CHAPTER 11

AFTER BRIEF NAPS, GIRTHA AND I SHOWERED and dressed for dinner. I donned my usual blue suit while she labored in indecision, her outfits spread on both beds as she switched tops and bottoms for maximum impact.

"No need to be so picky about your clothes, Girtha," I advised. "Toussaint will probably spill something on them anyway."

"Oh… I feel so sorry for that young man, Chauncey. He tries so hard, but he must have cheated his way through waiters' school. Hey…" she said, her voice trailing off in thought and her face brightening, "maybe *I* should get a job on a cruise ship. The tips have got to be better than waitressing at Cosmo's Diner."

"Be careful what you wish for, Girtha. You have some strange customers at Cosmo's, but nothing that remotely approaches Castrada and Arturo."

"You've got a point there." She decided on an ensemble, and we left the room, headed for dinner.

With the exception of Colonel Talbo, our dinner companions were being seated as we arrived. Del Muerto was decked out in a bright yellow leisure suit. Castrada, in contrast, was wearing her usual funereal attire: a floor-length black gown of undeterminable fabric, and much too heavy for a tropical climate. Lamont Darling was draped in yet another pastel-shaded, silk jacket and trousers that were several shades darker.

Fifi had been shoehorned into a little number that left hardly anything to the imagination—its hemline *almost* covering her derriere when she tugged it down and its bust line *almost* containing its cargo when she tugged it up. I was surprised to find that she could take enough of a breath to speak, but it was actually Fifi who broke the silence as we approached.

"It's been so hot these past few days that I haven't felt like wearing a bra or panties."

"Señorita, *please*, there is no need to apologize," Del Muerto said with horny magnanimity. He was already wiping the corners of his mouth with his thumb and forefinger, trying to remove the drool that started to form as he undressed her with his eyes.

"I must, for once, agree with the señor," I chimed in. "Don't overdress and be uncomfortable on our account."

My reassurance was immediately followed by a swift elbow in the ribs. I didn't know, however, if Girtha's reaction was caused by my comment or by the fact that the dress Fifi was almost wearing had attracted all the attention from her studiously selected outfit du jour. Rubbing my ribcage, I wisely changed the subject. "What exactly does a publicist do, Fifi?"

"Why, I take care of Mr. Darling's every need. I run his bathwater, give him messages and manicures, and—"

"She's still new in this position," Darling interrupted, patting her hand.

I obviously needed to change the focus, too. "How did you spend your day, folks?" I asked the Del Muertos.

"Me... I had a little business to take care of," Del Muerto responded with a shrug.

"Will we be reading about that business in the island's crime tabloids tomorrow?" I goaded.

Del Muerto smiled and lowered his eyebrows. "Not if the tide and sharks do their job..."

"And, did you have an equally eventful day as well?" I asked Castrada.

She maintained her normal facial composure, which was something between hostile indifference and a withering stare, while her husband answered in her stead. "My wife... she picks up a few herbs and spices for the kitchen; items hard to find in our country."

Girtha and I looked at each other. "Yeah," I said, "Girtha and I thought we saw her in town. We tried to get her attention but failed." I suddenly wondered if Madam Draconia's business card had been placed in my napkin by one of the Del Muertos.

Following dinner, Girtha and I adjourned to the nightclub to try our hand at bingo. After several rounds of no luck, we were exiting the room when a geriatric posse of uberserious spinsters in their seventies had to be physically restrained from pummeling a gentleman severely about his head and shoulders with their purses—he had made the mistake of claiming a bingo that was subsequently disallowed when his card was reviewed. Seeking a safer pursuit, Girtha and I adjourned to the casino and promptly lost a bucket of quarters in the slot machines.

When I escorted Girtha back to the room, the time was approaching midnight. After making sure she was comfortable, I excused myself to find out what Joey Morton wanted to see me about.

His cabin was one of the outside staterooms on Main Deck. I knocked and was greeted by an eyeball peeking through a small crack between the door and the jamb. Assured it was me, and only me, Joey poked his head out, looked up and down the alleyway, and pulled me inside.

"What's the matter, Joey? You look like you just found a prescription to treat VD in your true love's medicine cabinet."

Joey poured himself two fingers of ten-year-old single-malt Scotch and quaffed it in a toss. He pointed the bottle to me. I politely declined.

"McFadden, the word around ship is that you're more than an inspector. Rumor says you're actually a detective hired by the cruise line to find out who killed Lars Amundson. Any truth to this?"

"If it'll help you come to the point, let's assume it is. It's obvious you're in something over your head, Joey. You want to step inside Father Chauncey's confessional or continue to operate in panic mode?"

Joey didn't need much prompting. He rolled the whiskey glass between the palms of his hands for a minute and began. "Bruno and I had a business arrangement going, which you may've already suspected." He paused and poured himself another drink which he swirled in his glass for a moment.

"I have a feeling it isn't the kind of business that would earn you an SBA loan?"

"Probably not," he agreed without relish. He stared into the amber fluid he still swirled, watching it rotate like a hurricane pattern on the six o'clock weather report. "We were smuggling cocaine into the states from the Caribbean."

I was shocked by this unexpected and pointedly straightforward revelation, and I took a moment to digest it before carrying on like it was yesterday's news. "I don't suspect that you were freelancers, so who hired you and Helmje to smuggle the contraband into the country?"

Joey's pause was intensified by his obvious pain. "The Zunimbists. We collected the cocaine from their suppliers and delivered it to their distributors in Miami. It seemed like an easy enough way to build a pension."

"How did you avoid detection by customs personnel? Don't they search everything going on and off a ship?"

Joey smiled faintly. "The goods are smuggled aboard in the false bottoms of musical instrument cases and inside the sound equipment boxes that island entertainers bring aboard for their acts—you probably noticed that we feature local musical groups from ports of call for shows in the Carousel Lounge."

"So, as the ship's comedian, who doesn't play an instrument, how do you fit in?"

"All staff members have one or more part-time jobs in addition to their main one. In addition to being the comic-in-residence, I help Ingrid, the cruise director, hire and schedule Caribbean singers and musicians for our afternoon and evening gigs—the shows in the Carousel Lounge. I get the names of the musical groups from the Zunimbists via Helmje."

"Please tell me that Lawrence Welk was an exception. I couldn't bear the thought of him being a fairy dust mule for the cocaine cartel."

"You can relax. We'd never be able to book somebody like Welk on our limited budget. Anyway, I coordinate getting the groups and their equipment on board and settling the drug-dealing musicians into their backstage quarters. Once that's done, the cocaine, which is wrapped in waterproof packages, is transferred into small valises, which I turn over to Helmje."

"Why Helmje?"

"Since Helmje is the chief radio operator, he can roam the entire ship without arousing suspicion. With all due respect to the Captain, whoever controls the airwaves runs the ship. Bruno occupies a central, strategic position; he's privy to communications coming into or leaving the *Oslo Aphrodite*. He sees information before the Captain does—he even sees information that is never passed to the Captain. Also, any last-minute changes in delivery or transfer plans—times, amounts, locations—can be relayed in code from Zunimba's people to Bruno without fear of discovery.

"Once I turn the cocaine over to Helmje, he hides the cases in his cabin until the night before we are scheduled to arrive back in Miami. That night, during the early morning hours when it's deserted, he takes the cocaine to the galley and gives the packages to an associate—usually a waiter or some other food services person—who hides them in the bottom of specially marked garbage containers.

"The coded containers are then separated out at the waste disposal facility at the Port of Miami and delivered to the Zunimbists."

"That's a lot of people and coordination," I said in admiring summation. "But, something obviously went wrong on the last trip…"

Joey bit his fist. "When the distributors in Miami opened the designated garbage containers, they found only garbage: the packages with the drugs had disappeared."

"Then Victor Dubonnet must have been the galley connection. It would have been his job to hide the drugs in the garbage containers."

"Yeah, but he never got them because they were stolen out of Bruno's cabin. Victor didn't know what to do… he went ashore to get some direction…"

"But," I concluded for him, "he got iced instead."

"You got it. And, Bruno, who'd been ripped off was afraid to leave the ship. He searched high and low for the drugs but never found a trace of 'em…

"Then, on Sunday night, the second day after the *Oslo Aphrodite* left port, he got a call from one of the Zunimba clan. It was a death threat telling him he was next... and... that... I would follow in short order. It wasn't until then that Bruno told me about the missing drugs. He disappeared on Monday, and I've been stir-crazy ever since."

"Why don't you try explaining the truth to Zunimba and pledge to work with him and the Zunimbists to find out what happened to the drugs?"

Joey gave me a look usually reserved for the village idiot. "Zunimba isn't much into forgiving and forgetting. You don't get a second chance with those guys. I can't raise my hand and ask for a do-over."

"Then why don't you turn yourself in to the authorities?" I suggested. "You've got no police record and this is a first offense. You'd probably serve minimal time at worst and then get the remainder of your sentence commuted for good behavior."

"Possession of more than ten grams of cocaine, powder or crack, is a first-degree felony punishable by up to thirty years in the can and a $10,000 fine. I don't want to spend my retirement making license plates.

"Besides, I wouldn't live to see the penitentiary in my rearview mirror. The cell blocks are crawling with Zunimbist inmates. The warden would find me in the exercise yard with a shiv in my back before I'd taken my first jailhouse crap."

"Then what's your plan?"

Joey eschewed the glass and took a swig directly from the bottle. "We dock in La Guaira tomorrow and I'm jumping ship. I've got some friends in Caracas who are fixing me up with a fake passport, international driving license, and other documents. Money is being wired to me at a local *banco* from my branch in New York."

"I wish you good luck, Joey. This does prompt a seminal question, however: why are you telling me this?"

"I'd like you to find out what happened to the cocaine. If you do, I'll wire you five grand for the information. Restitution is the only thing that can square me with Zunimba. Until that happens, I've got no choice but to change my name, grow a beard, and hide out in a monastery somewhere.

"I'll get your office phone number from the long-distance operator and call you in a few weeks, after I get settled, to see if you were able to turn up anything."

"If I run across anything, I can pass it along but I have no vested interest in the recovery of the drugs. Why are you asking me to bird-dog the drugs anyway? You might be able to get better value from a Miami-based PI."

"I'm not going back to Miami and I don't know any detectives there I can trust. Besides, you're an insider and you're here *now*," Joey explained. "Anders Erickson and Captain Nelson have apparently given you carte blanche on this vessel, and the answer to the disappearance of those drugs is somehow connected to this ship. You're in the best position to snoop around 'til you find something.

"*I* think the drugs may still be aboard. Unfortunately, if they're not found soon, any chance of recovery becomes slimmer and slimmer."

I reflected on the new information and how it might fit into the overall case. "Okay. Let's say that I buy your story and its explanations—and that I even understand your course of action— none of it explains Amundson's murder. Was he working with you and Helmje?"

"Nah, Lars wasn't involved in *our* operation. But, he could have been working for the Zunimbists in some other capacity. Or he could have found out about our operation and had his lip zipped… which reminds me of something else I should explain…

"The Zunimbists are a real tight, clandestine organization. Bruno and I are considered satellites. That means we have a specific role as part of the general organizational umbrella but we aren't trusted enough to be part of the inner circle… we aren't privy to the secret handshake, the mystic mumbo jumbo, or the chicken and snake rituals."

"Doesn't smuggling drugs cause you and Helmje some moral discomfort?"

"You want the stock reply? Here it is: if we weren't doing it, somebody else would be. Besides, we weren't dealing crack cocaine outside of school grounds or selling it to downtrodden vagrants in cardboard boxes in the city park. Our powdered cocaine goes to overpaid celebrities—professional athletes, film stars, musicians—

who have nothing better to do with their money than sniff it up their noses."

"Putting the stock reply aside—why did *you* get mixed up in something like this, Joey? Drug dealing is such a nasty business; it doesn't appear to be your shtick."

Joey looked in the bottom of his whiskey glass, as if trying to find the answer there. "I don't ask myself that question because I'm not certain that I'd like the answer." He paused. "I have a list of possible reasons, though.

"For instance, maybe it's because comics are risk takers by nature and drug smuggling is a risky business. Maybe it's because the big money I used to command stopped flowing and I'm now grabbing any available job for chump change." Then, Joey's voice dropped to a whisper. "Maybe it's because I've seen my entire career ebb, from Vegas headliner... to warm-up for mediocre acts who wouldn't have been allowed on stage in my heyday. When your name drops to the bottom of the billing... when you aren't mentioned in the trade rags anymore... when customers walk out in the middle of your act... when the only time your autograph is requested is to sign an IOU...

"It's like the first time I visited my mother in the dementia ward at the nursing home. I talked for two hours, but she had no idea who I was. After my visit, I went out to the parking lot, sat in my car, and cried like a baby. It's the same way with the twilight of a comic's career. When you laugh and they don't laugh back... you're never the same again."

I couldn't help but feel sorry for him. My first impulse was empathy, but how do you console someone who's reached the end of the line; someone who's staggering to find a sanctuary for their depleted soul and been led astray by the lethal lure of easy wealth? How do you assist someone who's crouching at the door of eternity—too afraid to enter, yet too timid to retreat.

I searched for something poignant and eloquent to say, but all I managed was, "I see you've got some packing to do, so I'll run along. And, Joey..."

"Yeah?"

"You may want to sleep in another cabin tonight. There's one under the name of Buck Tolleson that may still be vacant. And keep the door locked—Helmje's murderer may still be aboard the ship. I don't want to see a duffel bag containing *your* compacted remains floating past my porthole tonight."

CHAPTER 12

THURSDAY, THE SIXTH DAY OF THE CRUISE—ALREADY. While I could finally report something positive to Captain Nelson when the occasion presented itself—that a major drug-smuggling ring aboard the *Oslo Aphrodite* had been uncovered—I was no closer to finding the killer of Lars Amundson. In addition, I was no closer to finding the killer of Buck Tolleson, or to having a motive. I was no closer to finding the killer of Bruno Helmje; and I was no closer to finding the killer of Victor Dubonnet. I also had other mysteries on the radar screen: who heisted the cocaine, and where was it stashed?

Girtha and I got up early, about six and I filled her in on my meeting with Joey while we got dressed. After I told her about his involvement in the drug-smuggling operation, she brought up the ethical component of the equation that I, in all honesty, had not considered: "Chauncey, how could you let Joey go? If he was smuggling drugs, you should have had him arrested."

"Girtha, don't make this any more complex than it is. Simply put, I'm hired by people to solve problems they're unable or unwilling to solve for themselves. If I succeed, I've fulfilled my mission and earned my pay. Sorry, honey, but I'm not a moral avenger—self-appointed or otherwise—crusading to right the wrongs in the world. I'm not qualified to perform that role so I leave it to a higher moral authority. And, who said Joey is going to avoid punishment? You can't easily escape a web of evil the size of Zunimbism. If Joey's alive this time next year, I'll be surprised."

"If you find the drugs, will you tell him?"

"Not likely because *now* you're talking about a moral code to which I do subscribe. Joey is, after all, just another disillusioned drug smuggler. I don't accept cases from those people, however personally appealing they may be."

Girtha nodded her head. I was glad we had reached an accord of sorts.

"By the way," Girtha teased, inspecting her fingernails but looking at me out of the corner of her eye, "did Mr. Erickson give you an advance on your fee? You should see the bargains in the ship's gift shops."

Since I was constantly borrowing from Girtha between paychecks back home, I took the hint and reached in my pocket for three twenties. "No, but here's a little something to keep your shopping machine purring. I guess I can always pad the expense account." Well, no one said my moral code was perfect.

"Girtha, I'm going to test your powers of observation. Did you notice anything different about Toussaint's appearance at dinner last night?"

Girtha scrunched her face and tapped her lower lip; tangible signs of attempted recollection. "Nothing out of the ordinary. He was his usual jovial self."

"You didn't notice that the stud earring in his left ear was missing a small stone?"

"I guess I would make a poor detective. I never even noticed the earring. Is that significant?"

"It could be a matter of life and death for someone."

Girtha looked out the porthole and exclaimed, "Look, we've already docked. Where are we today?" she asked, picking up the day's *Sea Compass.* "I've forgotten."

"La Guaira, the port of Caracas, Venezuela's capital. What did you sign up for?"

"There are a couple of six-hour tours that leave at ten o'clock: a city tour and a German village tour. I chose the city tour." After glancing at the tour brochure, she continued, " It has a lot of interesting stops listed like the capitol and other government buildings, Simon Bolivar's house, the Pantheon—mausoleum of heroes, the Quinta Anauco colonial museum, the Hotel Tamanaco for lunch, and the Murano Venetian Glass Factory. It's a good combination since you learn a lot about the country and its history *and* you get in some shopping, too. Aren't you coming with me?"

"I have to follow someone ashore today. In fact, I may be following two people," I said, putting on a curly blond wig, Panama hat, and oversized sunglasses. "What do you think?" I asked, striking a modeling pose.

"I would hardly recognize you, Chauncey," Girtha said in genuine amazement.

"That's what I'm counting on." I slipped my Smith & Wesson into the right front pocket of my slacks and a sheathed hunting knife into the left one, both while Girtha was looking away. I then attempted to adjust the brim on my straw hat.

"Are Panama hats really made in Panama?" Girtha asked.

"Actually, no. They're made in Ecuador and the better ones can take up to eight months to make. They only became associated with Panama after Teddy Roosevelt wore one when he visited the Panama Canal."

"That's what I enjoy about you, Chauncey. You're a walking encyclopedia of little-known facts," Girtha said. "I'm going to grab a quick snack at the breakfast buffet by the pool," Girtha said. "I'll see you tonight."

After Girtha left, I called the food and beverage manager. "Jean-Charles, this is Chauncey McFadden, the ship inspector. Is Toussaint L'Enfant working this morning?

"Oh, so he's off… When's he due back?

"'Late this afternoon, before dinner.' Thanks a lot."

I next dialed Captain Nelson. "McFadden here. At what time are passengers allowed to leave the ship this morning?"

"At nine…"

"Can you have the guard at the gangway instructed to let me disembark at 8:30? I have some urgent business ashore. I'll be in disguise but I'll flash my ID. Thanks a lot."

At 8:30, sharp, I identified myself to the gangway attendant and walked over to a line of cabs that were queued at a distant curb. A transportation coordinator with a clipboard and beige pith helmet yelled at me, and pointed to the lead cab. That was fine with me. The driver was a shapely young black woman who was leaning back against the front bumper with her elbows on the hood. She was wearing skin-tight jeans and an even tighter Mickey Mouse T-shirt. Because she was so well endowed and bra-less, Mickey's ears were the size of Dumbo's. A set of dreadlocks, long and shiny, fell gracefully from underneath a frazzled New York Yankees baseball cap. She smiled and opened the back door of an old Mercedes Benz that looked as if it had rolled off the assembly line about the same time Hitler was hunkering down in his Berlin bunker.

"Do you speak English?" I asked.

"I am most excellent English speaker," she proclaimed proudly. "I translate American television reruns for my *mami* and *papi*."

"Great. I want to rent your taxi for half a day."

"That will be fifty American dollars or 2,150 bolívares, *jefe*," she said, flashing a broad smile which was almost as bright as the rays of the morning sun off her long dangling earrings. "I am Florita, your most excellent driver."

I handed her two twenties and a ten since it sounded less painful than two thousand bolívares. "Wait here a minute, Florita. I have to make a purchase at the *carnicería* across the street." A few minutes later, I exited the butcher shop and accepted Florita's offer to slip into the back seat.

She closed my door and slid into the driver's seat before jingling her keys in front of the rearview mirror. "Where Florita take you?" She flashed her smile into the mirror. "I go as far north as the Rio Grande and as far south as Tierra Del Fuego."

Looking around at the worn interior of the taxi, I had my doubts she would go so far in *this* car. "I don't know yet, but hopefully it won't be that far. I'm waiting for a passenger to get off that ship," I said, pointing to the *Oslo Aphrodite*. "He may be followed by another passenger. I want you to tail them both without being detected. Think you can do that?"

"I am most excellent tailer," Florita said with her grin.

"Glad to hear that," I said. "Let's move your taxi out of line and park in that alley facing the ship's gangway.

In ten minutes—at nine sharp—Joey Morton scurried down the gangway ahead of the passenger exodus. Ten feet behind him, sporting sunglasses and a surprisingly colorful guayabera, was Toussaint L'Enfant. Joey tossed two suitcases inside the trunk of the first taxi in line and jumped into the back seat without looking around. Toussaint jumped into the next cab, which eased into traffic two cars behind Joey. Florita followed suit and we were underway.

It was a shame my ride through La Guaira was for business rather than leisure. The seaside resort of fifteen thousand, La Guaira is also the principal international port of Venezuela. It sprawls on a narrow strip of coastal land bordered to the north by the winding coastline of the Caribbean Sea and to the south by a coastal mountain range. The architecture in much of the city, aging under massive royal palm trees, preserved the atmosphere of the colonial period and was particularly evident in the forts of El Vigía and La Pólvora that we passed.

Within minutes of leaving the city, we ascended into a pre-mountainous tropical forest that formed a strip parallel to the coast. The two taxis ahead veered off onto the recently completed superhighway that connected La Guaira to Caracas. "Before completion of the highway, the trip to Caracas takes *four hours*," Florita explained. "Now, only forty minutes. The straight distance only seven miles; but actual distance twenty-three miles because of mountains."

The highway was in excellent condition and proved to be an engineering marvel as it negotiated the rugged topography with one hairpin turn after another. Bordered by dense forests and huge rock formations, the road carved through majestic green-clad mountains and soared above deep valleys. The topography was sprinkled with modern high-rises and clusters of dilapidated shacks called *ranchitos* that clung precariously to the sides of the mountains.

Each time we rounded a curve to enter a long gradual climb, I could see the two taxis ahead of us gliding up the incline. Clouds eventually wafted over the roadway, and the fog grew increasingly heavy as the humidity of coastal air masses collided with drier mountain air. I welcomed the fog and the winding mountain road as allies in my attempt to shield our surveillance. In addition, Florita did indeed prove to be a "most excellent tailer" as she maintained a quarter-mile distance behind the second taxi.

"Where do you think they're headed, Florita?"

"To Caracas, maybe; is still about twelve miles away. Or maybe they go to Maiquetia."

"What's Maiquetia?'

"The Simon Bolivar International Airport."

I froze at the later possibility. This is something I hadn't anticipated. While I had my passport and money with me, I couldn't very well leave the ship at this point in time and abandon Girtha to continue the cruise alone. Besides, I had too much unfinished business onboard. I broke out in a cold sweat and began to fidget; my anxiety escalated with each passing mile. Just when I began to feel chest pains kicking into gear, Florita proclaimed good news.

"Look—they are turning into the Hotel Miramar."

"What's that?"

"It's a resort for *turistas—muy caro.*"

Muy caro seemed an understatement. The Miramar was a sprawling palatial hotel, white with a red tile roof that was built into the side of a mountain. Even the parking area offered gorgeous panoramic views of the coastline and the Caribbean Sea in the distance. We passed by clay tennis courts that were busily in use and two swimming pools whose sparkling water shimmered in the overhead sun. Above the hotel, small whitewashed *casitas*, also with red tile roofs, were nestled in the side of the mountain, as well. Each of them appeared to connect with the hotel by narrow gravel paths.

Joey's taxi stopped under the porte-cochere in front of the lobby, and a crew of uniformed bellmen hustled to the trunk and removed the luggage while Joey paid the driver. Twenty feet back, Toussaint waited until the object of his prey approached the lobby door before exiting his taxi and entering the hotel. I couldn't imagine why Toussaint was being so cautious—he had just joined the ship's crew for the current cruise and was one of a hundred waiters. There was little chance that Joey might recognize him.

As they entered the hotel lobby, I instructed Florita to park under an adjacent tree while I inserted bullets into the cylinder of my Smith & Wesson.

Noticing my pistol, Florita asked suspiciously, "How long you want I wait?"

"Until the meter runs out or you see them wheeling my body out on a gurney, whichever comes first." I grabbed my purchase from the *carnicería* and exited the car.

After checking my disguise one final time in the glass door, I entered the hotel lobby and looked around. Joey had just received his key and some brochures from the front desk and was following his bellman out a side door. Toussaint tossed a newspaper he'd been using to shield his face and followed Joey at a brief distance. I gave Toussaint a lead and joined the rear of the caravan.

The bellman led Joey up a long path that ended at one of the remote *casitas*. The unit sat in the midst of a scenic palette of color that was shaded by a sprawling jacaranda tree whose branches were loaded with orange blossoms and peppered by bougainvillea bushes, their woody vines and bright red and purple blooms climbing over wall-mounted trellises. The bellman unlocked the door, held it open for Joey, and followed him in with the two suitcases. In a moment, he came out folding some currency, which he slipped into his pocket.

In evaluating the scene and watching Joey, I momentarily lost track of Toussaint. Fortunately, before I could panic, I saw him emerge from a room marked *"Empleados"* wearing a waiter's jacket emblazoned with the hotel's logo. Balanced atop his right palm, he carried a beverage tray holding some tropical concoction in a tall glass crowned with a straw, orange wedge, and tiny red umbrella.

As he progressed up the path to Joey's *casita*, I moved forward, too. Out of curiosity, I stopped in front of the *"Empleados"* room, pushed the door ajar, and peeked in. As I expected, an unconscious Latino in a wife-beater T-shirt was slumped in a corner on the floor with blood dripping from a gash on his head. I eased the door shut, glanced around nervously, and began the arduous trek up the path.

Managing an unpaved incline in a mountain-high atmosphere wasn't easy for someone my size—I had to stop every ten yards or so to rest my knees and catch my breath. One of these wheezing spasms was suddenly interrupted by a sharp noise that shattered the encompassing stillness.

The sound seemed to come from the *casita*, so I took a deep breath and quickened my pace. When I got to the room, I pressed my ear against the mahogany door to listen for sounds, but it was quiet inside. I drew my pistol and tried the handle of the door—it was unlocked, so I pushed it open a crack and peered inside. There was no sign of Joey, but a sliding glass door out the back was open and the thin curtains that framed it were still stirring from the sudden draft.

I stepped inside and found I wasn't alone. In the center of the floor, on his side and doubled up in pain lay Toussaint. A dark red spot was spreading rapidly across the white jacket.

"Toussaint," I said, removing my hat and wig and turning him onto his back, "did Joey shoot you?"

He moaned as blood seeped between his quivering fingers, which were pressed against the bullet hole. His eyes widened in surprise at seeing me, but then he gasped a couple of times and nodded affirmatively.

After I turned him over, I noticed a long-bladed knife on the floor beside him. "This looks like a case of self-defense. You followed Joey here to kill him, didn't you? Are you a Zunimbist?"

Toussaint's eyes widened again and flickered but he said nothing. I reached inside the *carnicería* sack and removed a dead chicken.

Toussaint's body jerked stiffly. He was either having pre-death pulmonary tremors or I'd gotten his attention.

"Toussaint, your time is running out. You have two choices and not much time to consider them. You can tell me what I want to know, and die a happy martyr to your faith. That way you can kiss snakes, dance with vestal virgins, or do whatever else it is that Zunimbists do in the hereafter. Or, if you remain silent, I'm going to *pase poul* this chicken all over my body to remove the impurities, cut out your tongue, sever this chicken's head, and stuff it in your mouth." I reached into my pocket and removed my hunting knife, then slowly slid the edge of its blade across the chicken's neck to illustrate my point. "What's your decision?"

Terrified by the eternal consequences of the threat, Toussaint's eyes were wide open and he nodded his head in cooperation.

"Did you kill Bruno Helmje and dump him overboard because he didn't deliver the cocaine to your Miami distributors?"

He nodded, confirming the first of my suspicions.

"And did you come here today to kill Joey Morton for the same reason?"

He nodded again.

"Did you kill Victor Dubonnet and Jacque Destang in Miami because of the disappearance of the drugs?"

Toussaint nodded a third time and gasped haltingly, "Yes, and to take Victor's place… as waiter… on ship… so I can avenge Zunimba."

"Do you know where the drugs are and who took them?"

This time, he shook his head from side to side.

"Who killed Buck Tolleson? Was he murdered by a Zunimbist? Did he have anything to do with the drug operation?"

Toussaint looked genuinely confused so I let that string of questions pass.

"Did you leave the card in my napkin to direct me to Madam Draconia?"

Toussaint nodded up and down.

"Were you trying to scare me off the case?"

The nodding continued, but with considerably more pain.

"Did you leave the chicken head in my water glass at the Sand Conch hotel in Miami for the same reason?"

He slowly moved his head from side to side.

"Then that must have been done by an employee of the hotel," I thought aloud. I wasn't expecting a reaction, but Toussaint nodded. "And that person must have found out about me from someone in Erickson's office…"

Toussaint nodded some more.

"How about Lars Amundson—who killed him?" The waiter hesitated, so I severed the chicken's head and dangled it back and forth over his face.

Encouraged to speak, he coughed instead and blood spurted from the corners of his mouth. His body shuddered and his arms fell limp at his sides.

Well, so much for the barnyard lie detector test. Though, I had to admit I was fairly impressed with the results.

I stood and wiped the blade of my knife on a towel, then stripped a sheet from the bed and covered the body. I was tempted to mumble a few words of eulogy, but what do you say over the corpse of a pathological serial killer?

I looked around the room and nothing caught my attention, so I started to leave. I noted that Joey hadn't bothered to leave a tip for the maid, to atone for the mess he'd left, so I tossed the worn chicken on the mattress: at least she could get a Sunday dinner out of it.

Retracing my journey was far easier going downhill. Nonetheless, I was huffing and puffing by the time I got to the taxi and Florita. She seemed genuinely pleased to see me and jumped from her seat to open the back door with a sigh of relief.

"I start to worry," Florita said. "That man we follow in the first cab… he run from the hotel with his suitcases five minutes ago, throw them in a taxi, and takes off. I have not seen the second man."

"The second man will be staying here until room service turns down the sheets tonight. Then he'll get a free ride in an ambulance and an autopsy courtesy of the Venezuelan medicos."

"I see spots of blood on the knees of your pants but I will ask no questions," Florita said, looking into a downward adjusted rearview mirror. "What should I tell police if they ask me questions about this trip? I do not want to get you in trouble, but I am very afraid of police."

I picked up on the hint and leaned forward, passing her a couple of twenties over the front seat. "Your silence is appreciated but you're in no danger from the police. As it turns out, I was only performing room service by dropping off a chicken."

Florita took the twenties and grinned.

"You have a nice smile, Florita." Then, visualizing her stretched T-shirt, I added, "And, I like the way Mickey twitches his ears."

CHAPTER 13

W HEN I GOT BACK TO THE *Oslo Aphrodite*, the red
message-waiting light was blinking on the phone. Since it
was only mid-afternoon and Girtha was still touring
Caracas, I dialed the Radio Room and was instructed by a message
to see Captain Nelson upon my return. The stoic helmsman was on
the bridge, puffing on his meerschaum and initialing some
documents that were being held by a perky blonde who was
wearing a Nordic Caribbean leisure suit with a whistle dangling
from her neck.

"You asked to see me, Captain?"

"Yes." He nodded and waited for the blonde to skip off before
turning to me. "I was talking to Erickson this morning and he told
me to expand your assignment. The Miami press linked the
murders of Tolleson and Helmje to the *Oslo Aphrodite*, so he's now
requesting that you find out who murdered them—he said he'll
double your payment."

I did my best to suppress my excitement but it wasn't easy. After
years of low-paying jobs as a gumshoe, I had backed into a
lucrative $6,000 payday.

"If I get killed after lunch, do I get paid for the whole day?"

Nelson looked puzzled, and I assured him it was a joke.

"There's more," Nelson added with a somber look. "Bruno
Helmje's been found."

"Where?"

"The duffel bag containing his body was spotted yesterday by the crew of a C-130 Hercules that was flying a low-altitude search-and-rescue mission. The bag was snagged on a coral reef off one of the small, uninhabited micro-islands off the Jamaican coast. The airplane crew called in a U.S. Coast Guard cutter, which retrieved it.

"Bruno's remains were still inside. His identity was confirmed by a preliminary autopsy performed by a Kingston medical examiner. It'll be some time before the coroner convenes an official inquest, but the ME did declare the death to be a homicide. That'll permit the FBI and Coast Guard Criminal Investigation Division to be called in. They may want to interview you since you reported finding the corpse."

"I'm surprised they ruled out accidental death or suicide so quickly. After all, Helmje could have met the same fate by choking on a chicken head while backing into an airplane propeller."

"But how would he have gotten into the duff... el b..." Nelson slowed his words as he caught himself mid-sentence and smiled sheepishly.

I cloned his grin. "I was being facetious. Sorry. Did the coast guard find anything else inside the duffel bag?"

"They didn't say. Apparently, the corpse wasn't in very good shape, but their guess was that he hadn't been dead for more than a couple of days. I wonder how they knew that?"

"Bodies dumped into water after death initially sink, but eventually float to the surface because of internal gases that build up as putrefaction occurs. The temperature of the water determines how long this process takes: in the warmer waters of the Caribbean and Gulf of Mexico, probably only a couple of days.

"The forensics folks also have some telltale signs they look for. For example, the hands and face start to swell after two or three days. The skin starts to separate from the body after five or six days. The fingernails detach after eight to ten days and so forth. If none of these physical deteriorations had occurred, then a recent time of death can be reasonably established."

I noted surprise on Nelson's face at this knowledge of forensic science, so I explained. "I only know this because I had a client who was found floating off the Santa Monica Pier a couple of years ago. Since she had no next-of-kin, I was called in to identify the body. The corpse was a former beauty contestant but after a week in the ocean, she'd started to resemble an exorcist candidate under the throes of demonic possession.

"I've got some news for you as well. Joey Morton left your employ this morning. He apologizes for not being able to give two weeks notice."

Nelson turned to me, clearly stunned. "That's not like Joey. He's been with the cruise line for several years. I had no idea that he was unhappy with his job."

"His departure was only indirectly employment-related. He's running for his life, trying to stay one jump ahead of Zunimba and his merry band of cutthroats—no pun intended."

Nelson took the pipe from his mouth and pushed his hat back from his forehead. "Why would the Zunimbists want to kill Joey?"

"Joey and Bruno Helmje were working for Zunimba. They were engaged in a large-scale cocaine smuggling operation, using your ship to transport drugs from Caribbean and South American suppliers to Miami distributors. Unfortunately for them, the last shipment got hijacked before it reached Florida. Zunimba evidently is not a merciful god… anyone who breaks one of his cocaine commandments will, along with a chicken companion, be carved up like a Halloween jack-o'-lantern."

Nelson was genuinely crushed. He looked as if a judge had just discovered a worm in his prized 4-H Club apple. He removed his cap and ran his fingers through his thinning hair. "How do I know this is true? What proof do you have?"

"A face-to-face admission from Joey before he took off and a deathbed confession from another source."

"What other source?"

"That's another piece of regrettable news I have to report. Your wait staff has also experienced a sudden vacancy—a fellow named Toussaint L'Enfant."

"How do you know that?"

"I pulled a sheet over his dead body a couple of hours ago in the room of a swanky resort in the mountains above La Guaira."

Nelson shook his head in disbelief. "Another death somehow connected to the *Oslo Aphrodite*. This is a real tragedy."

"Not really. Toussaint was a lousy waiter. Any replacement is bound to be better. I've had better service from a broken vending machine.

"Another thing: before he died, Toussaint confessed to the murder of Bruno Helmje so at least I have that one cleared up for Erickson."

"If Helmje was killed by Toussaint, that may complicate things somewhat," Nelson said.

"Complicate? In what way?"

"Your country has a law called the Death on the High Seas Act that's been around since 1920 or so. Whenever the death of a person has been caused by a wrongful act committed more than a marine league from the shoreline of any American state or territory, the victim's heirs can file a suit for compensation based on economic damages, but not pain and suffering, against the responsible party. Though Toussaint is the one who killed Helmje, I wonder if Bruno's widow can come after Nordic Caribbean using the 'deep pocket' strategy."

"You've got me. I have as much experience in admiralty law as I do counting calories. I don't see any apparent negligence on the ship's part, though. If there's any liability, it would appear to be that of the crewing agency that should have screened Toussaint before placing him in your service.

"In addition, I'd suspect that any potential judgment would be nullified or severely reduced by the fact that Helmje met his demise while engaged in an unlawful activity."

Nelson was wrestling with this new information, trying to see if a positive spin could be salvaged. He brightened and said, "At least the drug-smuggling operation has been stopped in its tracks. That's good news."

Nelson could tell from the look on my face that his optimism wasn't shared. "I wouldn't count on it, Captain. We've put a temporary crimp in it at best. But I imagine that in no time at all, Zunimba will have fresh recruits aboard and another pipeline in place." I thought for a moment before adding, "Drug dealing *has* given this case a different look, however, and I'd like to discuss that with your security officer and get him involved."

Nelson nodded. "I'll call Bo and ask him to meet you in your cabin, for privacy's sake. Remember: I don't want a word of this drug-trafficking news spoken to anyone other than Bo—passengers or crew. We've got to keep a tight lid on this. I must confess that I'm relieved Toussaint was killed on shore; at least that clears the ship of any jurisdictional liability."

"Plus you don't have to bury him at sea which would, at the very least, be a distraction to the fun-loving passengers." This slipped out before I realized my sarcasm could have been more muted.

I returned to my cabin and, ten minutes later, opened the door in response to a solid knock. A muscular, tanned fellow who looked to be in his early- to mid-thirties ambled into the cabin as I held the door open.

No stranger to a gym, he had the physique of an inverted pyramid. He initiated a firm handshake, which left my fingers with a numbing sensation, and I couldn't help but follow a formidable forearm to a bulging bicep and powerful pectorals, all exerting considerable stress to a white short-sleeved shirt. This upper body tapered rapidly to a small waist and slim hips, which were covered in black pants. His large brown eyes were darker than his close-cropped, sun-bleached hair.

"Mr. McFadden," he greeted while folding his arms and leaning against the wall. "I wondered when we'd get around to a powwow."

His slow Southern drawl was as mellow as aged bourbon.

"I'd intended to consult you earlier, Hatfield, but unforeseen events moved the case along at an accelerated pace. If you don't mind, tell me a little about the security officer position—what are the qualifications and what it is that you do?"

"I joined the U.S. Army at age eighteen and served for eight years. I spent most of my time as a drill sergeant at Fort Polk and then Fort Benning before volunteering for a couple of tours of duty with the Americal Infantry Division in Vietnam. I was a cop in Columbus, Georgia, for a year after I got out.

"The cruise lines don't require much in the way of qualifications," he continued. "But they like their candidates to have military or police backgrounds, speak English, have security and firearms experience, and have received maritime certification."

"I understand you have a security assistant?"

Hatfield smiled. "Yeah, I got this dink by the name of Phat Nguyen. He weighs about one-twenty soaking wet and couldn't knock a sick baby off a bedpan."

He certainly offered an interesting evaluation. "It sounds like he might have gotten his law enforcement experience in Mayberry with Sheriff Andy."

"I'd be afraid to give him even one bullet, though. When it comes to security, he's as helpless as a monkey trying to fuck a wet football."

I tried not to smile outwardly, but I was amused by his ability to express himself in such clear visual images. "What kind of situations *do* you get involved in?"

"Most of the stuff is minor and we smooth everything over with some public relations work. Primarily, we get a lot of cabin burglaries—the locks are outdated and they aren't re-keyed frequently like hotel rooms. The doors are also open a lot while cleaning crews or cabin stewards service the rooms. That all leads up to beaucoup reports of thefts and loss of luggage or personal belongings.

"People also tend to tilt the jug too much on cruises which can lead to assaults and rapes. We have video cameras installed in the larger public areas, and we try to watch the nightclubs, casinos, Jacuzzis, and swimming pools—they tend to be the areas where predators hang out. Date-rape drugs are a growing problem, too, although I don't see why anyone would need them."

"Why do you say that?"

"Cruise ships are a horny man's paradise. A lot of women come on cruises and let it *all* hang out. They like the idea of getting humped without everybody in their hometown finding out about it. Gettin' laid on the *Oslo Aphrodite* is easier than shootin' quail over a baited field. Good thing I'm divorced." he confided. He lowered his voice before continuing. "There's this one little broad from Korea who's been chasing me around the whole cruise—I finally nailed her last night. I got this thing for Oriental women," he explained. "We had a saying in the army—'they can do more tricks on a six-inch pecker than a monkey can do on a hundred-foot vine.'"

Anyone speaking with Bo didn't need much imagination, that's for sure. "How about murders?"

"Once in a while you hear about a murder being committed, especially by crew members on crew members. Most of these people are transient and seasonal workers who receive squat in the way of background checks or employment screening. They're from different nationalities, they're clustered together in close quarters, and they work long hours for low pay. These melting pots can sometimes flare up in a hurry."

"How would you handle a passenger murder?"

"It all depends. Shipboard crimes fall into a 'no man's land' when it comes to enforcement. In fact, reporting a crime on board a cruise ship doesn't mean that anything will ever be done or that the crime will even be investigated.

"People think, because they board a ship in a U.S. port, that they're protected by our justice system. But most ships are actually registered in foreign countries and spend most of their time traveling in territorial or open waters where our laws don't apply.

"Let me give you an example because it can get complicated. Say, a crime occurs between two passengers of different nationalities; they boarded the ship in a third country; the ship is registered in a fourth country; and the crime took place in the territorial waters of a fifth country.

"The governing law is the International Maritime Law, but it's not as well developed as U.S. law. The FBI is the only U.S. law enforcement agency that *can* investigate a major crime in such a situation, but it can only do so *if* the crime occurs in international waters. Otherwise, crimes are reported to the jurisdiction of the closest foreign country and to the embassies of the parties involved. Prosecution of crimes is left to the local port authorities—and that shouldn't give you a huge sense of relief."

"Then I gather you are not investigating the murders of Buck Tolleson or Bruno Helmje."

"You got that right. I got no dog in those fights. Tolleson was killed in a foreign country and Helmje was found floating in the waters of a foreign country."

"What do you know about drug smuggling aboard this ship? I don't know if Captain Nelson told you, but the *Oslo Aphrodite* was being used to transport drugs from Caribbean ports of call to Miami. It seems that Bruno Helmje, Joey Morton, and a waiter named Victor Dubonnet were involved."

"So I heard, but stopping the flow of illegal drugs is a thankless task," Bo said with obvious frustration. "It used to be that the bulk of narcotics entered the states in the containerized cargo of commercial ships. But customs and the immigration guys started cracking down with content searches and canine teams.

"FBI statistics say that sixty-five percent of the heroin in the U.S. now comes from Colombia and that much of it enters through south Florida. It was only a matter of time before drugs found their way aboard cruise ships—and I'm not just talking about personal use by passengers and crew members.

"Drug security on cruise ships is pretty lax, you know? We've found cocaine, heroin, and weed smuggled on board in the strangest places: within artificial limbs, false compartments in luggage, the lining of hats, tubes of art prints purchased at auction, hollow sculptures bought from local artists on shore… you name it."

"What can you tell me about the Zunimbists? How far into the cruise line has their organization penetrated?"

Hatfield looked cautiously around, even though he and I were the only two bodies in the cabin. "Zunimba's gang is outta my league," he spoke quietly. "Those guys are mean enough to do the knuckle-shuffle with barbed wire, so I leave them to the federal boys. Only the feds have the organization and firepower to take them on. I wasn't raised on jerk juice; I'm not anxious to have my headless body found draped over an ice sculpture at the midnight buffet.

"I can tell you one thing I've heard—I'm told that Zunimba doesn't kill for thrills: he seeks revenge only on those who've been an obstacle or direct threat to his operation. That's fine with me. Live and let live.

"As far as the organization's presence on this ship, I'm sure it's here, but it's hard to pinpoint since the group's members are so damned secretive. If you ask me," Hatfield added, leaning close to me, "I think Zunimba's smuggling his people into the U.S. on cruise ships to expand his drug and weapons businesses on our continent. If cruise lines keep attrition records, they keep the results secret; but I see too many home boys who work only one cruise and then disappear in Miami. They blend in real easy there and can hide out in halfway houses until they get settled or relocated. That's my theory anyway."

"Have you shared your theory with the Captain?"

Hatfield smiled. "When it comes to drugs, the Captain is—as we used to say in the army—eat up with the dumb-ass. He can be a little naïve: I don't think he believes a cherry's ever been popped in the honeymoon suite. But, it's not just him; it's the entire industry. They don't raise questions that they don't want to have answered their own way."

"What can you tell me about Lars Amundson?"

"He was a good officer and a pretty regular guy, traveling around the Caribbean and Mediterranean, living it up—waiting for his old man to take a dirt nap. He didn't mess around on the ship because of his position and the fortune he was heir to, but once he got on shore, he did the dirty boogie with the best of 'em—if the time and place were right."

"What can you tell me about his little scrape in the Dominican Republic?"

Hatfield grinned. "The way I heard it, Lars met this hot little number at a cruise line function at the embassy. They had a few drinks and ducked into an empty room to compare anatomies. One thing led to another and they were caught doing the belly shuffle by a family member. In his defense, I'm told that the girl looked a lot older than she was; but she turned out to be only sixteen."

"What was her family's reaction?"

"According to Lars, they wanted him to accept responsibility and pay compensation for the damage done to her reputation. However, Little Bo Peephole was later discovered to be pregnant and the family *really* turned up the heat. It seems you can't get much in the way of a dowry from a local groom if the bride is considered to be damaged goods."

"That's understandable—new cars sell for more than used ones. Did Lars financially appease them in some way?"

"Not that I'm aware of. He admitted to the affair, but denied that the baby was his. He felt he'd been set up by her family to weasel some serious green out of him once he got his inheritance. He felt that maybe they were using their daughter's cherry as leverage to get their hands on some of his old man's estate once it got settled."

"So Lars refused to be entrapped or blackmailed by a proud, upper crust Hispanic clan," I concluded. "Since they would have no desire to have their blackmail scam *or* their daughter's sullied honor publicized, they were left with few options..." I sat this scenario and its possible ramifications aside and changed the conversation to explore the existence of a connection between Amundson and the Zunimbists. "Lars appeared to have been killed Zunimbist-style. *Could* he have been part of the drug smuggling operation?"

"No way. Lars could step off the deep end once in a while, and even blow a little ganja, but a large-scale drug operation had nothing to offer him. The only thing I can think of is maybe Lars was killed because he found out about the operation and had to be zipped."

"How about Bruno Helmje and Joey Morton? Were you surprised by their involvement?"

"I never would have thought Bruno and Joey to be nose-candy mules. But, in looking back, it helps to explain some of their behavior."

"What kind of behavior?"

"Bruno was one close-mouthed dude. His grip on the Radio Room was tighter than the chastity belt on King Arthur's old lady. A couple of months ago, Boyd Fowler told me confidentially—after a few drinks one night—about Bruno's secretly coded radiograms. I suspected that something was afoot, but all I could do was keep an eye on him. In retrospect, it seems he was a key traffic cop for moving contraband in the Southern Hemisphere. I would never have suspected that.

"I became suspicious about Joey when a passenger found an account book from a Swiss Bank in the men's room. After he turned it in to security, we discovered it was Joey's. He had deposited more than fifty thousand dollars in the past year. I kidded him about the balance when I returned the book, and he said it was his stockpiled salary; he was getting free room and board on ship plus collecting the royalties from comedy albums and joke books that were offered from time to time in the AARP magazine."

"Moving in another direction, do you check out passengers after the boarding list for a cruise is compiled? I'm specifically thinking of Arturo and Castrada Del Muerto."

"I saw them at your table when I was checking you out the other night. That woman is ugly enough to turn a freight train up a dirt road. To answer your question, ship security doesn't do passenger screening. It would take too long and, really, what would it accomplish?"

"Thanks, Hatfield. If you hear or discover anything else related to the topics we've discussed, give a holler."

Hatfield smiled at my colloquialism. "You got it, old son."

He had barely stepped out into the alleyway when he was knocked back into the cabin by a wobbly mound of packages staggering in the door. Hatfield flashed his pearly whites at the struggling Girtha, stepped around her, and was gone.

In a move that was becoming all too common, Girtha dumped her cargo on my bed and collapsed on hers. "I didn't think... I'd make it," she wheezed, fanning her face with a magazine. "The prices—I couldn't pass them up! Look at these little pipes, for example," she said, reaching into a bag. "They're genuine Mayan artifacts—made out of ceramic. And each one has a picture of a gorgeous quetzal bird. I got one for each of my nieces and nephews in L.A."

I had to chuckle as she unwrapped one for me to see. "If you give those out, you better plan on skipping the next family reunion."

"Why?" She looked at me, dumbfounded, taken aback.

"To avoid the wrath of your siblings, Girtha," I laughed. "Those aren't ancient artifacts. They're head pipes; they're used to smoke dope."

Girtha's chin dropped and she slammed the table with her fist. "That lying little bastard! He told me these were ancient pre-Columbian peace pipes." She paused to reassess her situation and wondered, hopefully... "Maybe *my* nieces and nephews won't know the difference."

"Don't kid yourself. Cannabis cultivation and consumption is a required course in the junior high schools of East L.A." The look on her face told me I had to offer a solution, which I just happened to have. "Why not sell them to your low-brow customers at Cosmo's? They'll be a big improvement over the homemade water bottle and rubber tube contraptions they use now.

"And think of the boost you gave the local GNP."

"The Gross National Product?" Girtha asked.

"No—Girtha's Nutty Purchases—" I managed to duck a sandal that bounced off the wall above my head.

After a few more laughs, I told my soul mate about the morning's events in La Guaira. Girtha was shaken and looked at me with her big Bambi eyes.

"Chauncey, let's go back to L.A. This is getting way too dangerous. You could have been killed."

"Not likely. Toussaint was only after Joey, but his intended victim got the drop on him first. I wouldn't be surprised if Joey didn't pick up on his tail as he left the ship, then used the taxi ride to lure Toussaint into a controlled environment where he could be terminated."

"Where is Joey now?"

"In a witness protection program of his own design. I hope it's a good one because it won't be long before Toussaint's replacements are scurrying over the countryside like fire ants."

"You want to order room service?" Girtha asked with a yawn. "I'm too tired to change for dinner."

"Be my guest, but I'll have to take a rain check. I've got a few questions I need to ask a couple of our fellow diners this evening."

"Okay," Girtha yawned again. "Say, what's on tap for tomorrow? Do you want to go to the spa with me? I was thinking about taking a mud bath followed by a relaxing sauna."

"I stopped by the spa and asked about a massage but they said that because of the amount of my flesh, their masseur would call me with an estimate." I picked up the *Sea Compass* and checked the next day's scheduled events. "Tomorrow is a day at sea, but it's followed by three successive days in ports: Bridgetown in Barbados, Fort-de-France on Martinique, and St. Thomas in the U.S. Virgin Islands."

"Great. I can relax by the pool all day tomorrow. My sunburn is almost gone."

She picked up the phone to dial for her dinner and I headed out to our table. I arrived and joined in the salutations that were already in progress. Darling was, as usual, engaged in flashing his pearly whites and scribbling autographs for a line of his faithful fans. Fifi, his anorexic waif with the high-beam headlights, was wearing a hot little backless and strapless number whose cups could only have been held up by reverse gravity. Del Muerto was eyeing Fifi and panting palpably as evidenced by a napkin which jumped up and down in his lap. Castrada, his behavioral antithesis, sat stoically with her hands folded in her lap, resisting reaction to anything around her. Colonel Talbo finished twisting a finer point on the tip of his handlebar moustache before straightening his pocket handkerchief.

After responding to everyone who inquired about Girtha's absence, I began my line of questioning. "Señor Del Muerto, did you go ashore today?"

"Ashore? Yes… yes… we went into port. The country reminds me in many ways of my own land. I heard that the murder rate is lower in Venezuela than in Colombia. We are thinking of moving there."

"Don't be *too* hasty," I advised. "Your move to Venezuela would just jack up the murder rate in that country and you'd be back where you started."

Del Muerto laughed and slapped Castrada on her back. "This McFadden… he is a funny man. I want to take him home with us. I wonder if I could fit him inside a suitcase." He turned to his wife and repeated his little witticism in Spanish.

Castrada Del Muerto continued to look straight ahead and replied without emotion.

Arturo guffawed and slapped the table.

Looking at me, he explained. "Castrada said you could fit if I cut you into many small pieces."

I felt my rectal sphincter contract. This broad could be scary. I was thankful Girtha had skipped the meal.

Mercifully, Colonel Talbo asked. "Where's our waiter? If that boy worked for me, he'd be running down a dusty dirt road with my bullwhip snappin' at his heels."

"I'm afraid we've lost Toussaint's services for the remainder of the cruise," I said. "I heard that he went ashore and had an accident."

"Was it serious?" Fifi asked.

"As serious as it gets. The local medical examiner is probably tagging his toe as we speak."

Del Muerto raised his hands up, palms outward, and slid back from the table. "Do not look at me. I can account for all my time today."

"I'm inclined to believe you, Arturo. I wouldn't dream of resorting to... 'defecation' of character," I said, referring to his earlier malapropism. "Tomorrow, we're at sea but the next day we dock at Bridgetown, Barbados. What are your plans for *that* port?" I asked, my curiosity aroused by the entry I recalled from his appointment book.

"Bridgetown... Bridgetown..." Del Muerto said, rubbing his chin. "Ah, he exclaimed, looking up and smiling. "I have some business to transact there. After that, this cruise is all play and no work."

"Please excuse delay," a small brown man with black hair and dark eyes said as he circled our table, distributing an armload of menus. "I am Taboul and I am your new server. I will handle your table for the remainder of the cruise."

"We were just commenting on Toussaint's absence," Darling remarked. "We heard he met an untimely death."

"So sorry, but I know nothing of the details. I will return to take your orders." Taboul backed away in genuflection and rushed to another table.

"What a coincidence," Fifi said. "On the way to dinner, we saw a 'cancelled' sign slapped on Joey Morton's poster by the Carousel Lounge. It seems he's not available tonight, either."

"That's too bad," I mused, tongue-in-cheek. "If Toussaint had been able to catch the show, I'm sure Joey would have knocked him dead." After enjoying my cleverness for a moment, I turned to the svelte actor. "Mr. Darling, we used to see your movies all the time and then it seemed you dropped off the face of the Earth."

Darling smiled, but it was a smile born from sad resignation rather than joy. "The film studio to which I was under contract for thirty years was taken over by a media conglomerate. Unfortunately, the arrogant new boss was an upstart who felt I was getting a little long in the tooth for major roles and no longer capable of filling enough theater seats so he gave me the old pink slip.

"On top of that, I lost almost all of my wealth when the investment company managing my assets went under. It seems the strategy the company used was little more than a Ponzi scheme involved in siphoning off investors' money. When they became unable to attract enough new capital to meet redemptions and dividend payouts to stockholders, the SEC shut them down. I don't mind telling you it's been a rough time.

"I've managed to get by on residuals, cameo roles and bit parts and guest appearances on television that have been thrown my way."

"Are you ever planning on making a comeback?" I asked.

"Fortunately, things *may* be picking up. Public interest in my career is starting to return, courtesy of the current nostalgia wave. I was just a step away from the theaters of Branson, Missouri, and being relegated to serving as emcee for afternoon matinees.

"I don't know if I could have spent the rest of my professional life waving the flag, kissing up to veterans and retirees, and reminiscing about 'the good old days,' a time when hard work and family values were the rule rather than the exception."

I pondered Darling's viewpoint a moment before offering an opposing one. "Using scripted appeals to generational values for the purpose of stimulating positive audience reaction *has* been a legitimate career-extender for a number of artists over the years. As an art form, it's admittedly closer to square dancing than ballet; but its wholesome folksiness is, to many, a welcomed departure from the trite and prurient which has cascaded over contemporary audio and video airwaves."

The rest of our dinner passed uneventfully without the bungling Toussaint, and I rejoined Girtha in time to feed some metallic monsters in the casino and laugh at the passenger talent show. A few hours later, we were finding our way to… you guessed it—the midnight buffet.

CHAPTER 14

"DO YOU HAVE ANY ROOM IN YOUR SUITCASES, sweetie-kins?" Girtha asked the next morning. "I can't get all my souvenirs inside my bags anymore."

"I hope you kept all your receipts. Customs will be checking the cost of your purchases when we dock in Miami. You'll have to pay duty on everything over the exemption limit."

"What's the limit?"

I answered after scanning the cruise brochure. "We can each bring in three hundred dollars worth of merchandise duty-free, six hundred dollars if purchased in the U.S. Virgin Islands. We can also bring in one carton of cigarettes each—five cartons if four of them are purchased in St. Thomas; and one quart of liquor each—one gallon if purchased in St. Thomas." Reading further, I said, "Here's some good news, Girtha. You may not have to pay duty on your ancient artifacts, or even open them up for inspection—they would appear to fall under the 'island-made goods' exemption."

"That *is* good news," Girtha said after breathing a sigh of relief at the customs disclosure. "Making license plates for some banana republic would probably ruin my manicure, not to mention this little bit of a tan I've got started.

"I think I'm gonna spend all day by the pool again. I'll have breakfast and lunch there. Care to join me?"

"I'll catch you this afternoon. I have some leads I want to pursue first." I immediately noted the scowl on her face and quickly added, "But, I'll be careful."

My first stop was the Radio Room, to see Boyd Fowler. "Mr. McFadden," Boyd greeted as I entered the room. "I was just about to call you."

"Really? What about?"

"Two things. First, you have a package from the Miami police which they overnighted to the ship in La Guaira." Boyd handed me a thick legal-sized envelope which I tucked under my arm.

"Second, after we got word that Bruno's body had been found, Leif Jurgens, the new COS, told me to clean out Bruno's office. The drawers in his desk were locked so we had to pry them open. I found a big stack of radiograms in one of them and Mr. Jurgens instructed me to give them to you. They're in that code I was telling you about that's impossible to understand."

I thumbed through the stack which must have numbered fifty or sixty. Fowler wasn't kidding. The radiograms contained strings of numbers, letters, and special characters that defied cognition.

"These are going to require some analysis and decoding. If you have a large envelope, Fowler, send these to Lieutenant Alameda in Miami and ask that they be forwarded to the FBI's cryptography lab. If the meaning of these messages can be unlocked, we may be able to put a sizable dent in Zunimba's drug operation." I scribbled a note detailing my desire for the messages to be deciphered and addressed the envelope the radio operator handed me.

"Has a passenger named Arturo Del Muerto made any ship-to-shore phone calls or sent any radiograms? Look for activity after we disembarked from Jamaica; say late Monday to early Wednesday."

Fowler scanned his outgoing communication logs, which were intended to be used for billing support purposes. "Nope, nothing here for Del Muerto."

I thought that to be unusual. Surely, Del Muerto would have notified his employer in some innocuous fashion that the mission had been accomplished.

"Thanks, Boyd." I left the Radio Room and returned to my cabin to examine the contents of the envelope from Miami PD. I ripped the end flap open and dumped the contents on the table.

The first items that seized my attention were the eight-and-a-half-by-eleven stills that spilled out—photos I'd requested of Zunimbist victims murdered in the Miami area. I examined each of the dozen torsos closely, carefully studying and comparing the markings on the chests of the victims. After a while, my eyes were starting to blur, and I removed my glasses to wipe the thick lenses. With a clean field of view and some rest, I placed the photo of Lars Amundson on the table and slowly compared it, one at a time, to each of the other photos using a side-by-side visual analysis.

Suddenly, I stopped—I had spotted it—a telltale difference.

The design on Amundson's chest was not the same as the markings on the other eleven cadavers: the markings inside the carved circle on his chest looked more like tentatively dabbed thumbprints than confident, distinct symbols drawn in blood. Now that I saw the difference, I couldn't believe it had taken me so long to notice.

But, now I had to wonder... Was there a reason the style was different on his chest? Was it possible that Lars was not killed by a Zunimbist? Was a copycat killer responsible? If so, I'd be back to square one as far as perpetrator and motive were concerned.

I tucked the pictures back in the envelope and hid them in the bottom of my suitcase—they were not the sort of divertissement I would want Girtha stumbling across. Then I moved to the bed to consider the other items Lieutenant Alameda had sent.

First, I reviewed the data on the Del Muertos. As I knew, Arturo had a long history of arrests for suspected homicides; but, as I also knew, he had never been convicted on any of the charges. Castrada's juvenile record was equally lengthy and lurid; but it was relatively free of skirmishes with the law once she reached adulthood. Next, I scanned the copies of their birth certificates—and I made a major discovery. Excited, I slid the documentation into the desk drawer. One thing was now quite clear.

I left the cabin and went to see Bill Graham, the chief purser. His staff had control over the ship's safe into which passengers were strongly encouraged to store their valuables. I found only one man in the purser's office.

"I'm looking for Bill Graham."

"You've found him," Graham answered with a smile.

"I'm Chauncey McFadden." I flashed my Nordic Caribbean ID. "I believe Captain Nelson has told you about me."

"Yes, indeed, Mr. McFadden. How may I be of service?"

"I'd like to see the list of passengers who've deposited and withdrawn items from the ship's safe and, if possible, what those items were."

"That's easy enough to produce," Graham said. He pulled a key from his pocket, unlocked a drawer, and removed a ledger, which he placed on the counter. "Information on items deposited with us for safekeeping is recorded in five columns: the date, the passenger's printed name, the passenger's signature, the passenger's cabin number, and the item deposited or removed."

The ledger was full, but I didn't have to scan very long before a familiar name appeared for Saturday, May 15—the first day of the cruise. Mr. Lamont Darling had deposited two envelopes, each one purportedly containing $20,000 in U.S. currency. Scanning further, on Monday, May 17, he had removed one of them. I completed my review of the ledger without detecting any other activity for Darling or anyone else I knew.

"Thanks, Mr. Graham. Now, may I ask that you call me, immediately, when Mr. Darling removes his other envelope from the safe? I'm in cabin 700."

"Will do," the purser replied.

I could do nothing but wait, so I returned to our cabin, changed into shorts and sandals, and wandered out to the pool area. On the way, I inched through the buffet line, stacking a large paper plate with hamburgers, hot dogs, and barbeque sandwiches before joining Girtha. I found her slathered with oil, reclining under an umbrella and holding a book with a lurid dust cover.

"Are you free for the day now?" Girtha asked, peeping over her sunglasses.

"I'm afraid I'm just taking a break." The words were nearly inaudible as they squeaked from a narrow fissure between my two packed cheeks. "What're you reading?" I squeaked some more.

"One of those chick-lit best sellers. Boy, have these books changed."

"How so?" I mumbled, pushing the caboose of a hot dog into my mouth.

"Years ago, they just talked about 'smooth alabaster thighs' and 'heaving bosoms' and 'male firmness pressing against writhing flesh'."

"And, now? What do they talk about now?" I asked, wiping my mouth with a paper napkin.

"Since you asked, listen to this," Girtha instructed.

"The muscular pirate wrenched Lady Clarisse's gown off and threw it at her feet. He then ripped the petticoats, camisole, and underdrawers from her tremulous body and slung them across the room. She modestly tried to cover her nakedness with her hands, but he slapped her across her taut nipples and threw her down upon his bed. Although terrified, she didn't resist as he jerked her timid thighs apart. He scrunched his apple-hard buttocks and thrust his raging manhood deep into her rapacious love-canal, stretching its walls to accommodate his length and width. Only intense pleasure from her now sopping passion hole could compensate for the pain of being impaled by this handsome corsair."

"Have you ever heard anything like that before?" Girtha asked.

"Can't say that I have, but it sounds like the pirate fell into a vat of Madam Draconia's erection elixir and had to swallow his way to escape."

Fortunately, I was able to duck Girtha's book as it whizzed by my head.

"Chauncey McFadden, have you no sense of romance?"

We spent the next couple of hours soaking up rays and enjoying the calypso band. Just as the band ended one set and I prepared to order another drink, we were interrupted by the arrival of Boyd Fowler.

"Mr. McFadden, you got a phone call from Miami police a few minutes ago, and, since you weren't in your cabin, I jotted down a message."

I thanked the departing radioman and unfolded the sheet of paper he had given me. Miami police had run Simon Cartier's name through the federal databases and awarded him a spotless criminal record. He was a Caucasian male, aged sixty. Born in New York, he had lived in a number of places around the world—London, Paris, Hong Kong, and Tokyo. My interest, however, was piqued by his ten-year residency in Beverly Hills, and his concurrent position as CEO of Global Media Enterprises, Inc., in Hollywood. Global Media had purchased Galaxy Films in 1960 and sold it to Imagination Pictures in 1970. Cartier had taken his buyout and moved to Bridgetown, Barbados, where he had opened a chain of clothing stores. His telephone number and office address were provided.

I looked over at Girtha as I thought about this information and how it might fit into the bigger picture. At least some of the puzzle pieces were starting to come together.

"What's the message? Who's it from?" Girtha asked.

"Some information on someone I asked the Miami police department to check out. It does necessitate a change of plans, I'm afraid. You're going to be on your own again, tomorrow. I have some urgent business to take care of in Bridgetown."

Girtha struggled to position herself upright in her chaise lounge and said softly but firmly. "No way, Chauncey. You're not going to risk your life again like you did in Venezuela. I'm starting to really stress out. I'll admit that I was proud of you for solving those murders in L.A. I know how much you wanted to lift your detective practice up a notch and do work that required greater skill and provided more satisfaction.

"But, you were almost killed solving that case. I only came along on this trip because I thought you were just going to be the ship's babysitter for two weeks. Plus, how dangerous could a cruise be? Boy, was I wrong! This has gotten totally out of hand. The bodies are piling up like my grocery cart in a bakery."

Girtha's remarks were not to be taken lightly. More than once, I had thought about dropping the case, too. It did seem to be growing more ominous as the cruise progressed. When faced with mortal danger and no safe exit, how would I react?

I wondered, in retrospect, if I had not trudged slowly up the path to Joey's *casita* because I wanted an obviously deadly encounter to play itself out before my arrival. Mop-up duty was one thing; ducking knives and bullets was another. Not only did I wrestle with these self-doubts concerning personal courage but I had Girtha's well-being to consider as well. This case had assumed more lethal overtones and expanded beyond its original boundary, and I knew I had no right to place her in jeopardy.

The wild card was the Zunimbists. I had tried to avoid direct confrontation with them, opting to solve the murders by providing information to invoke the action of surrogates. At what point would Zunimba consider me a threat and order my dismemberment by the Caribbean Chicken-Chasers Club? I suspected that the only reason I was still alive was because my death would bring a string of replacements and an expanded investigation.

"How about a compromise?" I propositioned. "If I take Bo Hatfield, the ship's security officer, with me tomorrow would you feel more at ease?"

Girtha's reaction was quicker and more light-hearted than I expected. "If you lock me in his bedroom, I'll even let you go ashore by yourself! I've seen that guy and he's a hunk. Why, if you painted him green, he'd look like the Incredible Hulk." Then, after giving it some serious thought, she did acquiesce. "I guess it would be better—okay."

"Sounds like we've got a deal. I'll call him when we get back to the cabin."

"Hey, I forgot to ask. How was the new waiter last night?"

"He seems to be the real deal. He was really hopping since he had to take on our table in addition to his normal workload. No serious mishaps so far."

Having received enough sun, we returned to our cabin. While Girtha showered, I walked to the security office and caught Bo Hatfield as he was departing. "Bo," I hailed. "I need your help in Bridgetown tomorrow."

"Tomorrow? No can do, old son. I'm meeting a vacationing geisha girl in town. She's tired of washing all those Jap businessmen and their little penises. I'm gonna show her my Georgia white snake and bang her like a cap pistol."

"This is important, Bo. You and I are going to prevent a murder and catch a killer in the process."

"Hmmm," Bo pondered. "You mean do some legitimate police work?"

"You got it. Think of it: it'll be like old times again. Besides, you can still pencil Lotus Blossom in for later in the evening."

"Do I have to turn the killer over to the local cops right away, or can I beat him like a rented mule first? The courts down here don't make much of a distinction between a voluntary confession and one obtained after some administered pain."

"Alive is better. Besides, we may not be dealing with a 'he.' I'll tell you more tomorrow morning. Meet me at the gangplank at 8:30 so we can be the first ones off the ship. Remember to wear street clothes; you'll want to look like any other tourist."

"You got it, old son."

CHAPTER 15

THE NEXT MORNING WAS SATURDAY, OUR EIGHTH DAY of the cruise. I was stirred to consciousness, not by our normally requested wake-up call, but by the blast of the ship's horn and the feel of the engines downshifting to allow the side thrusters in the bow and stern to initiate lateral movement and improve maneuverability so the ship could edge nearer to the dock. I woke Girtha and bid her adieu, donned the disguise I had worn in La Guaira, grabbed some breakfast at the buffet, and headed to the gangway forward. Bo showed up five minutes later wearing a short-sleeved Hawaiian shirt, Bermuda shorts, and sunglasses.

"I almost didn't recognize you in that Panama hat, curly blond wig, and walrus mustache," he said. "You dress like that in an army stockade and your hemorrhoids are gonna take quite a beating."

"The people we're going to tail today know me by sight, so my disguise is a necessary precaution," I explained. "We want to be the first people off the ship. Then, we'll duck out of sight and wait for our unsuspecting leaders to guide us into town. Any idea how much longer we'll have to wait?"

"The ship's gotta be cleared by the Barbadian authorities. It shouldn't take longer than fifteen to twenty minutes."

"Good. We'll be watching for a passenger named Arturo Del Muerto and his wife, Castrada. I suspect they'll be getting off the ship as soon as they can."

"Which one do you want me to follow?" Bo asked, clenching and unclenching his fists.

"We're both going to follow Castrada."

"Why her and not him?"

"I believe she's going to meet someone today: a businessman named Simon Cartier."

"Why do you need my help?"

"A couple of reasons. "First, there's less chance of losing both of us if she spots the tail."

"What's the second reason?"

"It could be a fatal mistake to underestimate her. I have reason to believe that she's a world-class assassin and highly skilled with a knife. In fact, it's reported she can make more cuts on a six-inch pecker than a monkey can perform on a hundred-foot vine," I said, borrowing one of his gaudier military metaphors.

"You got *my* attention," Bo said. "I got no desire to sing high notes in the Vienna Boys' Choir."

In five minutes, the cord across the gangway entrance was removed and Bo and I led a handful of early passengers down to the quay. Even before we reached solid ground, we became the targets of pouncing vendors hawking their wares and tour guides offering their services. We finally succeeded in convincing them of our disinterest and shooed them away.

"How far is Bridgetown from here?" I asked Bo.

"We pulled into berth number two at the Port of Bridgetown. The center of the city is about a mile away—twenty minutes if you hoof it."

"I don't know if the Del Muertos will walk into town or take the taxi or a shuttle service, so let's get out of sight, behind those busses, and watch for them."

To pass the time, I engaged Bo in some idle conversation. "What can you tell me about Barbados?" I asked. "I read that it's a smaller, warmer version of England."

"She's been an independent member of the British Commonwealth for the past fifteen years or so. They have a statue of Lord Nelson in the middle of Trafalgar Square, just like in London, only Barbados put theirs up first. Most of the churches, landmarks, and government buildings are modeled after English architecture. Even most streets and public places have English names. The people here speak English, too, and drive on the left side of the road."

I nodded. "I also remember reading that Barbados has one of the highest literacy rates and standards of living in this part of the world and…"

I was cut short by the noise level from the dock which picked up and I turned to see a large group of passengers stampeding down the gangway. Many held maps and sauntered off on foot towards the shopping district to browse and do some sightseeing on their own. Most of them, however, boarded waiting busses for cruise-sanctioned tours of the island.

Several minutes passed and Bo began to squirm. "Are you sure they're coming down this morning? They're slower than pond water backin' upstream."

I was beginning to have reservations myself when I saw a tall couple emerge from the ship and slink down the gangway. First was Arturo, dressed in a beige suit and sporting a matching pinch front fedora. Next was Castrada, conservatively dressed in dark slacks and blouse and holding a carry-on bag. They waded through the hoi polloi and headed into town on foot, which suited me just fine. Bo and I waited for a proper distance to form, and then hopped into the crowd to begin our trek.

The twosome headed east along the Princess Alice Highway; the Fontabelle District stretching to their left and the harbor to their right. At Wharf Street, they took a right toward the Careenage or Constitution River. When they got to the river, they walked along its bank.

The water of the estuary was only deep enough to allow fishing boats, small yachts, and other pleasure craft to enter. On the water, officers of the harbor police were attired in eighteenth-century naval garb: middy blouses and bell-bottomed trousers. One of these patrols was rowing a longboat under the two bridges that connect the halves of the city. To the left of us, I heard the clip-clopping of a horse and turned to see a spike-helmeted member of the mounted regiment on the road hugging the waterfront. Crossing in front of him, a dozen small black children decked out in white cricket uniforms sprinted down the sidewalk.

The Del Muertos stopped walking and talked for a moment before continuing along the picturesque waterfront. After walking two hundred yards farther, they took a left turn. They paused again as they reached Broad Street, Bridgetown's bustling main avenue and center for shopping and commerce. Fortunately, the street was congested enough that we could easily follow the couple without being detected.

From what I could tell via quick glances, Barbados was definitely upscale as Caribbean islands go. The windows of the stores and shops displayed a broad selection of high quality, duty-free merchandise from around the world: Parisian-designed clothing, French perfume and cosmetics, South American precious and semi-precious stones, Spanish porcelain, Swiss watches, Irish crystal and embroidery, English pottery, and German and Japanese cameras were only a few of the wares beckoning from behind elegantly furnished windows.

In a couple of blocks, the pair stopped once more, near the Parliament buildings, and spoke again before going their separate ways—Arturo strolled off a short distance before turning into the Shepherd's Gate Pub; Castrada continued past the Norman Centre, to an office building on St. Ambrose, where she stopped and looked around before ducking inside.

Bo and I quickened our paces to avoid losing her inside the building, approached the entrance without much caution, spun through the revolving glass door, and halted to scan the lobby; I spotted her walking past the concierge's desk and some shops and pointed her out to my cohort while pulling him back behind some decorative foliage. Here, we had few people to provide cover, only a couple of browsers and a quartet waiting for an elevator. As my heart rate slowed, I realized we could have used sonar at this point, rather than visual observation, to track the distinctive sound of her stiletto heels crossing the shiny marble floor.

Bo and I moved in closer as Castrada approached a pair of restroom doors. To our surprise, she walked up to the men's room door and opened it wide enough to peek inside. She abruptly withdrew her head, backed up, and edged down the wall. Several moments later, a custodian exited, followed by a well-dressed man who was straightening his jacket and tugging on his French cuffs.

Castrada approached the door again, opened it slowly, and peered inside. Satisfied the restroom was empty this time, she ducked in with alacrity. Bo and I waited a few minutes and quietly followed her in. The room was empty but we heard rustling sounds coming from the last stall at the end. Creeping noiselessly across the floor, I peeked under the door and saw a pair of bare feet. I motioned for Bo to follow me outside where we took refuge behind a column.

"Care to explain what's going on?" Bo asked, genuinely puzzled.

"I believe, my friend, you are about to witness an amazing metamorphosis."

Bo still looked puzzled.

"—a physical change."

Five minutes later, the restroom door opened and there, before us, was none other than a twin of Arturo Del Muerto. The figure wore a beige suit, identical to the one Arturo had worn off the ship. An identical fedora was pulled down low over her pulled up hair partially covering a face that now had long, dark sideburns, a scar, and no moles on the corners of her mouth.

"Voila," I said in admiration. "Arturo's doppelganger."

"His what?" Bo asked.

"His physical double."

We watched Castrada—now Arturo—walk to the elevators, the bag still in hand, and push the third floor button. I grabbed Bo's arm in restraint. "We'll take the next one up," I whispered. "I know where she's going."

We jumped into the next car, got off at the third floor, and strolled down the hall until we came to room 360—Cartier Fashions. I pressed my ear against the upper smoked glass panel of the door and heard a deep voice say, "I'm Luis Montevista from the House of Beaumarchais. I have an appointment to see Mr. Cartier at 10:00 A.M."

I opened the door a crack and saw the disguised Castrada standing in front of a young woman who was seated behind a small desk. "Yes, I have you here, Mr. Montevista, from ten to eleven. Please go right in Mr. Cartier's office and make yourself at home. It's at the end of the hallway to your left. He'll be with you in a few minutes—he's just wrapping up a meeting in a conference room next door. Care for some coffee?"

"No," Castrada-Arturo tossed over a shoulder while heading for Cartier's office. As soon as she was gone, Bo and I walked in.

When the secretary saw Bo, she removed her reading glasses and brushed back strands of long blonde hair from her face. She arched her back to flaunt her full cleavage, twitched her swollen red lips, and batted two large, smoky green eyes that could have popped the lid off a dead man's casket. "And what can I do for you?" she asked, oblivious to my presence but soaking in every detail of my companion's physique.

Bo leaned over her desk and smiled which caused the top two buttons on her silk blouse to pop open and the hem of her skirt to retreat an indecent expanse. "We need to speak to Mr. Montevista, but it can wait until after his meeting with your boss is over, sweet thing."

At that moment, a side door opened and a man of medium height and build, mid-fifties, with wiry, salt-and-pepper short hair swooped in.

The sultry blond interrupted her swoon. "Mr. Cartier, Mr. Montevista is waiting in your office."

"Thanks, Daphne. Hold all my calls, please." With that command, he scooted down the hall.

I turned to the secretary who was again transfixed by Bo's gaze. "Daphne," I said, quickly flashing the Nordic Caribbean badge in my wallet. "I want you to remain quiet and perfectly still. We're investigators here on official police business."

She was startled when I pulled my Smith & Wesson from my pocket, but Bo's follow-up action of placing his index finger against her lips and blowing her a kiss calmed her and enabled Bo and I to creep to the closed door of Cartier's office.

"It's good to meet you as well," were the first words we heard through the door. "So, Mr. Montevista, am I to understand that the House of Beaumarchais is interested in wholesaling some of my island fashions for worldwide distribution?"

"Not exactly, Mr. Cartier. But, let me get to the point."

So, she *can* speak English, I thought.

"Buying clothes… that is not why I am here."

She even talks like Arturo.

"Then why are you here?" Cartier asked. His voice reflected curiosity.

"It is with much regret that I have to give you some bad news."

In fact, her English is *better* than Arturo's.

"Bad? In what way?" His voice now reflected concern.

"I am afraid I must be the first to offer my condolences."

"Condolences? On what?"

"Your death."

"My death?" Even through the door, I could tell that his voice had reached panic mode. "Are you crazy?"

I raised my arm and motioned for Bo to be ready for action. He nodded in acknowledgment.

"This is nothing personal, I assure you," the conversation continued. "It is purely a business matter."

"This is preposterous. I'm calling the Royal Police Force... wait... what—put that knife away!"

That was the signal I was waiting for. I nodded to Bo, who twisted the knob to the office door. A moment later, we had lowered our shoulders against the door and burst in.

Cartier was on his feet, darting back and forth, trying to keep the desk between himself and Castrada. She held a sliced phone cord in her left hand and a long switchblade in her right, coolly stalking him around the desk. Surprised by our sudden entry, she spun around, changed her grip on the knife, and raised her arm as if to throw it. I pointed the barrel of my Smith & Wesson and fired, but my trembling hand caused the shot to veer left. Fortunately, Bo had leaped toward Castrada and sent her reeling across the room with a hard right to her chin. She slammed against a bookcase and slowly slid to the floor.

Cartier was wide-eyed. "What... why... who are you?"

I caught my breath, waited for my own palpitations to subside, and responded. "We're security from a cruise ship, the *Oslo Aphrodite*, which berthed this morning."

"And, who... who... who is he?" Cartier asked, pointing at Castrada, "and... and, how did you come to be here?"

"The 'he' is actually a 'she' who was hired to kill you. Let's just say we got wind of the plot and showed up to prevent it."

"Who... who would want me dead?"

"I'm still working on that piece of information. I expect it to be cleared up shortly, however."

Cartier collapsed in his chair. Perspiration rolled down his forehead until temporarily stalled by his bushy eyebrows. Firm grips on the armrests of his chair still didn't prevent his hands from shaking. "I don't know how to thank you."

I was delighted that he had taken this attitude. If he had known the facts, he could just as easily have taken us to task for using him as live bait to catch a killer.

Hatfield looked at me and grinned. "Remind me never to take you on safari, bwana. If I had to depend on your marksmanship, the lion would have plumb ate my country ass up."

"That was a warning shot. It's a professional courtesy," I mumbled weakly as I walked toward Castrada's unconscious body, phone cord in hand.

"What're you doing?" Bo asked.

"I'm going to tie her up."

"That ain't necessary. When I hit 'em, they stay hit. By the time she wakes up, her trial will be over."

"Mr. Cartier, are you all right?" Daphne asked. She was standing in the doorway with her palms on her cheeks.

"Yes, thanks to these gentlemen," Cartier replied. He leaned back in his chair and loosened his tie, still in the throes of recuperation.

Bo placed his hand on Daphne's behind and guided her out of the office. "Let's you and I go to your phone and call the police, sweet thing."

The Royal Barbados Police Force arrived within ten minutes. They quickly secured the scene, revived Castrada with smelling salts, and cuffed her before getting statements from Cartier and me. During my statement, I also told them about Arturo, her accomplice, and suggested that he might be apprehended in the Shepherd's Gate Pub or one of the other local watering holes. Or, if that tactic failed, he could be taken into custody later as he reboarded the ship. In addition, I alerted them to the Tolleson murder in Ocho Rios and suggested that they coordinate prosecution with the Jamaican authorities.

Before leading Castrada away for her short trip to their version of Old Bailey, the investigators sought statements from Bo and Daphne, but both had been missing for a while. I volunteered to search for them and, on a hunch, began looking behind closed doors. Eventually I saw him sneaking out of a back room with Daphne, wiping lipstick from his mouth.

"Bo, don't tell me you were compromising a material witness before they could even get the crime scene processed," I teased.

Bo checked his zipper, looked up, and smiled. "Sweet thing was *so* upset I felt obliged to spend a few minutes comforting her..."

"It was nice of you to console her," I praised, impressed with Bo's unexpected sensitivity.

"Actually," he added with a lower voice and a wink, "I consoled her twice—on top of the copy machine. While I was giving her the 'Georgia shuffle' and the 'boar-hog grind', the damn machine got accidentally turned on and took this great picture of her ass." He handed me Daphne's posterior portrait for my review.

"This would make a great item for a Rorschach test," I commented. Then looking up, I added, "The police need to get statements from you and your patient, that is, if your physical therapy session is over..."

The police soon released us but cautioned that we might receive subpoenas to return to Barbados if a deposition for the arraignment or testimony at the trial were needed. As Bo and I neared the quay, we ran into a handcuffed Arturo, who was being escorted away from the ship by two stalwart members of the RBPF with solid grasps on each arm.

"Arturo!" I greeted in mock surprise. "What happened? Did they catch you slicing holes in the life jackets again?" I removed my hat, wig and mustache to reveal my true identity.

"Ah, señor McFadden," he replied, shaking his head, "you will not believe it—someone, I guess, was murdered today and when the police learn that the affable Arturo is in town, they arrest me. The alibi... I have one, of course. Castrada... if you see her, tell her I return after I answer a few questions."

"Tell her yourself. She was apprehended trying to carve her initials into the pacemaker of a fellow named Simon Cartier. It seems your little murder-for-hire operation will be shelved for a while."

"This is big misunderstanding," Arturo said, shaking his head. "I will explain and bail her out."

"I don't think you're going anywhere anytime soon. Once they read you your rights, I suggest you call your attorney, Pedro Mason. Castrada is probably spilling her guts out right now, trying to get a lighter sentence by implicating you as the mastermind of the operation."

"The law... I know a little about it. A wife... her testimony against her husband is not admissible in a court of law."

"That may be true, but Castrada isn't your wife: she's your sister. And, I *do* hope you two haven't been enjoying connubial relations. Murder is one thing, Arturo, but incest—that's a little gamy. Even Bo draws the line there, and he raced through puberty on Tobacco Road, where family ties fly out the window once you get sister Sophie naked in the barn."

Taking on a more serious demeanor, I turned to the two constables, flashed my badge, and asked if I could speak with the prisoner in private for a moment. They looked at each other, shrugged, and released their grips. Bo and I guided him about ten feet away.

"Arturo, my dear friend," I said, "as part of the plea-bargaining process, I suspect you're going to be asked to rat out your employer. The police like to get the top guy, you know, even if they have to give a little on the sentence of the hired hand. Therefore, *amigo* to *amigo*, tell me: who hired you and Castrada to kill Simon Cartier?"

Arturo looked at me with amusement before shrugging his shoulders. "You know, *gringo*, I think I would tell you because you are a funny man but I have, as you say, one problem: The contract... I don't know who put it out."

Realizing that his cover was blown, Arturo's English became noticeably better. "I am hired through personal ads run in the Bogotá newspaper. I convey my acceptance of the contract by replying with an ad of my own. I am then sent a package which contains pictures of the person to be hit, their family members, close associates and bodyguards if any. There is also a recording that tells me personal details like the victim's habits, their travel schedule and routes, home and business locations, the time frame in which the contract is to be carried out, and how I will be paid. For this job, I was to be paid in cash by an envelope delivered to me in my cabin after the kill was confirmed.

"It is a very simple business. No link in the chain knows the other links connected to it." He turned and started walking back toward the policemen by himself.

"Arturo," I yelled. "I have one last favor to ask."

The departing desperado stopped, looked back and asked, "And, what might that be, funny man?"

"Since you won't be at dinner tonight, can I have your dessert?"

When we got back on the ship, I proceeded to the Purser's Office while Bo corralled a cabin steward to have the Del Muertos's belongings packed for removal by the Barbadian authorities.

"Mr. McFadden," Bill Graham said as I entered. "I tried reaching you earlier about your request of yesterday—I have an update for you. Lamont Darling removed the second money pouch from the ship's safe right before lunch."

"That's what I suspected. Thanks a lot. By the way, have you seen Captain Nelson recently?"

"He was in the engine room a few moments ago, talking to Arnolf Hansen, the chief engineer."

When I asked directions, he found a map of the ship and traced a route with his finger. I was navigating my way to the engine room when I bumped into Nelson getting off the elevator.

"Got a few minutes, Captain?"

"Let's go to my cabin," he said, taking the lead.

"What do you have to report?" he asked, after we had both seated ourselves.

"The next time you talk to Erickson, you can tell him that the Tolleson murder has been solved."

"Was he killed by the Zunimbists?" the Captain asked, articulating his worst fear.

"On the contrary, he was killed by one of your passengers, Castrada Del Muerto, an international assassin who was arrested in Bridgetown today along with her brother, Arturo, an accomplice before the fact. They were attempting the murder of a local man, Simon Cartier. Hopefully, the RBPF will obtain enough information from this attempted homicide investigation to be able to link the

Del Muertos to the Tolleson murder. Bo Hatfield assisted me in their apprehension and is taking care of any legal formalities that might be required to protect the cruise line. Since all criminal activity happened on shore, Barbados has territorial jurisdiction and the ship's departure won't be impacted."

"That's a relief. You said the Del Muertos were assassins. Who hired them?"

"I'm still working on that one."

Nelson shook his head in bewilderment. "… A brother and sister assassination team."

"Arturo was the mastermind and the decoy, his sister, was the naughty ninja. Apparently, it never occurred to authorities to check for a marriage license, dig up their birth certificates, or reconstruct their genealogies. I became suspicious when I noticed their similar physical features, which they tried to differentiate with gothic makeup. I was also puzzled at seeing identical pairs of suits in their closet when I searched their cabin the other day. Then I realized the reason—one suit was for him to wear and its twin for her to murder in. Any witnesses to an assassination provided a description that matched Arturo's features and clothing. However, when apprehended, he always had a substantiated alibi for being elsewhere at the time of the killing even though he was in the same general vicinity."

Nelson sighed. "Cruise ships used to attract the nicer social elements. These days, I'm starting to feel like a bus driver shuttling riffraff between jail and the courthouse." As I rose to leave, he asked one last question: "Are you making any progress on Amundson's murder?"

"I have some ideas," I bluffed. "That case should be wrapped up by the end of the cruise."

"That's good news. Before you go, we gained thirty-two passengers today in Barbados, the jumping-on point for the remainder of the cruise's itinerary. Here's a list of their names and cabin locations."

I slipped the list into my pocket and left.

When I got back to the cabin, I found Girtha soaking her feet. Only a few bags graced the credenza—I was relieved to see that she had scaled back. "How did it go today?" I asked while looking through her bags.

"What are you looking for?" she asked warily.

"I just wanted to make sure the vendors didn't sell you a bunch of dildos by passing them off as antique Arawak Indian rolling pins." I ducked the tossed pillow and sat on my bed, leaning against the wall. "Did you have a good time?"

"Fantastic. I took this interesting tour of the island." She picked up the shore excursion brochure and scanned it to refresh her memory. "We started off checking out all the historical stuff in Bridgetown and then crossed the Charles Duncan Onea Bridge, went past the Queen Elizabeth Hospital, and stopped at this sugar plantation to tour the great house, Villa Nova. We continued to St. John's Church, which is built on the edge of a cliff overlooking the sea. We then stopped at a beach hotel for lunch and a drink—I had steamed flying fish, believe it or not, and a salad made of picked-green bananas. We returned to Bridgetown along the south coast highway, which took us past the airport and through some picturesque little villages named Oistins, Dover, Worthing, and Hastings. Oh, and we stopped at the Mount Gay distillery and did some tasting. Boy, is that stuff strong. How was your day?"

I recounted how I—with able assistance from Bo—had stopped a murder in progress and gotten the Del Muertos taken into custody. Girtha was starting to pale, so I opened a box of chocolates from the gift shop and passed her a few since that always seemed to bring her around.

"So you see, Girtha, I was never in any real danger." I got up to pour us a drink and Girtha picked up a piece of paper that had fallen out of my back pocket.

"What's this?" she asked, unfolding her find.

"Oh, that. It's just a photo of Daphne's naked ass."

An hour later on our way to dinner, I was still rubbing the lump on my head, rethinking how I might have explained the photocopy a little better.

CHAPTER 16

THE AUTOGRAPH HOUNDS AROUND OUR TABLE SEEMED to multiply each evening. Tonight, even small children, awkwardly clutching pads and pens, were pushed into the line to fulfill a mission still hazy to them. Girtha and I wedged through the crowd to join the resplendent Lamont Darling, the pulchritudinous Fifi, and the harrumphing Colonel Talbo.

To my surprise, our dining entourage had expanded by two: Bo Hatfield *and* none other than Lieutenant Alameda! Bo was in uniform and introduced himself as the ship's security officer. The lieutenant quickly offered me her hand to obviate any verbal reaction. "I'm Constancia Alameda from Miami. I just joined your ship today for the second half of the cruise. I've been so needing a vacation." Other introductions made their way around the table until our waiter, Taboul, appeared to distribute our menus.

"Good evening. Tonight's menu features traditional Caribbean dishes prepared with a personal touch by our chef. I will be back in a moment to see if you have any questions and to take your orders."

Fifi looked puzzled. "How do we have room for two new diners? Where are Arturo and Castrada? It's not like them to miss dinner."

"The Del Muertos won't be joining us this evening," I replied.

"Did they make other dining arrangements?" Darling asked casually while unfolding his napkin.

"They'll be eating later, after the Barbadian police have finished booking and interrogating them," I announced.

"They've been arrested? What did they do?" Fifi asked, exchanging glances with Darling.

"Castrada was nicked trying to skewer some local businessman they'd been contracted to kill. She and Arturo ran a murder-for-hire partnership dedicated to pruning the human population of those poor souls unlucky enough to have made it to the top of someone's snuff list."

"I knew there was something mighty strange about those two," Colonel Talbo declared, "but I never thought I'd be breaking bread with a couple of chain-gang Charlies."

"They weren't plantation aristocracy, that's for sure," I agreed.

"I can't say I'll miss them," Fifi added. "It was creepy the way she never spoke or opened her mouth. Do you think it was to hide her fangs? I told Lamont she always seemed to be looking at my neck. I was going to start wearing a scarf wrapped around it with a clove of garlic stuffed inside."

"If your supposition is correct, once confined with a captive population she could make a sizable dent in the island's recidivism rate," I injected.

"And that Arturo," Fifi continued, "every time he stared at me, I felt like he had X-ray vision that could see everything I have."

"He wouldn't have had to see through your clothes to do that!" Girtha said sweetly. "You expose enough flesh to give anyone a good idea of your girlish charms."

Fortunately, Taboul's arrival to take dinner orders ended any impending cat fight, and as soon as he left, I changed the subject.

"This Del Muerto business would make a great movie script, wouldn't it, Mr. Darling?" I probed.

"A little too melodramatic for my taste," he retorted without relish.

I turned my attention to Constancia Alameda, which wasn't hard duty. She'd looked good in Miami packaged in an official dark blue suit. But, this evening, her straight black hair, which hung to her waist in a shimmering luster, and her pale almond skin focused attention on her large, brown eyes and full carmine lips. Her strapless, backless dress looked as if it had been sprayed on. The entire package was stunning enough to leave any man breathless and woman envious.

Needless to say, poor Bo was beside himself. Flanked by the physical charms of Fifi and the overpowering beauty of Constancia, his raging libido must have been racing like a NASCAR engine on its last lap. Fifi would have doubtlessly given him a pit stop to remember, but any untoward advances directed at Constancia could result in a snapped fuel line and a bent tailpipe.

Girtha's voice pulled me from my trance. "I can't imagine why people would kill other people for money. There must be some other reason."

I thought a second and replied, "I think Gertrude Stein said it best when she penned, 'There ain't no answer, There ain't going to be any answer, There never has been an answer, That's the answer.'"

"Are you a poet, Mr. McFadden?" Constancia asked, in whimsical tease.

"I can rhyme defective with detective but that's about it. I'm a ship's inspector, performing an audit of certain aspects of the vessel's operation. How about you, Miss Alameda? What do you do for a living?"

"I work for a commercial insurance company; in fact we insure the Nordic Caribbean Cruise Line. I had a week's vacation coming and I had to use it or lose it, so, here I am." Now that she was finally speaking, she continued making small talk by turning to Lamont Darling. She fanned herself and said, "I never dreamed I would have the honor of meeting you, Mr. Darling. You have been the favorite actor in my household for some time."

Darling smiled, "You mean your mother has faded pictures of me in her drawer hidden under her lingerie?"

Constancia gave him a smoldering pout in return. "You have the type of look and sex appeal that is ageless. I found your pictures in my mother's bedroom some years ago, but now they're safely tucked away under *my* panties."

This was better than phone sex. In reaction to her comment, Darling was beaming, Bo was overheating, my heart was racing, and even the Colonel blushed and loosened his collar.

Talbo was next in her sights. "Colonel, you're such a distin-guished-looking gentleman. You remind me of my father in many ways. He owned a large plantation in Cuba until the fall of Batista in 1959."

Colonel Talbo's glands were already stirring and his mustache twitched as he jerked his head up. "*Your* folks had a plantation?"

"Yes, it had been in our family for ages. Five thousand acres of fertile land near Camaguey devoted to coffee beans and tobacco. Castro confiscated it when he seized power and distributed the land to his supporters. When my family fled to Miami, we were lucky to have the clothes on our backs."

I smiled at the irony: she didn't have anything on her back this evening either.

"The same thing happened to the Talbo plantation," the Colonel replied bitterly. "Most of our land, which had been in our family for generations, was stolen from under our feet and given to people we wouldn't have allowed to sink a plowshare into it."

Constancia reached over and patted his hand, then turned to address Darling's companion. "If you ever leave California, you should consider relocating to Miami Beach, Fifi. It's simply crawling with stunningly beautiful runway models and you would feel right at home."

Fifi blushed and thrust her cleaved cargo forward. "Modeling would be nice, but I would have to lose some of this baby fat to slip into a revealing bikini."

All this saccharine was going to cause my diabetes to flare up, so I interjected. "Constancia, may Girtha and I buy you a drink after dinner? I have some reinsurance matters I'd like to get your input on."

"I'd prefer not to talk shop on vacation," Constancia said in mock pain, holding the back of her hand against her forehead, "but I'll make this *one* exception." She smiled and lowered her hand. "But I do have one condition…"

"What's that?"

"That Girtha tells me where she got that lovely dress she's wearing this evening. It flatters her features so well."

Girtha, startled, straightened up in her chair and thrust her own cleavage forward as if to tell Fifi, You don't have anything that I don't have more of!

"After you've been bored to death by McFadden, maybe I could escort you to the disco for some dancing," Bo offered. He leaned across the table and gave her a look I normally reserved for a medium-rare, marbled prime rib-eye cut at an upscale steak house.

"That sounds like fun, Mr. Hatfield," Constancia cooed. "I haven't been dancing in ages. Besides, I have a special affection for men in law enforcement."

I couldn't help but smile—Constancia was *good*. I don't believe I had ever seen a table worked so well. Within minutes, she had created four boners without alienating any of the distaff diners, which was no small feat.

It did cross my mine that I should warn Bo that if he wasn't on his best behavior with Constancia, he could find his penis twisted into a poodle, like the ones clowns make with balloons at children's birthday parties. But then I decided, ah, what the heck. Let him try to stick his wiener in a pencil sharpener… it may be healthy for his rampant ego.

An hour later, still basking in the glow of Constancia's compliment, and understanding that my need for a discussion with her was urgent, Girtha allowed me to huddle with the sexy siren without a chaperone. I met her in the Skytop Lounge at a table in the corner, far from the madding crowd.

"Have you found the drugs yet?" Alameda opened after we gave our orders for two vodka martinis to the waitress.

"I haven't a clue," I replied, "but that hasn't been a primary focus of my investigation. Tell me, what really brings you aboard this ship of fools?"

She smiled. "I really am on vacation—really. My presence is purely unofficial; after all, I'm out of my jurisdiction. I had some time coming, so I decided to join your little sojourn. I've been intrigued by your requests for information—so much so that I'll admit I may have misjudged you."

"In what way?"

"My initial impression was that you were a harmless third-rate gumshoe seeking a payout by borrowing my watch to tell Erickson the time."

"But now that you've been enlightened?"

"I'm starting to think that maybe you're not the bumbling buffoon I had originally perceived you to be."

"Lieutenant, please, you'll turn my head with all this flattery."

The waitress brought our martinis and we clinked glasses in a silent toast. "Give me a recap of what you've uncovered so far," she asked.

"In a nutshell, Bruno Helmje, the ship's chief radio operator, and Joey Morton, a contracted comedian, were smuggling drugs from a variety of Caribbean ports into Miami by hiding the goods in equipment brought aboard by island entertainers. They then used marked garbage containers to transfer the drugs ashore in Miami. When the last drug shipment didn't arrive as scheduled, two parties on the delivery end felt the wrath of Zunimba: Victor Dubonnet, a ship's waiter whose job was to hide the drugs, and Jacque Destang, a worker at the waste management facility whose role was to extract them from the garbage and get them into the hands of the distributors. Victor was replaced by Toussaint L'Enfant, who killed Bruno and dumped him overboard. The Coast Guard found what was left of Bruno's remains in a canvas bag off a Jamaican cay, bouncing back and forth among coral stalagmites like a pinball.

"When Joey jumped ship in La Guaira, Toussaint followed him with the intent of murdering him as well. Joey must have spotted the tail and lured Toussaint into a trap—he turned the tables by killing his pursuer."

"How do you know this?"

"I was following Toussaint who was too busy tailing Joey to notice me."

"Since you suspected what Toussaint was up to, why didn't you act to prevent any murder from occurring?"

"It was a long uphill climb to the scene of the crime," I confessed, my hands folded demurely on my ample paunch. "By the time I got there, Joey had slipped out the back door and Toussaint was spurting blood like a Yellowstone geyser. He was waiting for last rites, but I didn't have my sacraments with me—a dead chicken took his confession."

"Where is Joey now?" she asked.

"Your guess is as good as mine. By now, he's probably changed everything but his jokes. I wouldn't be surprised if he's gotten himself elected village medicine man by some aboriginal tribe deep in the heart of the Amazon, keeping them amazed with his Zippo lighter and card tricks."

"When you were discussing the murders in Miami, you didn't mention Lars Amundson," she probed.

"The more I learn about Lars, the more I'm convinced he wasn't involved in the drug-smuggling operation. If you accept that premise, then it's not likely he was killed by Zunimbists. It's possible, I suppose, that he may have learned of the operation and been killed to insure his silence. I've uncovered nothing to support this hypothesis one way or the other, though. I actually have another theory, which I'll share with you once I obtain some evidence to support it."

"What's the story on Buck Tolleson?"

"Tolleson was a hostile raider who had amassed a fortune using corporate blackmail. One of his past victims, apparently chaffed at being exploited by him, hired an international hit team, Arturo and Castrada Del Muerto, to murder him in Jamaica. The Del Muertos got away with that one, but were apprehended in Barbados while attempting to murder a second victim, a businessman named Simon Cartier. Fortunately, Bo and I were able to apprehend them before they could succeed.

"By the way, have you gotten the decoded results of Bruno's radiograms back from the FBI?"

"Not yet. The radiograms were sent to their Cryptanalysis and Racketeering Unit in Quantico, Virginia. I'll follow up when I get back."

"It would have been nice to have that information to work with." Then, in as offhanded a manner as I could muster, I invited her to join me for some potential fun. "Say, if you have nothing better on tap for tomorrow morning, how would you like to help bring a guilty party to justice?"

"Hmm," Constancia murmured as she slipped the olive off its toothpick with her full, ripe lips and played with it with her athletic tongue. I was mesmerized by the way she could turn an innocent gesture into an absorbing sensual experience. "I was planning to work on my tan lines on the beaches of Fort-de-France, but I suppose I could lend a hand… unofficially, of course. What do you have in mind?"

"I'm expecting to trap the culprit who hired the Del Muertos to kill Buck Tolleson and Simon Cartier."

"Do you have a plan or are we going to wing it?" she asked in lieu of an outright acceptance.

"Meet me at the gangway on level four tomorrow morning at 8:30 with swimming attire and comfortable shoes. I'll fill you in then. We'll be going ashore to take the *Kon Tiki* excursion, which takes us over to a secluded beach."

"Count me in. That reminds me, have you revealed my real occupation to anyone?"

"Girtha, of course, has known since our meeting in Miami. If you have no objections, I'll also inform Bo in confidence since I suspect that I'll have additional need of both your services before this cruise is over."

Constancia glanced at her watch. "Speaking of Bo, I have a date to trip the light fantastic with your new sidekick, so *I'll* give him the news: I'm dying to see the look on his face. But, I do have one question about him…"

"Fire away."

"Bo is certainly a studly specimen, but do any parts north of his navel work?"

"He's not a dazzling, sophisticated urbanite, but don't be taken in by his cornpone ambience. He's as solid as he wants to be. As for tonight, just hold a nickel between your knees and you should be safe."

Constancia stood and brushed her hair back from her face. "I never take loose change on a date. Besides I'm a little curious—I could feel him poking my knees at dinner, and he was sitting on the other side of the table."

She smiled, smoothed imaginary wrinkles from the abdomen of her sheath dress, and sashayed across the floor, a wave of turning heads following each and every sway of her curvaceous hips.

CHAPTER 17

T HE NEXT MORNING WAS SUNDAY, THE NINTH DAY of the cruise. Girtha and I got up early to shower and watch the ship ease through Fort-de-France Bay and dock in the capital of Martinique. Birds, drawn by the promise of food scraps, gracefully circled the arriving ship, whose horn had rudely rousted them from their coastal sanctuaries. From our rail, some ten stories above the water, a mountain peak, unobscured by clouds, could be seen in the distance north of the city. At some fifty miles long and twenty-two miles wide, Martinique was one of the largest islands in the Lesser Antilles.

"Look at the buildings on shore, Chauncey. They look like those I've seen in pictures of the French Quarter in New Orleans."

"Not surprising. According to the *Sea Compass*, Martinique's been under continuous French control since 1814. In fact, it's a department and region of France and it's represented in the French Parliament."

"I thought Columbus discovered Martinique. Why isn't it Spanish?" Girtha asked.

"While Columbus was the first European to land on Martinique, he was—as in many other cases—run off by the natives, in this case, the Arawaks and the Caribs. I'm surprised old Christopher didn't develop a complex. He was run out of more places than a rent collector in a ghetto tenement building."

"Whatcha got planned for today?" Girtha asked, already assuming we would be going our separate ways, as usual.

"You and I are meeting Bo and Alameda in the Carousel Lounge at 8:30—I signed the four of us up for a scenic boat ride around the island that includes a stop at a beach. There, you should be able to swim, sunbathe, collect shells, or beachcomb. I'll be setting a trap for Lamont Darling and Fifi with Bo and Constancia along as backups."

"Why?"

"I'm going to try to wring a confession from Darling for funding the murder of Buck Tolleson and the attempted murder of Simon Cartier."

"You're taking another chance, Chauncey," Girtha exclaimed in anguish. "You promised me that you wouldn't put your life in jeopardy anymore."

"That's why I have Constancia and Bo along. They'll be armed and they're both crack shots should that be necessary. Either one could pop the testicles off a sand gnat at twenty paces."

While we had breakfast by the pool, Girtha's spirits gradually returned. "Well, I guess I can use this as an opportunity to try on my new bathing suit," she said. "It's supposed to have special panels that provide uplift support for the cups and contraction support for the stomach."

I didn't say what I was thinking, for once. The thought that came immediately to mind was, *that's a pretty amazing engineering feat for a swimsuit!* But, what I ended up saying was, "Sounds like you got your money's worth on that purchase." Thankfully, she took that as a compliment.

After breakfast, we returned to the room to pack for the day and proceeded to the Carousel Lounge to meet Bo and Constancia. The lieutenant was wearing a thin tank top that left little to the imagination and tight white shorts—I saw no way she could have been concealing a gun in that outfit, so I hoped it was in her beach bag. Bo was wearing loose-fitting Bermuda shorts and a muscle-revealing T-shirt that displayed his buff profile to maximum advantage. I handed them their boat-tour tickets and we merged into the rest of the group, which trickled down the forward gangway to the dock.

Keeping Darling and Fifi in sight was easy as we followed them onto the *Kon Tiki*, which had been modeled after the original raft. The crew began serving an unlimited supply of free rum punch as soon as we boarded, and everyone got in a festive spirit without delay. A steel drum band comprised of island natives contributed to the party mood by cranking out local renditions of Caribbean ballads. The lyrics of one particular little ditty caught my fancy:

> In Martinique there was a family
> With much confusion as you'll see.
> It was a mama and papa and a boy who was grown
> Who wanted to marry a wife of his own.
> He found the young gal, who soothing him nice
> He went to his poppa to ask his advice
> His papa said, 'Son, I have to say no,
> That gal is your sister
> But your momma don't know.'
> The weeks went by and the summer came down,
> And soon the best cook in the island he found.
> He went to his poppa to name a date,
> His poppa shook his head and to him he did say,
> 'You can't marry that girl, I have to say no,
> That gal is your sister but your mama don't know.'
> He went to his momma and covered his head,
> And told his momma what his poppa had said,
> His mama, she laugh—she said, 'Go, boy, go,
> Your daddy ain't your daddy,
> but your daddy don't know.

In addition to music and punch, the boat contained large glass-bottomed viewers that allowed passengers to see the spectacular underwater palette beneath them. Featured were schools of brightly colored tropical fish that flitted among coral, sea fans, and sponges. Sunlight added its own spectacle while filtering through the clear water to highlight vibrant hues to an intensity that was beyond description.

Before too long, effects of the rum elixir became evident. First, couples shed their inhibitions and took to the dance floor; then, before everyone became too exhausted, a limbo demonstration was announced. Everyone returned to their seats to enjoy this island specialty.

"Limbo looks pretty interesting," Constancia said, after watching one agile dancer inch his way under the stick. "I'd like to give it a try."

Bo laughed and nodded at her healthy bust. "Sweet thing, the only way you could get under that stick is face down. But, I may give it a try."

Constancia looked at Bo sweetly, smiled, and counterattacked: "Pocket rocket, the only way *you* could get under that stick is to tie your willy to your leg!"

"Tit for tat," Bo replied, enjoying this repartee.

"You wish, tat," Constancia shot back.

Girtha and I were in stitches. "You two ought to take your testosterone-and-estrogen act on the road. You could be a contemporary update of Nick and Nora Charles, replete with raging hormones, who spar with each other more than they fight with criminal forces."

"That sounds like a great idea to me," Bo said enthusiastically. "Can we start rehearsing the love scenes now?"

"Let's wait for the script. Oh," Constancia exclaimed, touching Bo's arm sympathetically. "That may be a problem for you—you'd have to know how to read—and act."

Bo laughed. "They can do a voice-over unless we're in bed; then, I'll do my own voice *and* stunts. I'll have you know I was in a couple of plays in high school—I even played King Lear."

"Bo," Constancia laughed, "the closest you've been to royalty is watching reruns of *The Dukes of Hazzard*."

This sparring match would doubtlessly have gone on forever if I hadn't reluctantly stepped in. "I hate to interrupt while you two are fanning the embers of lust, but we need to get down to business. As I mentioned, we're here today on a serious mission— to follow Lamont Darling and Fifi, and we're doing so for two reasons. First, I want to make sure they get back on board the *Oslo Aphrodite*—I don't want them jumping ship in Martinique. Second, I want to force Darling's hand and get him to commit himself. I'm going to pretend to blackmail him for the murder of Buck Tolleson. That's where you two come in. Once Darling knows that I'm on to him, I'll need you to cover my back, which is where the guns could come into the picture.

"Remember, too, that we need to keep our eyes on Fifi as well since I don't know to what extent she may be involved."

"I think we can handle that," Bo said. "And, Constancia," he added with a grin, "don't overestimate your charms. While I am glad to see you, that's actually a snub-nosed thirty-eight in my pocket."

"*You'd* get deeper projectile penetration and better accuracy with a long-barrel .357 magnum," Constancia teased back.

"As I was *saying*," I weighed in again, "as soon as the *Kon Tiki* docks, let's follow Darling and Fifi to the beach and spread our towels near theirs. When the opportunity presents itself, I'll get Darling alone and set the trap."

By the time the boat arrived at the pier, most of the passengers were in high spirits. They hustled to spread out along the blended white, ochre, and silver volcanic sand of the beach to claim their spots, dump their gear as quickly as possible, and speed-walk directly into the inviting waters.

"That looks like a good idea," Girtha said. "I think I'll take a stroll into the surf as well."

"I'd go farther down the beach if I were you."

"Why is that?"

"A lot of booze was consumed on a boat with only two restrooms, so I suspect a lot of that processed rum punch is being released into the water right about now. I hope all that ammonia doesn't kill the aquatic plant and animal life."

Girtha propped her hands on her hips and gave me a look of exasperation before straightening up and pointing down the beach. "Chauncey! Look!"

I followed her pointed finger to a number of statuesque young women who were emerging from the water. Their tanned wet bodies, glistening in the morning sun, were naked from the waist up. They adjusted their thongs, leaned over to squeeze excess water from their hair, and sauntered to their beach chairs.

"This is a topless beach, you dog! You didn't tell me that."

"Honestly, Girtha, I'm sorry. I had no idea." It was probably the most insincere apology I've ever uttered. This captivating view of wet semi-nudity was like being in the dressing room of a Vegas show after the overhead sprinkler system had gone off.

Bo, fortunately, came to my defense. "It's actually a clothing optional beach. You can strip naked or keep your swimsuit on: it's up to the individual. Martinique is the number one Caribbean destination for French nationals, so this ain't nothin'—you should see the beaches in front of the big hotels. Eighteen-year-old French girls play volleyball topless there. It's quite a sight, particularly when they serve and spike."

While Bo was talking, Constancia had removed her shorts and T-shirt, revealing a black string bikini that had less cloth than a pirate's eye patch. An undraped Constancia was a vision to behold. She'd be a runaway selection for the cover shot in *Playboy's* next "Women in Law Enforcement" spread.

Seeing what he'd missed momentarily, Bo whistled softly in admiration. "How about you, sweet thing? You want me to untie your top or can you reach it?"

"Girtha and I will maintain decorum and *not* sink to the level of tawdry exhibitionism displayed elsewhere," Constancia replied, largely in jest.

"You got *that* right, girl," Girtha said, breathing a sigh of relief at having procured an ally on such a sensitive subject.

"However, I'll toss you some table scraps, Bo, and allow you to rub suntan lotion on me. *But*, first, you have to go wash your hands in the ocean."

"Why's that?" Bo asked.

"Because, I don't know where they've been… or who they've been on," Constancia replied, smiling innocently.

"Sweet thing, I have no problem with your request. As my daddy said in his proposal to my mama, 'I'd crawl across a burning desert, over barbed wire, and through a field of broken glass just to kiss the spot where you peed last week.'"

I cringed at this latest visual of Bo's homespun remembrance. "I really do hate to miss this little vignette, but Darling's wading in the ocean and now's a good time to rattle his cage." I struggled to my feet, removed my shirt and hat and waddled out into the surf.

"Mr. Darling," I hailed, "Mr. Darling." As I approached him, the floor of the ocean sloped until I was wading through chest-high water.

Darling had turned towards me as a wave of salt water washed into my open mouth. "McFadden, what brings *you* into the realm of Neptune?" he greeted.

I spit the salt water from my mouth, tried to disguise a cringe of pain from stepping on a shard shell, and did my best to carry on with some dignity. "There's a little business matter I need to discuss with you."

"Oh? What business is that?"

"I have something extremely valuable to sell."

"What do you have to sell that I'd be interested in?" he asked suspiciously.

"My silence."

Stalling for time, he pushed his wet hair back from his forehead. "Why would your silence be of value to me?"

"Because it'll keep you out of prison."

"I'm sorry, McFadden. You're obviously playing some sort of game and I'm not privy to the rules."

"This is no game, my thespian friend. You hired the Del Muertos to kill Buck Tolleson. You also hired them to kill Simon Cartier, but the killers were apprehended before that murder could be carried out. The rules are simple once you know them."

Darling was still trying to look relaxed, but the look wasn't convincing. "Who told you such a preposterous tale?"

"Arturo Del Muerto." I paused for a breath and to observe his reaction. "We want twenty thousand dollars—five thousand for me and fifteen thousand for the Del Muertos."

I had clearly taken Darling by surprise, and he scurried to find a response. "Even if this absurd idea were true, why would Del Muerto confess to being my hired killer? And, why would he confess to you?"

"Because I'm a private dick, not a ship's inspector. After he found out I had his partner-in-crime nailed in the act of attempted murder, he was convinced to take me into his confidence. After the Barbadian authorities cuffed him, he confessed to the Tolleson murder—to me, confidentially. He needs money to post bail and cover some legal fees; he had no way of contacting you personally, so he enlisted my help.

"So, let's cut the crap and get down to business, Darling. I don't have the time or patience to continue this little charade." The waves had cooperated until that moment, but, as if they knew I was making an important point, I was slapped in the cheek by a small breaker. Fortunately, my mouth was closed this time.

"Again, just playing along with you, how do I know Del Muerto won't turn me in to get a lighter sentence? Once you submit to a blackmailer, they say you're always in their pocket."

I blinked the salty water from my eyes. "Del Muerto has no interest in seeing you nicked *if* you show your goodwill by helping him out. He's confident that a good attorney will enable him to beat the charges on both islands. Besides, giving you up in a plea bargain wouldn't be good for future business: who'd be willing to hire a cold-blooded killer that ratted out his employer?"

His facial grimaces showed that Darling was clearly struggling with a decision. Then, as another wave bounced by, he suddenly brightened. "You're overlooking one important thing, McFadden."

"What's that?"

"Proof. All the information you've presented is purely circum-stantial. There's not one bit of evidence to link me to Del Muerto or these crimes. It's the word of a brutal hired assassin against the denial of a beloved screen legend."

I decided to run my bluff for all it was worth. "Ah, but I do have the proof… The serial numbers of the hundred-dollar bills in the envelopes you gave the purser to hold for safekeeping were copied for security reasons while in the purser's custody. Some of those same bills—the ones from the first envelope that you used to pay for the Tolleson murder—were confiscated from Del Muerto when he was arrested."

In surfer slang, I'd 'shot the gnarly curl'—Darling slumped and he was the one now spitting out sea water. Wiping his face he muttered, "Even if I agreed to your blatant extortionary demands, I couldn't come up with that kind of money."

"Darling, I told you I'm a detective. I *know* there was a second envelope with another twenty grand entrusted to the purser—an envelope that you never gave to Del Muerto, first, because Cartier wasn't killed and, second, because Del Muerto was arrested before he could return to the ship. *That's* the envelope you'll give me tonight.

"I also have a couple of questions for you. The first one— was Fifi involved in these murders in any way?"

"Fifi?" Darling managed a weak smile. "The only thing she could kill is a flute of champagne."

"My second question concerns motive. May I assume that Cartier had something to do with your expulsion from the studio and that Tolleson was responsible for the loss of your investments?"

Darling sighed and began his story. "I had a lot of my money invested in a couple of 'can't miss' start-up companies in the early sixties. Each of those companies was eventually taken over by Buck Tolleson, who achieved some amazing results for shareholders in the beginning. But, as we were later to find out, after he had inflated the market values of the stocks with false rumors, crooked accounting methods, and overstated performance measurements, he quietly sold off his shares and bled the companies dry. All that was left for us small investors was a few carcasses and a few bleached bones. The money I'd put away during the good years of my career was gone in the twinkling of an eye."

"And Cartier?"

"Cartier took over the studio and decided that because of my waning box office popularity, I didn't figure in future production plans. Veteran actors like me were put out to pasture while the studio retooled and changed its focus to the eighteen to twenty-five demographic. The new roles didn't go to those who could breathe life and drama into their screen creations, but to those who could 'hang ten' on a surfboard and play 'beach blanket bingo.'"

"Two decades is a long time to hold a grudge."

"Not when you've had a wonderful life snatched from your fingers and thrown into the trash bin of oblivion with the other has-beens. It's only because of recent income from my 'comeback' that I've mustered the funds to belatedly pursue revenge."

He straightened as he finished and stared straight at me. "I have a 'business' question for you, McFadden—How do I know that I won't be blackmailed by others?"

"Very simple: I'm the only one who can trace you to the payoff. I didn't tell anyone else because I have no interest in splitting my paltry share with them. Your secret is safe with me... as long as I get paid tonight."

"I confess to some surprise, McFadden. You never impressed me as the type to engage in something as repugnant and despicable as blackmail."

"Don't mount your moral horse so quickly, Darling. Blackmail's not the type of thing I'll boast about at my family reunion, but it's a schoolboy prank compared to murder-for-hire. Extortion isn't pretty but it's a damn site better than hiring someone to do your killing for you.

"Another reason is that blackmailing you instead of sending you to the pen allows me to cut you some slack. I've done some reading on Tolleson and, as my friend, Bo Hatfield, might say—'he needed killing.' In a tug-of-war with my conscience, I finally convinced myself that maybe you're the avenging angel for thousands of little folk who wouldn't be picking through a can of cold Alpo for tonight's dinner if not for financial rape by Tolleson.

"I'll meet you in cabin 1080 at nine o'clock tonight, after dinner. It used to belong to Tolleson and it's still vacant. I thought you'd appreciate the irony."

"All right, McFadden; it appears you're holding all the cards." Darling turned and slowly trudged dejectedly to shore, his stooped back slapped by incoming waves.

When I got back to my group, I saw Girtha reading a paperback, sitting under one of the many coconut palms that fringed the beach. To avoid further burn, she had also wrapped herself from neck to toe in two beach towels, reminding me of one of those Navajo squaws in an R. C. Gorman painting.

Constancia and Bo were nearer the water. She was laying face down on her blanket, her face resting on her crossed arms and the string to her bikini top lying listlessly at her side. He had worked himself into a straddling position over her thighs and had advanced from lotion application to massage.

"Sweet thing, your little old body is just full of tension. You must have a stressful job. Good thing you took a few days off when you did. It's going to take me a while to work out all these knots."

Constancia's only response was to purr and say, "I must admit, for a man with such a hard head you do have soft hands..."

"I was raised on a farm. I had to milk thirty cows every morning before breakfast. Turn over and I'll show you my technique."

Constancia smiled. "I rather suspect your technique was developed in the back seat of a '57 Chevy at the Hoot 'n Holler Drive-In—*not* in the family barn."

"There, too. In both scenarios, I had 'em mooing contently, begging for more." Noticing my return, Bo asked, "Well, old son, how did it go?"

"The trap is sprung courtesy of a few yarns which Darling has no way of checking. Tonight, after dinner, I'll make Darling tip his hand one way or the other." I sat down and outlined the plan, detailing the roles the two of them were yet to play. When I finished, I left them alone and went to join Girtha in the shade.

Thirty minutes later, the horn from the *Kon Tiki* shattered the stillness which prompted the passengers to towel themselves dry and brush off sand for our return trip across the bay. Many were still drowsy from sunbathing naps and slowly packed their beach gear. Others raced back into the water one more time before reluctantly preparing to leave their newfound paradise.

As some of the sun worshippers stood, they unwittingly revealed pink skin in places usually reserved for the pictorial spreads in men's' magazines. Constancia stood and attempted to tie the string to her bikini top. Ever the gentleman, Bo quickly jumped to his feet and volunteered his assistance.

"Ouch!" Constancia shrieked. "You're tying it too tight. You'll have me spilling out in the front—"

"I'm not sure I see a downside to that complaint," Bo snickered. Even so, he loosened his tug.

Once on board, the open bar and infectious island music soon restored the festive atmosphere and revived the party to full swing. Passengers formed a conga line and snaked around the perimeter of the boat—three steps followed by a kick—with one hand on the shoulder in front of them and the other clasping a large paper cup. I began to wonder if free rum punch wasn't the answer to all the problems being experienced around the world. Anytime an international or internecine conflict threatened to erupt, NATO could pass out free samples of rum punch and get the combatants to drop their weapons and form a conga line.

I usually get these thoughts when I experience concern about the outcome of an impending event. Although it seemed I had everything covered, nothing always works according to plan. While I tried to outwardly exude confidence and command of the situation, the reality was that I was still a penny-ante gumshoe with limited homicide experience. My bluff had been successful to this point, but what if my luck ran out? Having Bo and Constancia—and their more extensive law-enforcement experience in this area—as colleagues helped me to rest a little easier.

When the *Kon Tiki* reached the dock, Darling and Fifi headed towards town instead of returning to the ship.

"Aren't you afraid they'll skip?" Bo asked.

"Not any more. The hook is in too deep. Whatever Darling plans to do, he *has* to do it tonight. He'll be back on board before departure."

Dinner that night promised to be an interesting affair. Girtha and I were the first arrivals for a change, followed by Darling and Fifi, Colonel Talbo, Constancia, and Bo in succession.

Our affable waiter, Taboul, appeared and distributed the evening's menus. "Good evening, my esteemed guests. Tonight, our chef is featuring some Martinique specialties, a mix of classic French and Creole."

"What would those be?" Colonel Talbo grumbled.

"Our appetizers are *oursins*, or sea urchins, and *lambi*, or conch; our second course is *callaloo*, a soup made from greens and West Indian herbs; our main course is *colombo*, an Indian curry dish cooked with goat and served on rice with *boudin*, a spicy blood sausage; our featured desert is *amour cache*, a pastry made with coconut jam. While you're thinking and reviewing the menu, may I take your beverage orders?"

"Anything *but* rum punch," our side of the table groaned in unison.

"Perhaps local ale—*biere de Lorraine*, or some bottled Didier Water?"

"I'll have a Manhattan without the sweet vermouth and bitters," the Colonel ordered.

"But," questioned the waiter, "that will be straight bourbon…"

"You're catching on right smartly," the Colonel complimented. "And, I don't eat stuff I can't pronounce. I'll have me some fried ham, rice with red-eye gravy, an ear of silver queen corn, speckled butterbeans with ham hock seasoning, and cornbread. For dessert, I'll have the peach cobbler."

Poor Taboul was scanning the menu in panic mode, clearly befuddled. "I will see what I can do, sir."

"Where have you folks been today?" Talbo asked, looking around the table and seeing all the sunburned faces. "Y'all are as pink as the belly of a newborn sow, especially you, Miz Constancia."

Bo shook his head. "Sweet thing, I tried to get you to turn over and let me put something on your front side."

"What did you have in mind other than your muscle-bound body?" she taunted.

Turning to Colonel Talbo, I answered, "All six of us took a boat ride and went to a remote beach to do a little relaxing." I then turned to Darling and asked, "How about you, Mr. Darling? Are you still relaxed?"

"I expect to be soon," he said soberly, "after I resolve a small contretemps."

I wasn't crazy about the sound of that.

The rest of the dinner was without incident. As usual, the kitchen had even managed to scramble through the larder and find several of the culinary items the Colonel had requested. On cue, Bo and Constancia excused themselves immediately after dessert and left. Girtha and I waited a respectable interval and rose to depart as well, leaving only the Colonel, Lamont Darling, and Fifi finishing a conversation at the table.

"Girtha, I'm afraid you need to go on to the show by yourself," I told her when we were out of earshot. "Bo, Constancia, and I have some business to attend to. I'll see you back in the room tonight." Surprisingly, she responded with a gentle kiss and turned toward the theater. I watched her walk away, and then headed for my meeting.

When I got to cabin 1080, I found Bo and Constancia already waiting inside.

"Did you bring your hardware?" I asked.

Constancia opened her purse and showed me her Beretta, and Bo whipped out his Glock from an ankle holster.

"Very good. As we discussed, you two wait in the bathroom where you can hear everything and come out when you're needed.

Don't be too anxious, though; give Darling enough rope to hang himself. Any thoughts, Bo?"

"Old son, it's your hand—play it. I'm no kibitzer."

"Okay, get in there and keep quiet. Lock the door from the inside in case he gets nosy."

They shut the door and I was alone in the vacant cabin. I paced for a few minutes, then sat down on one of the beds and waited anxiously. An occasional voice in the alleyway got my attention, but the voices faded and the room itself remained eerily quiet. Five minutes passed, then ten minutes—and still no Darling.

I started to worry about imaginary things—like Bo and Constancia making the beast with two backs in the bathroom and her delirious but muffled cries of orgasm drowning out the sounds of me being shot by Darling... like Darling not showing up because he had opted to call my bluff... like him using the twenty thousand to hire another assassin to punch *my* ticket. It was even entirely possible that Darling had alerted the Bogotá-based crime syndicate of my plan and that they agreed to take me out as a freebie—I had, after all, been responsible for removing one of their favored sons from circulation.

As my panic attack grew, I thought of another possible outcome: What if Darling *did* show up and gave me the money? What would I do then? I couldn't take the money because that would make me an accessory after the fact and expose me to extortion charges. On the other hand, I couldn't refuse the money or he would know my evidence was bogus.

This was all getting too confusing. I wish I had thought this out better before I hatched this plan.

Fortunately, my descent into despondency was interrupted by a knock on the door. I got up to admit my visitor and, to my surprise, was not greeted by Darling alone, but by Darling and Fifi who was carrying a bag. Adding further to my surprise was the gun Darling pulled out of his pocket.

"Cruise ships have so many guns on board these days," I said with false bravado. "Does the Screen Actors Guild know you're toting a rod? If they find out, your liability insurance is sure to go up. But I won't say anything if you put it away..."

"That would be wasted effort since it's going to be used."

Ignoring that statement for a moment, I greeted Fifi. "I'm surprised to see you here. I didn't think you'd be involved in the Tolleson murder or the Cartier attempt—"

"She wasn't," Darling answered for her, "but she'll be involved in yours. After our *tête-à-tête* in the ocean this afternoon, I filled Fifi in on my predicament. While she abhors violence as much as I do, she's not anxious to see me serve jail time or to see her standard of living plummet. She's reluctantly agreed to help me with your demise."

"I'm sorry, Mr. McFadden," Fifi said.

I had to admit that she did look genuinely despondent.

"I wish there was some other way, but Lamont's convinced me that you can't be trusted. Wherever we go, we'd have to be looking back, over our shoulders, wondering when you'd put the bite on us again."

"Oh, that's quite all right, Fifi—I totally understand," I said disingenuously. "Does this mean I'm not going to get the twenty grand?" I asked Darling.

"That's a reasonable assumption, McFadden. They say if you want something done right, you have to do it yourself. I would normally prefer to leave these types of sordid things to professionals, but you've backed me into a corner and I don't have time to locate a specialist."

"I don't suppose it'll do any good to say that I'll forget about the money and drop this whole matter if you drop the gun?"

"That's another reasonable assumption. I've heard that you're smarter than you looked. I've also heard that all you have to do is cock these things, point them at the victim, and pull the trigger. With a target as large as you, a miss at this distance is unlikely. Would you agree?"

"You have the physical logistics down pat, Darling, but if you don't mind me offering a few pointers, there are a few other details that need to be considered."

"Such as?"

"Noise for one. Gunshots make a lot of racket, and you pulling the trigger would likely bring a boatload of morbidly curious people trampling over each other to see what was going on."

"A valid point, however, it's one that I've already considered. You see, the *Oslo Aphrodite* has started her engines and is hoisting her anchor as we speak. In a couple of minutes," Darling said, looking at his watch, "those infernally loud horns will blow several times to announce embarkation. A shot during that time is not likely to be heard."

Daunted by his rebuttal, I scrambled for another potential concern. "You also need to consider motive. The suddenness of my death will prompt the authorities to learn everything they can about the cases I've been working on, and they're already aware of my involvement with Cartier and the Del Muertos. It won't take much digging to discover the trail leads to you."

"I've thought of that as well, my good friend. That's why we have to give them a false trail to pursue."

"And, how do you propose we go about doing that?"

"Will you dump the contents of your bag on the bed, dear?"

Fifi walked to the bed and turned her bag upside down. A butcher knife fell out, but she continued shaking the bag—and, out plopped a chicken head.

"I see from the look on your face that you're beginning to get the picture, McFadden. I read about a murder and a drug cartel called Zunimbism in the Miami newspapers. Then on several occasions since we've boarded, I've overheard French-speaking crew members discussing some of the details among themselves. As you know, I was born in France and I speak the language fluently.

"I don't pretend to know *all* the details about Zunimbist executions, but I think I've learned enough to give the authorities an easy explanation for your death. Simply put, my plan is to shoot you, cut your throat, remove your tongue, and insert a chicken head in your mouth—don't worry about salmonella, it's fresh. I just bought it this afternoon in town. I'll then have to remove the bullet and stab you a number of times to mess up the fatal wound. Forensically, it's not foolproof but I doubt they'll do much of an autopsy on you anyway under the circumstances. Finally, there's the matter of some markings on your chest—oh, and I believe they're drawn in your own blood.

"So, it'll be assumed that you were just one more of the many victims of Zunimba. Any other concerns or last thoughts?"

"Yeah, it wouldn't be fair to shoot me right now."

"Why not?"

"I've only got two car payments left."

"Then you won't be around to object to its repossession by the lender. Anything else?"

I rubbed my chin and looked studious. "Well, I could help by drawing a bull's-eye on my chest so you couldn't miss, but it seems that you have other plans for that part of my anatomy. I do like your Zunimbist ritual murder idea, though—all that slicing and dicing will make it impossible for my insurance company to allege suicide and deny the claim."

"I think I can accommodate your—" The first blast of the ship's horn interrupted before he could finish.

"I'm sorry, McFadden, but the bell has tolled and you know what that means." He raised his pistol and pointed it at my head.

"It means the next sound you hear will be my gunshot as it blows your head through the porthole," Bo said as he stepped out of the bathroom, arm extended and braced, gun in hand. Constancia followed him out with her Beretta aimed at a startled Fifi.

"What the..." Darling exclaimed.

As he whipped his head around, I snatched the pistol from his hand. "*Now* who's playing it close, bwana?" I said, admonishing Bo while dabbing the perspiration off my face with a handkerchief. "In another second, I would have been chewing chicken."

"Old son, you were never in any danger," Bo scoffed. As he cuffed Darling and Fifi, he added, "If anything happened to you, sweet thing and I would feel plumb terrible."

"That's right," Constancia added, slipping her Beretta back into her purse.

"And those reassurances are supposed to make me feel better?" I joked with them. Then I offered some sympathy to Darling. "Maybe the warden will cut you a break and let you stage some plays in your spare time—that is, if you're not too sore from being the object of booty bongo at the hands of your fellow inmates in the penitentiary shower room.

"As for you, Fifi, I'm afraid your standard of living *is* going to take a big tumble after all. With your looks, I'd advise you to seek the protection of the biggest dyke you can find once you get inside the cell block. The sex will be frequent and skanky, but at least it'll be monogamous."

Bo stepped forward to lead a dour Lamont and his wailing sidekick to the ship's brig. "Here's an added surprise—I taped this little episode for you." He removed a cassette from a recorder and slipped it into his pocket as he hustled the odd couple out the door.

"Well done," Constancia complimented. "I assume Bo will handle the paperwork and the notifications to the appropriate authorities?"

"Yeah, but he'll be calling on you and me to give written statements on the events preceding the arrest," I answered. "You know... I was just thinking..."

"About what?"

"Two things, actually. First, how much I love the word 'skanky.' It's so onomatopoeic."

A double-take reflected on Constancia's expression at my sudden change in conversational direction, and she shook her head in wonder. "Who would guess you to be an educated man, McFadden?"

"Very few, but I'd rather be an intelligent man."

"What's the difference?"

"I once read that an educated man is one who gets his thinks from someone else. An intelligent man is one who works out his own thinks."

She smiled and asked, "What's the other thing?"

"I hope Colonel Talbo is above reproach."

"Why is that?"

"He's the last person left at our dinner table who hasn't been thrown in jail."

CHAPTER 18

T HE NEXT DAY WAS MONDAY, THE TENTH DAY of the cruise. Girtha, wearing her usual bathrobe and towel-turban ensemble, rousted me when she got out of the shower.

"I figured you would be an early bird," I yawned. "When I got back to the cabin last night, you were dead to the world. You were snoring so loudly, I wedged a towel under the door to keep people in the alleyway from stampeding in fear."

"I do *not* snore! I was pooped! All that sun and rum really did me in."

"I'm not surprised. Bo told me that Martinique is the rum capital of the West Indies. They grow all the ingredients on the island and distill some seventeen different varieties."

"Hurry up and shower, sweetie-kins. I want to go to the early breakfast seating—I'm starved since I missed the midnight buffet."

I briefly filled her in on the events of the previous night but omitted the part about Lamont packing some heat since she was already uptight about my previous brushes with mortality. I simply told her that we had tricked Lamont into a confession and had recorded it on tape for the authorities.

We arrived at our table and were surprised to find Constancia and Bo at the early seating, too. Not surprisingly, Bo was all over her like a three-day tattoo.

"Did you have any problems with Lamont and Fifi?" I asked.

"Nah, they're locked in a couple of cells down below in the off-limits High Security area. My faithful sidekick, Tonto the Tet Wonder, is seeing they get fed and cleaned up. The FBI has some agents on St. Thomas who'll be coming aboard this afternoon to take'em into custody until any jurisdictional issues can be resolved."

"I forgot about that," I mulled. "What a conundrum. They're American citizens outside of U.S. jurisdiction being charged for murder in Jamaica, attempted murder in Barbados, and a second attempted murder aboard a Norwegian ship in the waters of Martinique."

"Most of the Caribbean islands are usually agreeable to extradition requests. They're eager to avoid the expense of lengthy and costly trials," Bo said.

"You were pretty rough on poor Fifi last night," Constancia said with a grin.

"I was trying to prepare her for the rough nights ahead. You know as well as I do that with that face and figure, she'll be passed around like kielbasa hors d'oeuvres at a Polish wedding reception."

Constancia smiled. "Sadly, that's true. If you ever visit a women's prison, you'll hear a lot of them refer to themselves as a 'LURD.'"

"What's a LURD?" Girtha asked innocently.

"Lesbian Until Release Date," Constancia replied.

"Speaking of weddings, I'll never forget the last one I went to," Bo said.

"I'll bet you've never been to a wedding where the bride wasn't eight months pregnant, waddling down the isle with four little barefoot bastards picking their noses and hanging on to the hem of her dress, and marrying a close relative who was being nudged to the altar by a shotgun held at his back." Constancia teased.

"That's true for most of the weddings in my part of the country," Bo acknowledged. "My own wedding had to be postponed a couple of times until enough bridesmaids could be bailed out of the slammer to attend it."

"You were married?" Constancia asked in disbelief.

"That's a fact, sweet thing."

"How long did your marriage last?"

"One day."

"One day? What happened?"

"Right after the wedding ceremony, my mother-in-law opened the bathroom door at the church and caught me with my pants down."

"What's wrong with that? She should have knocked first."

"I was in there with the naked maid of honor."

I shook my head. "That must be some kind of record, Bo. I've had bowel movements that lasted longer than your marriage."

"My intentions are good; it's just that I get easily distracted," Bo said, shaking his head in comic introspection. "By the way, do you need me or Constancia today? She wants to go shopping and I told her I'd go along and carry her packages."

"That good deed shouldn't go unrewarded," I praised.

"My thoughts exactly, old son. Every good boy deserves favor."

"I'll do you a favor and let you rub my feet when we get back to the ship from St. Thomas," Constancia teased.

"Sweet thing, the best thing you can do for your feet is to wrap them around my waist."

"Wait—did you say we were in St. Thomas today?" Girtha interrupted.

"You got it," Bo replied. "It's the best shopping destination in the Caribbean for Americans. They have free port status and have one of the highest duty-free quotas of any place in the world."

"Weee!" Girtha squealed. "Just what I was waiting for. I was afraid that after missing Martinique, I wouldn't have another chance to shop on this trip."

"Martinique's not good for shopping," Bo said. "They only give you a twenty per cent discount on credit card and traveler's check purchases. You can save some real coin in the shops of Charlotte Amalie. They've got great bargains on jewelry, cigarettes, and perfume, but especially liquor."

"Why don't you come with us, Girtha?" Constancia asked. "We'd love to have your company. Plus, I would prefer to have a chaperone, anyway."

"Chauncey, can you come with us?" Girtha asked.

"No, I'm afraid I'll have to skip your little spree. I've got some business to take care of aboard the ship. I'm sure the three of you will have a good enough time. Constancia, let's talk tonight. I'll need your help tomorrow in Santo Domingo when we dock in the Dominican Republic."

"Some more loose ends to tie up, old son?" Bo asked. "I thought you'd nabbed all the evil-doers."

"The puzzle's still missing a few pieces. I'd love to go with you guys, but duty calls."

After the shore-bound threesome finished their eggs Benedict, they left, already planning some destinations. I sat a while longer, nursing my orange juice before heading to the bridge in search of Captain Nelson. I found him in front of the control panel, just as the engines were being cut and the anchor was dropped.

"Good morning, Captain. I thought I'd check in and have a quick visit. Have you seen Bo's morning report?"

"Yes, I have," he mused, "and I must say, you're cutting a pretty wide swath though my passenger list. If this cruise lasts much longer, I'll be steering a ghost ship back into the Port of Miami." He exhaled a partial chuckle. "Your visit is timely, though; as soon as we got docked, I was going to have you paged. The FBI called and alerted me that they would be aboard this afternoon to take the two prisoners into custody. They want to talk to you as well. Can you make yourself available at fourteen hundred hours?"

"I was wondering when I'd be dragged in by their net. Two o'clock is fine. Almost all your passengers will be in port today, so the feds should be able to hustle Darling and Fifi ashore without a lot of fanfare."

"That's my hope, as well," Nelson said with relief. "I'm glad to see that you evaded another attempt on your life. I hope when the ship gets back to Miami, you're able to leave under your own steam and not be carted off in a black vinyl body bag.

"By the way, how's your investigation into Amundson's murder progressing? That is, after all, the reason you were hired in the first place."

Recalling one of Bo's earlier statements, I repeated, "My intentions are good; it's just that I get easily distracted. I've been working on his case on and off. I should have a better report after I do some research tomorrow in the Dominican Republic." My business finished, I turned for the door. "I'll catch you later. I need to see Boyd Fowler."

When I reached the Radio Room, I found another crew member at the console and Fowler in Bruno Helmje's old office. "Did you get promoted, Boyd? If so, congratulations are in order."

"No such luck. I'm just filling in until a decision is announced."

"By any chance, did a response ever come in from the FBI's cryptology lab? They haven't had a lot of time I suppose but I'm anxious."

"Nothing for you yet, Mr. McFadden," Boyd replied after scanning his log. "Do you want me to send a follow-up to Lieutenant Alameda in Miami?"

"I'll tell you what," I said, after weighing several courses of action. "Lieutenant Alameda's not in Miami at the moment. Send a radiogram directly to the FBI's Cryptanalysis and Racketeering Records Analysis Unit in Quantico, Virginia. "Here I said," writing the addressee information on a piece of paper and handing it to Boyd. "Ask them to send a status report on their decryption progress on Helmje's coded radiograms to the *Oslo Aphrodite* and sign Lieutenant Alameda's name to it. When their response comes in, give it to me. I'll be sure she gets it."

"You got it, Mr. Ship's Inspector," Boyd said with a smile.

I patted him on the back and left.

After partaking of a little blackjack at the casino and some lunch at the poolside buffet, I returned to my cabin with the hope of catching some quiet relaxation. A resulting descent into drowsiness was shattered by a knock on my door at a quarter past two. I opened it and greeted a distinguished-looking black gentleman in a dark suit. His close-cropped hair and mustache were well along in their transition from black to gray, suggesting that he was on the other side of fifty. He reached inside his coat pocket and flashed a photo ID.

"I'm Special Agent Broomfield Tatum with the FBI. I presume you're Chauncey McFadden?"

"You got me!" I raised my hands. "Are you here about the Gideon Bible I stole from that Miami hotel room or the invalid child I tossed in the ocean to gain a seat on the lifeboat?"

"You can keep the Bible," he replied, chuckling. "We don't investigate thefts of less than $10,000. As far as chucking the crippled kid into the briny deep, as long as it was in international waters and he wasn't an American citizen, you'll never appear on our most wanted list."

I invited the agent inside and he picked up some brochures from my nightstand.

"This is a pretty swanky ship," he said, thumbing through some pages. "I'm always surprised when a homicide occurs on one of these floating palaces."

"Murders don't consult bank accounts before they occur. Have you ever been on a cruise?" I asked.

He smiled. "Never had the desire. My ancestors had some bad experiences with one-way cruises from Africa to the colonies back in the seventeenth and eighteenth centuries."

"I understand," I said, returning the smile. "My forebears were shackled to oars and forced to row Romans around the Mediterranean. That must have been a real bitch, especially when the Captain wanted to water-ski." Since I didn't get as hearty a response as I'd hoped for, I jumped to another discussion.

"Before your inquiries begin, can you take a minute and explain FBI jurisdiction regarding crimes committed on cruise ships? The ship's security officer gave me a thumbnail sketch, but it's still a little muddled."

"It's confusing to me as well, and I've been an agent for better than thirty years," he confessed. "The authority of the FBI to investigate crimes and enforce laws on cruise ships—on the high seas or territorial waters of the U.S.—depends on several factors: the location of the vessel, the ownership of the vessel, the nationalities of the victim and the perpetrator, the points of embarkation and debarkation, and the country in which the vessel is flagged.

"Generally speaking, the U.S. has jurisdiction over crimes committed on a ship when any of the following factors are present. The first is if the vessel has U.S. ownership and it's within the territorial waters of the U.S., *and* out of the jurisdiction of any other particular nation. Another is when the crime is committed by or against a U.S. national and occurs outside the jurisdiction of any nation. Another is when the crime occurs in U.S. territorial waters—within twelve miles of the coast—regardless of the nationality of the victim, the perpetrator, or the vessel. A final one is when the victim or perpetrator is a U.S. national on any vessel during a voyage that has departed from or will arrive in a U.S. port.

"Where it really gets complicated is when the crime occurs outside the territorial waters of the U.S.," Tatum continued. "Our ability to investigate an incident then depends on the laws of, and treaties with, other sovereign nations *and* international law, as well our own maritime code.

"In these cases, FBI legal attachés, who're posted worldwide in offices known as legats, work with local officials and authorities in conducting investigations. Most countries welcome our help in collecting evidence and frequently invite us to play a larger role."

"Does the FBI have any legats in the Caribbean?"

"Bridgetown, Barbados, and Santo Domingo on Hispaniola."

"Are many crimes reported aboard cruise ships?"

Tatum shrugged. "Not when you consider the number of passengers who sail each year. I was reading some statistics the other day in a regional bulletin and, if I remember correctly, the FBI opened about two-hundred and fifty cases of crimes on the high seas in the past five years, or fifty a year. About seventy percent of those happened on cruise ships; the rest took place on private vessels, commercial ships, and oil rigs.

"Of the cruise ship crimes, over half were sexual assaults and about a quarter were physical assaults. Only about five percent were missing persons cases. While foul play was suspected in a few of them, the majority were deemed to be accidents or suicides. The bodies were rarely found and there were no prosecutions due to lack of conclusive evidence and the scattering of witnesses once the ships reach their points of origin. There were thirteen death investigations on cruise ships during this five year period but only one conviction, to date. The rest are still pending."

I soberly reflected on this data. "Based upon my limited cruise experience, and what I've learned about the drug-smuggling industry, I have a feeling that the murder rate is getting ready to pick up. It seems the cartels and drug bosses now think it's easier to smuggle drugs into the U.S. aboard cruise ships than to sneak them into the Florida Keys on speedboats in the dead of night."

"Actually, it's that experience I'm here to talk to you about, Mr. McFadden," Tatum said, removing the wrapper from a cigar. "To start off, what can you tell me about the murder of Bruno Helmje?"

"Not much. I was searching a cabin when I was knocked unconscious from behind. When I came to, I discovered a gray duffel bag in the closet. I opened the drawstring and saw a bloody face looking up at me from inside the bag. I went to fetch Captain Nelson but when I returned with him, the bag was gone. Later, when Helmje turned up missing, I realized it was him in the bag— I'd only met him once, briefly, before that."

"I understand that you also identified the killer."

"Yeah, a waiter by the name of Toussaint L'Enfant. He was a Zunimbist disciple placed on board to discover the whereabouts of a missing drug shipment. He was shot in the act of committing a crime. His confession was made on his deathbed so I have no proof to offer you other than my humble testimony."

"That's not a problem. The Haitian authorities have already closed the case, happy to be rid of him. He was a petty criminal with a record longer than a walk to a urinal at a football stadium. They don't even want a statement from you."

Tatum paused to light his stogie and get it started. "However, the FBI might have some interest in L'Enfant's killer. You indicated to Captain Nelson that he may have been an American."

"I found the waiter dying in a room where, just moments before, he'd been with a comic by the name of Joey Morton. Joey is running for his life and I doubt he'll ever be discovered by anybody other than some intrepid explorer who's hacked his way through five hundred miles of dense jungle."

"We'll leave him to the mosquitoes and alligators, then. Venezuela won't even give lip service to an investigation since the victim isn't one of their citizens.

"Moving on, according to the security officer's report, you set a trap and snared the party who hired the infamous Del Muertos to kill Buck Tolleson and Simon Cartier."

"That's right," I replied with more than a tinge of insuppressible pride in my voice. "We have three eyewitnesses and a tape recording of the confession."

"I have the recording already," Tatum acknowledged. "I left Hatfield forms on which you witnesses are to record your statements. Because of the logistics involved, they can be returned to me at this address." He handed me his business card.

"Though Darling and his consort, Fifi, are both American citizens, I assume you involved the Norwegian and Martinique authorities since the ship is owned by and sails under the flag of the former and is located in the territorial waters of the latter?"

"You're a quick study, Mr. McFadden. Did you ever think of law enforcement as a career?"

"Occasionally, I yearn for the stability of sustained employment and regular paychecks, but I don't handle authority very well and hate working in a structured environment with defined procedures and processes. While I might generate my share of arrests and convictions, my methodologies and work ethic would probably cause me to be under constant investigation by Internal Affairs."

"Message received," Tatum laughed. "Well done; keep up the good work," he commended while shaking my hand. "Your efforts have kept my case load from growing larger."

And, with that, he was gone.

My ego sufficiently fluffed, and my work with the FBI complete, I made myself comfortable and resumed my nap.

I was ready to rise when Girtha arrived back in the cabin right before the five o'clock deadline. She staggered through the door and plopped on her bed as I lifted myself up onto an elbow. "I... am... bushed," she said, easing her shoes off and fanning herself with a magazine. "I've never walked so much in my life!"

"Where are your purchases? I thought you'd be wobbling behind a teetering stack of boxes."

"Believe it or not, I just bought a few pieces of jewelry, which are in my bag. I also bought you some of that expensive brandy you like—it was half the L.A. price. And, the liquor store delivers directly to the ship. The room steward will deliver it to our cabin the morning of our arrival in Miami. I even stayed under the exemption, so we won't have to pay customs duty on it. But... Chauncey... when will you be through with this case? We've only got a couple of days left on the cruise and we've hardly spent any time together."

"I *could* have it wrapped up as early as tomorrow, but my expectations have been thwarted in the past.

"You have to remember that detectives have muses just like authors, poets, composers, painters, or any other artist. The detective's muse is different, though. While our muse is also a source for inspiration, it doesn't always manifest itself in impromptu creative genius. Rather, it delights in having us sprint after red herrings and form false conclusions from misleading evidence. Our muse is frustrating in that it appears on its own timetable, not at the points in an investigation when its guidance is most sorely needed. Although I've frequently prayed to my muse for direction, it has proven to be dilatory at best and indifferent at worst.

"So, to respond to your plea, I assure you I'm working toward a resolution as promptly as possible. But enough of work already; let's get changed and tie the feedbag on."

Our dinners were getting increasingly intimate since attendance had dwindled down to a quintet. Tonight, Colonel Talbo continued his education of Taboul on the joys of cooking with lard, while Girtha and Constancia regaled us with information about the bargains they'd captured through their aggressive negotiating techniques.

After dinner, I pulled Constancia aside. "I need your help tomorrow. Can you go ashore with me to Santo Domingo? I want to rent a car and visit the Sotomayer family in Santa Cruz de Concepçion, a little town north of the capital. I believe they can provide some insight into the murder of Lars Amundson. Since they're located in the boonies and my Spanish isn't all that fluent..."

Constancia shrugged. "How can I refuse? After all, I have an interest in Amundson, as well—he was killed in my backyard. I'll be glad to go along with you as an interpreter; but, remember, I have no jurisdiction in Hispaniola."

"Nor do I, but both of us will be acting in an unofficial capacity and I'll make that clearly understood. Let's go to the Radio Room, call the Sotomayers, and ask to see them late tomorrow afternoon. Tell them it's a matter of utmost urgency and concerns their son, Julio. Amundson had a little episode with their underage daughter a few months back and it may have some bearing upon his death. I'll explain all of this to you tomorrow."

Constancia called while I fidgeted. She started the conversation off in Spanish but switched to English after a moment, grabbed a pencil and pad, and began writing. I looked over her shoulder and saw that she was jotting down directions. She spoke a little more Spanish, then hung up and looked over at me.

"We're in."

CHAPTER 19

T HE NEXT DAY WAS TUESDAY AND THE ELEVENTH DAY
of the cruise. According to the itinerary, we were to arrive in
our final port at noon and not depart until two the following
morning.

I got up, showered, dressed, and studied the map of the
Dominican Republic. Santo Domingo was on the southeast corner
of the island, hugging the Caribbean Sea and sprawling around the
mouth of the Ozama River. Santa Cruz de Concepçion was twenty-
five miles northeast. We should be able to get there and back before
dark.

Girtha stirred, removed her sleeping mask, and mumbled, "If
this is Tuesday, we must be in…"

"Santo Domingo," I finished. "I have business ashore so, I'm
afraid you're on your own again."

Girtha raised herself and leaned back against her pillow incline.
"There's not going to be any danger is there?"

"No, I simply have to interview a few people. Constancia is
going with me, anyway, so I'll have someone watching my back in
any event. What do you have planned for today?"

"I've run out of money so serious shopping's out of the
question. Santo Domingo is so full of history though that I think
I'll take a couple of tours." She reached over to the table for the *Sea
Compass* and began reading. "They have a colonial old city tour that

looks interesting. It visits the Cathedral of Santa Maria La Menor, the oldest cathedral in the Americas; oh, it also has the tomb of Christopher Columbus. There's also the Alcazar, the palace built for Columbus's son, Diego, and his wife, the niece of King Ferdinand of Spain. We'll also see the Casa Del Cordon, the oldest house in the western hemisphere; Atarazana, the oldest commercial street in the New World; the oldest university in the Americas; and—"

"Thanks," I interrupted with a laugh. "Remember, I used to teach history in East L.A., before we ran out of students due to the mandatory sentencing law that extended jail time for drug peddlers and those using firearms in commissions of felonies." I left her to her reading and headed out the door.

I met Constancia in the public lounge a few minutes before two and we descended the gangway to the pier. A crew member stationed at the bottom directed us to a rental car agency at a hotel a few blocks away, but after completing the paperwork, I was having second thoughts about renting the car.

"What's the matter?" Constancia asked noting my frown.

"I hope I'm being charged in local currency because I see too many zeros here. I also had to buy a local license."

Constancia looked at the contract. "The exchange rate is thirty pesos to the dollar so you're paying about twenty U.S. dollars, big guy."

"I also noted that I'll have to drive on the left side of the road."

"Not to worry. It only takes a few minutes to mentally adjust."

"It also says here that Dominican law allows visitors to be detained if they're involved in an accident in which injuries are sustained."

Constancia shrugged. "In that case, if you hit someone, back over them again and we'll prop the dead body up by the side of the road with a couple of woven baskets—people will think it's a vendor."

I wasn't totally reassured but, with Constancia providing directions, we left the daring architecture, spacious boulevards, beautiful parks, and sun-drenched beaches of Santo Domingo and found the Autopista Duarte, the highway that connects Santo Domingo with Puerto Plata on the northern coast. Before long, I started to relax and enjoy the geography of the island's interior, which was exceptionally diverse. We drove through mountains of lush foliage dappled with coffee plantations and a few distilleries. Beyond the mountains were fertile valleys of tobacco, bananas, sugar cane, and coffee. It was easy to see why Columbus had left testamentary instructions to be buried here on Hispaniola.

Our exit was a dirt road that eventually meandered through several small villages and farms. Docile cows crossing the road paid scant attention as I braked to permit their passage. I did manage to speed by a few chickens and roust them into flight from the fresh meadow muffins they were pecking in the middle of the road, deposits plopped down by their bovine hosts.

At the crest of a hill at the end of a gravel road was a resplendent hacienda. Its sparkling white stucco reminded me of the hillside abodes of Santorini and was enlivened by a red tile roof and arched windows that were nestled securely behind black steel bars.

We parked our car on a circular brick driveway and walked up to a massive dark wooden door. A minute after we rang the doorbell, a diminutive elderly lady wearing a black dress and white apron opened the door. The skin on her face and hands was wrinkled and deeply tanned, the result of genetic inheritance, I thought, rather than the ravages of outdoor work in the tropical sun.

"*Vinimos a ver al señor y señora Sotomayer,*" Constancia said.

"*Los están esperando. Por favor síganme.*"

We followed the maid into a large *sala* and responded to her hand gesture by taking a seat.

"Don't look surprised by anything I say," I warned Constancia after the maid's departure. While I have a *few* facts," I continued while squirming my way into the tight leather chair, "they're sprinkled among pure conjecture—this is largely a fishing expedition."

"Just don't expect me to hold the bait bucket. My presence here could subject me to professional inquiry and sanction, even if I am off-duty."

While waiting, I looked around the formal living room. The windows reached from floor to ceiling and were framed by heavy drapes, billowed at the top and indented at the waist by tiebacks of golden cord. The dark wood furniture looked old, expensive, and hand-carved. The upholstery was sumptuous but threadbare, which suggested that the family fortune may have declined from a cascade to a trickle.

Unusual were the dozens of pictures, many in gilded frames that sat on every imaginable surface—the mantel, credenzas, tables, shelves. A few were yellowish prints of older couples—presumably ancestors—in stiff poses, formal surroundings, and dour faces. The women wore flamboyant silk hats, the size of Mexican sombreros, and the men had pomaded black handlebar mustaches that spanned from ear to ear. Many of the men were dressed in dashing uniforms with epaulets on the shoulders and medals pinned to their chests. I wondered whether the medals had been earned or purchased.

Most of the pictures, however, were contemporary photos of two children and ranged from infancy to young adulthood. The boy looked a few years older and was quite handsome. His dark hair, sparkling eyes, and flashing smile were very camera-friendly. The young lady, whose stunning beauty was equally as photogenic, was his distaff counterpart. The similarity of physical features suggested a sibling relationship. Equally obvious was their affection for each other, which I based on their gestures and facial expressions—many photos showed them embracing and they seemed to go everywhere together: in bathing suits by a pool, under a pergola by tennis courts, on horseback, leaning against a sports car, in soccer attire, or in formal clothes.

Equally as captivating were the dozens of paintings in ornate frames which fought for wall space. From my previous experience as a security guard at a museum art gallery, I recognized the pictures as reproductions of works hanging in the El Prado Museum in Madrid. Nonetheless, I was impressed with the selection, which included erstwhile members of the Spanish school—Bartolomé Bermejo, Pedro Berruguete, Luis de Morales, El Greco, Alonso Cano, Zurbarán, Murillo, and Goya.

My admiration of the remarkable faux brushwork was interrupted by the appearance of a distinguished looking couple who entered the room together. The man, bearing a remarkable resemblance to Gilbert Roland, was attired in a black silk suit, black shirt, and black tie. The woman, bearing an equally remarkable resemblance to Katy Jurado, was draped in a conservative black taffeta dress, which covered her body from neck to floor. Her dark hair was piled on her head and held in place by several pearl combs. I suspected them to be in their early fifties, but they appeared to have, at least temporarily, stonewalled the physical manifestations of advancing age.

The gentleman greeted us in a quiet voice. "Good afternoon, Miss Alameda... Mr. McFadden. I am Rigoberto Sotomayer and this is my wife, Isabela." She nodded and waited dutifully as he held the back of her chair, insuring that she was seated before selecting a matching wing chair for himself.

"May we offer you a *bebida*—something to drink?"

"No, thanks," I responded. "We won't be taking up much of your time. I appreciate you granting us an audience on such short notice. I 'm also grateful that you speak English, since my Spanish is somewhat rusty."

"Isabela and I both attended college in your country. In fact, that is where we met," Rigoberto said, exchanging brief smiles with his wife.

I waved my hand around the room. "These are some great pictures you have there," I complimented, ending my sweep by indicating the more recent photographs.

"Thank you. Those are of our son, Julio, and our daughter, María Cristina," Rigoberto replied. He then decided to dispense with further introductions and get directly to the point. "Your call intrigued me," he said with more weariness than intrigue. "Miss Alameda, you mentioned that Mr. McFadden is a private detective from Los Angeles and you are a police official from Miami."

"That's correct," I answered to draw the attention away from Constancia.

"She also said that you had a matter to discuss which involved my son, Julio."

"That's correct as well." Since he wanted to get to the point, I decided to hop on board beside him. "Did you know Lars Amundson? He was second-in-command of the *Oslo Aphrodite,* a Nordic Caribbean Cruise Line ship."

The couple exchanged pained expressions before Mr. Sotomayer replied stiffly. "We met Mr. Amundson on one very unfortunate occasion, yes."

"Did you know Mr. Amundson was murdered in Miami about two weeks ago?"

The Sotomayers again exchanged glances, their discomfort visibly mounting. "We were aware of that as well, yes. We receive the *Miami Herald* here in the Dominican Republic. But what does that have to do with us and our son, Julio?"

"Folks, I regret being the bearer of bad tidings but I believe your son, Julio, may be responsible for Amundson's murder."

Mrs. Sotomayer gasped and Mr. Sotomayer's face grimaced and hardened. "Why would my son want to murder Mr. Amundson?"

I replied with as much empathy as I could muster. "I'm aware of the 'embarrassment' that Mr. Amundson's liaison with your young daughter, María Cristina, caused your family and of your inability to get him to accept his responsibility—financial and otherwise—in that matter. Since your family's honor could be restored by Amundson's death, your culpability in his demise is not an unreasonable suspicion."

"What proof do you have to support this allegation?" Mr. Sotomayer asked quietly.

"I had the passenger records of every airline that flies between Santo Domingo and Miami checked out. Your son flew to Miami two days before the murder on American flight 604 and flew back to Santo Domingo on American flight 605 the afternoon of the murder."

"I recall that my son was in Miami on business during that time but that does not make him a murderer."

"The doorman at the hotel where your son was staying flagged a taxi at Julio's request to take him to the parking garage at the Port of Miami, the place where Amundson was killed."

"That is still little more than circumstantial evidence—can you place my son at the scene of the crime at the time of death?"

"The CSI unit found a baggage claim ticket underneath a car adjacent to Amundson's. They checked it out with the airline and discovered that it belonged to Julio. He was there all right. And, I'm afraid men have gone to the gallows on far less evidence."

"Why wasn't my son arrested if your case is so…" he paused, searching for an appropriate English term, "… ironclad?"

"The district attorney wasn't aware of the situation involving Amundson and your family. While opportunity for the crime had been established, motive was not known at the time."

The Sotomayers looked at each other yet again, once again exchanging pained expressions. Several moments passed before Rigoberto sighed deeply and spoke. "This is all a rather moot point now, Mr. McFadden." He reached down to a coffee table and handed Constancia a Spanish newspaper folded to the *Obituario* section.

Constancia scanned the page, her brow furrowing further with each line. She finally looked up at me in surprise. "It seems that Julio died two weeks ago, here in the Dominican Republic. He was killed in an automobile accident."

My mouth dropped as I struggled to process this sudden piece of information. I finally managed to stammer, "Please accept our sincere condolences on the loss of your son. We were unaware of his death…"

Mrs. Sotomayer dabbed at the corner of her eyes with a handkerchief while her husband patted her arm.

"He had just returned from Miami and was on his way home from the Las Americas International Airport in Santo Domingo when his car ran off the road and rolled over a precipice. We are still puzzled by this occurrence—Julio was a good driver; in fact, he raced professionally on the international circuit. He knew that road like the back of his hand and had taken it a thousand times. It does not make any sense. We are puzzled which has made our mourning more difficult."

"Were the authorities able to pinpoint the *cause* of the crash— a contributing factor like mechanical failure, excessive speed, alcohol, drugs, hit-and-run… anything that might offer an explanation?"

"No," Mr. Sotomayer replied. "They found only the tire marks where his car left the road."

"Then I share your bewilderment. We just took that same road and it didn't appear to contain any undue risks, particularly to a knowledgeable driver… Further begging your pardon, I must ask: How did María take his death?"

The Sotomayers looked at each other again; their grief even more palpable. "She was devastated by the news, of course," the father began. "... She and Julio were so close. We think her brother's death... caused her to lose the baby."

"Please accept our condolences again," was all I could manage. The grief was starting to pile up like wet leaves in a clogged gutter. "Would it be possible to talk to your daughter?"

"Absolutely not," Rigoberto snapped. "She is undergoing psychiatric care at a sanitarium and is not to be disturbed. Her emotional condition is very fragile."

"We're sorry to hear that," I said in a condolatory mumble, as sorry to find that we couldn't speak with her as I was to hear about her condition. "I guess that ties up all the loose ends..."

"How do you mean?" Rigoberto asked.

"On Lars Amundson's death. While it's not the resolution we expected, it does close the file. It's one less unsolved murder for Miami Homicide and one more collected fee for me." I winced in embarrassment at the last words as soon as I said them.

"There is one problem with your explanation," Mr. Sotomayer said, ignoring or not grasping my insensitive social gaffe.

"What do you mean?"

"My son did not murder Amundson."

Startled again, I struggled to respond. "Please, tell us; why do you think that?"

"It is true that Julio went to Miami: Isabela and I thought the purpose of his trip was business. It wasn't until later that we learned his plan had been to kill the defiler of his sister, our daughter. Julio had contacted a friend in Miami; someone named 'Rubio', who found the garage where the cruise ship staff parks their cars while they're at sea. He also obtained Amundson's license number. Once Rubio located Amundson's car in the garage, he parked in a vacant space nearby and called my son at the hotel. However, my son—after reaching the garage and upon further reflection—could not carry out his vengeance. He called it off and they left the garage without further action.

"Julio phoned me from the Miami airport; he was very distraught and apologetic that he had not completed his mission. I was thankful that he had not and urged him to come home immediately. That was the last time I talked to Julio. He arrived in Santo Domingo from Miami that afternoon but never made it home."

I looked at Constancia, searching for a reaction. It was possible that Rigoberto had concocted this story in an effort to save his son's reputation. However, I was inclined to believe him since nothing in Julio's background suggested he might be capable of such a cold-blooded act.

"I guess that takes us back to square one. Do you have any questions?" I asked Constancia.

"Just one," she answered. "Did María Cristina consider having an abortion after her pregnancy had been confirmed? That would have been a solution to the problem."

"No," Rigoberto replied firmly. "We are staunch Catholics. Such an act would have been against our faith."

I'd gotten pretty much what we came for so I motioned to Constancia and we got to our feet. I shook Rigoberto's hand while Constancia embraced Isabella and kissed her cheek.

The drive back to town and the rental car agency was quiet for the first few miles. Then Constancia turned to me and broke the silence.

"Do you know what went down back there?"

I pushed back from the steering wheel and took a deep breath. "I think so. I suspect that the reason Julio could not go through with Amundson's murder was because he knew Lars was not the father of María Cristina's baby."

"Then who was?"

"Julio."

My conclusion led to another period of silence, which was again broken by Constancia. "Incest is a nasty accusation—particularly, since it involves a minor *and* a respectable culprit who's already deceased."

"That's why I backed off. The idea didn't occur to me until I saw all those pictures of Julio and María Cristina. My guess is that María Cristina and Julio had unprotected sex in a moment of passion. Then, afraid that María Cristina might become pregnant, they panicked and devised a plot to conceal their incestuous act—the *other* kind of love that dares not speak its name as Oscar Wilde might say—and replace it with a less damaging explanation.

"Then Amundson was just in the wrong place at the wrong time," Constancia concluded.

"I believe María Cristina picked the unattached Lars out at that embassy party, seduced him, and lured him into a compromising situation. She and Julio used Lars as a cat's-paw and set him up to hide the intimacy of their own relationship. When Maria and Lars were 'discovered' doing the dirty boogie—an event the two siblings had prearranged—the family and society assumed that the innocent cloistered youth had been taken advantage of by an older, experienced man of the world.

"If pregnancy from her union with Julio did result, they not only had a fall guy already set up to take the paternity rap, but a wealthy source of child support even if Lars rejected a matrimonial solution."

"McFadden," Constancia said, shaking her head slowly, "I'll grant you one thing: you sure can build a sand castle from a bucket of dirt."

"Wait,—the castle gets bigger. When it became clear that Amundson was going to balk at playing daddy, he had to be silenced to prevent any medical and legal inquiries into parenthood that Amundson might initiate in response to their charges. When Julio realized he couldn't kill an innocent man, he committed suicide rather than face the disgrace and consequences of his sexual misdeed. In essence, he took his own life out of shame. Why else would a skilled driver's car swerve over a precipice on a road he knew so well?

"The sad part is that Maria's recovery may take considerably longer than her doctors think."

"Why is that?"

"My guess is she's not grieving for her lost fetus, but for her lost love—Julio. While Maria Cristina might be subject to *some* social stigma as the single mother of a love child, it would have been much worse if the child's true paternity had become public knowledge. Society may disapprove of children born out of wedlock, but they are downright nasty where incest is concerned.

"And, you know the crazy irony of it all? Since Maria Cristina lost the baby when she learned of her brother's death, poor Julio sacrificed his life for naught."

Constancia wiped some imaginary tears from her eyes. "This is getting more melodramatic than I can stand."

"Keep your hanky out. The irony goes even farther. If Julio had just waited, he wouldn't have had to commit suicide. Lars wound up getting murdered that same day anyway."

"So, who's your suspect now? Haven't you ruled out the Zunimbists?"

"Initially, I doubted their involvement because the markings on Amundson's chest seemed inconsistent with those on other victims. But, now, I'm not so sure. I keep getting this strange feeling that someone is playing with my mind."

"Well, I must admit that I'm impressed with your powers of deduction. I readily confess that it would have taken me longer to reach the conclusions you were able to draw on the spot."

I was buoyed by Constancia's comments. Her recognition of me as a fellow professional was important to my self-worth. I don't know whether it stemmed from my basic insecurities or from my desire to wrest approval from such a formidable force.

"Thanks, but I have a confession to make—a couple of facts helped guide me toward my brilliant hypotheses."

Constancia laughed. "*Now* the truth comes out. Spill it."

"The first is that Julio could not physically have murdered Lars."

"And, why is that, hotshot?"

"At our initial meeting in your office, you reviewed the ME's report, which stated that the killer was right-handed because of the left-to-right angle of the slash across the throat."

Constancia reflected a moment. "That's right; the report did contain that statement."

"Now, do you recall the picture we just saw of Julio playing tennis?"

"Not in any detail…"

"Julio was holding the racket in his *left* hand—he was a southpaw."

"Very good, McFadden—that, he was. Okay, what's the other fact?"

"When I was reading through Amundson's personnel dossier in Erickson's office, I noticed something interesting in the medical portion of his records."

Constancia paused for a moment before slowly providing a logical guess. "I think I know where this is headed. Amundson was firing blanks—he had a medical condition that would have made fatherhood impossible."

"Congratulations! You get to move on to the bonus round. You're right on target. Lars had a vasectomy three years ago. That's why he ignored the accusations and demands of the Sotomayers."

"It sounds like you have things pretty well wrapped up."

"Not quite. There's still the matter of finding the identity of Amundson's killer, which may reveal some other information of value to law enforcement authorities."

The rest of the trip was spent in idle chatter, and Constancia and I parted ways after we returned the rental car. She was meeting Bo at a nightclub to have a few drinks and do the *merengue* before returning to the ship. But I wasn't really in a partying mood, so I returned to the *Oslo Aphrodite* and headed to the Viking Lounge, hoping a few drinks might coax an appearance from my reluctant muse. While nursing my second refill, the public address system came on and paged me to the Radio Room.

When I arrived, Boyd was there completing a pink sheet from a notepad. "This just came in for you, Mr. McFadden."

The telephone message was from the FBI. I read it and shook my head. My suspicions had been confirmed, and the last pieces of the puzzle were beginning to fall into place. I tucked the note into my pocket and returned to my cabin to wait.

Two hours later, at 7:00, my phone rang. "McFadden, I've just been informed that I'll be coming into some important information later this evening that you'll want to have. It's confidential, so can you meet me in my cabin at midnight?"

"Sure. What's your cabin number?"

"It's Suite A on the VIP Deck."

I whistled. "That's pretty rarified atmosphere. They must pay you cops more than I thought."

She laughed. "I don't vacation often, so when I do, I go first-class. The suites are bigger and have a door leading to a private deck overlooking the ocean. Speaking of private, remember to come alone."

After we hung up, I called the Security Office. "Bo, I need to ask another favor. I'm meeting Constancia at midnight in her cabin—Suite A on the VIP Deck, and I need you to serve as a backup again. At five after midnight, after I'm inside, I want you to wait outside in the alleyway and keep your ear to her door. If I yell, use your passkey if necessary and barge in—*with* your pistol loaded and cocked."

"Sounds like you're expecting some trouble, old son."

"It's just a precautionary measure at this point."

"Did she say why she wanted to chew the fat at that time of night?"

"No, but I have an idea, and she did say to be alone. I'll explain my hunch to you later."

"All right; you got it, old son."

Just as I hung up, Girtha walked in. "How was the tour?" I asked.

"I *loved* it! Everything was the first, or one of the first, in the Western Hemisphere and at least four- to five hundred years old. How was your day?"

"Not as well, I'm afraid. It looks like Julio Sotomayer didn't kill Lars Amundson, so I'm back where I started. I have an appointment at midnight that might shed some light, so you'll have to entertain yourself this evening. Here's fifty dollars—why don't you go to the bingo parlor and slug it out with the blue-haired rottweilers or feed the one-armed metal midgets in the casino?"

"Well," she said, taking the money, "since I won't have your company, I'll have to console myself somehow."

We went to dinner and found ourselves alone at our table. Dining by ourselves for a change was quite pleasant, and we lingered over our bowls of *sancocho* and *la bandera*. After finishing our conversation and her sangria, Girtha wandered off to a Broadway review.

I returned to our cabin to wait.

CHAPTER 20

AT TEN MINUTES BEFORE MIDNIGHT, I REVIEWED a map of the ship's layout to confirm the location of Constancia's suite. It was the equivalent of a city block from my cabin, but I managed to knock on the door of Suite A at the magic hour.

Constancia opened the door and my eyebrows cocked as I took a second look. Barefoot and braless, she was wearing tight white shorts and an unbuttoned pink shirt that was tied in a knot below her ribs. Okay, so she warranted a *third* look!

"I must say, I've been dying of curiosity for the past couple of hours trying to imagine what information you have to share."

She walked to the two windows facing the private deck and closed the curtains, then crossed the room to a dresser and opened the top drawer. When she turned around, she was holding her Beretta.

I had halfway expected something like this; still, I had to tense the muscles in my legs to keep them from shaking.

She wasted no time. "Where is Joey Morton?"

"As I previously told you, I followed him to a mountain resort but lost him when I stopped to get L'Enfant's dying confession. I had no authority to detain Joey nor did I have any vested interest in pursuing him."

"Have you learned anything about the missing cocaine shipment?"

"No. I wasn't commissioned to look for the hijacked narcotics nor have I uncovered any information regarding their whereabouts."

"In that case, you have no further value to me. I really regret having to cap you, McFadden. I've actually grown fond of you strangely enough, but all my other options have expired. I think you're well on your way to figuring things out and your continued existence places me in escalating jeopardy. You understand my position, don't you?"

"It became pretty clear when I learned from the FBI that you never submitted the coded radiograms from Bruno Helmje for analysis. I had to ponder, of course, what you had to gain from suppressing such important information. And I could only come up with one answer: you had something to lose if those documents were made public… and, that meant you were somehow involved with the drug-smuggling operation aboard the *Oslo Aphrodite*."

Constancia smiled. "I was afraid you would figure that part out. And, once you made *that* connection, I didn't expect it would be long before you deduced the rest."

"Which is…"

"That I am Zunimba."

My mouth dropped and my knees buckled. Wobbling, I reached out to a chest-of-drawers and braced myself with my extended arm before stammering, "You… mean, *you* are the *capo di tutti i capi* of the Zunimbist empire?"

"That's a Mafia title, but it fits pretty well."

My mind was still swarming in confusion, but I had to ask: "How did you get to be Zunimba? And, *why*?"

Constancia looked impatient, but she couldn't resist the opportunity to talk about herself. "It all started with a phone call that came one day from a distant aunt in Panama. Her husband had been diagnosed with a terminal illness and wanted to talk to me.

"I was surprised by the call because I'd never been especially close to either of them—my family had long avoided those relatives because of suspicions and gossip surrounding the source of their wealth. But I was interested in finding out why he might suddenly want to see someone in the family, and why me in particular, so I took some time off and went to see him.

"By the time I got to Panama, my uncle was in a hospice and not in very good condition. He'd already received last rites from a priest and was in a confessing sort of mood. He emptied the room and began talking... he talked non-stop, in fact, and I was floored by what he told me—how he had been a small-time drug peddler in his youth... how he'd been exposed to voodoo rituals and beliefs during a visit to Haiti... how he got the idea of building a tight-knit organization that would combine the devotion and religious fervor of its followers with the ruthlessness and profit maximization of a drug cartel.

"As he neared death, I suppose he wanted to try and salvage what little bit of a soul he had left. Knowing that I was with the Miami police, he spent his last hours giving me a complete rundown of the organization, its members, and the location of its records with the expectation that I would use that information to dismantle the Zunimbists and put the organization out of business.

"He could have had no idea that I was already looking for another career path, something where the advancement was faster, the rewards better, and the power—most importantly the power—was greater. Yes, I'd had some success in the police department, but I constantly had to dance to the tune of the good old boys. You could say that the timing was perfect for a new opportunity like the one falling into my lap."

"I think I can guess the rest," I said. "It didn't take long for you to figure out that it would be folly to shut down such a booming business. Why turn the money spigot off when all that was needed was a new CEO?"

"You got it, shamus. Why innovate from the bottom when you can start at the top? After my uncle's death, I easily convinced the flock that he had appointed me to succeed him as Zunimba, the head *mambo*. He had no children and I, his niece, was his only natural heir apparent.

"As soon as I took control of those country bumpkin drug pushers, I introduced some Harvard business school knowledge, some organizational theory, and some more extensive enabling technology."

"Of course, your position in the Miami Police Department hasn't hurt either," I added. "As head of the Zunimba Task Force, you have unquestioned access to information that is vital to Zunimbism itself. No wonder Zunimbists are rarely arrested and the organization has flourished so successfully of late. You're advantageously positioned to see that none of your Zunimbists are *ever* in the wrong place at the wrong time with the wrong stuff, and that your advantage is maintained over competitors.

"My requests for information were starting to make you nervous, so you dropped everything for a sudden vacation, providing you with a firsthand look at—and finger on—what I was doing"

"Bingo."

"So, indulge me one question… you *did* have Lars Amundson killed…"

"Bingo again."

"Even though he wasn't involved in the drug-smuggling operation?"

"Bingo, again. He was merely a signal to Bruno and Joey that I meant business, and to show what they could expect if the cocaine wasn't located."

"Then why," I asked with a truly puzzled expression, "were the markings on Amundson's chest different from the markings on the chests of the other victims?"

She smiled. "The markings were only different in the picture I sent you. That was not Amundson's picture I sent you. It was victim on whom we painted misleading markings after I received your request for pictures."

"For what reason? Why would you want me to think that Amundson was killed by someone other than a Zunimbist?"

"Think about it. *You're* the detective."

I took a moment to reflect. "You obviously wanted to misdirect me by diverting suspicion away from your group." Another moment produced a conjecture. "You wanted to distract me away from the Bruno Helmje investigation since finding out Bruno's role in the smuggling ring, and for whom he was doing it, would be a direct threat to your goal of finding the missing cocaine. You wanted to draw my attention back to the Lars Amundson murder, which had *no* significance to you or the missing drugs since he wasn't involved."

"You're batting a thousand, gumshoe," she complimented. "And, now can you also see why I can't let you live?"

"Hey, when you're good, you're good. But, why tonight on the ship? Why not wait until we get back to Miami, or until I get back to L.A.?"

"A Miami execution *was* my original plan. But you were learning too much too fast. If I wanted to kill you at sea, I couldn't wait any longer since the cruise wraps up day after tomorrow."

"Okay, but why midnight?"

"There are fewer people around at that time. Tonight, most passengers are still in Santo Domingo because of the 1:30 A.M. boarding time and our 2:00 A.M. departure. The people who are on board are at the midnight buffet which, as I believe you are well aware, is at the other end of the ship. You're a modest man, McFadden, and I know you wouldn't want your death to be the subject of fanfare."

"Your planning has been faultless so far, I must say. I assume you chose to host my murder in your suite for a reason, as well?"

"It gives me privacy to plug you, and easy access to the open sea, where I'll dump your body once we leave port." Constancia glanced at her watch. "I hate to be pushy but it *is* getting late. I have to dispose of you before Girtha realizes you've disappeared and sounds the missing persons alarm." She looked into my eyes. "I have to admit that you're taking this much more easily than I expected. Aren't you going to plead for your life or try to give me some good reasons why I shouldn't kill you or stall some more with additional questions?"

"My confidence isn't due to personal courage, I assure you, but to advance planning. "Bo!" I yelled. "Care to join us?"

The door opened and Bo walked in with his pistol leveled at Constancia. "Hello, sweet thing," he greeted before walking over to her, gently tugging the Beretta from her hand, and slipping it into his pocket.

Turning to Constancia, I explained. "I assumed you might be up to something not conducive to my welfare, so I took reasonable precaution." I beamed at my cleverness. "Bo, it might be a good idea to go ahead and cuff her."

"Why not use the restraints from earlier this evening?" Constancia asked with a twinkle in her eye.

Before I could comprehend what was happening, she turned to Bo and they melted in each other's arms in a passionate embrace. To my complete surprise, they were suddenly engaged in a frenetic tongue duel, fueled by white-hot lust.

Completely devastated, my knees started to wobble for the second time, and I reached out to the wall again for support. It took a full minute for me to stop my head from swirling. "Bo, I hate to be a spoilsport, but 'you got some 'splainin' to do, Lucy.'"

The heated lovers finally disengaged and while Bo wiped lipstick from his mouth, Constancia turned to me. "You're not the only one who believes in the value of advance planning—in my line of work, it's essential.

"You see, after I invited you to my cabin earlier this evening, I called Bo. His line was initially busy, but that was because of your call. When I got through, I asked if I could meet him in his cabin. I showed up with a bottle of champagne, wearing a low-cut sundress and—oh, well, nothing else. Needless to say, one thing led to another and it wasn't long before he was plowing me like his beloved forty acres. The bed must have moved ninety degrees around that room."

"I really am sorry, old son." Bo's face was as downcast as an orphan peering into an empty Christmas stocking. "This scent for women," he said apologetically, "is inbred in me like the smell for rabbits in a huntin' dog. I knew what she was after when she called and came over, but I couldn't help myself. You know what they say: a stiff prick has no conscience. Plus, I gotta tell ya, I was impressed with sweet thing. I've never had a woman go four rounds with 'Bodacious Bo' and hop out of the sack without limping."

"That sounds like a great addition for your résumé, Constancia. How about Bo? Did he live up to *his* billing?"

Constancia gave Bo a yearning look... "Let's put it this way... If he was wearing a suit of armor, he'd have to use the hood of a '57 Volkswagen Beetle for a codpiece."

"I can see why I'm the odd man out in this mutual admiration society," I muttered dejectedly. "I'm puzzled by one thing: were you just hoping to neutralize Bo? Or did you intend to involve him as an accomplice in my murder all along?"

Constancia looked at Bo and smiled. "If you must know, I went to his cabin to give him a little Cuban coochie—after all, he's had his nose under my skirt since I came aboard. Following our sexual marathon, I gave him a glass of champagne doctored with knock-out drops.

"I'd only intended to knock him unconscious, to keep him out of the way until I could deal with you. After I thought he passed out, I went in his bathroom to get cleaned up and presentable. However, when I came out, he was propped up in bed with a smile on his face and a gun in his hand. It seems he'd dumped his champagne when I wasn't looking.

"I then had to fall back to Plan B, which was to make him an offer he couldn't refuse: an ongoing relationship filled with sweaty, non-stop sex. Plus, I can always use a right-hand man like Bo to help me govern my rapidly expanding organization." She looked at Bo longingly and trailed the back of her fingers softly down his cheek.

Lame levity was not going to be enough to hide my disappointment, but I wasn't going down without a fight. "Bo, you could at least have sold me out for something of value, say thirty pieces of silver… Betraying me solely for splayed legs that wrap around you like a cummerbund is a blow to my ego."

"Old son, be reasonable, and put yourself in my place. I have a chance for a high-paying management position during the day and a chance to crawl on top of this every night." He ran his hand over Constancia's booty squeezing gently as he went. "What sane man could turn down an opportunity like that?"

"Not many, I expect," I said, sighing in surrender. "Where do we go from here?"

Bo handed his gun to Constancia. "Here, sweet thing, use this one. It's equipped with a noise suppressor and it's small caliber and quiet. Just put a shot in the center of his forehead. That way, the bullet won't exit and leave a mark in the wall. Also, it's not registered and can't be traced if found."

Constancia took the gun and said to me, "Normally, I give a victim the opportunity to say some last words but, knowing you—you'd probably start reciting *Evangeline* which wouldn't end until noon tomorrow."

"Remember, sweet thing, after you plug him, you have to strip."

Constancia looked at Bo with fevered curiosity. "Why do I have to remove my clothes? Not that I mind… since I *have* been thinking how great it would be to celebrate our new relationship by having the fuck of the ages."

"Because I have to slowly rub a plucked chicken all over your bare flesh, so we can cut its head off and put it in Chauncey's mouth. Isn't that the way it works?"

Constancia shook her head. "I wasn't planning to leave the Zunimba signature on McFadden. If his body should be found, I don't want any connection between his death and my organization. However," she suggested in her sexiest smile, "I have an alternative proposal regarding something you can rub all over my body which is anything but dead."

They kissed again and started groping each other like two blind pickpockets in a dark alley. It was almost enough to make me want to shoot myself! But, by that time, my mind was paying scant attention to them because it was inundated by a swirling cloud of self-doubt and recrimination. Why had I left the marginal-paying but safe job of low-rent peeper for a more lucrative but dangerous career path? How could I have thought that successfully performing mundane investigative tasks requested by ordinary people would be preparation for taking on the darkest deeds of which the human soul was capable? I suppose I was looking for personal and professional redemption but at what cost? Memories of Girtha flashed before me like a 35mm slideshow. Had I put her in harm's way as well? I was expecting memories of my life to flash before my eyes, but the only thing I could think of was if I had turned my room air conditioner off before I left L.A.

Click… click… click.

The sounds abruptly returned me to reality and my eyes quickly refocused on Constancia's face, which was straight ahead with a confused look on it. She turned to Bo—"This gun is empty!"

"That's right, sweet thing." He grabbed her around the waist with one arm, pulling her to him and kissing her, while his other hand reached in his pocket and pulled out her gun. When their lips parted, he placed the gun against her heart and pulled the trigger. She jerked and stiffened momentarily, then slumped soundlessly against his shoulder. I still hadn't grasped the situation when he picked her up, carried her to the shower, and propped her against the tile wall.

When he walked back into the room, he looked at me. "She'll keep there right nice until we get well out to sea and everybody's asleep. Then I'll sneak her out that door," he continued, indicating the exit to the suite's private deck, "and toss her and the gun over the rail." He looked around the carpet. "No blood; that's good." Then, acknowledging my pallor, he asked, "What's the matter, old son? You don't look to be in very fine fettle."

"Give me a minute to sort this out," I wheezed between heavy breaths. I'm a little perplexed at the moment..."

"Take your time, old son. We got a couple hours of downtime."

I sat, dabbed my damp face with my handkerchief, ran my fingers over my barren pate, checked my body for blood or holes, and scratched my head for several moments. Finally, I had recovered enough to ask two silly questions. "Then... you never bought into her plan? You never intended to kill me?"

"Oh, I thought about it; I surely did." He glanced back toward the bathroom, where we could see Constancia-Zunimba still slumped in the shower. "Yes, I did... I've bedded over a thousand women, I'll bet, since the age of twelve. The actual number is probably higher but I didn't learn to count 'til I was twelve," he said with a grin, "and *she* almost won me over. She's the only woman who's had a garage big enough to park my Cadillac in.

"But then I started thinking—what if she's just leading me on to get out of her current predicament? When we got back to Miami, she could easily have me bumped off by one of those chicken-chopping, body-carving jungle druggies.

"Now, I like my Dixie delight as well as the next man, but I'm not going to lose my head over it, no pun intended. Besides, I got tired of her pissing in my ear and trying to tell me it was raining."

"Then your mind was changed by thoughts of your own self-preservation," I charged with mock disappointment, "not by any regard for your professional responsibility or my well-being."

"Well, not entirely. I also had to accept the fact that Constancia... Zunimba... or whatever she calls herself couldn't stop with your murder. Afraid of pillow talk, she'd also have to kill Girtha. Then, she'd have to kill Boyd Fowler, Jurgens and anyone else who knew about the radiograms. Then, at some point, she'd probably get around to killing me if something cropped up that made her question my loyalty. I had to be realistic and accept the fact that she was a black widow.

"It became as clear as the glass balls on a gift shop monkey that the only way to stop this string of murders was to whack her first, and do it before she got back to Miami. As you've heard, hardly any missing persons cases on cruise ships ever get solved, so now seemed as good a time as any. She'll be shark shit long before anybody knows she's missing—which is good, since we can't leave the Zunimbists any clues that point to us. If we miss any evidence, we'll have to live the rest of our lives counting rosary beads whenever we see a Popeye's chicken joint."

At that moment, he paused and looked into my blank eyes. "Say, what's the matter, old son? You look pained, like you've got chigger bites on your scrotum."

"I'm wrestling with the moral dilemma of how I can not report a death that I've witnessed."

"Because that death saved your life and the life of your girlfriend. Don't make this situation any more complicated than it is."

"Did you know that Constancia was Zunimba before tonight?"

"I wouldn't have known that any more than a hog knows it's Sunday. I found out the same time you did; when I heard her tell you through the door. I should have suspected something, though. It was clear from day one that she was a bell-cow, clearly superior and different from the rest of the herd."

"And, why in the world did you wait until she pulled the trigger before springing into action? I could have died of a heart attack when she pointed it at me."

Bo thought a minute. "I can best explain that this way. Years ago, I was squirrel hunting with my ten-year-old nephew when we ran across a rattlesnake in the woods. My nephew screamed for me to kill it, but I explained to him that, while rattlesnakes *are* dangerous by their nature, this one wasn't doing anybody any harm at that moment; I advised him to just ignore it. But, when the snake coiled and reared its head back to strike my nephew, I shot it. I had to wait until the snake committed itself... 'til it made its intent clear... before I could kill it."

"That must be some kind of hunter's code of ethics. I don't completely understand it, but I am indebted to it."

"You better get back to Girtha. She's probably as nervous as a long-neck whore at a vampire convention. I'll stick around and mess up Constancia's bed, dirty up some towels and scatter some makeup items around the sink. That way, when the room steward comes in the morning, he won't realize anything out of the ordinary. By the time anyone realizes she's missing, we'll be safely in port."

I managed to form a grin and ask, "Are you sure you haven't done this before? You've come up with a tidy disposal strategy in record time. The only other person who could give you a run for the money is a guy I heard about in a previous case: he called himself 'The Cleaner from Chicago.' He could make all traces of a body disappear faster than a bevy of buzzards going back to work after a six-day fast."

"Hey, old son, that's pretty good—I'll have you using Cracker-based similes and metaphors in no time."

As I walked up to the door of the suite and prepared to leave, I realized how close I had come to death. I turned and put my hand on my partner's shoulder. "Bo, I think this is the beginning of a beautiful friendship."

CHAPTER 21

GIRTHA WAS ASLEEP WHEN I RETURNED TO THE ROOM, and I turned in without waking her. While the day had already turned, I refused to concede it was Wednesday until daylight peeked in the porthole, a moment that came all too soon. It was the thirteenth and final full day of the cruise. We would be at sea all day and arrive back at the Port of Miami around 8:30 tomorrow morning.

Girtha and I slowly sat up in bed, though I noted that we were strangely quiet. She was probably depressed by the end of duty-free shopping. My reasons lay in the myriad of secrets that I was suddenly holding from her. I had never kept anything from her in the past but, for her own safety, I could tell her nothing about the events of earlier that morning. My absence was explained by the need to interview members of the ship's crew.

We arrived at breakfast just a few minutes late and joined Colonel Talbo and Bo, who were already enjoying some sausage, eggs, and grits.

"Where's Miz Alameda this morning?" the Colonel asked.

Bo and I exchanged glances, but I spoke first. "She mentioned something about looking at some real estate in Santo Domingo, so she may have gotten off the ship and remained there." The rest of the meal was eerily silent, as if even Girtha was sleepwalking with Bo and me.

After Colonel Talbo left for the library to do some reading, and Girtha headed for the cabin to change into her sunbathing garb, I asked Bo for an update. "You didn't get much sleep this morning. Did everything go okay?"

"She hit the water at 3:00 A.M., old son. I put her fingerprints on a couple of empty wine bottles before I chucked her. The assumption will be that she got a little tipsy and fell over the rail. That's happened before so the investigation should be short and sweet."

"I had an uncomfortable thought during the night," I confessed. "What if she had contacted members of her organization in Miami and divulged her plan before she died? If so, we'll have to spend the rest of our lives sleeping with one eye open and our beds surrounded by chicken hawks."

"That same thought crossed my mind, too, but then I decided it was highly unlikely—for a couple of reasons. First, I checked with Radio Room personnel and found that she made no calls from the ship while she was on board. In addition, she didn't make any calls while we were on shore in Martinique or St. Thomas because I was with her at all times. Did she make any calls from Santo Domingo when she was with you?"

"No, she didn't. So we're safe on that front. You mentioned another reason?"

"To be honest, I suspect that killing you was a personal thing with her; something she wanted to take care of herself. Letting other people in on the act would have cheapened the experience. I think she got a hoot out of working her way into our confidences, knowing that information gained from her deception would be used against us. Constancia was a bona fide ball buster—a feminist on steroids."

"Tell me one final thing, Bo. Killing somebody is a horrific experience regardless of its legal justification. If you killed Constancia solely to save lives, that's one thing. If, in fact, you killed her because you were never able to bed her on your terms, that's something else. Are you—even if just faintly—troubled by any 'motivational' concerns?"

Bo paused as if choosing his words carefully. "I'll tell you the truth, old son. I learned a long time ago not to wrestle with ethical pigs—in the end, you just get muddy and besides, the ethical pigs love it."

I went to the bridge and found Captain Nelson in a familiar pose, puffing on his pipe and staring out to sea with his arms behind his back. "Case closed, Captain. It turns out that Lars was killed by Zunimbists after all, but *not* because he was involved in cocaine trafficking—his death was a warning to Bruno and Joey Morton, a warning of what lay ahead for them if the missing drug shipment was not handed over."

The Captain shifted the pipe to the other side of his mouth. "In an oddly comforting way, that's good news. I never thought that Lars was capable of being involved in anything like that."

"He's been cleared on another charge as well: he did not father the baby of the Dominican Republic girl."

The Captain chucked. "I wasn't so sure about that one, but it's important in that it keeps the reputation of the officers of the *Oslo Aphrodite* unblemished. By the way, we have an opening for a security officer. Are you interested? We could use a good man."

"An opening? What happened to Bo?"

"He turned in his resignation this morning. It's effective tomorrow when we reach port. I was surprised by the short notice."

This was an interesting development. "I appreciate the offer, but I'm a confirmed landlubber."

"Then," taking my hand, he added, "tomorrow you'll be leaving us, so I wish you Godspeed."

"Likewise, Captain, to you and the *Oslo Aphrodite*. May you always have the wind in your sails, may you face quiet seas free from tempests, and may you always steer your vestal vessel across the oceans of the world without taint or tarnish."

"That was nice, Mr. McFadden. Did you find that inscribed in the Seafarers' Chapel?"

"No, it was tattooed on the butt of a drunken sailor in the holding tank of the San Diego jail. I always hoped I would get to use it some day."

The rest of the day, I finally got to spend some uninterrupted time with Girtha. Turned out, she was a little depressed that we hadn't gotten to spend much time together, but she understood that my work had to take priority. We had our last dinner—a table for eight reduced to the two of us and Colonel Talbo, the sole survivors… almost literally! Bo's absence was noted, but I suspected he was cleaning up some last minute details since it was his last day on the job.

The next morning, we cleared customs, disembarked, and checked in at the Sand Conch Hotel. Girtha had spread her clothing purchases over the two beds and was luxuriating in her new wardrobe when I left to hail a taxi to Erickson's office.

I was announced by his secretary and found the energetic old redhead pacing back and forth across his carpet dictating into a tape recorder. He shook my hand energetically and offered me a chair.

"Captain Nelson tells me your missions were successful."

"Yes, it turns out that the Zunimbists killed Lars after all. They were using his murder as a scare tactic for Bruno Helmje, Joey Morton, and any other yet-to-be-identified souls on the ship who were involved in the missing cocaine shipment."

"Then that spat Lars got into in Santo Domingo never figured into this affair."

"No, that's a separate tragedy, which had no bearing on this case. Lars was cleared of any wrong-doing there, too, though just for the record."

"That's good to know. By the way, I got a call from Captain Nelson right before you walked in the door. He mentioned that one of the passengers was missing—someone by the name of Alameda. I believe that was the name of the police lieutenant who was in charge of Amundson's murder investigation—what a coincidence, huh? Did you know the missing passenger?"

Erickson had tapped an oil gusher but I managed to keep the lid on. "Yes… yes, as a matter of fact, I did. She joined the cruise somewhere in the middle. She even ate at our table a few times."

"That could be a job for you, McFadden. Contact her relatives; maybe they'll hire you to find her."

The gods must have been rolling over with laughter right about then, enjoying their little joke at my expense. "Possibly, but, unfortunately, I have to get back to L.A.—I have some previous commitments."

"Well done, then," Erickson said, "well done." He sat down and opened his desk drawer to pull out a checkbook. "That was $3,000 wasn't it?"

"And $3,000 for solving the Helmje and Tolleson murders, plus $1,672.41 for expenses," I said, handing him a list of expenditures incurred while working on the case.

After printing with deliberate speed, he signed and handed me a check for $7,672.41.

"I'm glad to get that behind us," Erickson said with relief. "Amundson's murder and the threat of additional violence have had the board of directors and officers of the company worried sick."

I tried breaking the news to Erickson as gently as I could. "I'm not confident that this business is entirely behind you."

"What do you mean?" Erickson asked, jerking his head forward and leaning across the desk.

"Based upon my observations, cruise ships are easy targets for use as transporters of illegal drugs. You're never going to be able to stop drug trafficking entirely, but you can help the situation by putting a choke hold on it so that the drug cartels will opt to switch to other, easier approaches. I'd suggest you assemble a task force to develop measures for tightening the lax security on all your ships, thereby making smuggling as difficult as possible."

"Your advice is well-taken. I've made a note of it already," Erickson said, scribbling on a notepad. "See?"

I wanted to tell him that although the head of the monster had been severed, one or more would grow back in its place. However, for the safety of all concerned, my knowledge of the death of Constancia and her alter ego could never be revealed to anyone under any circumstances.

I just hoped that my mental suitcase proved to be strong enough to carry the emotional baggage that I was anticipating.

CHAPTER 22

A MONTH AFTER RETURNING TO L.A., I WAS SITTING in my office working crossword puzzles to pass the time. Unfortunately, no plaintive cries from potential clients had been found on the answering machine upon my return. The phone rang that afternoon, though, and I grabbed it with the hope it might lead to some gainful employment.

"Hey, Chauncey! How's it hanging, baby? Do you remember me?"

I leaned back and put my feet on my desk. "How could I forget the irrepressible Joey Morton—it's only been a few weeks. Before you go any further, if some cannibals are holding you for ransom, don't come barking up my tree. Tell them you're Jewish and that they can't eat you until Rosh Hashanah. That'll buy you some time."

"You're a pistol, truly you are. Actually, I wound up down in Bolivia because nobody knows where Bolivia is. Hey, pal, the reason for this call—"

"No luck, Joey," I interrupted. "I didn't find the cocaine. To tell you the truth, I never really looked for it. And if I found it, I'd push it back in its hiding place because of the ruthlessness of the people who're after it. There's a mounting trail of bodies where the searchers have been and I don't plan to be one of them. I heard some talk going around that it was *you* who had absconded with the cocaine—something about you jumping ship with two big suitcases even though your clothes were still hanging in your cabin…"

"No, no, no. The suitcases were full of cassettes and videotapes of my comedy routines. That's my stock in trade and I wasn't about to leave them behind. I peddle them to make a buck or two when I can. But, you're not being a ganef, are you pal?"

"Joey, I'm being as right with you as I know how. There are simply some issues in life where I draw a line that I won't cross over, and drug possession and distribution is one of them."

"I know you're a mensch, pal, so thanks anyway"

"Be careful. In case you didn't know, that guy you shot in La Guaira was a Zunimbist. They don't accept their losses graciously."

"You ain't kidding. I had just gotten to the room when I heard a knock on the door. I looked through the peephole and saw it was a waiter bringing me a drink. I thought it was a welcome cocktail from hotel management, so I opened the door; but as soon as the guy was inside, he pulled out a knife and starting chasing me around the room like it was Thanksgiving and I was the turkey. I had no choice but to pull my rod out and pop him a couple of times. It scared me to death since I've never shot anybody before."

"Good luck, Joey. It's probably best for both of us if you don't call again."

"Take care, pal. Give my best to Girtha."

I had just hung up when the phone rang again. "Old son; Bo here. Just calling to see how you're doing—making sure you're still alive."

"That I am. Where are you, Bo?"

"I'm on an island in the South Pacific that's only accessible by boat—and we only see one of those weekly, when it drops off an occasional tourist and supplies for the thatched-roof hotel and grocery store. I can't pronounce the name of the place but it has a lot of vowels."

"It sounds like you've adjusted to the life of a beach bum with relative ease."

"You got that right. I'm laying here under a coconut palm with a bottle of dark rum and a bunch of half-naked native girls—one for each day of the week."

"You're servicing seven women?"

"More like sixteen. They got a different calendar here. Hey, I'm sorry I had to take off without saying good-bye."

"No apologies necessary. I pieced together the reason for your haste."

"You did? And, what did the pieces tell you?"

"That the cocaine you hijacked on the previous cruise was now sold and the proceeds of the sale wired to an account where the bankers aren't too particular."

Bo laughed. "How long have you known?"

"I figured it out on the plane ride back."

"What gave me away?"

"Three things. First, you wouldn't quit your cushy job with its generous sexual benefits *that* suddenly without a good reason— enough money to last you the rest of your life is the best reason I could think of. Second is the drugs themselves. If they weren't delivered to Zunimba in Miami, and if Bruno and Joey didn't have them, they still had to be aboard the ship. You perceptively put two and two together, based upon Boyd Fowler's information about the coded radiograms, and searched Bruno's room while he was ashore. You found the cocaine and stowed it away in your cabin."

"How did you get it off the ship, though—if you don't mind me asking?"

"That was the easy part," Bo said, chuckling. "I took the plastic waterproof packages that held the cocaine and, when we arrived in the Port of Miami at four in the morning, I tossed them overboard into the ocean from the stern of the ship to a buddy who was waiting below in a fishing boat. He snagged them out of the water with a gaff and the rest is history. But you said three reasons."

"I was never completely comfortable with your explanation for Constancia's murder. Maybe you *were* simply following your self-preservation instincts or maybe you *were* trying to prevent the loss of innocent life, but I had a hard time accepting either of those explanations. Constancia offered you a deal, Bo, the kind of deal that *your* libido would never have been able to turn down. To walk away from that offer, you had to have a more powerful incentive— something like the wealth promised from brokering a stolen drugs shipment.

"To keep the drugs, though, you quickly realized that you had to kill her—especially after you discovered that she was Zunimba—before she returned to Miami. You knew that once the relentless *mambo* queen found out you had left the cruise line, she would have put two and two together and unleashed her horde of soldiers to track you like midnight cockroaches on a dirty kitchen floor."

"Old son, you got it right again. My decision to snuff her was made spur of the moment but it's something I can live with, considering the circumstances. Another way to think about it is to understand that I intercepted an illegal delivery that was headed to one of the biggest bunch of cutthroats in modern times. From there, who knows what innocent lives would have been affected. I, at least, kept it out of the U.S. by selling it to foreign buyers. Besides, it wasn't like I stole money from the church poor box."

I took off my glasses and rubbed my face with my hands. "I recall having a similar discussion with Joey Morton. That distinction is clearer to you than it is to me. God knows, detectives have no special insight when it comes to ethical behavior, but it doesn't take a whole lot of thought to realize there's something wrong with your argument. The people to whom you sold that cocaine to fund your retirement will *still* target vulnerable neighborhoods and lost souls to spread their special brand of misery and degradation. You saved my life, for which I'll be eternally grateful, but the friendship didn't turn out to be as beautiful as I had hoped.

"Remember, Bo, when you dance with the devil, he's going to step on your toes sooner or later. I hope the amorous attention of the island lovelies helps console you in the years ahead when you wake up screaming in the middle of the night." I didn't give him the chance to say anything else. I just said "Good-bye, Bo" and hung up.

The case was finally over, or over at least as far as my participation was concerned. Hopefully, the decoded radiograms of Helmje would be found and provide the feds with enough evidence to make a serious dent in Caribbean drug-trafficking. After I hung up the phone, I sat back in my chair trying to sort out feelings that wouldn't go away; feelings with which I was still coming to grips a month later.

Clearly, one was disappointment. Constancia was a luminary who could have succeeded in any chosen field. Instead, she fell victim to a fatal flaw in her character, a flaw that compelled her to reign in hell rather than persecute its minions. If only she could have been comfortable with the considerable power of her persona rather than the obsession for more...

After the disappointment, I was left with a feeling of regret. I've never had many male friends, but I could have easily bonded with Bo. Until the dark, greedy side of his psyche took control, he had been a unique, unforgettable, and welcomed presence in the largely humdrum human melodrama that was my life. Having never had such a relationship in the past, I never missed it; but now...

It would take some time to shrug off these feelings. Yet, I knew they would pass with time, as all feelings eventually do. As sure as the bills mounted and the stack of completed crosswords grew, yes, they would pass...

The End

Dan Anderson has two favorite subjects: mysteries and comedies. His interest in comedy surfaced in elementary school and resulted in frequent time outs in the corner for misbehavior. It continued with his election as Wittiest Senior in his high school (too chubby for Most Athletic, too ugly for Most Popular, and too dumb for Most Likely to Succeed).

Being academically deficient because of suspensions for disruptive behavior, he bluffed his way through college and graduate school thanks to curricula outlines (think *Cliff's Notes*) and buying the notes of students who had actually attended class.

He milked academia until his G.I. Bill benefits ran out (drafted by the Army, he served in Vietnam but was shipped back to the states after it became apparent that his lethargic military skills had no discernible impact upon the war).

Forced to seek employment, and lacking demonstrable talents, he found a career with high pay and low demands: an executive position with a large US corporation. When it became evident that he was an imposter in the area of leadership and decision-making, he was downsized. Having honed his writing skills completing unemployment applications and fictitious résumés, it was natural that he would become an author.

Bad Vibrations, his first work, not only delighted mystery lovers, but was a reminder of how much fun reading can be in the hands of an irreverent craftsman. *Death Cruise* continues the investigative escapades of Chauncey McFadden, a reluctant PI who surprises everyone including himself.

Read on for a sneak peak at

Dan Anderson's next exciting mystery,

VIETNAM VINDICATION

Coming soon from INDI PUBLISHING!

Chapter One

"We're being murdered one by one!

"Each year for the past five years, one of my fellow squad members whom I served with in 'Nam's been killed. That's why I'm so scared, Mr. McFadden, and that's why I came to your detective agency for help."

In his case, an acknowledgement of fear wasn't necessary. My visitor squirmed in his chair like a petulant child with rectal rash and dabbed his face from time-to-time with the back of his wide tie. He had wiped his sweaty palms on the thighs of his light beige trousers so often that the resulting dark spots had begun to resemble the silhouettes on a Rorschach test. Sweating profusely, he used his palms to slake the perspiration on his forehead back over his bald head which made it glisten in the mid-morning light.

"Your anxiety is understandable, Mr. Coleman. Let's start at the beginning shall we? Briefly, give me some of your military background." I reached in the drawer of my desk and removed a small spiral notebook and ballpoint pen to jot down pertinent information.

He took a deep breath and clasped his hands. "I was in the army from '68 to '70. I took Basic Combat Training at Fort Benning, Georgia and AIT—Advanced Individual Training—at Fort Polk, Louisiana. In May of '69, I was ordered to 'Nam for a tour of duty. I stayed in country until May of '70 when I returned to the states and got my military discharge."

"You only served two years?"

"I was drafted when my student exemption expired; draftees served two years while volunteers served a four-year enlistment."

"What did you do in the army?"

"I shipped over as a PFC but made sergeant by the time I DEROSed. My MOS was eleven bravo forty."

"Can you put that in English that a civilian can understand?"

"DEROS is date eligible to return from overseas. MOS stands for military occupational specialty. Eleven bravo forty meant you were a grunt, a ground pounder in the infantry."

"What outfit were you with?"

"The Americal Infantry Division; the 198th Light Infantry Brigade—the 1st Battalion of the 6th Infantry."

"The Americal doesn't ring a bell."

"It was the largest military division in the RVN with three light infantry brigades and a squadron of armored cavalry." Coleman paused before continuing. "I studied the history of military units deployed in 'Nam. Military science is a hobby of mine. The Americal has a long and distinguished history. They had originally formed in 1942 during World War II on New Caledonia to hold the island against enemy attack. After hopping around a number of South Pacific islands like Guadalcanal, Fiji, Bougainville, and the Philippines, they were deactivated in December of '45 after the war ended. For 'Nam, they were reactivated again in '67 when the 198th and 11th brigades left Ft. Hood, Texas to join the 196th which was already in I Corps."

"I Corps being…"

"The northernmost tactical zone; 'Nam had 45 provinces divided into four tactical zones and I Corps was the zone closest to the DMZ."

"How many soldiers were in your squad?"

"There were eight of us in '70 when I got out."

"Why do you suspect that the deaths are homicides and that they're related?"

Coleman rubbed the stubble on his chin and squirmed some more. "We're a tight group and have stayed in touch every since we all got stateside. We attend the American Veteran's Association annual reunion where we play catch-up and swap lies. We were uncomfortable at the first reunions because almost all of the attendees were from World War II and, due to our paranoia, it seemed like many of them regarded 'Nam vets as second-class warriors since the conflict ended without victory. We were eventually welcomed into the military brotherhood on equal footing.

"Starting in '77, things began to unravel. We started losing one squad member every year. In the beginning, we didn't think much of it since a clear pattern hadn't formed that we could recognize. Then it hit us like a tsunami; these deaths were always the result of a freak accident or suspicious suicide, never homicide or natural causes."

"Tell me about them."

"The first to die was a kid from Milwaukee named Kasmir 'Kos' Koslowski, a big, strong Czech who could pick up the end of a jeep with one hand and change a flat tire with the other. He was absolutely fearless of everything except snakes. He was strong as an ox but dumber than a sack of lug nuts." Coleman leaned back in his chair, and seemed to relax for the first time. "I'll give you an example. When we went out on search-and-destroy missions, all squad members helped carry ammo belts for the machine gunner because if you stumbled into a firefight, the M-60 was your best friend. It was hard enough carrying your own gear in weather hot as hades and more humid than an outhouse after a hurricane so we paid Kos worthless Vietnamese currency to carry all the ammo belts. He still was able to step through the bush faster than the rest of us."

"What happened to him?"

"Get this: he died from a snake bite. He was found dead in his garage by neighbors who hadn't seen him in several days. He was working out doing bench presses when he was bitten on his thigh by a snake. It took doctors a while to identify the species which turned out to be a Russell's viper."

"A Russell's viper? Where would you get a viper in Milwaukee? They're one of the deadliest snakes in the world, but they aren't found outside of tropical climates such as Southeast Asia. Was it a pet of someone else in his family?"

"Kos was single. He hated snakes so much that he talked of retiring in Hawaii or Ireland where there aren't any."

I had some difficulty absorbing this information. "It's for certain that the viper didn't escape from a pet shop or fall out of a herpetologist's pocket. It's illegal to even own one of those things. How do they know that the bite was administered by a viper—did they find it at the scene?"

"The snake was nowhere to be found, but the venom is unique to the species. Kos had apparently been bitten during weight training and died of kidney failure before medical help was called. The venom doesn't usually kill immediately, but he was bitten several times. Koz probably froze up in fear and was unable to react. The coroner says he died in a day. In any event, the cops couldn't find any evidence to the contrary so they wrote it off as an accident."

"Just as well. The viper would probably have beaten the rap with a good attorney."

I swiveled around in my chair and pulled out an encyclopedia volume from my bookcase. I thumbed through the tattered pages until I found the object of my search. "It says here that the Russell's viper is the most dangerous snake in the world. It kills more people than any other snake. It ranks fifth in toxicity of venom, but it is easily excitable and can inject up to 250 milligrams per bite. For most humans a lethal dose is 40 to 70 milligrams."

I took some notes and asked, "Who was the next squad victim?"

"A black kid from the south side of Chicago; a gang banger by the name of Jerome 'The Shank' Manigault. He claimed to be a member of the Blackstone Rangers, a group of street criminals that later morphed into black power militants, but that might have been a crock of bull. What wasn't debatable was his skill with a knife. He'd taken a piece of metal from a bombed APC—armored personnel carrier—and honed it into the sharpest, most well-balanced knife that you've ever seen. He could sever the gonads off a mosquito at twenty paces.

"I'll never forget the time a few of us were sitting around LZ Cook outside of Phu Bien leaning on our shovels. We'd been working all day fortifying the perimeter—diggin' trenches, fillin' sand bags and stringin' concertina wire—when we stopped to take a break and have a smoke. We hadn't seen a VC sapper who had crawled through our Claymore mines and sneaked up behind us. When he was no more than thirty feet away, he jumped to his feet and leveled his AK-47 at us. No one saw him but Shank who coolly whipped out his shiv and let'er fly. He caught the gook dead center in his left eye; Charlie was dead before he hit the ground.

"He was also one of the best gamblers I've ever seen. He'd bet on anything if he felt he had an advantage. The guy never seemed to lose. After a while, no one would shoot craps with him. At poker, he enjoyed winning streaks that lasted all night even using other people's decks of cards.

"His favorite sport, though, was horse racing but there weren't any horses in 'Nam so he had to improvise. Before he transferred to our unit, he had been an aerial door gunner on a 'Firebird' gunship and manned one of the two M-60s on board. While in flight, if the crew saw a herd of water buffalo on the ground, they'd get a stampede going by firing at their feet. The winning buffalo earned the privilege of surviving for another day while the losers were shot."

I experienced some moral discomfort with this wartime sport and was now the one squirming in my chair.

"Was it necessary to execute the slower afoot? Why not let them retire from the fields and be put out to pasture to perform stud services like old racehorses?"

Coleman apparently didn't share my concern for the sanctity of animal life. "Shooting at 'Vietnamese tractors', as they were called, is more humane than peppering dinks in the rice paddies. Besides, they use the hides of water buffaloes to make tips for pool cues."

I was learning more about war than I cared to know. I had also developed a newfound reverence for billiard cues. "Changing the subject, how did Shank die?"

"His body was found in his bookie's parking lot in a section of town you wouldn't let your sister walk through. It was well-known that Shank loved to play the horses and he'd stopped by to place some bets. He was found slumped over on the pavement; his gut had been opened up with a knife and he'd been disemboweled."

In an attempt to lighten this morbid turn in the conversation, I quipped "Live by the knife—die by the knife. Placing a bet of my own, I'll wager that the police ruled it suicide by *hara-kiri*."

Coleman's eyes widened and he gaped at me with what appeared to be professional respect. "How'd you know? A knife was gripped in Shank's hand and there were no eyewitnesses or evidence of foul play."

Changing my approach to keep his new perception of my competence intact, I nodded my head knowingly. "I imagine the police did an onsite evaluation of the neighborhood and the victim and wrapped up the investigation in record time. We have areas like that in south-central L.A. where the ice cream men make their rounds in used armored cars accompanied by an armed guard riding shotgun. I gather you don't think Shank was the suicide type."

Coleman laughed. "You got that right. The only way Shank would take his own life is if the Dallas Cowboys cheerleaders were waiting for him stark naked behind the pearly gates. He was even thinking of converting to the Muslim faith so that seventy-two virgins and a river of honey would be waiting for him in the afterlife. Shank claimed that his high school hadn't had seventy-two virgins graduate since the founding of the school back in the '30s as a WPA project."

"Who was victim number three?" I prodded, finishing my notes and flipping the page of my notebook.

"'One Nut' Negrón"

I looked at Coleman suspiciously. "I suspect there's also a story behind that nickname."

"You're catching on quick," Coleman said. "Francisco Negrón was the best point man in the Americal. He had a keen nose and good eyesight which worked to our benefit time after time. I'll never forget the day he was ditty-boppin' down a jungle trail and suddenly stopped, pointed to an area off the beaten path, and told us to clear the vegetation away. We pulled camouflaging branches aside and discovered a tunnel which contained more than two hundred Chicom grenades, forty satchel charges, two dozen AK-47s, ten AK-50s and six RPGs—rocket propelled grenades."

I could never get over the fact that while veterans may not be able to remember what they had for breakfast that morning, they could mentally hurtle back in time and, without pause, rattle off military minutia like the lyrics of a dirty limerick.

"In addition to munitions, he could also smell NVA regulars and VC a half-mile away. On more than one occasion, his keen nose and good eyesight kept us out of a horseshoe ambush. If you wander into one of those, you better have a 'Blue Ghost' gunship standing by to rake fire over the area or Charlie will tighten your shit for you.

"One Nut got the nickname after his first enlistment ended. After a duffle bag drag and bowl of cornflakes…"

I interrupted. "In civilian jargon, please."

Coleman nodded and explained. "That was the final meal at Tan Son Nhut Air Force Base prior to boarding a freedom bird for the flight back to the land of the big PX. Before the soldiers were allowed to board the plane, they were told to throw any drugs in their possession into amnesty boxes since MACV—the Military Assistance Command Vietnam—had a hard-ass attitude about the exportation of drugs out of country. Most of the guys went through their pockets and duffel bags and complied with the order. Francisco decided he'd take the risk and attempted to board the plane with a bag of weed shoved down the front of his pants. One of the drug-sniffing German shepherds broke away from its handler and jumped Francisco ripping off part of his crotch. One testicle was still intact but the damn dog ate the other one. Despite rolling around on the floor in agony, One Nut looked up at the MP and asked, 'Do I get a purple heart for this?' One Nut was the toughest little *dinky dau*—that means crazy—bastard I ever met."

"That's an interesting story, particularly because of the delicious irony."

"Irony? What do you mean?" Coleman asked.

"It's ironic that One Nut was undone by something with a better sense of smell than his."

Coleman frowned, apparently not as amused as I by irony. "Moving on, what did One Nut do to warrant taps?"

"His body was found in a room of a motel he owned in San Juan, Puerto Rico—the *Cabro* Inn."

"And…" I prompted by moving my hand in a circular motion.

"The toxicology report said he'd died from an overdose of heroin."

I reflected on this briefly. "Then the cause of death doesn't appear to be unreasonable. One Nut did have a history of drugs, didn't he?"

"One Nut would puff a little ganja now and then but he didn't do hard drugs at all, much less being addicted to the point of overdosing."

"This is getting curiouser and curiouser. Tell me about the fourth victim."

"That's Woo-Suk Kim otherwise known as the 'Masan Monkey or 'M&M' for short.

"I hate to keep repeating myself, but there's got to be a story behind that nickname as well."

"M&M was a little oriental kid born in a city in southeast South Korea called Masan, but raised in Bakersfield by his grandparents after his folks died. He was short, about five feet tall, and weighed no more than one-ten soaking wet. Because he was so small and wiry, the army made him a tunnel rat and he became one of the best in the brigade. He discovered more weapons caches hidden underground than anybody I can remember. He was also responsible for producing dozens of *hoi chans* whom he found hiding down there."

"Hoy what?"

"*Hoi chans*. They were VC and NVA soldiers who surrendered and were proselyted to our side as part of the *Chieu Hoi* program. We processed thousands of them because the NVA forced kids as young as twelve into military service. Constant bombing from our B-52s and long-range artillery prompted a lot of them to change their allegiance once they received an official invite.

"Getting back to M&M, he got his nickname from his amazing ability to climb trees like a monkey. He could scoot up a tree faster than you could fall out of one. He was a hit with the villagers because of his ability to shed his gear and rescue trapped kittens and kites and pick high-hanging fruit.

"His skills had an important military application, too. A lot of the time when we were out in the field, we were covered by a triple-canopy of overhead vegetation and couldn't be seen from the air. If we got lost, or encountered enemy fire while in this kind of terrain, our choppers couldn't find us. In those instances, M&M could climb a tree and, clear of the branches, shoot off a flare to indicate our position below."

"Where did M&M live and how did he die?"

"He moved to Seattle after his enlistment was up. He'd met a little Oriental girl at a USO and moved to Washington to be near her." Coleman then sighed and said, "You'll find this hard to believe also, but he supposedly broke his neck when he fell off the roof of his house while trying to connect his TV antenna to his chimney."

"You're right; that explanation does have a certain amount of credulity strain attached to it. My guess is that someone broke his neck and dumped his body by the ladder. This is another accident that appears to fly in the face of the facts. How about the last victim?"

Coleman sighed and looked increasingly pained. "That would be the 'Professor', Jordon Vandergrift. He was a pale, skinny kid with big ears and bright red hair from Gainesville, a town in northeast Georgia—the Poultry Capital of the World as it's called. He'd no sooner got his degree in Veterinary Medicine from the University of Iowa when his draft notice showed up in the mailbox. His family didn't have the political clout to extend his educational deferment—and he didn't have the money to flee to Canada or Denmark to avoid service—so his college days came to an abrupt halt."

"It sounds like he may have had to make some intellectual adjustments to the rigors and realities of warfare," I said.

"When he first arrived for orientation at the Chu Lai base camp, he was a cherry who appeared to be an unlikely candidate for a rifle company," Coleman said, shaking his head. "He was a pacifist like Sergeant Alvin York but without the marksmanship skills. To look at him—gangly arms and glasses—you'd think he was a chaplain's assistant or 'chairborne ranger' working at division headquarters. He always looked scared, even when buying ice cream in the PX during a three-day stand-down."

Coleman paused as if struggling to pick the right words to string together. "He had that look of death that you sometimes see on certain guys. It's hard to describe. It's a combination of a number of things: body language... facial expression... voice... personality... The accursed don't know they have it, but people around them can sense it, even if they can't define it, and it makes them uneasy. The grim reaper has his hand on their shoulder but they don't feel a thing, even though the reaper is laughing as he always does when he takes a life before its time. Even money said that the Professor would be in a body bag before he'd taken his first dump in a latrine."

There was silence for a while which was a welcomed interruption. I could imagine Coleman's consciousness wandering to the Vietnam Veteran's War Memorial in D.C. and his mind's eye slowly scanning across the names carved in granite.

Before the quiet proved awkward, Coleman perked up and actually smiled. "But then the Professor found himself. In the heat of a pitched battle on Nui Yon hill south of Tam Ky, we discovered he had a skill that no one else possessed: a photographic memory. Out of boredom, back at camp he'd memorized the topographical map of the area and the location of everything of significance: roads, trails, cities and villages, military installations, and geographic features like mountains, hills and lakes. When our company commander, a shake n' bake—an officer right out of OCS without any combat experience—and the FO—forward observer— got killed, he picked up the Prick—nickname for the PRC-25 field radio— and relayed coordinates to an artillery battery at a distant fire base to bring smoke. The Professor's directions were so accurate that the NVA's position at the crest of the hill was obliterated within minutes. It wasn't until later that the Professor realized that if his calculations had been off, we could have received the pounding and been another one of those 'friendly fire' casualty stories you hear about."

"That is impressive," I acknowledged. "It's too bad he's not available to work with my newspaper delivery man who can't hit a driveway through the open window of a slowly moving van."

"How did the Professor expire?"

"When he got out of the army, he returned to Gainesville and entered the family business which was processing chickens. They received live chickens from regional farmers and produced whole fryers, roasters and packages of chicken parts for the meat departments of butcher shops, gourmet markets and grocery stores. They found him hanging from a rope one Sunday morning when the plant was closed. The coroner ruled it a suicide"

"What justification did they give for that finding?"

"There was no evidence of foul play and the only witnesses were dead chickens."

"Looking at the marital aspect; were the Vandergrift's having any relationship problems?"

"To the contrary, they'd only been married a year and were trying to have a baby. At the reunions, Jordan was as happy as I've ever seen him… putting the death of the squad members aside, that is.

"I don't know if this is important, but he did mention that he had taken out a big life insurance policy when he got married..."

I shook my head. "That wouldn't be a factor. If they got married a year ago, the benefits wouldn't have been payable the first two years because of the suicide exclusion clause. The Professor was a bright guy: if he was contemplating suicide, he isn't likely to have overlooked that key provision."

"Was he having business difficulties or any type of financial problems?

"You can rule that out. The business was privately owned and operated—no stockholder or management hassles to worry about—and had been around longer than General Electric. Plus, he'd just landed some big contracts with the state of Georgia school system to provide chicken nuggets to the high, middle, and elementary schools."

I scratched my head. "The Professor wouldn't appear to fit a suicide's profile to be sure."

My pen had run out of ink and, after scrounging another one from my drawer, I said, "Let's move on to the three survivors."

Coleman looked more relaxed now, probably because he would be talking about the living rather than the dead. "I'll start with Dominick 'Dog' Duquesne. Anticipating your next question, he's called Dog for a simple reason: you could never catch him without a puppy under his arm or walking beside him on a leash. There were plenty of orphan pooches in "Nam which he adopted to save'em from the stew pot. Post-army, he raises pedigreed dogs for sale and trains them for the Seeing Eye Foundation. He has a spread outside of San Arroyo Seco, a desert town eighty miles northwest of L.A."

"What kind of soldier was he?"

"He was a typical grunt. Being drafted, he complained about everything: the heat, the humidity, the cold in February, wearing the same underwear and socks for days on end, the food, the weight of the packs we had to carry, having to clean his rifle every day—the M-16s jammed a lot if you didn't, the pay—$320 a month plus $60 hazardous duty pay for a PFC and his hometown girlfriend whom he suspected of infidelity.

"But when shit happened, he was as solid as they come. He could empty the M-16 clips from his bandolier faster than anyone

I'd ever seen. I think that he hoped everyone would run out of ammo at the same time so that the remainder of the fighting could be conducted via fixed bayonets."

"How about the second survivor?"

Coleman got up and stretched his back before reseating himself and replying, "That's Lester 'Lifer' Luckingbill from Swamp Cabbage, Kentucky."

"Lifer sounds like he may have been the elder statesman for the younger recruits."

"That he was," Coleman confirmed with obvious admiration and respect in his voice. "Lifer was a career soldier who was on his last tour of duty before retiring with thirty years under his belt. He lost his military cherry in the waning days of the Korean War, picking up a cluster of purple hearts and silver stars in the process. He first came to 'Nam in '63 as an advisor but switched over to the infantry in '65 at the first sign of troop build-up because it was more fun killing people yourself than telling other people how to do it."

"What was his rank?"

"He was a First Shirt—Sergeant First Class—three times. Every time he made E7 rank, he'd get drunk and start a fight at the NCO Club or ignore a direct order in the field which earned him a reduction in rank and forfeiture of pay and allowances. He actually enjoyed a successful military career which couldn't have been predicted considering the circumstances surrounding his enlistment."

"You mean he wasn't a passionate patriot volunteer anxious to plant our flag on foreign shores?"

"He was probably that as well, but the direct reason for his interest in the military was provided by a judge. Lifer was caught making moonshine in the woods behind his farm by the revenuers and given the choice of either joining the army or breaking rocks at the Kentucky State Penitentiary in Frankfort for ten years. It seems the federal boys don't take kindly to rednecks brewing their own libations without paying liquor excise taxes.

"Lifer was respected by everybody including the senior officers for a couple of reasons. First, he looked the part: GI crew cut, square head, granite jaw, and more scars than a nervous butcher. He always had a cigar in his mouth, even when eating. He would push his stogie to the left side of his mouth with his tongue and funnel C rations through the right side. Secondly, he had more time in country and combat experience than anybody else. You ignored his advice at your own peril as his platoon leaders quickly learned. He'd earned so many medals and service ribbons that he'd run out of display space on his dress uniform jacket.

"His love for combat was legendary. When other soldiers got R&R or seven-day leave, most would go to Bangkok, prostitution Mecca of the Orient, to shake the dust off their willies via 24x7 unrestrained sex. Lifer disdained this creature comfort and instead offered his services to PICs—Prisoner Interrogation Centers— to help the Military Intelligence boys from G-2 interrogate VC and NVA prisoners. I can't comment upon his methods—although I suspect they may have involved some incidental pain—but I do know that he got more information for the intelligence unit than a bug planted by the CIA under a rubber machine in a Kremlin's men's room."

"It sounds like anyone planning to kill him will have his hands full. It's hard to imagine him dying at the hands of any man born of woman," I said in quasi-jest. "What's he up to these days?

"He's drawing his pension from the army and collecting disability payments from social security. That income, plus what his wife brings in from the textile mill, is enough to maintain their modest standard of living. These days, he spends his time suckin' shine from a Mason fruit jar on the front porch during the day and going out to his barn with a shotgun and flashlight at night to shoot rats."

"An unusual hobby wouldn't you say?"

"Not for Lifer. He picked up the practice during his first tour of duty when he, acting as an advisor, and some ARVNs came across a Montagnard village in the Central Highlands right after the NVA had left. They found men and women whose ankles and elbows had been smashed with rifle butts and rocks and rendered immobile. They had been dragged to a river bank by the communist gooks and left to die. When Lifer got there, the bodies, many still alive, were being eaten by river rats the size of armadillos. Ever since that experience, Lifer has had this vigilante thing for rats."

I was going to quip something about Mickey and Minnie having to get a restraining order on Lifer but wisely let it pass.

"You mentioned a disability…"

"He left a couple of toes in a minefield explosion in a rice paddy outside of Tam Ky. He still gets around on his own two legs, though."

"I believe that brings us to you, Mr. Coleman."

"The least interesting of the bunch," he said modestly. "I was born and raised in Glendale and attended grad school at USC until I ran out of money. The draft board moved faster than the student loan company so I wound up in army greens. After I got out of the service, I became a recluse, smoking a little weed in the mornings, sleeping in the afternoons and stocking a department store at nights. After a year, I woke up and escaped this funk when my brother-in-law suggested that we open a barbecue place. We started 'Pig and Pit' in Woodland Hills and have added three more restaurants in the past two years."

"What was your nickname: I know you must have had one."

"Yeah," Coleman chuckled, "I was afraid you'd get around to that: it's Porky."

"Like Petunia's boyfriend in the comic strip?"

"One and the same."

"How did you warrant that particular moniker?"

"From my looks as you can see. I'm short, bald, have a plain face, snub nose and carry excess weight I don't need."

"That makes two of us, Mr. Coleman. Uncle Sam tried to draft me, but I was classified 4-F because of my poor vision." Instinctively, I reached up and adjusted my black, horn-rimmed glasses on my nose.

"If that concludes the bios of your squad, I'll need the addresses and home and work telephone numbers for yourself and the other two surviving members of your squad. I'd also like the last known addresses, phone numbers and names of the closest next-of-kin of your five deceased comrades."

"I anticipated your request; it's all here for you," Coleman said, handing me another sheet of paper.

"When did the eight men in your squad leave Vietnam and get out of the service?"

"As I mentioned, I left 'Nam in '70. The others were out by '72. Most of us were draftees and left 'Nam and got out of the army at the same time. The policy in effect then was if you served your year in "Nam and had less than six months left in the army when you returned to the states, you would be released from further active duty. The army figured it wasn't worth their time, expense and effort to assign you to another outfit or a National Guard unit for periods less than six months."

"That makes sense. All right, Mr. Coleman, let's assume for the moment that these deaths aren't accidents or suicides. I'll admit that it's somewhat unlikely that in an eight-man control group, five men in the prime of life would each die under such questionable and mysterious circumstances. However, other than the fact that all five decedents were in the same army outfit and serving in Vietnam at the same time, what makes you think these deaths were triggered by something which happened there?"

Coleman nodded as if he had been expecting this question. "Each of the victims was found by the crime scene investigators to have a Vietnam Service Medal ribbon bar pinned to his clothing."

"Ribbon bar…?

"Each soldier who served in 'Nam, Cambodia, Laos or Thailand from '65 to '73 received a ribbon bar. It's yellow with vertical wide green stripes at both ends and three thinner red stripes in the middle. They're normally worn on a military uniform."

I was startled by this revelation and asked excitedly, "Are these ribbon bars available for public purchase?"

"Yeah, they can be found in any pawn shop or bought at any military supply store or surplus depot."

"I'll grant you that the ribbon bar does appear to be a common link which suggests a common perpetrator but it leads to the next question: how do you know that the causes of deaths are attributable to something which happened in Vietnam?"

"There's more," Coleman said quietly. There was another long pause but I didn't mind because I sensed that we were finally getting to the heart of the matter.

"In early '70, we returned to Chu Lai after several rough months in the bush for a couple of days of rest and relaxation. Our squad cleaned up and went over to the club to have a few beers and listen to Led Zeppelin. There was a Vietnamese girl at the bar, a hot little number named Mai Tai, who we started talking to. We were happy with this development since Mai Tai was well-known around base camp for her version of the Soldiers and Sailors Relief Act if you know what I mean. What made it even better was that she was looking real good that night. She was wearing a slinky *ao dai*—the traditional slit skirt and trousers—that left little to the imagination. After a few drinks at the bar, the eleven of us moved to a table and continued to work on her, buying round after round until none of us was feeling any pain. When the club closed, they threw us out and we staggered back with Mai Tai to our hootch. When we got there, she did a little striptease and dance which put everybody in the mood for a little boom boom. She was obviously looking for more than drunken conversation, so we decided to pull a train and played rock-paper-scissors to determine humping order. She was clearly enjoying the non-stop sex until the seventh or eighth guy. Then, all of a sudden, her sexual defense system kicked in and she started to resist. We were taken back by this sudden change in behavior and thought she was putting on an act, but we were too far along to change plans. In retrospect... in the light of day and with clear minds... we realized that she wanted us to stop. But, with our bellies full of beer and no recent sex in weeks, we weren't in a frame of mind to abort the mission once well underway. To make it short and sweet, what started out as a consensual orgy blew up in our faces."

I was numbed by the impact of his confession. Coleman's stared down at his feet and looked as sorrowful as I have ever seen a man look.

"We all knew it was wrong, not because of the way it started, but because of the way it ended. Not a single day has passed that we haven't regretted it. We went into denial at first, searching for rationalizations to show that our actions had some justification. We blamed it on combat stress... we reasoned that non-consensual sex wasn't that much worse or different than her frequent consensual sex... anything to trivialize the act of rape to the point where we could live with it. After all, she had encouraged us with her words and behavior and once the genie is out of the bottle, it's a bitch to put it back in.

"Each year at the reunion, we struggle to avoid discussing it but it always manifests itself in some form or another—a heavy ache in your heart or the lingering pain of remorse in your conscience that flairs up whenever it's provoked by the reminder of memory. We were further haunted by the knowledge that Mai Tai used to help out at the 27th surgical hospital and had, so to speak, help save lives and provide medical and spiritual comfort to casualties. In effect, we had committed an outrage against an ally which was unconscionable no matter how you slice it. In the U.S., we would have stopped at the first sign of resistance since we live in a country with laws and penalties for breaking those laws. In 'Nam, we learned that once you got in the bush, different rules applied which is to say you could create your own laws. After a few life-altering experiences, we came to learn that the first casualty in 'Nam was not a body bag sent home, but the loss of innocence, decency and humanity."

Coleman slumped in his chair and I gave him some time to complete his soul-searching before saying, "Funny thing about evil; it has the amazing capacity to reinvent itself. It can be at a different time, in a different place, and in a different form, but it never misses an opportunity to disable a conscience and steal a soul." Then I prompted, "What happened next?"

"Mai Tai reported us to the Judge Advocate General's office and we were charged with rape and arrested by the MPs. They held a hearing and determined that there was enough evidence to proceed with a court-martial so we were locked up and provided with legal counsel."

"What was the verdict?"

Coleman wiped his brow. "The court-martial was never held."

"Why not?" I asked, puzzled by this unexpected response.

"The day before the court-martial was to have begun, Mai Tai committed suicide. We couldn't believe it; why go through all that hassle to file charges then take your life. The JAG office deliberated for a few days and then dropped the charges for lack of a plaintiff who could present testimony and be cross-examined."

"Was Mai Tai her real name?"

"Her first name was Mai and her middle name started with a 'T' so everyone called her Mai Tai to keep it simple. We never did know her last name."

"Thanks," I said while scribbling. "Go on."

"While the cancellation of the court-martial removed the immediate legal problem, we continued to be haunted by the fact that while Mai Tai had been a willing accomplice in the act early on, she was ultimately forced against her will and we've lived with that every day of our lives. We never intended to do anything which could have fatal consequences; it's just that a good time got out of hand. We'd give anything if the events of that night could be changed but while God might have the capacity for forgiveness, He's not much into do-overs."

I scratched my head. "Talk about a gray area: this case is full of ethical snares and legal traps. On one hand, the legal resolution could be construed as being a bit generous for the defendants," I confessed. "Even though Mai Tai was dead, she *had* filed charges alleging to have been the victim of a crime and that, after all, may deserve some justice even if it's just a fair and impartial review of the facts of the case. Her suicide could be interpreted as the result of the shame she had been caused by the sexual violence. On the other hand, her suicide may have been prompted by personal remorse for her own responsibility and conduct in leading to a precipitation of the act."

I sighed in confusion at all the conflicting nuances of this act. "I'm not a jurist but I suppose it can be argued either way. I'm not very good with legal math so I wonder how do you pursue an act that is seventy percent consensual and thirty percent forced?"

Coleman appeared to be just as lost in legal wasteland as I. "I should mention that there was another event in play which had a far-reaching impact upon the operation and conduct of the war; one which I believe may have had a direct bearing on the decision to quash our court-martial."

"What was that?" I asked, my curiosity having been piqued.

"The My Lai Massacre."

"I'm listening."

"In March of the previous year, one of our sister Americal brigades—Charlie Company, 20th Infantry, 11th brigade to be exact—received some intelligence that NLF—National Liberation Front—guerrillas had massed and established a stronghold in My

Lai 4, a little hamlet in the My Song village complex in Quang Ngai Province. Quang Ngai had been the location of some of the fiercest fighting in the war which was further intensified by the Tet Offensive which began in January of '68. Prepped for revenge, the troops were told to attack the village and kill any NLF soldiers, supporters and sympathizers whom they encountered. However, the only people found by the 11th brigade were 350 to 500 women, children and old men who they herded together and shot. Civilians always bear the brunt of any war, and they received even less protection in this conflict."

"Duly noted but what is this leading to?"

"The American had first attempted to cover up the fiasco at My Lai but when the truth leaked out, and the press and public got word of the intentional massacre of unarmed and nonresisting people, the shit hit the fan. The American brass circled the wagons and hunkered down in contain-and-control mode. I believe our court-martial was dropped because they couldn't afford to be distracted by a comparatively minor offense."

"You're probably right. I can't help but reword something Reinhold Niebuhr once said: man's capacity for good makes justice possible; but man's inclination to evil makes justice necessary."

"Please forgive my foray into Protestant theology. So you think that the incident with Mai Tai is the reason for the vendetta being experienced by your squad members?"

Coleman paused again and tapped the desk with his finger tips. "That's right. We think that we're being systemically killed by someone seeking revenge for what they feel is the rape of Mai Tai."

I studied this conjecture for a moment. "Let's look at possible suspects shall we? Does Mai Tai have any close relatives who, motivated by 'justice delayed is justice denied', might want to see her violation avenged?"

"We don't know anything about her family, sorry."

"Where was Mai Tai from?"

"She was from Saigon originally and took some nurses' training there. She relocated to Chu Lai in the late '60's and volunteered to work with the medical core of the Americal Division. She was Eurasian, part Vietnamese and part French, which probably accounted for her good looks."

I nodded and tapped my pen on the desk in frustration. "Her family history will be hard, if not impossible, to track at this point in time. The North Vietnamese won't respond to a records request even if those records existed. Our only chance is the documentation which had been assembled in preparation for the court-martial. The Judge Advocate General's office may still have it.

"Looking at another possible source, did she have an ardent admirer in the military who may have sought revenge on her behalf?"

Coleman shrugged. "As I said, she reputedly had beaucoup lovers but I don't know if any one of them was smitten enough to become a self-appointed personal avenger. Most guys can tell the difference between a one-night stand and eternal love."

I leaned back in my chair and looked at my notes. "Let's stop a moment and see where we are. You've provided four common threads or denominators: the deceased were members of the same military organization in the same place and at the same time, all died from causes that are at the very least suspicious, all had a Vietnam service bar attached to their corpses, and they all participated in the same sexual attack of a foreign national. Other than the service bars and the rape, do you have anything to connect the deaths of your squad members to service in Vietnam?"

"Just one thing: each of the five men was killed at the same time each year."

I jerked upright in my chair again and scribbled hurriedly. "Now we're getting somewhere! That's conclusive evidence of serial killer involvement. What's the common day of death?"

"All five were all killed on the first day of Tet: Vietnam's Lunar New Year."

"When is that?"

Coleman reached in his jacket pocket and pulled out a piece of paper which he handed to me. "It varies each year but it will always fall between January 21 and February 19."

I scanned the paper which contained the following:

1977	Kos	February 18
1978	Shank	February 7
1979	One Nut	January 28
1980	M&M	February 16

1981	Professor	February 5
1982	?????	January 25
1983	?????	February 13
1984	?????	February 2

"When a buddy didn't show up at the reunion, we'd call him to find out why. If he was dead, we got the dates of death from his spouse, parents or other next-of-kin. We then compared the dates of death to look for a pattern but the only thing they had in common was that they fell in the first two months of the year. As you might suspect, the Professor was the one who figured it out after M&M was killed."

"That's a nice piece of detective work by the professor," I complimented. "Few people could have made that connection other than a Vietnam vet, a Vietnamese citizen or someone immersed in the culture of Southeast Asia."

Coleman fidgeted in his chair and dabbed his forehead with his handkerchief. "That's all well and good, Mr. McFadden, but the most important piece of information is the one we don't know: which one of us is next?"

I nodded understandingly. "I appreciate your sense of urgency. This appears to be the work of a precise, organized killer. If so, the key to breaking the code of his methodology may be right here in front of us. Walk around and stretch your legs and give me a few minutes to work with your list."

I reviewed my notes and the obituary list which Coleman had given me. He got up to stretch his legs and walked to the dirty window of my office to look down on the nearly deserted streets below. When I finished, I spun around in my chair for the second time and pulled out the encyclopedia volume which contained the letter "T". I read the entry under 'Tet' for a few minutes and then added a couple of lines and a fourth column to the sheet.

By now, Coleman was pacing back and forth, his anxiety falling somewhere between that of an expectant father and a condemned man waiting for a last-minute reprieve from the governor. Finally reaching the end of his patience, he turned to me and asked, "Have you figured anything out yet?"

"I think so. I can tell you when you're going to die."